James Wilde is a Man of Mercia. Raised in a world of books, he studied economic history at university before travelling the world in search of adventure. It was while visiting the haunt... fenlands of Eastern England, the ancestral home of He.. ...endary Englis........... should be the subject of his debut novel. The first in w....... would become an acclaimed six-book sequence, *Hereward* was a bestseller. His most recent novel, *Pendragon*, explores the origins of what would become the myth of King Arthur. *Dark Age* continues this remarkable adventure.

James Wilde divides his time between London and the family home in Derbyshire.

To find out more visit, www.manofmercia.co.uk

Acclaim for *Pendragon*

'*Pendragon* has all the hallmarks of a traditional historical adventure story – there are battles, swords and the bantering of violent men – and these are all done with style. However, there is also intellectual heft to this story, with its themes of myth-making and the nature of power.'
Antonia Senior, *THE TIMES*

'Not since Bernard Cornwell took on the Arthur myth has a writer provided such a new and innovative view of the Arthurian story . . . a fast-paced, action-packed book . . . a wonderful tale.'
PARMENION BOOKS

'On the shadowed frontier between myth and half-imagined history, James Wilde paints a vivid and gritty picture of the genesis of one of the greatest legends of all time.'
Matthew Harffy, author of *The Bernicia Chronicles*

'Skilfully deconstructs the myths of Arthur and Camelot . . . creating a stunning prequel.'
THE ELOQUENT PAGE

Also by James Wilde

HEREWARD
HEREWARD: THE DEVIL'S ARMY
HEREWARD: END OF DAYS
HEREWARD: WOLVES OF NEW ROME
HEREWARD: THE IMMORTALS
HEREWARD: THE BLOODY CROWN

PENDRAGON: A NOVEL OF THE DARK AGE

For more information on James Wilde and his books,
see his website at www.manofmercia.co.uk

DARK AGE

A NOVEL OF
THE DARK AGE

JAMES WILDE

BANTAM BOOKS

TRANSWORLD PUBLISHERS
61–63 Uxbridge Road, London W5 5SA
www.penguin.co.uk

Transworld is part of the Penguin Random House group of companies
whose addresses can be found at global.penguinrandomhouse.com

Penguin
Random House
UK

First published in Great Britain in 2018 by Bantam Press
an imprint of Transworld Publishers
Bantam edition published 2019

A CIP catalogue record for this book
is available from the British Library.

ISBN
9780857503220

Typeset in 10/13 pt Plantin by Jouve (UK), Milton Keynes.
Printed and bound in Great Britain by Clays Ltd, Elcograf S.p.A.

Penguin Random House is committed to a sustainable
future for our business, our readers and our planet. This book
is made from Forest Stewardship Council® certified paper.

1 3 5 7 9 10 8 6 4 2

For Elizabeth, Betsy, Joe and Eve

Goddess of woods, tremendous in the chase
To Mountain boars, and all the savage race!
Wide o'er the ethereal walks extends thy sway,
And o'er the infernal mansions void of day!
Look upon us on earth! Unfold our fate,
And say what region is our destined seat?
Where shall we next thy lasting temples raise?
And choirs of virgins celebrate thy praise?

Geoffrey of Monmouth

The gods too are fond of a joke.

Aristotle

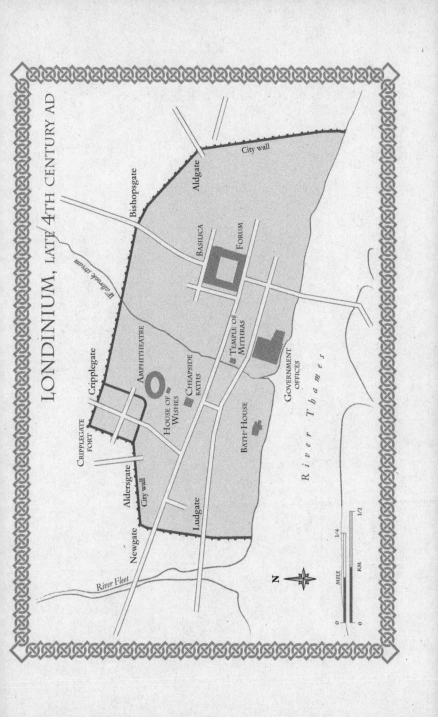

LONDINIUM, LATE 4TH CENTURY AD

Walbrook stream

City wall

Bishopsgate

Aldgate

BASILICA

FORUM

Cripplegate

Cripplegate

AMPHITHEATRE

HOUSE OF
WISHES

CHEAPSIDE
BATHS

TEMPLE OF
MITHRAS

CRIPPLEGATE
FORT

Aldersgate

City wall

BATH-HOUSE

GOVERNMENT
OFFICES

River Thames

Newgate

Ludgate

River Fleet

N

MILE   1/4

KM   1/2

0

0

PART ONE

The Blasted Land

'What man is the gatekeeper?'

The Black Book of Carmarthen

CHAPTER ONE

The World is Ending

AD 367, *South of Lactodurum, southern Britannia, 26 July*

'WHO IS THE KING WHO WILL NOT DIE?'

The desperate words floated in the warm night air. Apullius looked down at his young brother and tried to force a reassuring smile. Morirex had seen only eleven summers, and was small for his age: the Mouse, the other children called him. He was allowed to be frightened. Five years older, Apullius was tall and gangly, awkward but strong, with an unruly mess of brown hair. They had other names for him, and he cared about none of them.

'You remember the stories we heard in the village?'

'Yes.'

'The King Who Will Not Die will come when we need him most to lead us out of these dark times.'

'Don't we need him now?'

Apullius didn't answer.

'But who is he?'

This time Apullius felt a pang of frustration. He wanted to say it was nothing but a story, one told to the weak and the frightened so they didn't feel bad about their failure to be strong enough to save themselves. But that would be cruel.

3

Raising his eyes to the slab of sky, sprinkled with stars between the black high branches, he breathed in the calming honeyed scent of the golden resin bubbling from the trunks. They should have been tossing and turning in summer sweat under a familiar roof, not out there in the woods. But the safety of home was gone now.

The world was ending.

In wave after wave, the enemy crashed across the fields they once knew. Burning and raping and slaughtering. He'd seen their numbers, that cold, pink dawn. The charcoal smudge had shadowed the horizon, growing larger by the moment, and wide, as far as he could see in each direction. That vast line swept down, silhouetted against wavering angry red under the black pall of smoke.

The world was ending.

Around him he could hear the snuffling of the others, like pigs waking in their sty at first light. A baby mewled and the mother desperately tried to silence it. An old man hawked up phlegm and someone hushed him in a harsh tone. Other children whispered questions like the one his brother had uttered.

Where is the one who will save us?

If they could not save themselves they did not deserve to survive this night.

'They call him the Bear-King,' he told Morirex. 'No one knows his name, but we will know him when we see him.'

'And he'll come tonight?'

'Or in a hundred years' time.'

Morirex choked down a sob and Apullius realized his mistake. 'Come, you little mud-crawler! Why would we need a king to save us? Father is out there with his cudgel, and all the men of the village.'

'And Mother? Why has Mother gone, and all the other women?'

Because they need every hand they can get.

'Because the women have better eyes and they can see in the dark. You know that. Now, hush. Sleep. It will be dawn soon enough and we'll be on our way.'

'But not home.' The voice grew thin and Apullius could hear the tears lacing it.

'A better home. A grand home with mosaics and warm floors in winter and ovens to bake bread. Go to sleep, mud-crawler. Sleep!'

Apullius fumbled in the dark and pressed his hand on his brother's eyes to close them. After a moment, he felt Mori-rex's lashes flutter shut and a moment after that his breathing soughed in a regular rhythm.

Pulling away, Apullius crept past the prone bodies. Few of them were sleeping. He could smell the vinegary fear-sweat. No, they would not be returning home, because their home had burned to the ground along with the rest of the village. They'd all barely had time to flee into the woods after the watchers posted half a day's walk away had raced back to tell of the barbarians' relentless advance.

Among the trees, he could just make out the hazy outline of a figure hugging its knees under a twisted hawthorn. The soldier who had stumbled into the village, begging for food. Now barely a soldier, barely a man.

When he'd staggered up, he'd been streaked with filth and grass stains, his cloak tattered, a beard like a lark's nest tumbling down his chest. His eyes had ranged, never at peace. He'd abandoned his post, as had all the army, when the barbarians had thundered across the land. Saxons, and Scoti and Picts, and names he didn't recognize. Surging across the great wall in the north from Caledonia. Sweeping in on ships from the west and the east. All those far-flung tribes, who had thrown aside their petty disputes and joined into one unstoppable force to take Britannia from the empire.

Unheard of, his father had muttered. The tribes hated each other. 'They hate Rome more,' his mother had whispered, 'and all who shelter under its banner.'

If the army – the finest fighting men in the world, his father had always called them – if they could not resist, what hope for the rest of them?

'Britannia has fallen,' the soldier had raved. 'Only blasted land remains in the barbarians' wake. Burned villages. Men and women and children slaughtered, or taken slave. All riches looted.'

Apullius remembered how his father's face, usually so strong and filled with mirth, had drained of blood, and grown drawn, so that he looked like an old man. That was worse than any words.

After that soldier's message of terror, they'd had some thin hope for a while. The refugees streaming through their village carried on their backs what meagre belongings they'd been able to rescue. They said that the barbarians had come to a halt on a line from Ratae.

'Perhaps they've seized all the loot they can carry,' his father had said. 'They'll return to their homes and spin tales of their great victory in the years to come.'

But midsummer passed and the invaders had set off again, advancing more slowly this time, breaking into small groups so they could roam across the countryside to pillage, and retreat at speed if they were resisted. But they never were. The army was shattered.

Apullius crouched on the boundary line they had decided on in the last of the light. The other sentries stood silently away in the dark, the five younger men like himself who had been chosen to lead the old and the sick and the mothers with young away should things take a turn for the worse.

Before he had left, his father had hugged him tight as if he would never let him go. But he did not look back as he marched into the gloom. His mother kept her face turned away too.

As he looked out into that ocean of night, a light gleamed away in the grassland beyond the wood's edge.

He felt a cold blade in his heart. It was a torch appearing over a ridge of higher ground. Another one flared suddenly, like a star fallen to earth. Then another, until an entire constellation glimmered in that gulf.

Not the folk from his village. They were all in hiding, in the ditches and the long grass, waiting to mount one last desperate attack if the barbarians chose to follow their trail from the ashes of their village.

Apullius' throat felt as narrow as a piece of straw. Those torches danced inexorably forward. Perhaps they would pass the hiding places. Perhaps there would be no battle.

And then the first scream rang out.

It was not the cry of a man stabbed through the heart. This one tore the throat as if the victim had stared into the horrors of hell.

The torchlight swirled, and Apullius swooned at a vision of summer fireflies in the fields near his home.

Another scream echoed.

Another.

Another. Those awful cries merged into one long howl.

For a moment, Apullius clutched his ears to smother the sickening sound. But then his fury seared like a furnace and he threw himself towards the fray.

A hand clamped on his shoulder and dragged him back.

Apullius whirled. A giant wolf loomed over him. Fangs bared. Maw wide.

He yowled, then stifled it when he realized his mistake. No wolf. Only a man. The beast's grey pelt hung across the stranger's back, the head set on his own, the snout pulled down so his features were thrown into shadow. In his right hand he clutched a bronze sword. Moonlight plucked black tracings of runes from the blade. A barbarian.

'Stay,' the man-wolf growled.

Apullius kicked out for the intruder's shins.

The warrior clenched his iron fingers and held his captive at bay. He cuffed Apullius once round the ears to bring him to his senses.

'I'm not your enemy.'

Apullius realized he could understand the words – this was not some guttural barbarian tongue – but the accent was heavy and unfamiliar. Letting his limbs grow slack, he peered under that wolf's head. The face was strong and as yet unlined, serious but not cruel. Eyes of fierce intelligence glowed from the black pools of the sockets.

'Who are you?' he croaked.

'My name is Lucanus Pendragon. Some call me the Wolf.'

'Pendragon?' He knew that name from somewhere. A title. Was this the war-leader he'd heard his father discussing?

More screams jerked him from his reflection and he twisted round. 'My father . . . my mother . . . we must help them.'

'Your father and mother are not coming back.' The voice was low, but not unkind.

'Please—'

'It's too late for them. But not for you.'

Apullius sagged, almost falling against the warrior. He'd known it the moment the first scream echoed, but grief surged when he heard it stated so baldly.

Lucanus loosened his grip and squeezed Apullius' arm. It was a silent communication that said this strange man understood the torment that lay within him, the lad knew. But the warrior was already searching the night for the enemy.

'What's to become of us?'

'You're with us now.' The Pendragon's voice had grown as cold and hard as stone, the voice of a man who did not readily give in to adversity. 'Come,' he said, tugging the boy towards where the other villagers cowered.

Apullius squinted. Dark shapes shifted among the trees, stooping every now and then to whisper reassuring words to the refugees and to help them to their feet. The lad felt a glimmer of comfort, but then his sorrow surged again and the tears came.

'Time enough for that later,' the warrior said. 'Now you must be a man.'

'Let me tell my brother—'

'We cannot wait,' Lucanus interrupted. 'The Attacotti are coming, and that will be an ending worse than any you can imagine.'

CHAPTER TWO

Running With Wolves

'**M**AKE HASTE!'
Lucanus whipped his arm forward to encourage the refugees. The final scream had ebbed away. Now there was only the silence of the grave.

The Attacotti filled him with dread and he was not afraid to admit it. They could track across the wildest landscape, never slowing, never tiring. Fierce warriors. Silent, relentless. Not men at all, some said, but daemons. Few knew where their home lay, or understood their tongue, or could divine what gods they worshipped, or what they truly believed, or why such monstrous beings had agreed to join the barbarians in this war.

The Scoti ... the Picts ... they were fearsome on the battlefield. But they did not eat human flesh.

'Make haste,' he urged again.

He counted only a few more than twenty refugees. Many were old, and the rest were mothers carrying babes or towing bawling children who had only just learned how to walk. A few older boys and girls, trying to seem grown.

One hunched figure refused to move. Lucanus shook the man's shoulder. 'You have to come now. Your life depends on it.'

As his filthy cloak fell away, the Wolf realized he was looking down at a soldier still dressed in the rags of his military tunic. His eyes flashed open, and for a moment Lucanus thought he was looking at a wild beast about to attack. But then hot tears brimmed and the soldier shuddered with deep sobs.

'I can run no more.'

'You must.'

'No. No.' The soldier collapsed on his side, wrapping his arms around himself. 'I'm done with it all. I want it to be over.'

Lucanus looked through the trees to where those lights burned, brighter and closer. He had no time to argue; there were others who needed him more.

As he turned to leave, the broken man croaked, 'There's still hope for you. I haven't got it in me any more. But if you keep going . . . to Londinium . . .'

The Wolf crouched beside him. 'Why do you say Londinium?'

'Sanctuary . . . safety . . .' The soldier began to mumble and Lucanus shook him, a little too hard. 'Any of us left . . . soldiers . . . fighting men . . . those who can still walk are making their way to Londinium. To wait for fresh men to arrive from Rome . . . to make a last stand if need be.'

Lucanus had never before ventured this far south of his home in Vercovicium. Yet he had heard tell of Londinium from those who had travelled to the cold north. It stood on a river, easy to supply, walled and defensible.

'Ho! We must be away!'

Mato dashed from the throng and beckoned him. Taller than any man there, and slender, he had the soul of a poet and his eyes normally twinkled with humour, but now his expression was grim. Their friendship had been forged when they roamed the wild lands beyond the wall in the brotherhood of the *arcani*, the scouts of the Roman army who watched for any threat from the tribes in Caledonia. Five of them were in their band, the Grim Wolves, each wearing the

11

pelt of one of those majestic beasts that he had killed himself. Of those five, only Lucanus and Mato were here. And every night Lucanus offered a prayer to the gods that the other three would be brought back to them from that dangerous territory beyond the barbarian lines where, he hoped, they still lived, still fought.

'We have no hope of outpacing the Attacotti with these in tow,' Mato whispered.

'We can't leave them behind.'

'No. But the men aren't fools. They'll see creaking legs and women laden with children, and they'll know it'll be like tying a rock to the ankle of a drowning man.'

Lucanus looked around his war-band. They weren't fighting men: far from it. He saw the pale faces of money-counters and the paunches of merchants, the leathery cheeks and mop hair of farmers, the broad shoulders of blacksmiths and butchers. They were levied from the towns and villages that were yet to face the advancing barbarian horde. The people of Britannia had not had to fight to defend themselves for centuries, not since Rome had sent its invincible army, and they'd grown soft.

But Rome was falling into twilight now, and Britannia would need to learn to fight again if its folk were to survive.

Lucanus looked up to the heavens. Not too long ago his life had been simple. He remembered laughter and the warm company of his friends in the fort at Vercovicium on the great wall that divided the empire from the barbarian lands to the north. Scouting in that wilderness, with clear skies overhead and the other Grim Wolves loping at his side. And Catia, the woman he had secretly loved since they were children. She had been married then, with a husband and a son, but tragedy had taken both of them away. A tragedy born the night the vast horde of barbarians had crashed over the wall, smashing Vercovicium to dust.

From then, it had been endless fleeing for their lives,

always towards the south, with the other Grim Wolves, and Catia and her father and brother, and Amarina who had run the house of women in the settlement. That would have been bad enough. But no, he had been caught up in a plot of wood-priests and witches, entranced by a prophecy that this time of blood and fire was the beginning of an age when a great saviour would return, the King Who Will Not Die.

His fingers closed around the gold crown he kept tucked away in his cloak. It had been given to him by the wood-priest Myrrdin, who had insisted he had a part to play in their unfolding plans. He was to be the Pendragon, which was the ancient title of the great war-leader, the Head of the Dragon, who would lead the resistance against the barbarian horde and guard the bloodline of this mysterious king. And he'd been given the sword Caledfwlch, which the druid had promised was a gift of the gods. He'd accepted the role, reluctantly.

That was when his entire life had turned sour.

Myrrdin had sworn that Catia was the Chalice, the source of that royal blood, and her son Marcus would carry the line forward until the saviour was born. And then it seemed everyone wanted to lay claim to both of them, to grasp that power and control it. And in that conflict Marcus was murdered – a death for which Lucanus had to accept some responsibility – and Catia was wrenched away from him and taken captive by the barbarians. His friends, Bellicus, Solinus and Comitinus, those missing Grim Wolves, were hunting for her, but what hope was there of ever bringing her home?

Now there was nothing but running and fighting while the light died around him.

Apullius tugged at his arm. 'They're coming.' Grief had made the lad white as chalk, and his dark eyes seemed to have stopped blinking. But he wasn't crying, now, and that was good.

*

13

Sparks leapt from flints. Strands of blue smoke twisted and specks of orange glowed like tiny suns. Soon blades of flame stabbed up along the wood's edge. That summer had been hot. The countryside was tinder-dry, and the blaze rushed through the yellowing grass and dried bramble, the fallen branches and twigs, embracing oak and ash and holly along the way.

Raising one arm high, Lucanus snapped it forward. The old folk and the mothers trudged away from the trees and down the slope into the grasslands beyond. Behind them, the wall of fire roared along the high ground, growing broader and deeper with each moment.

Lucanus watched Mato stare up as the billowing black smoke engulfed the stars. His face seemed to be full of regret. 'I'm sick of choking on smoke from the villages they've burned, and turning away from streams pink with blood and poisoned by bodies. I've had my fill of this land they are creating.' He shook his head, and raced to join the men cutting a V through the sea of grass, while Lucanus watched the ragged band of refugees struggling to keep up. How many had they rescued now? Not enough. Never enough.

Now, though . . . could Londinium be the answer to their prayers?

'Lucanus!'

Mato's cry cracked back across the bowed heads of the stumbling refugees. The Wolf saw his friend pointing and whirled.

Stars were glowing in that thick bank of black cloud billowing across the high ridge. Growing larger, brighter.

Flaming arrows arced towards them. A score, perhaps more. His cry of alarm had barely formed in his throat before the shafts whined down.

In a sizzle of sparks, an arrow thumped into the back of an

14

old man. Flames leapt across his greasy cloak to his long grey hair, and then he was howling as the fire consumed him from head to toe.

Another shaft slammed into one of his men. And another.

Screaming, the refugees threw themselves down the slope. Some fell, trampled underfoot by those behind them. A crackle became a deafening roar. Fiery waves washed the scene, cresting higher than a man's head.

'Stand your ground!' the Wolf roared at his men. At the sound of his voice, they turned. 'Take the villagers with you!'

Fear-stricken, some still ran, but others scrambled back, hauling children on to their shoulders, grasping the wrists of the elderly, heaving the infirm into their arms before once again plunging down the slope on a narrowing path through the conflagration.

As he stumbled blindly in the choking smoke, Lucanus felt a hand grasp his arm.

'Apullius ran back to find his brother,' Mato shouted above the roar, eyes watering.

Lucanus looked over his shoulder at the swirling bank of smoke lit orange underneath by the raging fires. Soon enough the barbarians would be in pursuit.

'It's too late,' Mato cried, his grip tightening.

But it was not Apullius' face Lucanus was seeing in his mind's eye. It was Marcus, the boy who had been like a son to him, whose life he had failed to save.

He threw Mato off. Levelling his arm in front of his face, the Wolf ran into the inferno.

CHAPTER THREE

The Burning

LUCANUS STUMBLED ON, BLINDED BY WAVES OF SKIN-SEARING heat and choking clouds of acrid smoke. With each step, he felt his chest tighten. If he didn't find the brothers soon he would be burned to ashes, lost and forgotten, and all those who relied upon him would be lost too.

'Apullius!' he bellowed, but his voice was swallowed by that deafening roar, which he thought sounded like a woken dragon ready to consume all in its path. When he lurched away from the worst of the fire, however, the din receded a little and he realized he could hear the sound of coughing floating in the air.

Apullius was crouching down, forcing his brother to the ground where the air was clearer. 'Hush, Mouse, hush,' he was saying. 'Any sound will draw the barbarians to us.'

The Wolf dropped beside the two brothers and saw Apullius' face glow with hope. 'If the gods are with us, the smoke will be our friend,' he reassured them.

Urging his charges down the slope, he muttered a prayer that the barbarians would still be looking for a way past the wall of fire that his men had lit, but he had barely taken five paces when he realized the futility of that hope. In the corner of his eye, he glimpsed a grey shape half forming in the smoke before the folds stole it away again.

The Attacotti were already here.

Lucanus slowed his step, afraid to make the slightest sound. No point in running. Once the Attacotti sensed him there, they would be on him in an instant. He needed to be sly like the wolf now.

The brothers must have read his tension for Morirex whimpered, clinging tighter. Apullius tried to shush him, but that only made more noise. Lucanus pulled his cloak around them, praying that would be enough.

A half-seen ghost flitted by, fading just as quickly.

Another.

This side, that side.

Footsteps thumped, drawing so close he stiffened, and were then swallowed by the deadening smoke. How many of the Attacotti were out there – the whole advance guard, or only a few who had slipped by the fire?

Easing his hand inside his cloak, he drew Caledfwlch. That was a mistake. The younger boy began to whimper again, the sound growing louder despite the protestations of his brother.

It was enough.

Feet pounded at his back. Lucanus thrust the boys ahead of him and yelled, 'Run!' Whirling, he levelled his blade. A figure took on shape and solidity as it emerged through the folds of drifting smoke.

The Attacotti warrior's skin was the white of dead flesh, the eyes circled black, the cheekbones dark-lined. Though Lucanus knew it was only crusted mud and ashes, and char-coal for emphasis, a disguise to frighten enemies, he still shuddered.

Without slowing his step, the warrior swung his short

sword in a horizontal arc. Lucanus flung up his own blade and felt his arm throb as the vibrations jolted to his shoulder. Sparks flew.

The man was fast on his feet, ducking this way then that, faster by far than the plodding barbarians his tribe fought beside. Though he was little more than skin stretched over bone, Lucanus could see he would make up in agility what he lacked in brawn.

The swords clashed high, then low. The Attacotti warrior bounded, thrust, leapt back before Lucanus could land a strike upon him. Cursing, the Wolf pushed forward, slashing back and forth. He blinked away tears from the stinging smoke, but could see his enemy was untroubled. Cold, black voids, the staring eyes were twin wells that seemed to go on for ever.

Seeing an opening, Lucanus lunged. His blade ripped open his enemy's shoulder, red streaking the crusted white. Yet the warrior didn't cry out, and it was only as that ghastly face loomed close that Lucanus realized he had been lured in.

The Eater of the Dead rolled away, bringing up his sword to clatter Caledfwlch aside. In one fluid movement, he threw all his weight forward. The Wolf breathed in a queasy mix of raw meat and loam, and then his enemy ploughed into him. He felt his blade fly from his hand.

Lucanus slammed back against the hard earth, his breath whistling through clenched teeth. A weight like a sack of grain crashed against his chest. A forearm crushed his throat. He was pinned down, his fingers clawing at burned grass, unable to close on the hilt of his sword.

The features of the white devil swam above him, filling his vision. The crust of pale ash across the skin was cracked, the charcoal around the eyes and along the cheekbones smeared. The jagged teeth were red. But it was those black eyes, like the deepest, darkest wells, that chilled his blood. He could see nothing in them that he recognized.

The face pressed closer. The coal eyes became all, and then Lucanus felt the cold caress of steel at his throat. The warrior's knife, ready to unleash his lifeblood.

The Wolf bucked, but the Attacotti killer held him fast.

Images flooded Lucanus' head, and his thoughts flew back to that night in the far north, bound beside a campfire at the gathering of the tribes when others of this warrior's kind had sawed off his ear and swallowed it. The horror that engulfed him as he watched a part of himself being consumed.

The blade dug deeper, while around him the sounds of battle ebbed until he was floating in an eerie silence. Those black eyes were his whole world.

And with that realization it was as if a torrent rushed through him. Visions of his childhood, his father's face looming large, eyes as hard and cold as the frozen lakes of winter in the Wilds, but his grin as warm and welcoming as the hearth-fire. His father, lost to him for so long, disappeared in the vast wilderness north of the wall, with not even a body to bury.

And the old wolf he had killed, one-on-one in the moonlit glade of the deep forest during the ritual when he had been accepted into the *arcani*, the majestic beast's spirit rushing into him, transforming him into a wolf himself, a Grim Wolf, who could survive in the Wilds, and smell and see and race with all the powers of his namesake.

And there was Catia, and he thought his heart would break that he would never see her again.

All these thoughts rushed through his head in an instant and then he was back, feeling the pressure on his neck, swimming through the foul stench of meaty breath.

'I'm ready,' he croaked. 'I don't fear death.'

Yet in that moment he felt the pain in his throat ease as the knife pulled back a notch. Lucanus saw something odd in those eyes: questions, perhaps.

The Eater of the Dead pushed his head down, almost into an embrace. The Wolf felt the bloom of hot breath on his neck. The barbarian nuzzled him, and he heard the deep intake of breath. Once, twice, three times.

His spine prickled. His enemy was drawing in his scent, as a beast would do with the other animals it encountered.

The warrior's head pulled back, reared up. In his eyes Lucanus saw another look that he couldn't quite define. Recognition, perhaps? Or something deeper and more troubling?

The barbarian leapt off him and paused for an instant, those eyes locked on Lucanus' one final time. Then he bounded away into the night.

The Wolf sucked in a gasp of calming air. Why had that Eater of the Dead spared his life?

A cacophony of jubilant cries rang out nearby, and he realized that the barbarian horde had broken through the wall of fire.

As he staggered to his feet, a Scoti warrior crashed out of the smoke. His braided red hair flew, and he wore leather armour and furs crusted with lamb fat from the last cold winter. A round shield hung on one arm; a short sword was gripped in the other hand. In an instant, the Scot drank everything in – the dazed man, the weapon lying on the ground nearby – and grinned. Bellowing a battle-cry, he hurled himself forward. His blade swung high.

Lucanus stared, rooted, defenceless.

From nowhere, he glimpsed the flash of a blade. A gout of crimson arced, and the Scoti warrior spun back, clutching at his opened belly.

Mato lurched in front of him, his sword dripping.

'You should be with the others,' Lucanus hissed.

'That's the thanks I get?' Mato grabbed his arm and dragged him away.

Nearby, the boys crouched in the swirling smoke, clutching each other. As he loped past, Lucanus hooked a hand under one boy's armpit; Mato caught the other. And then they were careering down the charred slope a few steps ahead of the call and response whistles ringing out behind them.

Beyond the fires, night cloaked a countryside of thick woods running along the banks of the river Tamesis. Ahead lay the old Britannia, of peace and freedom.

Pausing in the brittle grass, where their fire-shadows danced and sparks twirled up on the air currents into the dark like the fireflies in the fields of his youth, Lucanus looked back. The bank of smoke with its orange furnace burning deep within was a wall, as daunting as the one the Romans had built across the north, and one that would be just as easily breached. There was no safety any more in this new world.

CHAPTER FOUR

At the Bridge

A FIERY RED SHADED TO PURPLE AND PINK ACROSS THE eastern horizon. Lucanus mopped the sweat from his brow as he scanned the cool emerald woods and shining lakes dotting the grassland, the last undefiled expanse between the invaders' lines and the sea. Even at that hour, he could tell another furnace awaited them.

At their backs, the jubilant cries of the barbarians rang out like the revels of drunk young men heading home from the tavern.

'Still following.' Mato cocked his head, listening to the distant calls.

Apullius hugged his brother close. 'Do we run and run until we die?'

'Don't lose hope,' Lucanus said, remembering what the soldier had told him. 'We have to get to Londinium. The army, or what remains of it, is heading there. We'll be able to shelter behind the walls. Better that than being run like deer in open country.'

Mato nodded. 'It will give us a slim chance to hold the barbarians off until the cold months. By then Rome might have remembered they have part of their empire here.'

'I want to fight,' Apullius said.

'Then you will.' Mato unhooked his belt and handed it over, with the sheath and scabbard attached.

'You'll need that,' the Wolf said. 'Let him find another weapon.'

'I'm not a fighting man, you know that. Solinus always said I should have been a priest instead.' Mato's smile tightened. 'I have no stomach for death. I'm not walking away, don't fear it. I could never abandon you, or my brothers, but I'll serve in a different way: as a scout. That's what I'm good at. Or a cook, if necessary, or a smith. But I've killed my last man.'

Lucanus nodded. He understood, if he didn't agree.

Apullius strapped the belt around his waist. It fitted him well enough.

'Don't draw the blade until you've had some lessons,' Lucanus cautioned. 'A novice with a weapon is as likely to kill himself as any enemy.'

'You'll teach me,' Apullius replied, looking down at his new prize with awe.

After a while they pushed through swaying willows to the banks of the river. A dragonfly darted, gleaming like a jewel in the first light.

'One thing I don't understand,' the lad went on. 'When that ... that thing ... that white-skinned warrior ... attacked, he had you pinned down. He could have killed you. But he didn't. He ran away. Why?'

Lucanus looked back and saw Mato frowning. There was a flicker across his features that Lucanus couldn't quite read, almost as if this news was both troubling and no surprise.

'The Attacotti are unfathomable,' he replied. 'Let's not waste time trying to plumb the depths of their minds. By rights we should all be dead by now, so let's celebrate our good fortune as a gift from the gods. We live to fight another day.'

'The Attacotti were our allies once,' Mato said, slipping an arm round each lad's shoulders.

'For one night only,' Lucanus said. 'Whatever Myrrdin promised them, it was not enough to turn them to our side for good.'

Mato flashed him a grin, but the expression seemed forced, and Lucanus was puzzled. He pushed on along the riverbank, his thoughts turning cold.

The bones of the bridge jabbed from the shimmering water like the remains of a great beast whose flesh had long since rotted away. Lucanus stood under a fluttering willow, shielding his eyes against the barbs of sunlight as he tried to divine a way ahead.

'At least we know your men can obey orders,' Mato said. His tone was wry despite the whooping calls of their pursuers.

'What's happened to the bridge?' Apullius gaped at the wreckage. The central section still stood, but both ends had collapsed into the water in a mass of jumbled timber.

'I commanded my men to destroy it once they'd got the people of your village to the other side,' Lucanus said. 'The horde will turn back rather than travel along the river to find a ford.'

'But shouldn't they have waited for us?'

'Protect the helpless first,' Mato said. 'That is our law. We can look after ourselves.'

Lucanus peered along the verdant banks towards the hazy distance. 'If we go now we'll lead them straight to the ford,' he mused, before turning back to the others. Crouching, he rested his hands on the younger boy's shoulders. 'You're a brave lad, Morirex, and I need you to be braver still. Whatever happens, you must remain silent. Do you understand?'

The boy nodded.

'Good. Quickly, then: follow me.'

To their credit, the boys hesitated for only a moment before splashing after him into the shallows. His skin throbbed at the coldness of the water. As he pushed out into the flow, he could hear the barbarians thundering through the brush behind them.

Morirex flailed, spluttering, and Mato, bringing up the rear, hooked a hand into the back of the boy's tunic. Holding his head above the water, he settled in to the strong current and let it pull them both towards the ruined bridge.

Once all four were hidden in the deep shadows among the ribs of shattered wood, Lucanus clung to a beam jabbing up through the surface and watched the trees along the bank. Morirex wrapped his arms around another timber, trying to stifle his spluttering, and Mato and Apullius held on tight, with only their heads poking above the lapping water.

One by one the barbarians emerged into the hot sun, looking all around. They were quiet now, certain that their enemies were nearby.

A Pict with a shaven head adorned with swirls of black tattoos crouched to examine the grass along the bank. After a moment, he looked up at another red-headed Scot swathed in furs and leather despite the heat of the day. Lucanus had learned the tongues of the tribes during his forays in disguise in the Wilds beyond the wall with the *arcani*, but whatever the Pict said was lost to the river's gurgling.

The two warriors peered across the Tamesis to the far bank and muttered some more: weighing, debating. Around them, more barbarians stepped out of the shade of the trees, blinking. Their weapons hung loosely at their sides, all of them seemingly comfortable in the undisputed assumption that they were the masters now.

Beside him, Lucanus heard Morirex moan in fear at the sight of the wild men, and he silenced him with a glance.

A huge figure loomed out of the woods, a man who was a good head taller than any other warrior there. Lucanus had seen this one before, when he was a prisoner at the barbarian moot-camp in the far north. His head was bound with filthy strips of cloth to cover a face that had been all but burned away, so the stories said. Arrist, the Pictish king of the Caledonian south.

Arrist turned his head slowly, his cold gaze drinking in the surroundings.

The tattooed Pict trudged behind his leader along the bank until he was close enough for Lucanus to hear. 'Where next?'

'Back,' Arrist growled. 'We have our booty. These Romans can fight all they want, but their numbers are few. They'll fall before us soon enough.'

Raised voices rumbled through the trees, and a moment later two Picts emerged dragging a bloodied man between them. Lucanus stiffened when he recognized Kobold. They had thought him dead, cut down when they had retreated from the advancing barbarians the previous day.

Kobold's face was crimson from a deep gash across his forehead and his tunic was soaked with blood. 'Help me,' he croaked.

The two Picts threw him to the ground, then one of them leaned in and said something to Arrist.

'Tell me what you told them,' the king said.

'I never meant to speak out. I'm loyal—'

'Tell me and we will stop the blood flowing from those wounds. Keep your lips sealed and you'll be drained dry before noon.'

Kobold's chin dropped to his chest. Lucanus could see him fighting with his conscience. After a moment, he replied, 'One of your war-bands has taken the Pendragon's woman captive.'

26

Lucanus felt his blood run as cold as the waters around him.

'Who has her?' Arrist demanded.

'I don't know, just that she was taken—'

Arrist took the man's head in his huge hands and snapped the neck. 'There. Your blood will now stop flowing.'

As Kobold crumpled to the ground, the tattooed Pict stepped over him. 'With the woman, we could bargain. The Roman war-leader would give up his resistance—'

'We do not bargain. The stories about this Pendragon are nothing more than that . . . stories designed to frighten children. He's no threat to us.' The king raised his head to the blue sky and seemed to think for a moment. 'Still . . . if he fell, all this land could be ours before summer is out. We will not bargain. But her head would send a message. He might realize how hopeless his fight is.'

Lucanus felt a rage born of desperation surge up in him.

'Send out messengers,' Arrist said with a thoughtful nod. 'Find who has this woman. We should have words, she and I.'

CHAPTER FIVE

Open, Locks, Whoever Knocks

'IT IS THE WITCHING HOUR.'

Decima's whisper was almost lost to the warm breeze rustling through the high branches. She was craning her neck up, and to Amarina she seemed one with the shadows. Only the whites of her eyes glowed in her dark skin.

Amarina followed her companion's gaze.

The charm was constructed from twigs bound together by leather thongs to form a star shape. Hanging from it, the skulls of four small birds clack-clacked.

Amarina pursed her lips. She'd seen them before, across the years, of course she had. Hanging from the trees in the Wilds. To most folk, their meaning was hidden, as was the witches' way. A marking of territory. A warning. A charm for good luck, hung and then forgotten.

But she knew the truth.

She tugged her cloak around her. It was the colour of moss, embroidered with golden spirals, perhaps the only fine thing she still owned since they'd all been forced to flee their homes in the north when the barbarians attacked. She felt acid in the mouth at the thought of those long weeks of running and hiding and crawling in the mud like beasts.

All those years struggling to build a life of comfort for herself, leading men by the nose to the girls she kept for their pleasure and then relieving them of the gold in their purse. Counting coin and hiding it away for a day when she would truly be free. All of it, washed away in one night. If she was to see these invaders drown in their own blood, it would be for that alone. She was not a woman who forgave.

But there was little hope of that. The end was coming fast. Back at the camp, the men still waited in silence around the fires. Lucanus hadn't returned. And if the Wolf had been lost, everything else had died with him.

'I told you – there's no reason to be afraid. The sisters are our friends.' She pulled a strand of auburn hair from her face and tucked it into her hood.

Decima eyed her, but said nothing. She'd brought her own superstitions with her when she had travelled from the hot lands in the south, and Amarina could see that at that moment they were haunting her.

'Bellicus told me Lucanus found one of these charms in his hut when the boy, Marcus, was stolen,' the third woman breathed. The silver streaking Galantha's black curls glinted in the moonlight. Amarina could hear the note of longing in her voice for Bellicus, the Grim Wolf who had faded away into the heart of the barbarian lands, possibly to his death.

How had it all come to this?

She glanced back down the slope to where the lights of the campfires flickered. A lone voice was now singing a mournful song that yearned for times past and loves lost.

The camp by the ford sprawled along the banks of the Tamesis. Each day more men straggled in to join the army. Myrrdin continued to send out word to all the free lands that the Pendragon was reforging bonds from an age ago. He called on the names of the old tribes that only a few grey-hairs still remembered, insisting they send their strongest to repel the invaders.

Little good would it do in the face of that advancing horde. They never slowed, never stopped slaughtering.

She was not about to make one last stand and die. There was always another way.

'Enough talk,' she said. 'We will never find the wyrd sisters. But they will find us when they're certain we're not a threat.'

Amarina pushed on across the soft loam beneath the clustering trees. Here and there shafts of silvery moonlight punched through the canopy, illuminating their way. Pulling her hood back, she listened. A brook tinkled as it tumbled over stones. That was good. Water and wood were the signs of the wyrd sisters' favoured habitat.

In a clearing she breathed in the aroma of sticky resin and warm vegetation and struck a flint. Her torch flared into life.

For long moments the three women watched the shadows swoop among the trees. The wyrd sisters did not always answer the call – they were mercurial. Mad, some would say, their thoughts dashed away by days and nights in the loneliness of the forest, feasting on toad's-stools and dreaming vivid dreams.

Amarina felt the hairs on her neck prickle. Away in the dark, she sensed movement. Though no sound reached her ears, her nostrils wrinkled at the scent of bitter herbs.

The gloom seemed to unfurl like a curtain. Grey, hazy shapes took form, solidifying at the edge of the wavering circle of torchlight. Three women: one young, one matronly, one a withered old crone. Moon-eyes glared, wild and white and roaming. Fingers flexed, claws ready to strike. Mud-caked naked bodies streaked with charcoal so that they could become as one with the forest. Each one's untamed hair was a halo clotted with leaves.

Clutching her hands to her chest, Decima muttered something in a guttural tongue that Amarina didn't recognize. Galantha stood rigid. One hand slipped into the folds of her dress where she kept her knife.

'Sister,' the youngest witch said.

Amarina kept her eyes fixed ahead. She had heard the note of recognition in that greeting and she could feel Decima and Galantha looking at her.

'Hecate,' she replied. *And Hecate, and Hecate. The same name, as if three were one, as if all the sisterhood across all the world were one.*

'We have been watching you. All of you.'

'Following you,' the mother added.

The crone cackled and spat a gobbet of phlegm on to the ground.

'What do you want, sister?' the youngest asked.

'Aid,' Amarina said. 'Escape. Safe passage away from this dark place.'

'It will grow darker still.'

'Of that I have no doubt. That night outside Vercovicium, you warned me of this age of blood and fire. You said your time was coming round again . . . that the Dragon was rising. Rome's power would fade—'

'It has. It will.'

'You see this plan unfolding.' Amarina moistened her lips, trying to ignore the dread that had been gnawing at her for too long now. 'You will be safe. But I see no way out for any of us. The barbarian horde will drive us into the sea. And if this Bear-King comes to lead us out of the dark, as you say, it will be too late for us three. Take us with you.'

'You'd abandon your friends?'

Amarina started at the masculine voice. She glanced back to see Aelius step up to the torchlight, his sword hanging loosely in his good hand, his withered arm hidden as always beneath his cloak. Catia's younger brother was handsome, with his sleek black hair and square jaw, and he had a wit that always entertained her. But these days he was too much Myrrdin's dog.

'This is no place for you. Leave us,' she said.

'But then I wouldn't be able to keep an eye on you.'

'Don't you trust us?' Galantha snapped.

'Were you not trying to run away and leave us to face this battle alone?'

'Still. We would never betray you,' Decima said.

Aelius only smiled, but Amarina saw his eyes flicker towards her. No one trusted her. And rightly so. Memories were still raw of that night when she had taken the boy Marcus from their band to barter for all their lives. Not a day passed without her regretting it. And though it was not her fault that Marcus had died – that stain lay on the soul of his father in whatever afterlife he now inhabited – the loss only added more poison to her betrayal.

He looked past her, to the witches, and said, 'Are you servants of the Fates, or are you the Fates themselves?'

'Aye. We are.'

'Are you agents or witnesses? Do you read the runes for what is to come, or do the gods act through you to make men dance to their will?'

'Aye. We do.'

Aelius grunted. 'We'll get no joy here.'

'If you choose your words, and open your ears, they'll tell you truth,' Amarina snapped.

'The only truth here is hidden in the web they weave. I've heard tell of their kind—'

'From the wood-priest, I suppose.' Amarina gritted her teeth.

'The wyrd sisters will lure you on by feeding your hope of uncovering that truth, but you will only find yourself trapped by your own wriggling until something decides to feast on you.'

'Would you anger us?' The younger Hecate's voice was honeyed, which, to Amarina's ears, only made it more menacing.

'We do not follow your rules,' the mother said.

Aelius raised his brows. 'The rules of Rome, or of men?'

For a moment, there was only the music of the night-breeze soughing through the branches. Then the youngest witch crouched like a beast. 'When the Romans first set foot on this land, when they slaughtered the wood-priests and drove the wyrd sisters deep into the forests, the gods stepped away from us. They saw straight lines drawn across the land, not paths where we walked serpentine as we had since the first days. They saw the groves cut down. The Wilds carved and ordered. And they sighed and went underhill and beneath the lakes. But they left the doors to the Otherworld open, against the day we grow wise once more and call them back. The forests and the moors and the high land are the home of daemons, and if you listen with the wind in your ears you can hear their voices. But beware, for they can drive you mad.'

Aelius nodded. 'And so you sow seeds of confusion. For in the chaos that has engulfed this land what you wish for will take root and thrive. The madness that is your aim, and death, and blood, and the falling apart of all that was.'

'Aye. For only then will something new grow. Or something old.' The youngest witch stood up and cupped her belly. She looked at Amarina with a sly smile.

'You're with child?'

'My days are waning,' the crone said throatily. 'And soon a new maiden will join us.'

'The season is turning, sister,' the youngest one said. 'Things that have been a long time coming are almost here. Be ready. When you hear the howl, deep in the woods, be ready. Let Cernunnos back into this world.'

Amarina saw Aelius shiver. She could see he had noticed that none of the witches was blinking, their pupils so dilated that their eyes were almost black. She knew well what that look felt like, as if they were peering through skin and bone and into the very essence.

'Will you aid us, sisters?' Amarina blurted. She took a step forward as Aelius lunged for her arm.

'Hecate hears your plea, sister. When you need us most, we will be there. But we will make demand of you in return. Are you in agreement?'

'I am.'

Amarina heard Aelius curse under his breath, but it was too late. The deal was done.

Before another word could be uttered, the Hecatae melted away into the night. Aelius sheathed his sword and snatched up his torch, waving it from side to side as he stalked into the trees. He was fearless, Amarina had to give him that.

After a moment's irritated searching, he marched back to the three women.

'I am a captive now?' Amarina demanded. 'A word of warning. A quiet one for ears wise enough to hear. No one should try to shackle me. Of all the things that could be heaped upon my shoulders, that is the one that will most likely see your balls removed.'

'You're no captive, you know that. But Myrrdin's wary. Every side in this war has their own plan, and they will all use us to win. Twisted words, lies, stories that have the ring of truth but are designed only to lead us down their path. In the end, the only ones we can trust are ourselves.'

'But you do not trust me.'

'I would like to.' He waved the torch to light the three women's path back to the camp. 'But you've just agreed to do the bidding of the wyrd sisters. Can anyone trust you now?'

CHAPTER SIX

Black River

THE DAWN CAME UP LIKE FIRE. AS THE LONG, LOW WHISTLE rolled out across the grey waters of the Tamesis, Amarina stood on the edge of the camp, looking towards the west. She felt a wave of relief. They were not done for yet.

'What little faith you have.'

Myrrdin had ghosted up behind her. The wood-priest leaned on his staff, a wry smile on his lips. Ringlets of black hair tied with leather thongs framed a tanned, thin face, and he scrutinized her with those dark, fierce eyes. The black tattoo of the snake curling along his cheekbone to his jawline seemed to be watching her too.

'I have plenty of faith. In myself.'

'Lucanus the Wolf may not yet have the greatness of the Pendragon in him, but he'll grow into it. You should listen to the Hecatae. They've watched him long enough to know his true worth.'

Amarina eyed the wood-priest as he stepped beside her. He always looked as if he was enjoying some private joke at everyone else's expense.

'The Hecatae and others,' he continued. 'Strong voices have spoken out for him.'

'I'd say a man like you doesn't leave much to chance, or faith.'

36

'I commune with the gods—'

'The gods have their plans and you have yours, wood-priest. And who is to say which one influences the other?'

Myrrdin laughed under his breath. 'Schemers come in many shapes and sizes. You would know that.'

They stood in silence as another blast of the whistle rang out, Mato signalling that all was well. The sentries would be ready for them.

'There's no need to run from us. You have a part to play,' the druid said.

'I have no stomach to play any part in your game. Not one that will likely have me dying in a ditch while you dance away to safety.'

'There is a need to usher the King Who Will Not Die into the world—'

'Your need, wood-priest. To bring you druids back into the position of power you once held before Rome came and cut you out like a canker.'

'All who live on this isle will gain when the Bear-King comes.'

'You wood-priests weave your plans across long years. That's how you've survived the Roman scourge, in the deep forests and the wild places far from man. Why should I care what happens after I'm gone?'

She glimpsed movement among the trees on the other side of the river, and four figures eased out into the early light.

'Lucanus has put his trust in you,' she said. 'But he's a simple man who lost his father too young. No one has told him the way of the world.'

'And you are much wiser, I suppose.'

'You keep up with this pretence of a prophecy for the sake of those whose wits are not sharp. It brings new recruits tramping to this camp to lay down their lives. If you told them the truth, that the royal bloodline ended when the boy

Marcus was killed, and that the barbarians will smash them into the mud and march over their shattered bodies—'

'Oh, there will come a King Who Will Not Die. Have no doubt of that.'

'Ah. You plan to set Lucanus' mare to breeding again. What if the barbarians have already done with her?'

Myrrdin said nothing.

Amarina swallowed her derision at the wood-priest's attempt to maintain his lie and watched Lucanus and Mato splash through the shallow water at the ford with two boys in their wake.

Once they'd squelched up the muddy bank, Mato said without introduction, 'Speak sense to him. He's my good friend, but he's also a jolt-head of some renown.'

Amarina narrowed her eyes at Lucanus.

'He is set to ride into the heart of the barbarian horde to find Catia and rescue her,' Mato continued.

Amarina sighed. 'This is your doing, Myrrdin. You've given him a gold crown and now he thinks he can do anything.'

'Don't mock me, Amarina,' Lucanus muttered. She could see the worry etched in his face now.

'Why would you think of throwing away your life?' the wood-priest asked.

'That Pictish king, Arrist, has learned Catia is a captive of one of the war-bands. He's planning to use her to make me surrender, or he will end her days.'

'And you think you should die as well?' Amarina asked. 'What good is there in that?'

'I have to do something—'

'You'd trust Bellicus with your life, yes? Is there any man stronger or braver?'

Lucanus didn't answer.

'If any can bring Catia home, it's Bellicus and Comitinus

and Solinus. Those Grim Wolves are risking everything to save her . . . and for you.'

'They might already be dead,' the Wolf spat.

'If they are, you wouldn't fare any better.' She softened her tone, watching him struggle with his emotions.

'Have faith. Your wolf-brothers don't march into the enemy's territory alone,' Myrrdin said.

'What allies are there?'

'The gods are on their side.'

Amarina saw the wood-priest's sly smile. More secrets. What was he hiding?

The druid pushed his staff forward as if it were a wand about to cast some magic spell. 'These words may sound harsh, but they come from the heart. Once you accepted the crown of the Pendragon, you gave up all rights of a common man. You are the war-leader now, the Head of the Dragon, and that is all you are. Not a lovelorn man desperate to save the life of the woman who holds his heart. Not a grieving father to a boy who was not your son. You lead, and you fight, and yes, if need be, you die, for the sake of the people of Britannia.'

'Not often do I say this, but I'm in agreement.' Amarina half turned and swung a hand out to the jumble of makeshift tents stretching away from the riverbank. The first blue wisps of smoke were winding up from the morning fires. 'You're the difference between life and death for these men. Walk away and they'll surely die. No one here has been forged in the fires of this war like you. No one else understands the minds of the barbarians. No one else has the authority to lead. You might not want this burden, Lucanus, but the wood-priest is right: it's yours.'

Amarina hoped her words were strong enough to steady him. If she were to buy some time to find a way out of this predicament, and keep her head on her shoulders, she'd need this army to protect her.

39

Lucanus looked across the sprawling camp. Her heart was as cold as stone, but for once she felt it go out to this man who had had responsibility thrust upon him. She could almost see the lines deepening on his face.

After a moment, he nodded and marched away towards his new army without another word.

Myrrdin leaned close and Amarina breathed in the sweet smell of herbs from the balm with which he anointed his skin during his daily ritual.

'See, you have a part to play,' he murmured. 'No king stands alone. They need good men and women around them to keep them on the path of virtue. We are all his strength in times of weakness. Would you turn your back on that?'

And the day ended with fire too. The western sky blazed crimson and gold, the trees stark silhouettes against it. In the camp, the sticky aroma of bubbling stew mingled with woodsmoke. Blades whined against whetstones, an accompaniment to the lilting songs of the men hunched over their hearths.

Amarina sat cross-legged in the entrance to her tent. Across the baked mud of the path, Aelius wiped grimy sweat from his father's brow. Menius was ashen, his rheumy eyes barely seeming to register anything that passed in front of him. The old man had been hollowed out ever since his daughter had been taken.

'If you choose to leave, you know we'll come with you.' Decima was lying on her belly beside her, chin resting on her hands.

'I'm still weighing where the benefit lies.' *Weighing where we are least likely to die.* Lucanus had decided they should march for Londinium at dawn. They would be safe there, he promised.

'Wait. Listen.' Galantha cocked her head.

40

At first Amarina thought the other woman had recognized some old song. But then she heard another high-pitched sound cutting through the music of the camp.

A distant shrieking, growing closer.

Hauling herself out of the tent, she stood for a moment, feeling her skin prickle to gooseflesh. Then she hooked up the hem of her dress and hurried in the direction of the noise. Towards the river.

At the water's edge, she shielded her eyes against the ruddy glare and realized the cause of the din. Upriver, birds, a cloud of them, blackening the sky.

Decima and Galantha ground to a halt beside her, breathless.

'I've never seen the like, not at this hour,' Galantha said.

'What ails them?' Decima asked.

Amarina's gaze dropped to the turgid grey waters. Black smears were drifting. Birds would swoop down to them, then soar up high. Others fought just above the surface of the river, a confusion of flapping wings and pecking beaks. She felt her teeth set on edge at the spiralling shrieks.

As realization dawned, she spun round, shouting, 'Away! We must be away!'

Her words had barely died when the low blast of a horn cut through the birds' frenzy.

Corpses were drifting in the current, so many of them they threatened to block the flow from bank to bank. In the wake of the bodies, what she had taken to be the reflected light of the early evening sky was a trail of lifeblood. Fresh kills.

The birds swooped and fed, swooped and fed.

'They've slaughtered their captives.'

Amarina looked round at the voice, low and heavy with anger. Lucanus was studying the river of bodies. 'They don't need slaves to slow them down. They're coming.'

'So we keep running,' Amarina said, hearing the bitterness in her voice. Like deer, herded and exhausted until the moment they would be cut down.

Another blast of the hunting horn rang out.

Mato raced up. 'Our scouts have just returned. What we feared has come to pass. The second attack has begun. The horde is pressing from the north and the west.'

Lucanus whirled. 'Break up the camp. Away!' he bellowed, picking up Amarina's cry. 'Away!'

Amarina watched the river for a moment longer, remembering the slaughter at Vercovicium when the invasion had begun. The ferocity. The relentlessness. The unimaginable numbers, wave after wave crashing down upon what had once been Rome's impregnable Fortress Britannia. Crashing down until their target had been smashed to pieces. Then she turned and hurried towards the din rising from the camp and whatever fate awaited her.

CHAPTER SEVEN

When the Trees Speak

Not far from Ratae, the Britannic heartlands

IN HIS TOMB IN THE COLD EARTH, BELLICUS STIFFENED UNDER the blanket of ashes and the charred bones of men he had never known. He choked on the reek of endings.

The ground thrummed. Horses riding by. Footsteps circling the hiding place he'd clawed out of the soil with his fingers, drawing across him the remnants of the burned village and the victims who'd once lived there.

He imagined rough hands dragging him out into the light. A blade slicing across his throat. He mouthed a silent prayer.

The footsteps thumped closer.

A gruff voice called out in one of the guttural barbarian tongues – he couldn't tell which through the earth pressing against his ears.

Silence for a moment. He stiffened again.

Then a splashing, a heavy stream. Taking a piss.

Bellicus held his breath until the warrior was done and his footsteps ebbed away. The barbarian bastard would be rejoining the war-band that Bellicus and his fellow Grim Wolves had seen riding across the sun-parched land.

This was how it had been ever since they had parted

company with Lucanus and Mato on that dismal June night beside Marcus' grave, when they had vowed to bring Catia home. Creeping through dense woods into a land thick with the enemy. Crawling along ditches. Crouching in the shallows of rushing rivers, waiting for the icy moment of discovery. Hiding. Sweating. Always knowing that death could strike at any moment if they let their watchful gaze waver.

He'd clung in the low branches of an oak while Picts had swarmed a spear's length beneath him, afraid their dogs would smell him out, or he would slip into their midst and be hacked to pieces. He'd submerged himself in a bog, with only a hollow reed in his mouth for breath. He'd cowered behind rocks in the dark of the night as their horses thundered by on both sides.

In the end, they'd learned that the safest hiding places were in the burned villages, among the bodies, or what was left of them. And there were plenty of those. At times it seemed all of Britannia was a wasteland. A kingdom for rats. The barbarians expected no threat from those villages they'd already destroyed. But still they came, closer, closer, always searching, for more plunder, or slaves, or to inflict more slaughter.

It was only a matter of time.

When he heard the beat of the hooves fading away, he waited for a few more moments and then dragged himself out of his grave. His mane of silver-streaked red hair was clotted with white ash.

Solinus was already sitting on charred timbers, cleaning the filth from under his nails with a knife. He looked up, wrinkled the scar that quartered his face, and returned to his task. 'If Galantha saw you now, you'd stand as much chance of a tup as that one-balled no-cock Decra. Not for all the gold in Rome.'

Not far from his feet, the earth heaved. Muffled cries echoed, growing increasingly frantic. Bellicus kicked some clods away, then leaned down and hauled another man out of his hiding place. Shuddering with panic, their companion sucked in a draught of fresh air.

'You stamped that dirt down, you bastard,' Comitinus gasped.

Solinus grinned. 'Arms like wet straw, you.'

Comitinus was like a sapling and would probably snap with a single blow from a strong hand. There was no meat on him, even less than there had been before they began their exhausting trek behind the enemy's lines.

Bellicus prowled to what had once been the village's edge and crouched among blackened wood punching through a sea of ash. The war-band was already riding towards where Via Devana carved through the grassland. Sometimes he dreamed he would see reinforcements from Rome marching up that road from the south, helms gleaming in the sun, standard held proud. But with each day that passed, he knew it was a fading hope.

This was the world they had inherited. No point wishing like children.

He whistled, and his dog Catulus bounded out from where it had been hiding. 'Good boy,' he murmured, scrubbing the shaggy fur of the Agassian. The hound was small and slender, but if any of those barbarians had ventured near him, they'd be missing chunks of flesh now.

As he tried to stop his fingers trembling by running them through the dog's rough coat, he looked out across the patchwork of woodland and grass and lake. He frowned. A smudge blurred in the distance, like a cloud-shadow though the sky was clear. He breathed in, and for the first time in many a day tasted fresh air not marred by the reek of new burning.

45

Back at their hiding place, Solinus and Comitinus were bickering and he cuffed them both before saying, 'The barbarians are moving. This might be our chance.'

A bubble of blood burst on filthy flesh. Frightened eyes ranged. Bellicus dug the tip of his knife a notch deeper into the neck of his captive.

'Answer my question,' he growled.

'We were allies once. Friends, even. You wouldn't harm me.' Laedo forced a gap-toothed grin, wrinkling the black spiral tattoos that covered the left side of his face. He shook his head, a little too hard, and the beads braided into his long hair rattled.

'You were no friend of mine,' Solinus said as he paced around the kneeling man. 'You'd have cut my throat in my sleep for the one coin in my purse.'

Laedo was one of the Carrion Crows, the group of *arcani* who had scouted for the army of Rome out of the fort at Vindolanda. The Crows spent more time alone in the Wilds than was wise, living on berries and roots. Too long out there turned men to beasts and brought a madness that was hard to shake, all the *arcani* knew that. Bellicus grunted as he looked into the man's roaming eyes. He'd never liked them.

They'd spied Laedo loping along beside one of the warbands and tracked him for most of the night and day as he scouted for any untouched villages to plunder. He was too confident, there in the heart of that ravaged land. His guard was down and they'd taken him easily.

'We're in this pit of shit because of you,' Bellicus said, unable to resist digging his knife a little deeper. The captive howled.

'You betrayed us all,' Comitinus added. 'The job of the *arcani* was to protect Britannia from attack. But you sold us all out. Taking the barbarians' gold to deceive those you had fought beside.'

'And your leader Motius is worse than any of you,' Solinus spat. 'Mad and fierce as a rabid dog. I hate that fucker.'

Laedo bared his teeth. 'We were betrayed long before by those we called master, you know that well. All the pay that never came, though we risked our lives daily in the Wilds. No respect—'

Solinus thundered a foot into the captive's leg and he howled again. 'It's the army, you whining cunt. Nobody respects anybody. We have a job to do and we do it.'

Bellicus held up a hand. 'I'll ask again. You were always a man who kept his ears open. What have you heard of Lucanus' friend Catia? Do your new masters still have her captive, or . . .' He let the question hang.

'Is she dead? No, she lives.' Laedo looked up from under his lids, his voice sullen.

'Where?'

'In the camp of Erca, a day's march south of Ratae, by the banks of a river, the Mease, not far from the line of Via Devana.'

'Has she been harmed?' Comitinus demanded.

'They're treating her well.' Laedo smirked. 'Erca favours her. Now, I have answered your questions, as old friends do. Set me free—'

Solinus thrust his sword into the Crow's chest and twisted it. Laedo's features jerked into a startled expression. Blood bubbled from his mouth. Once he'd slumped on to his back, Solinus dragged out his sword and wiped it on the dead man's tunic.

'Why did you do that?' Comitinus cried. 'We're not murderers.'

'Ah, what were we going to do?' Solinus wafted his hand as he turned away. 'Set him free so he could report back to

Motius? Then we'd have the whole horde on our heads. You know as well as I do, he was dead the moment we captured him.' He glanced back at the corpse, thought for a moment, then spat on it before he walked away.

'We didn't have to kill him,' Comitinus muttered. 'He was one of us. I drank with him in the tavern once.'

Bellicus sheathed his knife. 'We've got what we want. There's only one thing that matters now. Keep your thoughts on that.'

For a while they moved east through the fringes of shadowy woods of elm and ash and then made camp for the night, little more than shelters of branches and leaves. After they'd feasted on duck baked in clay, Bellicus slipped away.

Nestled in the twisted roots of a venerable oak, he looked up through a gap in the canopy to the night sky. His hound collapsed with a sigh next to him, resting his head on his master's thigh.

'Will this finally wipe the blood from my hands, Catulus?' he murmured. 'Will anything? It feels like a smith's tongs crushing my heart, this secret I've kept for so long. This secret only you know, boy. If I could make amends to Lucanus ... if I could unburden myself ... I might once again be the man I was, when there seemed to be light in the days to come. But how can I tell him I murdered his father, my true friend? A drunken night in the Wilds, a fight over a woman ... ah, I have a terrible temper, Catulus. And I am a fool who deserves all the punishment the Fates can give me.'

His thoughts rushed north across Britannia, beyond the wall, and into that long-ago night, as it had done so many times. That red rage. His fists pounding. And Lucanus the Elder, the then leader of the Grim Wolves, tumbling back over the crag, and down, and down, to the river below. He'd never found the body, and he'd hoped that some day his friend would walk back into Vercovicium and give him the thrashing he deserved.

But days became weeks became months became years, and he'd learned to accept the truth. And he'd stand with the young Lucanus, ruffling his hair, teaching him how to scout and fight and survive a bitter night in the Wilds as his father would have taught him if he had lived.

Every time he looked in the boy's face, and heard his prayer that the gods might bring his father back to him, he felt that pang bite deeper into his heart. It had never eased. No man should have to live that way. But he deserved it.

'We will bring Catia back to Lucanus, Catulus. Even if it costs me my life.'

'And well it might.'

Bellicus jumped to his feet at the low, rumbling voice. 'Who's there?' he growled, snatching out his sword. 'Show yourself.' Catulus scrambled upright, his hackles rising.

'Remember, when you make your plans, you are not alone.'

Snarling, Bellicus strode in the direction of the voice. 'I said show yourself.' He waved the sword from side to side, turning full circle as he peered into the gloom beneath the branches. The woods were deserted.

'Catulus. Find him,' he demanded.

The dog raced off, only to return a few moments later with nothing to show.

Bellicus stared into the dark. Had it been his guilt speaking?

You are not alone.

For a while, he stood beside the oak as the cool breeze whispered through the leaves, weighing those words.

CHAPTER EIGHT

The Messenger

THE RED BANNER FLUTTERED AGAINST THE CLEAR BLUE SKY. Beneath it, Scoti and Picts milled as tents were wrenched down and bales were loaded into creaking carts, horses whinnying as they were fed and watered for the journey to come.

Catia breathed in the reek of sour sweat and fruity dung; piss and shit and woodsmoke. The lavender scent of her villa at Vercovicium was a fading memory.

She snagged fingers through her matted blonde hair and gave up. They'd looked after her well enough since she'd been taken captive, but for the only woman in the camp there were no concessions or comforts. She lived as they did.

And yet it was not a bad life. In Vercovicium they'd always considered those who lived beyond the wall savages. Yet these men had fine songs and stories, observed their laws, loved their kin and were good farmers too, and they had some writing as well, to record their accounts.

Easing through the throng, Catia felt lascivious gazes settle on her. She pushed up her chin, swallowing her bitterness at the knowledge that she was safe only because their leader, Erca, had placed her under his protection.

And there he was, barking orders above the din of axes

and swords being sharpened. Sparks from the campfire glittered in a halo around his wild mane of black hair.

'You're going to take me into battle with you?' she demanded.

Erca narrowed his dark eyes. 'I'd wager you'd fight better than half the men here.'

'Give me a blade, then. I'll show you what I can do.'

The Scot nodded, his smile tight. 'If we were riding to battle with an equal foe, I would think twice about taking you with us. The field of blood, shit, mud and dying is no place for women. But the Romans have shown their true nature. At the first sign of a fight the army ran like whipped curs. Cowards, all of them. We will be at the sea in weeks. Britannia will be ours. And then . . .' He looked towards the horizon, dreaming, no doubt, of Rome and all its riches.

'Lucanus—'

Erca laughed. 'Ah, the man you love. A mud-crawling scout who thinks himself a warrior-king. He has some sense of strategy, I'll give you that, and a fire in his belly.' He swept an arm out to indicate the extent of his war-band. 'But we here are few and he'd still be hard pressed to defeat us. The rest of our army? The Saxons in the east, the Alamanni . . . the Attacotti? With a feeble band of farmers and merchants who have likely never lifted a sword until this time?'

'Will you think the same when you're staring down the length of his blade?'

'Put him out of your head. You will not see him again, not in this world.' She heard the irritation in Erca's voice and was pleased.

The bear-like leader snapped round to where two bickering men had come to blows. 'Logen!' he bellowed.

Catia watched a small, rat-faced man with long greasy hair thrust his way through the crowd. Logen of the Fire's Heart marched up to the brawlers and landed a vicious kick on the back of the right knee of the one nearest. As the man collapsed, howling, Logen whipped out a knife and stabbed it towards the chest of the other man. He hissed something that Catia couldn't hear. Whatever it was, the barbarian blanched and hurried away. Logen glanced back at Erca and nodded. Erca returned the nod.

When the leader turned back to Catia, he seemed to have softened. He glanced down at her swelling belly and she realized she was unconsciously cupping it with her hands.

'Has the sickness passed?' he asked, not without a hint of tenderness.

'The herbs your wood-priest gave me helped.' She thought of Lucanus and wished she had been able to tell him the child was his before they were torn apart.

'You will need a man to care for you when your child is born.'

'You? You would raise a child that is not your own?'

'You would rather do it by yourself? And starve?' Catia saw his cheeks colour, but he glowered at her.

'And your offer is not because then you have full control of the royal blood?' She heard the sardonic tone thick in her voice.

'Think what you will. My offer was true.' The Scoti leader looked up, thinking. 'Still, your child will have some value, that I can't deny. You were chosen long ago, by the gods, or the wood-priests, or the witches, or all at once, to bear the bloodline of the King Who Will Not Die, so we are told. By now you must have realized that there are many out there who will seek to take control of you and your offspring. A wise woman would know she needed a protector.'

'I don't need anyone.'

'You've already lost one child,' he spat, then caught himself.

Catia felt her face become like stone. The grief hadn't

gone. She wondered if it ever truly would. The only way to survive would be to make an accommodation with it, as she had with her husband Amatius, all those years when he had beaten her until she bled. The price then had been saving her father, and the family, after her mother Gaia had fled with her uncle, stealing everything they owned. Amatius' family money had allowed them to rebuild what they once had, and, she was sure, prevented her father from taking his own life in the pit of his despair.

Now she hoped Amatius was dead. She wouldn't mourn him. But Marcus, her beautiful son, murdered by Amatius' hand . . . every morning she felt as if her heart was being torn out when she thought of him.

But she would survive.

She held up her hand with its missing finger, taken by those Eaters of the Dead under Erca's orders, gnawed on, and then sent to Lucanus as a message. 'We know what happens when you seek to protect me.'

He had no answer to that, but it still didn't seem to trouble him unduly. For hard men like Erca, a little suffering was to be endured and forgotten.

'You will come round,' he said, turning away.

Once the camp was broken, she trudged beside the horses like some slave on the march south. Logen watched her like a hawk at all times.

A few times since her capture she'd tried to creep away in the dark of the night. They'd dragged her back and given her the hand to teach her a lesson. Erca knew she wouldn't relent. His men had been told that anyone who let her get hold of a blade would face his wrath.

As they lumbered along Via Devana, riders galloped up with word of the progress of other bands and then rode off to the next. Catia felt stunned by the level of organization. They had been planning this a long time.

They broke the journey before sunset. As dusk crept in, the sky darkened in a blink and a summer storm roiled overhead. The bonfire sizzled and spat as the deluge began. When night fell, she sat alone under the overhang of Erca's tent, listening to the drumming of the rain.

Through the trees, she could see the flickering lights of the small fires the warriors had lit under the sheets of their own shelters. She imagined them hunched around the flames, eyes down. Did they give any thought to the folk they had slaughtered? Did their hearts soar at the thought that Britannia with all its comforts and its kindnesses had been thrown into a pit, possibly not to recover until her child had grown old?

She thought she might feel hatred for what they'd done, but she didn't. Inside, she felt numb. She wanted nothing more than to escape, with Lucanus at her side, to a safe place where her child could be born.

Let the world burn.

As the squall settled overhead, she heard the sound of running feet splashing through the swelling puddles. Motius, the leader of the Carrion Crows, darted under the overhang. He was naked to the waist, as always, his torso and the left side of his face a mass of black tattoos that made him appear as if the darkness had half swallowed him. Though he was one of the *arcani*, like Lucanus, she had always feared him, and now she loathed him, for the treachery that had brought about the destruction of her home. He didn't give her a second glance.

'Erca,' he barked.

The leader of the Scoti eased through the flaps of the tent, a wooden cup in his hand. Catia eyed his cold expression and realized he didn't like Motius either; only tolerated him for his undoubted skills as a scout.

'What is it?' he grunted.

'Laedo is missing.'

'Probably sheltering from this foul weather.'

Motius shook his head. 'His trail vanished. That means either he hid it himself, or someone who knew about trails wiped it away so that wherever he is now he couldn't be traced. Either way it means we have enemies out there.'

Catia felt her heart leap. Could it be that Lucanus had come for her? The excitement was followed by a pang of fear and she prayed it couldn't be. What could he do but die here? No, better he left well alone and lived. She could shoulder her own fate.

Erca turned up his nose. 'Here? In the far north? This land is ours. No enemy could survive. We'd find them in no time.'

'Aye. So you think. But I stand by what I say.'

Erca shrugged and waved his cup, sloshing wine. 'Take your men, then, and see what you can find.' He stepped back into his tent.

Motius stood there for a moment longer. Catia suspected he was simmering with resentment at the casual way his concerns had been treated. When he did finally turn, he flashed one glance at her, and she felt a chill. There was murder in that look, and she was certain that if she had not been under Erca's protection Motius would have slit her throat there and then, just because he could.

She curled up where she sat, and weariness brought sleep quickly despite her racing thoughts. She dreamed of her child as yet unborn, so clearly that she could see the features, and he looked like Lucanus. In her mind's eye she saw him wielding that bronze sword of his father. But the night was pressing in around him, and when she jerked awake, her cheeks were wet with tears.

It was still dark, but the storm had passed. She could hear the steady patter of drops falling from leaves, but there was a stillness beyond it. She felt relief when she breathed in the cool freshness. Recognizing the sound of hoofbeats drawing nearer, she pushed herself up. Perhaps that was what had woken her. Motius returning with his missing Crow?

A moment later she heard a whinny, and then a guttural voice demanding directions. For some reason she couldn't understand, her spine prickled with warning and she crept around the side of the tent where she couldn't be seen.

The new arrival pounded up and she heard him bark Erca's name. The flaps slapped back. Erca would not be pleased at being woken.

'I've been sent by Arrist, the King in the South,' the stranger growled. 'You have a woman here. I've been commanded to take her, alive if I can. If not I'll just take her head.'

CHAPTER NINE

The Candle Gutters

T HE HAND CLAMPED OVER CATIA'S MOUTH AND A VOICE hissed in her ear. 'If you value your life, make no sound.' And then she was flying backwards, arms clamped against her sides, her feet kicking. Away from Erca's tent where the messenger was now deep in conversation with the Scot leader, past lines of rain-soaked shelters into the deep gloom of a cluster of ash trees.

She slammed into the sodden earth. For a moment she lay there, trying to decide whether she should fight or run. When she craned her neck round, she looked up into the rat-face of Logen of the Fire's Heart. He was peering back along the way they had come, head cocked, listening for any sound that would indicate they had been followed.

'Never touch me like that again,' she snarled.

'This is for your own good.'

'I'll decide what benefits me.' She dug her fingers into the wet leaf mould to stifle her temper.

'Erca has ordered me to keep you out of sight. To keep you safe.'

'Am I too valuable a prize to lose?'

Logen shrugged, gave nothing away. He turned his gaze back in the direction of his master's tent.

'That messenger—'

'Is from Arrist, the bastard king who rules the Pictish lands just north of the wall. He's heard of you. Thinks you might be useful to strike a bargain that will bring down the last of the opposition.'

'Then why doesn't Erca hand me over?'

Logen narrowed his eyes at her. 'No one knows much about Arrist. He came out of nowhere. Seized power through bloody slaughter. But we've heard enough grim tales of his rule to know you would not be treated as well as you are here. And then you would be killed.'

'Erca risks angering this Arrist by not handing me over?'

'You ask too many questions,' Logen snapped.

Catia stirred at the sound of voices. The messenger was leaving. Once he was gone, Logen reached out for her wrist, but she snatched her hand away and strode in front of him to Erca's tent. Throwing aside the flaps, she marched inside.

Erca watched her from under hooded brows.

'Am I supposed to thank you?'

'I expect nothing. I require nothing.' Erca flicked a hand to dismiss Logen.

'What are your plans for me?'

'I have none.'

'And I should believe you?'

'I don't lie. Your kind call us barbarians. But I have as much honour as any Roman.' He sniffed. 'More, I would say.'

'The only reason you would risk a battle with your ally Arrist is that you think you'll gain more power by controlling me and my child.'

Erca turned away. Catia grasped his shoulder and instantly regretted it. He spun round, his eyes blazing. 'I'm not interested in power, not like that. Those are the games the wood-priests play, not me.'

'Not so long ago you were ready to do anything to lay claim to my son . . . to Marcus.' She felt the blood pulse in her temples. For the first time she couldn't understand this man.

'And now I think differently.'

'Why?'

Erca retreated a step. He wouldn't meet her eyes, wouldn't look at her at all. Did he think so little of her?

'We'll take Britannia. Perhaps even Rome. I'll have as much wealth as any man could enjoy in a lifetime. Why would I need more than that?'

Catia studied him for a moment. She didn't want to believe a word that came out of his mouth, but her instinct told her he was speaking the truth. 'So what now?'

Erca poured a cup of wine and handed it to her, a kindness he'd never shown her before. She sipped it, enjoying the sweetness on her tongue. It seemed like a lifetime since she had tasted any.

'Arrist won't give up. He'll send the messenger back. Make some threats. If you're not handed over, he'll come and take you himself, war or not.'

'Then answer me: why would you risk a fight with your ally?' Her thoughts were racing, but nothing made sense.

And then he did look at her, fleetingly, and she was surprised by the rare softness in his eyes. 'It may be I'll have to send you away,' he said, as if he'd already answered her question.

'You could let me go. Back to my own kind.'

He shook his head. 'Soon enough there won't be any of your kind left.'

Anger flared and she silently cursed herself for treating this murderous dog like a civilized man. She hurled the cup of wine aside. 'I've had my fill of men telling me what the days ahead hold for me. I'll choose my own path, and you will not be able to stop me.'

She swept out into the dank night. Logen would be close at her heels, she knew that – she was a hound permitted just enough freedom to stop it going mad. There would be no point in attempting to flee. They'd only drag her back and beat her.

Catia weaved among the tents, trying to burn away her simmering rage so she could at least sleep. As she neared the edge of the camp, she heard raucous laughter and what sounded like a carcass being softened by a butcher's mallet. An angry epithet. More laughter.

A small group of men had gathered near a twisted hawthorn. Though it was dark, Catia recognized Motius poised like a spider ready to strike. The other Carrion Crows surrounded him. Three figures lay at their feet, all of them badly beaten.

Catia stepped closer. Her hand flew to her mouth.

One of the captives raised his bloodied head and saw her. She watched a defiant grin spread, despite the agony.

'We've come to rescue you.' And Solinus gave a throaty chuckle until Motius' foot slammed his wits away.

CHAPTER TEN

Age of Orphans

IN THE DISTANCE, THUNDER RUMBLED. THE WIND WHINING through the branches forced the storm away to the north-west. They would not have rain that night.

That was one small blessing. Mato looked out through the inky dark of the forest, where the red stars of what seemed like a hundred fires glowed. He was perching on a fallen tree, feeling his thighs burn and the wheeze of exhaustion in his chest. Lucanus had kept the pace hard in the face of the advancing wave of barbarians. But now he had given them leave to break for a while, to rest, to fill their growling bellies with the game they'd caught along the way.

How long could they keep running before they fell under those swords?

Sobbing could be heard and Mato heaved himself up and picked a path through the trees, following the sound. The crying came from the boy, Morirex, the one the others called the Mouse. His brother Apullius hugged him close, trying to comfort him. On the other side of the campfire Aelius lounged, his good arm stretched out along another fallen tree. He seemed unmoved by the boy's pain, his expression aloof and wry as always. But then Mato saw a shadow flicker across his face and knew it was just one of the masks he wore.

'Cry,' Aelius said. 'Cry until all the tears are gone.'

Apullius looked up. 'Don't be cruel.'

'Cruelty is to pretend what's gone is coming back. That hope will destroy you, in time. The only way to survive is to turn your face to this new world we've inherited.'

'I want Mother to kiss my tears away,' Morirex sobbed. 'I want Father to play-fight with me in the meadow.'

Mato watched Aelius' features soften. 'Your heart aches, I know. But you're part of a special brotherhood now.'

Morirex stopped sobbing and frowned.

'This is the age of orphans. Britannia is filled with ones like you now. Once the pain you feel ebbs away, and it will, you'll find that you've been given a gift—'

'A gift?' Apullius exclaimed in horror.

Aelius nodded. 'Death changes us all. We can't understand life, or ourselves, until we see it claim someone close to us. At the time it seems too harsh to bear, but it changes us. We were lead. We become gold. This is a great secret I'm telling you, one that only the wisest among us know, so heed it well.'

Mato smiled when he saw that Apullius and Morirex were rapt. Aelius had a way with words, from all those books he'd read. But the spell was affecting him too, he could feel it, and he remembered with a pang the day his sister left this world and travelled to the Summerlands. Lead into gold. He still carried the pain of that loss around with him, but he was a better man for it, a humbler man, a wiser man. What a cruel game the gods were playing, that this was the way to become the one you were always intended to be.

'Orphans are particularly special,' Aelius was continuing, his quiet voice still weaving through the crackles of the fire. 'The loss they endure ignites a fire in their heart. They go on to do great things. They have something to prove.'

Mato could see the Mouse was on the brink of tears again.

Aelius must have seen it too, for he wagged a finger. 'Listen carefully. I have a tale to tell.'

'About the King Who Will Not Die coming to save us?' Morirex gasped between two juddering breaths.

'In a way. But first I need to tell you how all this came to be, this misery, this world turned on its head.' He looked up into the dark among the branches, pausing for effect. It worked; the boys were rapt again. 'In the north, there is a great wall that runs from sea to sea. On one side, the empire. On the other, the land of the barbarians, of witches and dae-mons and curses and magic. For long years, battles raged along that wall like rolling summer storms, coming and going. And yet still trade flowed across it, back and forth. That lulled us. We thought we were cousins who fought and then made up. We never realized how much they hated us. The Scoti and the Picts held a great moot, and summoned the representa-tives of all the tribes scattered from where the sun rises to where it sets. They found common ground, and that was their hatred of Rome. Rivals became allies, because they knew, in that pact, they had the numbers they needed.

'And in Vercovicium, one of the great forts along that wall, and its settlement, we continued blindly with our mundane lives. Trading and fighting among ourselves and drinking and wooing. We were fools in many ways, all of us from the emperor Valentinian to the lowliest apprentice. We'd grown compla-cent. Rome was distracted by events elsewhere and it had stopped sending enough supplies and reinforcements and gold to keep our defences at their peak, so they began to crumble. There was no pay for the *arcani*, whom we relied on to scout the barbarian lands and warn us of impending attack—'

'Lucanus was *arcani*,' Apullius exclaimed. In his eyes Mato glimpsed the light of admiration, if not worship.

Aelius nodded. 'The *arcani*, the spies of Rome. Lucanus' band, the Grim Wolves, were the only ones who remained true.' He waved a hand, urging them to listen to his tale. 'And then there was the centurion Falx, now the most hated Roman in all of Britannia. He stole wages from his own men so that they became resentful and wouldn't fulfil their duties. All of this left us unprepared for the barbarian horde massing in the north. When they struck, it was like a wave of steel and fire that crashed over the wall, over all Vercovicium.

'Those of us who survived that slaughter fled south – and none of us would even have lived if not for Lucanus and the Grim Wolves. That vast horde came at our heels, looting and burning and . . . more.'

Morirex's eyes widened, Mato could see.

'Things look dark now,' Aelius continued, 'but this is a story of heroes.'

'And we are the heroes in this story,' Apullius said, giving his brother's shoulder a squeeze.

Aelius cocked an eyebrow, his smile wry and a touch sad, Mato thought. 'Are we, though?'

'We fight for what's right. We fight for the good people of Britannia.'

'You think the barbarians don't think they do the same? Fighting against the oppression of the empire. Driving back the ones who have plundered their villages and slaughtered their folk. Seeking revenge, perhaps even freedom from the yoke of Valentinian.'

'But . . .' Apullius gaped.

'Whoever wins will write the story.' Aelius leaned back and folded his arms. 'We've yet to know if we shall be cast as heroes and villains. No man knows that, until the judgement is made by other men after they're gone.'

'The barbarians think they are heroes?'

'All men do, my friend from the south. They learn and they love, and they fight and they strive, they suffer and they cry, and their hearts soar with the belief that they are the great Alexander or a Caesar changing the course of history. Cut-throats and beggars, princes and fools. Men who slaughter innocents, and priests who die for their creed. But whoever tells the tale will make the final decision.'

Morirex leaned forward. 'And you? You think yourself a hero too?'

Mato watched Aelius' mouth fall open to speak, and then he crunched it into another tight smile. 'I'll wait for the judgement of the teller of this tale.'

'You're strong, and brave,' Apullius pressed.

Aelius tapped his withered arm. 'I am half a man. Not one worthy of being the heir to any great prophecy. But . . . when I'm knocked down, I get straight back up again. That's how I make up for having only one good arm.'

'When the King Who Will Not Die arrives, all will be made right again, and we all will live in a new golden age,' Morirex breathed.

'Do you believe that?' Apullius said to Aelius, his eyes narrowing. He started to say more, but then glanced at Morirex and fell silent.

Mato leaned back against a tree, lost in the shadows. He was interested in the answer to this question. Aelius weaved his tale well, but did even he believe this so-called prophecy or did he understand that Myrrdin and his druids decided which story would be told, and made it real simply by telling it?

Aelius tossed some sticks on the fire and the sparks swirled up with a roar. 'The bloodline of the King Who Will Not Die runs through my family.'

'Is that true?' Apullius asked.

'It's true that my family has been cursed with bad luck. But perhaps that is the gods' way of finding a balance with the glory that lies ahead. In the months since the barbarians invaded, we have seen that history can be wiped away in the blink of an eye. Empires can fall. Oceans rise, mountains be

65

levelled by the hands of the gods. Yet we must never forget that it is men and women – their individual stories – which make up the pattern of the great sweep of events. And you are fortunate to be at the heart of the story of the King Who Will Not Die. You'll see it unfold around you, perhaps even help to bring it into being.'

A story, Mato thought. Aelius should be a senator for the way he played with words.

'But still, a family cursed.' Aelius glanced to the bundle of blankets nearby, making sure Menius was asleep. 'My father's wife Gaia left him and ran off with my uncle, taking much of what we owned. My sister Catia agreed to marry the son of another wealthy family. The price she paid for that sacrifice was to spend her days being beaten by her new husband. And then he killed their son Marcus.'

Aelius fell silent, staring into the fire.

'But Catia is strong,' he said quietly. 'She will rise above it.' His eyes gleamed when he looked up. 'When she was a babe, my sister was stolen from our home. Everyone searched high and low, but found nothing' – he shrugged – 'for days. By rights, she should have been dead. But when she was found she was being protected by wolves in the Wilds, and she had upon her shoulder a new mark, a brand, a dragon eating its own tail. The Ouroboros, the sign of the bloodline of the King Who Will Not Die. Catia had been chosen.'

'By a god?' Morirex asked.

Aelius only held out his hands.

'But if Marcus is dead . . .' Apullius began.

'The story yet unfolds. Let us wait for the ending.'

'Where is Catia?'

'The barbarians took her captive. Three of the Grim Wolves are bringing her back to us.'

Mato watched another shadow dance across Aelius' face. He saw worry there behind the glib words, anxiety for the sister he loved that carved deep into the heart of him. None of them knew if Catia was alive or dead.

'You're afraid for her?' Apullius asked quietly.

Aelius nodded. 'But I'm used to the hard knocks. It's Lucanus who deserves our concern. Only the gods know what torment must burn away inside him. He loved Catia from the time when they were children. He kept any hurt inside him when he watched her give herself to Amatius out of duty. And then, when it seemed he might finally find the path to that love, the world burned around him and Catia was stolen away from his arms. My sister was all that ever mattered to him. And now there is only sacrifice, duty and battle. However much he hopes and prays, he must know that the chance of his gaining happiness is fading fast.'

Mato jerked. Someone was standing in the dark beneath an oak's low branches. He'd not heard even a whisper of a footstep. The fire crackled and flames twirled up, lighting the face of Lucanus. Mato winced. Deep lines were carved in his friend's face, so deep that he seemed about to crumble. The pain of yearning for a love lost, one who might already be dead, whom he might never see again.

Mato felt his heart go out to him, this man who kept his own suffering hidden for the sake of his men's spirits.

The thunder rumbled again, closer this time. And then, on the back of it, further away. Mato frowned. He saw Lucanus stiffen, the raw emotion drain away, the cold features of a commander rise up.

Two storms. One distant, one nearing. But now Mato could tell that the closest was rolling, growing louder, the sound of hooves and feet making the earth throb.

'On your feet!' Lucanus raged, whirling through the camp. 'On your feet! We must be away! Our enemies are nigh!'

CHAPTER ELEVEN

The Workshop of the Gods

CROWS SWOOPED ACROSS THE BRIGHT BLUE SKY. THEIR shadows flashed over the line of kneeling men, hands bound behind their backs. Under the hot sun, sweat plastered fine tunics of Syrian silk to well-fed bodies. Faces twisted with fear and tears streamed down burning cheeks, while lips were constantly working, pleading, praying.

The jeers of the barbarians swallowed whatever the captives were saying. In their furs and with their wild hair and beards, the Picts and Scoti and Saxons looked like wolves about to fall on their prey.

Lucanus gripped the rough bark of the oak branch to steady himself. Through the emerald canopy, he peered down the long grassy bank to where the war-band had gathered.

The captives were leaders of their communities, used to opulent villas from the look of the gold thread that gleamed in their tunics. They'd come with sacks of coin and gleaming plate to try to buy the invaders off. Little good it had done them. The barbarians didn't need offerings. They took whatever they wanted.

The leader marched along the line, a blond-haired northman. At the end of the row, he turned and raised a hand. A

68

towering Scot stepped forward and swung his axe into the air. As the leader's hand fell, the axe swept down.

The first head spun away.

Now the captives shrieked, but the sound of their terror was lost beneath the jubilant roar of the bloodthirsty horde, which only soared louder as the axeman moved along the line.

When the grisly task was finished, Lucanus glanced at Mato lying on the branch next to him. His friend was mouthing a silent prayer, and it was with a cold grip on his heart that the Wolf looked back out across the war-band, over the lush countryside and gleaming lakes and thick forests to the hazy distance, where Londinium lay alongside the great Tamesis. The sanctuary they so desperately needed to reach.

The horde must have realized that all opposition was flowing towards the south-east. They had swept in from the north and the south, two horns of a relentless advance, to close off the way ahead.

Lucanus squinted into the brassy light, but he could see no way through. War-bands roamed everywhere.

His army was trapped.

Somewhere, an owl hooted.

A milky trail of stars flowed across the vast vault of the heavens and the full moon carved deep shadows into the silvery grassland. Lucanus leaned his head back and breathed in a deep draught of balmy air scented with the fragrance of cooling vegetation. Memories flooded back of similar nights in the Wilds beyond the wall, with his wolf-brothers beside him. He yearned for that peace.

'You feel it?' Myrrdin said, his voice low and rich. 'There is magic here.'

Lucanus thought he did. The hairs on his forearm were prickling erect and he thought he could sense a presence watching them as they trekked towards the cluster of trees silhouetted against that starry sky. Not man, nor beast; not a threat, but not welcoming either. It felt ancient, unknowable.

'The old gods are here,' Myrrdin murmured. 'This is one of their places.'

Or it was the druid himself who was weaving magic. That melodic voice plucked visions from deep in the cave of his head.

'The old gods,' Lucanus whispered. He felt awed by the silent majesty of that night world, as if he had been standing in a temple. 'Cernunnos, who stands deep in the forest and howls? The Morrigan, the Phantom Queen, the bringer of night?'

'Both of them and more.'

They'd left the army behind two days ago and journeyed south. Lucanus had been loath to abandon his men – the barbarians could attack at any time – but the wood-priest had pressed on him the importance of their going. 'A rite,' the druid had said. 'Putting the fire into your soul so you are ready for what's to come. You wear the gold crown of the Pendragon. Now you must let the serpent into your heart.'

He'd had no idea what the wood-priest had meant, but Mato had urged him to go too. The army was well hidden, camped in a deep, near-inaccessible valley at the heart of one of the old, dense forests. Mato would keep watch, and lead them away if any danger arose.

And so, reluctantly, he had set out under a rosy dawn, following a path that was ancient even in his father's father's father's time. Myrrdin knew the route. His people after all were the keepers of the old ways, and the old places. They'd followed the drovers' road due south between high banks topped with sweet-smelling blue flowers, planted there as offerings to the gods for safe journeys, so the druid told him. But where Myrrdin was concerned, Lucanus could never be quite sure what was true and what was some elaborate tale designed to lead him by the nose.

The wood-priest had leaned on his long staff as he navigated the meandering track, so unlike the straight roads of Rome. He kept his eyes high, watching the paths of sparrows as if they would reveal to him any dangers around the next turn.

They slept beside a still lake that was like a mirror lit by the moon. Myrrdin had told him it was one of the doors to the Otherworld, perhaps even the Summerlands, where the dead walked in fields of bliss. In the night, he'd woken and peered into those shining waters, and thought he could see a face just beneath the surface staring back at him. Oddly, he felt no fear. Instead his heart had soared.

When he woke the next morning, he convinced himself it had been a dream.

And now here they were at the second night. Myrrdin urged him on, determined to reach their destination before they slept. 'The lands around these places can be dangerous,' he said. 'They venture out from underhill and beneath springs and steal men away to their home, where one night passes in wild abandon. But here in the fixed world decades have passed, and all the folk the men knew have turned to dust.'

The druid did not say who *they* were.

As they crossed the grasslands, Myrrdin ground to a sudden halt. Lucanus followed his gaze. Between two black groves, a mound rose up. One bright star was suspended directly above it, almost as if it was lighting their way.

'Is that where we're going?'

'The barrow. This is where the weapons of the gods were forged in days long gone. Perhaps even that sword you carry, Wolf.'

'Caledfwlch?'

71

'That is one of its names.'

Strands of pearly mist drifted across the grass. It was cooler here. Lucanus pushed on, his hand unconsciously falling to the hilt of his blade. 'Does this place have a name?' he asked.

'Like all the old places, the names change across the years. When I was a boy, learning the ways of the wood-priests in our groves, I was told it was called Goibniu's Smithy. Goibniu forges the weapons of the gods.' Myrrdin's voice drifted out, but Lucanus found himself fixated on that silhouette of a mound with the sprinkling of stars falling across it. 'Folk have ventured here for a long time, just like us, to make offerings or learn wisdom. Beyond the smithy lie the downs, where the great old road the Ridgeway runs. It brought those seekers here from the east and west.'

'What will happen to us?'

'You will die.' As Lucanus' chest stiffened, Myrrdin continued with a note of dark humour at the game he had played. 'And be reborn, if the gods so agree. Or you will die and be welcomed to the Summerlands.'

'Then let's hope the wisdom is worth the risk.' Lucanus forced himself to show an unconcerned face as he clambered over mounds of rock half buried in the ground to where six standing stones guided the way to the black maw of the barrow.

Myrrdin stamped his staff three times, Lucanus didn't know why. 'It's said that if your horse has lost a shoe, then leave the beast here at night, with an offering, and in the morn it will be newly shod.'

'A fine story. For children.'

'There is always some truth in the old tales, Wolf. Remember that and you'll grow wise. In ancient times, teachers hid great learning in the heart of stories that stirred the blood, for folk were more likely to remember it that way. These days fools think they are just stories. But no stories are just stories.'

'You like your word-games, wood-priest.'

Myrrdin pointed his staff at the stone doorway and said, 'Enter.'

Inside, Lucanus shivered, either from the dank air or from the wood-priest's tales of gods and mysterious happenings. 'Are we alone here?' he asked, his skin turning to gooseflesh.

'We're never alone,' Myrrdin replied.

At the druid's urging, he crawled along the stone floor into a darkness so deep he felt he was floating.

'Enough.'

At the command, he stopped and leaned back against the cold wall. He sensed the wood-priest settle beside him, and a moment later fingers fumbled at his lips. Lucanus tasted the now familiar bitterness of the dried fungi that the druids used in their rituals.

'We're to fly?' he asked.

'We are to meet the gods.'

Lucanus felt as if the dark was swallowing him whole. 'How does this help us out of the barbarian trap? We can't stay in hiding. And if we emerge they'll slaughter us.'

'You have an army.'

'We have an army, growing but small. And a mass of old folk, women, children, sick and crippled. If we're wolves, we now move at the speed of three-legged ones.'

'You've been watched for a long time, Lucanus. You, and Catia, and her mother before her. This plan has been long in the making. It will not be allowed to fail, not now, when it is finally coming into the light. You were chosen as the guardian of the bloodline because it was decided there was no man better—'

'Who decided?'

73

'Powerful voices spoke for you. But that is neither here nor there. You were made the Head of the Dragon because you have a wolf's heart, and some wit. You'll be a great leader of men, whatever you might think. Use that wit and show us how the great wolf would bound free from this trap.'

Lucanus thought he heard a sudden flapping of wings in the dark. He was sinking into his toad's-stool dreams.

'You poke and prod me to get me to do your bidding. But I'm my own man and I make my own choices.'

Somehow he knew Myrrdin was smiling sardonically.

'Every man thinks he leads his own story. But all are merely players in a greater tale. Their actions chosen for them, their words delivered to their lips. Mere agents of the Fates, Wolf, who must bring about ends beyond their understanding.'

Those flapping wings seemed to be sweeping back and forth through the belly of the barrow.

'There are two worlds, Wolf.' Myrrdin's voice droned on, lulling him. 'The world of emperors and kings and armies and wars, and the world of secrets. You hear of one, but not of the other. Yet both have power. So let me tell you one of those secrets that truly shapes all things: there is only one story, one story that surfaces across the world in different forms. And there is only one source of wisdom, which takes on many faces.'

'You like the sound of your own voice. That's one thing I've learned.'

'You've had no schooling, but even you must have heard of the wise men of Greece from ancient times who have provided so much of our learning. Those teachers were forged by the Eleusinian Mysteries.'

'And if these Mysteries are so great, why haven't I heard of them?'

'The ritual has survived for near two thousand years,' the

druid continued, ignoring him. 'Think on that. What kind of thing lasts so long in this world, and why? From it, the followers of Mithras developed their own rituals, as did the new followers of the Christ. Aye, and so did we wood-priests, after a fashion. Plato's wisdom grew from it, and Pythagoras' music of the spheres. And Cicero too. You have heard of him? No, of course you haven't. Cicero said, "In the Mysteries we perceive the real principles of life, and learn not only how to live in joy, but also to die with better hope."'

Lucanus felt himself drifting now. He thought he could hear a resonant heartbeat, in the ground beneath him, or in the stone walls. Or perhaps it was only his own.

Slow, steady.

'For in that ritual . . . in our rituals . . . a man is purified, and initiated, and for a time dwells with the gods where he is taught great things, and to be a great thing,' Myrrdin continued. 'And the Mysteries do it through fasting, as we have fasted these last two days, and through stories, in which the secret wisdom is revealed, and through partaking of *kykeon*.'

'*Kykeon*?'

'*Kykeon* is the basis of all these rituals, Wolf, in Mithras, under the Christ . . . you yourself have eaten it this day.'

'The mushroom?'

'It is the base of all religions, for it's the way we speak with the gods. It brings about death, and then rebirth, and then divine inspiration. You have died and been reborn once, in the cold waters beside the Isle of Yews. This is the next step on your path to birthing the Dragon into the world. Here, in the dark of the smithy, you will die again. And if the gods are willing you'll be reborn with new wisdom, as many have died and been reborn in this place since the world was young.'

Lucanus fought the deep currents dragging him along. 'All of this is moot, wood-priest,' he croaked. 'Marcus is dead. Who will now carry the bloodline? Perhaps this is all for nothing.'

'No.' Myrrdin's voice cracked. 'There will be a saviour, come what may. It will be made to happen.'

'By the Fates?'

'By all who stand to gain by the end of Rome's rule and a return to the old ways. We are marching into the long night. The only light to guide our way is a king who will unite the old tribes. If he does not come into being . . . if our enemies destroy that thin hope . . . there is only darkness ahead.'

Those wings again, beating harder still. He could feel his thoughts slipping away on the brink of a deep, dark well.

'You're in the labyrinth now, Wolf. As are we all, to a degree.'

'In the stories I've heard, there's usually a monster at the end.' Lucanus felt his blood run cold. The flapping wings had died away and now there was only a deep, abiding silence. But in that quiet he felt sure he could sense some brooding presence.

'Think on this. What makes a king? Blood alone? Or is it, like the sign of the serpent eating its own tail, something more? What makes a king someone who will be heeded, and followed? Belief. Folk must believe that that royal blood has special qualities. They must believe the story. That is why kings wear crowns, for a crown is a story of a kind, that sets the man apart. Magic swords gifted by the gods. Words of power. Feats of legend. A man who is purer in heart, filled with greater honour, and greater courage, who will command the obeisance of all people, simply by being. Who will lead and they will follow, without question. The King Who Will Not Die will have all these things. A band of followers who will lay down their lives for him. A sword that shows his power. A great palace, so that all who look upon it will know what he stands for. For that is the only way the rule of Rome will be broken. This story has already been told. Now we only need to bring it into being.'

Lucanus turned his head, trying to pierce the oppressive gloom. 'Why me, wood-priest?' he muttered, distracted by his mounting unease. 'I'm nothing. A mud-crawler in the Wilds. A scout, not a warrior.'

'A warrior kills. A scout sees the dangers ahead and finds a hidden path.' When Myrrdin breathed a sigh, Lucanus thought he heard a deep sadness in it, perhaps even pity. 'Keep this candle burning in your heart: there is a mystical land, in the west, where the dead go. Avalon, it is called. There will be your seat of power.'

Lucanus turned to the sound of the druid's voice. It echoed further away now, as if rolling from the end of a long tunnel. 'The road to the west is cut off by the barbarians. We'll not be able to reach it until they are broken, or we're strong enough to cut through their lines.'

'Avalon waits for you, Wolf.'

Lucanus imagined a shining palace and felt warm. A place where they could all be safe. He slumped back against the wall.

In the dark, he thought he could see fireflies swirling, coalescing into a form. He half slid Caledfwlch out of its sheath, but his muscles felt like stone and his fingers fell away. Dim sounds reached his ears.

'I hear my father calling to me, wood-priest. He wants me to join him.'

A shiver.

'Wood-priest?'

He was alone.

CHAPTER TWELVE

The Second Dragon

Gaul, 25 August

THE CRIMSON TIDE WASHED IN.

Pink eddies swirled around jutting elbows and crooked knees. Pale faces stared like beached fish. Beyond the new reef of tangled bodies winding through the shallows, so many corpses drifted that a man might think it possible to walk from the beach to the moored ships without getting his feet wet.

Lucius Aurelius Corvus laughed and dug his heels into his horse's flanks. Across the wet sand he thundered, towards the Alamanni trying to form a defensive line in the surf. With their hair dyed red for battle, they looked like a splash of blood drifting on the heaving grey ocean.

He lived for moments like this.

Salt water splashed his face as his mount crashed into the incoming tide. Around him, a mad confusion of steeds and glinting armour churned. He only half heard the battle cries of his brothers-in-arms and the thunderous oaths of the barbarians. Cool and calm, he narrowed his attention to one target.

The warrior came at him, swinging an axe. Corvus dug

his heels in again, refusing to slow as he steered his mount just out of reach. As he passed the off-balance warrior, he leaned to one side and swung his *spatha*. The blade cleaved off the top of his enemy's head.

Corvus didn't see him fall. He was already riding on to the next, and the next.

And then the cavalry pulled round, pounding back up the beach to regroup.

As he turned his horse, ready for the next assault, Corvus flexed the cricks out of the muscles between his shoulder blades. His arms felt like stone, so much hacking and stabbing had he done. But now the fighting was almost over.

'You have a talent for killing, I will give you that.'

At his side, his constant companion grinned. Tiberius Annaeus Pavo was shorter, stockier, a hunk of meat and gristle with a remarkable capacity to survive any atrocity. His own *spatha* blade hung loosely in his fingers.

'Blood and death is no work for a man with the soul of an artist,' Corvus said. 'But Mithras has seen fit to bless me with these talents and so I shouldn't grumble.'

His gaze spun to the foot soldiers now striding in formation towards the ragged remnants of the barbarian warriors, helms shining in the dying light. The enemy, in comparison, were disorganized, dressed in rags and furs, roaring their fury, but half drunk as they always seemed to be when they fought.

When the emperor Valentinian first took control of the western provinces with his brother Valens installed in the east, the Alamanni had believed him unseasoned, a ruler who didn't know how to keep the tribes in line with gold, as past emperors had. They'd learned he planned an assault to stifle their restive ways, and thought if they moved first they would cut through the Roman forces, perhaps even deter them for good. And so, with some Franks and Saxon allies, they'd attacked along the border and the Gaulish coast. Little good it did having that first move. Led by Jovinus, Valentinian's favourite general, the army was now in sight of regaining imperial control of the coast.

'All is well in the world, eh, Pavo?' Corvus called as if his friend could read his thoughts.

'All is well, with better yet to come.'

And more than anything, Corvus hoped this would be the end of it. His destiny waited in Britannia.

An arm fell, an order was barked. Corvus dug his heels in once more and leaned across his mount's neck.

As he neared the foaming surf, one of the barbarians rushed straight at him, swinging a notched axe. His mind cooling, he raised his shield and levelled his sword.

The stone came from nowhere, ringing off the side of his helm.

Corvus spun backwards. Jagged bolts crashed through his skull from the impact of the missile. He slammed on to the wet sand, half realizing his sword was no longer in his hand. The barbarian loomed up against the rosy sky above him and flexed his biceps to bring his axe down.

Barbs of gold flashed across his vision: light shimmering off three blades in motion. One hacked through the barbarian's forearm. Another carved into the ribcage and the third cut into the neck. Corvus watched, fascinated. A red rain fell upon him. As the barbarian toppled backwards like an oak that had been felled, he felt hands grasping him, hauling him to his feet, pressing his sword back into his hand.

Bemused, he looked around at the three soldiers who had come to his aid. He knew them, of course, though he couldn't quite remember their names. All were secret worshippers of Mithras, like him; all ordered by Severus the Father to protect him at any cost. Their faces were serious, but their eyes gleamed with something close to adoration. He liked the feel of that.

'Our Lord smiles upon you!'

Corvus glanced round at the familiar voice. Theodosius the Younger was striding towards him, pulling off his helm to wipe the sweat from his brow. His friend was not a good-looking man, Corvus had to admit. His eyes bulged like a toad's and his sandy hair was already starting to thin, but no doubt his god loved him as much as any other.

'That's true. I will give my thanks in prayer tonight.'

Theodosius looked towards the three young soldiers throwing themselves back into the battle and shook his head in quiet bafflement. 'Your courage in battle appears to have earned the respect, even the love, of the men who fight beside you.'

Corvus only smiled. Humbly, he hoped.

The whoops of carousing soldiers rolled up from the twinkling lights of the camp in the valley. After the day's great victory, the order had been given for celebration. Ample quantities of good Roman wine had been brought in along the supply routes well in advance, and Corvus could still smell the sticky aroma of roasting venison.

'Ah, to wallow in wine, instead of traipsing into the dark for dull devotions.' He grabbed a branch and hauled himself up the steep slope.

'Nights lost in your cups are behind you now that you're a man of destiny.' Pavo's voice floated up from the trees behind him, thick with irony. 'There is only sacrifice, and struggle.'

Ahead, a shadow separated from the rest and Corvus whistled through his teeth to announce his presence. One of the men who had saved him on the beach stood guard beside a gash in exposed rock.

'And here is my first sacrifice,' Corvus muttered. 'Hiding away like mice while the cat prowls.'

'Those Christian cats have sharp claws, don't forget,' Pavo murmured.

The guard leaned in to peer into Corvus' face. 'Glory to Sol Invictus. You are alone?' he added, looking round.

'I am.' Corvus flashed a sly glance at Pavo, who grinned in return.

'Then enter, Heliodromus,' the guard said.

Wavering candlelight gleamed off slick stone walls as Corvus squeezed into a narrow natural tunnel in the bedrock. Behind him, he could sense Pavo's shade, always with him. Ahead he could hear the low rumble of voices. The crevice opened out into a cavern, the ceiling high enough to be lost to shadows above the orange glow of the torches on the walls. Corvus nodded approvingly. A temple in the earth's womb, perfect for the worship of Mithras who was birthed from the rock. The others had worked hard to find such a place at short notice.

'The Heliodromus has arrived.' A low voice reverberated from the far end of the temple. 'Let the Sun Runner step forward.'

The soldiers eased aside and Corvus marched forward to the makeshift altar. Behind it, the Hanged Man, Gnaeus Calidus Severus, peered down his nose, his head twisted at an odd angle from that long-ago failed attempt upon his life.

'Honoured Father,' Corvus said to the priest.

'The Invincible Sun has shone down on you this day. A great victory.'

'I wouldn't be standing here now if not for my brothers under Mithras.'

'Your brothers would lay down their lives for you, you know that. You are our great, perhaps last, hope as the Christians seek to crush us at every turn. The Dragon. It is your blood that will lead to the rebirth of our saviour upon this earth, great Mithras incarnated in the body of an undying man, who will lead us all out of this darkness in which we find ourselves.'

Corvus didn't know if the Hanged Man believed any of this, but he sold his story well to the gathered soldiers. They were simple folk. They didn't question that the Christians had the same prophecy of a saviour who would return, and the Egyptians with their strange beast-gods, and no doubt every other sect and cult whose followers raised their eyes up to the heavens in hope of salvation.

Whoever finally and completely laid claim to that story would own the power that accompanied it.

Corvus slipped off his tunic to stand naked, head bowed with suitable supplication, he hoped. He knew all eyes would be on the brand of the Ouroboros upon his shoulder, the serpent eating its own tail, the symbol of that eternal bloodline.

'I am only your poor servant, Father, and the servant of Sol Invictus.'

He stooped his shoulders and let the ritual wash over him. The chanting, the drone of Severus' voice as he spoke of the slaying of bulls, and the passage of the soul, and the great serpents who would fly from this world to the heavens to herald the king of kings made flesh.

Afterwards, there was no bull to slaughter and consume so he hunched with the others along the dank walls, gnawing on dry biscuit washed down by cheap wine. The sacrifices he had to make never ended.

As weariness settled on all of them, Severus beckoned Corvus to the dark behind the altar. 'I meant what I said,' the Hanged Man whispered. 'All our faith is in you. The situation in Rome is intolerable now for any follower of Mithras. They will have us crucified outside the city walls if they have their way. The emperor is too distracted by this business with the barbarians . . . not that he would care one way or the other what happened to us.'

'I value your guidance, Father.'

'You're ready for what lies ahead?'

'I will ensure any other pretenders to the saviour's blood-line will be swiftly dealt with.' *Particularly my half-sister Catia and any progeny she may have spat out.*

'You do not fear this news coming out of Britannia?'

'A few mud-crawlers with a grudge against Rome? You saw how quickly their resistance faded today.' He shrugged. 'We will be on our way soon enough. Jovinus is only waiting for his scouts to return from across the channel so he can prepare his strategy, which, I'm sure, will be nothing more than stab and thrust and shout loudly.'

Severus grunted. 'Don't expect any help from the emperor. Valentinian is still on his sickbed, I hear. News reaches me that yesterday his son Gratian was acclaimed Augustus by the troops at Amiens.'

'The emperor fears he might die?'

'Would he take steps to secure his dynasty in this way if he did not? Let us hope this doesn't interfere with our plans. For the love of Sol Invictus, we cannot continue much longer in this manner. The worship of Mithras is dying by the day.'

'Don't worry. All I require is that you watch over my mother.'

'Gaia and her child will be protected at all costs.'

Corvus saw the glimmer in the other man's eye and knew the priest wanted to say *your child*, but this was another of those matters which they had both chosen to allow to remain unspoken. His incestuous union with his mother was not born of carnal urges, only a desire to keep the bloodline pure so their claim to be the progenitors of the great saviour would carry more weight. But few would comprehend that, he knew.

Once they had finished their feast, if it could be described as that, the soldiers crept out into the night. Pavo was loitering among the trees. They stumbled down the slope together, but the twigs cracked under only one set of feet.

'I'm not sure how I'll survive in Britannia if the barbarians have looted all the good wine,' his friend said.

'There'll be more than enough for us. Besides, soon we'll have all the power and the gold that flows from it. We'll be able to buy enough drink to swim in. Did you not hear Severus? The Dragon will fly up from the earth to the heavens.'

'I forget you are a Dragon now. I bow my head to you.'

'No respect,' Corvus sniffed. 'Perhaps I should ally myself with someone who knows my true worth.'

'You'd be lost without me,' Pavo said, with truth.

Jubilant songs were still ringing out through the night as Corvus slipped into the camp. He skirted the fires where the men gathered, cups raised high. But as he flung back the flaps of his tent he sensed a presence waiting inside. His heart pounded when he saw Theodosius the Younger.

'Old friend,' Corvus gushed. 'You're missing the celebrations.'

He tried to read the other man's face to see any sign of threat, but the shadows masked it. He knew full well what would happen to him if a Christian as devout as Theodosius had learned he was a follower of Mithras, friendship or not.

'You know I have no time for drinking and carousing.'

'Of course. I was, myself, coming to prayer. Perhaps we could bend our knees together?'

'There's no time.'

Corvus flinched as Theodosius stepped forward, but the light dancing through the open flap showed only worry lines on his face.

'What's wrong?'

'We must ride tonight, on my father's orders—'

'Where?' Corvus blurted, unable to hide his relief.

'Now the coast is secure, the emperor is bringing the court to Trier to oversee the campaign from his sickbed. We must intercept them. Storm clouds are gathering, or so my father says, but he hasn't yet revealed the nature of his fears to me. I'm tasked with finding out what I can and bringing this news back to him.'

'The two of us?'

Theodosius nodded. 'My father trusts me, and I, of course, trust you.'

'Good. There is no one more loyal.'

Corvus damped down his frustration – he had hoped to be sailing for Britannia within days – but Severus had placed his mother and his bride, Hecate, with the court, for safety. If there was any threat to them, and his unborn child, then he should be there to protect them.

'Though it pains my heart, I will set aside my prayers for now,' he said. 'Let us ride so hard our arses hurt. I am at your command.'

His arse did hurt. Another sacrifice. Oh, for when he could sit at his own court, with his mother on one side and his bride on the other, with Gnaeus Calidus Severus standing behind him to advise, and all the heads bowed before him, offering fealty to this prophesied saviour. Then no one would make him ride for days and nights with only dry crusts to fill his growling stomach.

Theodosius kept his spirits up with his prayers, of course. They had time to pause for devotions at the side of the track through the baking countryside, but not to grab a little sleep in the shade.

Every now and then Corvus glanced back into the wavering heat haze. Once or twice he thought he saw Pavo following. He would be there somewhere, a ghost haunting their trail. His friend would not abandon him, whatever the risk.

They took the road south of Trier and a day later found the court camped for the night, a tent city surrounded by carts and wagons with the horses whinnying in their pens. When Theodosius led their own mounts to water, Corvus slipped away through the drifting smoke of the fires.

Following directions, he hurried to a sapphire tent on the edge of the camp. Inside, he felt his skin bloom from the heat. A brazier hissed in one corner, quite unnecessary for that time of year, but his mother felt the cold here in the west, away from the stifling Roman summer.

Gaia sat on a curved chair, hands clasped on her growing belly. A spiderweb of lines edged her eyes. She was not old, but this would be her final attempt to bear a child. And she was not used to travelling so far, or in the kinds of conditions endured by soldiers. Rutted roads, poor food, cheap wine. In Rome, she had only experienced a life of sumptuous ease, enjoying the wealth the family had made since they had fled Britannia when Corvus was barely formed.

'My beautiful boy,' she said, forcing a smile.

'Mother. I trust I find you well.'

'As well as can be expected in these hideous surroundings. Severus has made sure I'm well looked after.' Her face crumpled. 'My darling, why couldn't I have stayed in Rome? Our child would be safe there.'

Corvus sighed. 'Mother, I've told you. Britannia is where our destiny lies. Our heir must be born there, where the King Who Will Not Die has some meaning. That is where the power lies. That is where you were chosen, yes?'

She nodded, her head drooping.

'And if this child is born in Rome where the Christians are rampant, I wouldn't hold out much hope for it once they learn the followers of Mithras have a claim upon it too.'

Gaia kneaded her hands together. 'Are we doing the right thing? All these schemes and deceits—'

'The prize is worth it.' Corvus heard the snap in his voice and swallowed his irritation. Softening, he added, 'You've suffered so much in your life, Mother. All that hardship and striving. When Father died . . .' He winced, stifling the dream he had that he had pushed his father overboard in the storm that assailed their ship when they were fleeing Britannia. 'You deserve all that awaits us.'

'Corvus?'

He winced again, this time at the way the guttural notes of the barbarian still inflected the mellifluous Roman tongue. Turning, Corvus smiled at his new bride, Hecate, as she stood in the entrance to the tent. He had thought how beautiful she looked in that filthy shack in the Alamanni territory when he had rescued (*seized*) her after her sisters had been killed (*murdered at his command*). Now she had been bathed and massaged with fragrant oils and unguents and civilized by life in Rome, she all but took his breath away.

Corvus held out his arms and she stepped into his embrace. For a moment, he inhaled the perfume of her hair.

'Come to my tent,' she breathed.

'Stay here.' Gaia's voice was wintry. 'We have plans to make in preparation for Britannia.'

Corvus watched Hecate pull back and flash a honeyed smile at his mother. If his bride suspected that it was his child Gaia was carrying, she gave no hint. But she was clever, this girl, for all she'd had no schooling. She'd quickly grasped what was at stake. She knew the prophecy of the King Who Will Not Die, as all the barbarians seemed to know it, and she was prepared to do all she could to see her husband achieve his destiny. The thought of power and riches had a way of turning the heads of even the most innocent of people.

'Mother, you know I have spent little time with my wife since we were wed.'

Gaia glared.

Hecate leaned in and whispered, 'I will give you a night you will never forget.'

'If I didn't know better, I'd think she had you under a spell,' his mother said with a snort. 'Has she been slipping you some of those potions she conjures up in her cauldron when she thinks no one is watching? Yes, my dear, I've seen you at work.'

Another smile from Hecate. She knew she had the upper hand.

'We're family now. Let's not argue.' Corvus took Hecate's hand and reached out to Gaia. With a sullen girlishness, she grasped his fingers.

'Corvus!' His name echoed through the night.

He sighed. 'No rest for the wicked.'

Stepping out into the balmy darkness, he searched the shadows until he saw Theodosius stumbling among the tents. 'Over here.'

His friend lurched up and grasped his arm. 'Two riders have arrived. This is what my father anticipated. Bad news, I fear. Terrible news from the look of their faces. Come.'

Corvus wrinkled his nose as he stepped into the lush interior of the tent. It was the largest one in the camp, a glorious purple, filled with sumptuous cushions, gold plate, tapestry, places to sit and even a low bed so the emperor didn't have to sleep on the hard ground like the common herd. The air was perfumed, but he could smell the tang of sickness beneath it.

Theodosius tugged him on past the waiting guards. The tent had been divided by a sheet of gauzy material and beyond it Corvus could just make out a small crowd. He felt

Theodosius' hand between his shoulders, pushing him towards the rear of the group.

Valentinian lay on his sickbed. He was a tall man, and his bony feet hung over the end. A mass of premature wrinkles crawled across the yellowy skin of his face, and his eyes were rheumy. His head was turned towards two men, the new arrivals, no doubt. One feeble hand fluttered towards them.

'Speak,' the emperor croaked.

'We have a tale of horror,' one of the men said, bowing his head.

'The moment we set foot back in Gaul and told General Jovinus what we'd found, he sent us straight here,' the other soldier continued. He had the bluest eyes Corvus had ever seen, the lamplight flickering within them.

'Britannia is lost,' the first man said, his voice strained. 'The slaughter . . . it's beyond anything I've seen before. Heads on spikes . . . women . . . children! And rats, so many rats, whole fields of them, heaving.'

The one with the blue eyes rested a hand on his comrade's shoulder to silence him. When he spoke, he kept his gaze level and his voice clear as best he could. 'Our army has been defeated.' He paused for the intake of breath that rustled through the gathered council. 'As far as we could tell, the men saw the horde advancing upon them and refused to fight. All our forts are empty. Those who remain, the loyal few, are gathered in Londinium. Without reinforcements there's little hope of mounting any kind of campaign to retake the isle.'

'It may not be worth retaking,' the first man muttered. 'We wouldn't get far from the south coast without meeting resistance. The tribes own all Britannia now. But from what we could see, the towns, the villages, the villas, are all burned to the ground. The people who thrived under our rule slaves or dead.'

'We do not give up a part of the empire.' Corvus nodded in appreciation at the steel he heard in Valentinian's voice. Perhaps he was not half gone after all.

'The horde is advancing on Londinium,' the blue-eyed soldier said. 'If they take that – if they reach the coast – then it will be . . . difficult for any force to drive them back. They are better organized than I could ever have imagined. Infinitely stronger in total than any of the tribes standing alone.'

Corvus felt a chill in the pit of his stomach. This was worse by far than anything he had expected. But he couldn't abandon his plans now, not when he was so close.

'A strong commander is needed if Britannia is to be returned to the empire. A strong commander, and an over-whelming force,' the soldier continued. 'General Jovinus is ready—'

Valentinian shook his head. 'Not Jovinus.' He wheezed in a juddering breath, but Corvus could see his gaze harden. 'And not now. Not so late in the year. The channel is treach-erous. A disastrous storm at sea could wipe out most of the men we send. You know well the history of what happened when we first invaded Britannia. We must leave any attack to the spring.'

'But if Londinium falls—' The soldier bit down on his words.

Now Corvus felt his stomach knot so tightly he almost clutched at it. He couldn't afford to wait until the following year.

'Not Jovinus, no,' Valentinian continued as if he had not heard the other man. 'We will be fighting two campaigns – in Germania and Britannia. Jovinus must finish his work here in Gaul.' Corvus watched the emperor muse for a moment, but his own thoughts were racing and he almost didn't hear when Valentinian muttered, 'Theodosius the Elder. He will oversee the campaign. My trusted general.'

Corvus felt Theodosius the Younger stiffen beside him at the mention of his father's name. He glanced over and saw a soft smile lighting his friend's face. No doubt dreaming of family glory. Perhaps even greater things.

Outside in the night, Theodosius clapped his hands together. 'A victory in Britannia will ring down the years, my friend. And we will be there in that great battle, you and I, at my father's side.'

'But not until next year.'

'You heard the emperor. We need time to plan, to amass the troops that we will need—'

'I think it would be wise to prepare the ground, don't you? To let what remains of our army know that help is coming, put some steel into their spine. And to scout out the land and the barbarian forces so that when the time comes we can move like lightning.'

'What are you saying?'

'Tell your father . . . *I* will go. Proudly. Defiantly. I will do whatever I can for the empire.'

Theodosius grinned. 'You are a brave man, my friend. God has put courage in your heart and fire in your belly.'

'He must have listened to all my prayers.'

'I'll tell my father, and I'll accompany you on your glorious campaign. How could I not? To do God's work! To prepare the way for our Lord to smite the unbelieving barbarians. To ride into the very mouth of hell and look Death in its face. What a glorious undertaking!'

Corvus forced a reassuring smile, though the hell and death part didn't stir his loins. The road would be harder now, for sure, but at least he would be there, in the place where he needed to be. And if fortune and the Fates were on his side, he could find his sister Catia and rid her of any ambition to steal his destiny. And her life in the process, of course.

He watched Theodosius bounce away among the tents like an eager puppy. Corvus clapped his hands together and strode in the opposite direction. First wine, and then what a story he would have to tell Pavo of the adventures that lay ahead.

CHAPTER THIRTEEN

Trapped

Voices echoed through the trees. Guttural, low, questioning. The whinny of a horse. Then they came, like bears, hunched, thickset, heads turning slowly as they searched that shadowy emerald world. Five of them, Scoti, three on foot. Swords already drawn. Across the soft carpet of leaf mould, around the exposed fingers of roots, easing through the patchwork of sun and shade.

'How many?' one of them grunted.

'A few. An army, or what passes for one.'

Mato's breath burned in his chest. They were cautious, these barbarians. Always certain some kind of threat lay ahead. Lucanus' army had been so careful to cover their tracks, but something had clearly alerted this patrolling band. A hint of smoke on the breeze. A tang of sweat. The footprint of a careless scout in the mud by a stream. It mattered little now.

Their luck had run out.

From behind the tangle of a hawthorn bush, he stepped into full view and held out both hands. 'Brothers,' he called in the Scoti tongue he'd learned when he scouted the Wilds with the Grim Wolves. It was the first time he'd exposed himself to an enemy without a blade in hand. He felt strangely liberated, yet also terrified.

94

The warriors stopped, dark eyes glinting, caught off guard by his use of their own tongue and his unarmed presence. He could see the shadows of questions flickering across their faces.

Before they could reach any conclusion, he turned and ran. Skipping over a fallen tree, bounding across a brook, Mato ducked a low branch and skidded down the valley side along the familiar trail. Whoops and cries rang out at his back. They were enjoying this. The sport of a hunt after so many weeks of ceaseless slaughter.

Mato crashed against an oak. Hands on knees, he doubled up and sucked in a gulp of air. As the Scoti warriors thundered up, he wagged one finger at them to give him a moment to recover. They laughed.

Too soon.

One barbarian dropped from his horse, blood spraying from his shattered nose where the staff had slammed into his face. As the other rider fought to keep his mount under control, figures darted out of the dense undergrowth. Hands clawed for his furs, dragging him down. Knives flashed in a shaft of sunlight. Two throats slit in the blink of an eye.

The three remaining warriors swept back to back, blades levelled. Mato could see the incomprehension in their faces. He almost felt pity for them. Since they'd flooded over the wall at Vercovicium, they'd encountered no resistance.

Seven more of his men eased out of the undergrowth. They were cautious, remembering Lucanus' training; all but Aelius. He leapt in front of the others. Mato saw the young man's wry smile and knew he was enjoying himself too. He'd questioned Aelius' decision to fight – his withered arm left him at a disadvantage – but Catia's younger brother had insisted he was capable.

And he was. He danced beyond the tip of his enemy's blade, so light on his feet he made the barbarian look like a lumbering ox. A flick of his sword. A wound opened on the warrior's forearm. The Scot snarled, angry that such a weakling was making him look a fool.

Mato watched Aelius grin. How this young man had been transformed. Once he had been a drunk, consumed by bitterness, with little hope for the life ahead of him. And then, amid all the suffering, he had been reborn.

A step to the left, a lunge, a nick, a step to the right. And then the killing blow. As the warrior howled his frustration, his throat opened. Aelius stepped back from the crimson gush and sheathed his weapon. He bowed his head to Mato.

'A morning well spent,' Aelius said. 'I must confess, I have built up quite an appetite.'

The other warriors were dispatched soon enough, though not with as much aplomb. Mato ordered the bodies to be concealed. The wolves would dispose of the remains.

But it was still only a matter of time.

'How much longer do you think we have?' Aelius asked as they trudged back to the camp. 'Days? Hours?'

Mato wiped the sweat from his brow. 'Our scouts tell us the horde is massing to the west and north of where we're camped. Soon they'll realize that these five are missing. Others will come looking for them. Maybe only ten at first. Then a war-band when the barbarians realize the five didn't fall into a bog. Then the army, from all sides.'

Aelius sighed as if Mato had told him the last of the wine was gone. 'And the river holds us back in the south. Nowhere left to run. Things do not look good.'

Mato tried not to think what would happen once that barbarian horde swept through their camp. He still felt haunted by the slaughter at Vercovicium.

'Do you fear death?' Aelius didn't, clearly. But then in Vercovicium he had seen it as a way out of his miserable existence.

Mato shook his head. 'The first time we experience death, it changes us for ever. We turn from lead to gold, so the wood-priest likes to say. You're young, but you've heard tell of the Chain, yes?'

'Paulus Catena?'

'Sent by Rome to bring order to a restive Britannia. His men cut down my sister, Aula. Only eleven, she was.'

'I'm sorry.'

'That night, driven near mad by grief, I lay in the forest and . . .' He fought to recall the memory, but it was hazy now. 'The gods came to me, or sprites, or daemons, or some agents of the Otherworld, and they told me a truth, Aelius, one I can never repeat. But I know. Even amid death, there is joy, small sparks in the dark of the night, and on that we must always focus.'

A fox slunk out from behind a wall of bramble, looked at them briefly, then moved on.

'You're more priest than warrior. Amarina told me that. And now I can see she's right.'

'I've learned to love life, that's true.'

'You see things others don't. Not strange for a scout, I suppose, but still . . . strange.'

'Strange I am. And content to be so.'

'You counsel Lucanus well, I'm told.'

'If the wood-priest is in one ear, then I would be in the other. At least then there's some hope for him.'

'Ah. A battle for his soul. How grand.' Aelius licked one finger and smoothed his eyebrow. 'The druid who walks through the shadows and will have aught done, however terrible, to see his great plan realized. And you with your road of light and honour. That balance will keep him on the right path.'

'If he ever returns.'

Down into the deepest part of the valley they trekked,

along a near-invisible trail into an area of ever-present shadow. Silence hung over the camp. Mato felt his chest tighten in apprehension. But then, as he stepped past the first row of tents, he saw everyone waiting for him, trying to read his expression, desperate, praying. He nodded, and relieved grins rushed across their faces.

They thought there was still hope.

Flies droned across the camp. Under the thick canopy, men slumped by their tents in the furnace heat. Mato mopped the sweat from his brow as he inspected the meagre remnants of their stores. Starve or be cut down. What kind of choice was that? He didn't have the mettle to be a leader and make those kinds of decisions.

When the call of the curlew rang through the trees, he stiffened. A warning from one of their scouts. Aelius bounded to his side in an instant.

'Is this it?' the young man asked, already drawing his sword.

Mato cocked his head, but no tramp of feet or battle cries reached his ears. A lone scout?

Striding to the edge of the camp, he peered along the trail, the only way in or out. The curlew didn't cry again.

A moment later, a lone figure shambled into view between the head-high banks of briar. A traveller, shoulders hunched from deprivation on the road, broken by the threat of the barbarians. But as the man neared, Mato felt a hollow in the pit of his stomach and he ran forward.

'Lucanus?'

He grasped his friend's shoulders, and for a moment the Wolf didn't seem to recognize him. And Mato, his brother Grim Wolf, barely recognized him, even then.

Lucanus was dripping wet – from the river no doubt – and his face was drawn as if he were suffering from a long sickness. But his eyes burned with a light that Mato had never seen before.

'Where's Myrrdin?' he asked, his voice hollow.

'He's not with you?'

The Wolf shook his head slowly, as if waking from a dream. But then he smiled and some colour returned to his cheeks. 'I'm not the Lucanus you once knew, my friend. I'm sorry for that.'

'What happened?'

'There's no time. We have preparations to make. An army to raise to its feet.' He pulled out his crown and set it on his head. 'I'll speak to them now.'

Mato searched Lucanus' face. His friend was indeed changed, there could be no doubt, though Mato couldn't tell quite how. He sounded more confident, certainly; clearer of mind, less burdened. Less scared.

'You know a way out?'

A wolf's smile. 'We will not be trapped here. We will reach Londinium. And then we will bring this barbarian horde to its knees.'

CHAPTER FOURTEEN

The Raid

STRANDS OF MIST DRIFTED AMONG THE TREES ALONG THE riverbank. In the early light, the first birdsong of the new day rolled out across the grey waters of the Tamesis. For a while, nothing disturbed the morning peace. Then, slowly, figures eased out of the rolling clouds of white. Silent, they were, like ghosts.

In the barbarian camp, the warriors slept. Only fourteen of them rested in their tents by the cold ashes of the fire. There was no need for more, not yet. But soon the rest would come and see what gain was to be had from the jumble of vessels moored along the quay. A couple were the larger flat-bottomed boats that could navigate coastal waters and the deeper stretches of the river. Others were currachs made of hide stretched over a wickerwork frame. And bumping against them were a few planked rowboats and logboats.

Lucanus prowled ahead of his men. He never once took his eyes off that camp. In his hand, Caledfwlch sang to him, and the power of the gods thrummed through his veins. He glanced to Mato, then to Aelius, a silent communication of strength. One by one, he caught the eyes of the men nearest to him, and they nodded and passed it on.

In times past, these barbarians would have had a man on

watch. They'd grown too assured of victory. That would be their downfall.

His head had cleared now. Whatever he had dreamed, or experienced, in the dark of the smithy had started to fade. But its effect upon him had not. Myrrdin had been right. He felt reborn.

Ahead, a bare-chested barbarian lurched from his tent, stretching and cracking his bones. Bleary-eyed, he farted loudly. Probably still half drunk.

Lucanus threw himself forward, his feet barely making a whisper on the ground. The Scoti warrior stared at him, blinking stupidly, no doubt unable to comprehend the sight of this half-man half-wolf racing out of the shadows. He turned to grunt a warning, too late. Caledfwlch ripped through his gut and he died spitting showers of crimson. All around, the tents were torn apart as the barbarians scrambled to defend themselves. Lucanus' men fell on them, hacking and cutting.

He stepped back and watched, pleased to see how these quiet men had grown into their new role, as he had grown under his father's tutelage when he had first been groomed to lead the Grim Wolves.

True to his word, even in battle Mato no longer carried a blade. Instead, he swung a staff as long as Myrrdin's, cracking skulls and whipping legs out from under their enemies. It was down to Aelius, no longer a drunken callow youth, to finish off the fallen, which he did with an unnecessarily theatrical flourish of his sword. He shadowed Mato everywhere, ensuring the older man was never in any danger.

Finally it was done. The bodies of the barbarians lay among the tattered remnants of the tents and the strewn ashes of the cold fire.

'I think I've found my purpose here,' Aelius said, sheathing his sword.

Lucanus raised his brows. 'Killing is not much of a purpose.'

'You say killing . . . I say smiting the enemies who would draw the light out of the world. And perhaps helping to bring about a better one.' He cocked an eyebrow, smiling wryly. 'If that's not too grand. I wouldn't wish to raise myself too high. But someone has to clear the ground for the King Who Will Not Die.'

Around them, the men were bowing their heads, sucking in steadying draughts of air and trying to hide their shaking hands. For many, it had been their first raid.

'You did yourselves proud, all of you,' Lucanus said. 'This morning you've given hope to the women and children and old folk waiting in the camp. Heroes all.'

Awkward grins flashed. Eyes brightened. These soft-muscled merchants and farmers seemed to straighten as he watched.

'But we are not done yet,' he cautioned. 'The jaws of the trap are closing fast. Back to camp.'

The pounding of Lucanus' heart was like the beating of a war drum. The enemy was nearing. His nostrils flared at the reek of sweat on the few wafts of air that drifted through the furnace heat. Avian shrieks filled the air as birds took flight from the high branches. As each bout died away, a new one replaced it, drawing closer. And under that cacophony, if he listened intently, he could make out the low drone of hunting horns, the blast of full-throated battle-cries and the whistled call and response of war-bands communicating as they carved through the dense forest from different directions.

'Hurry!' he yelled as he marched around the camp.

Women scooped infants into arms and old men lurched on staffs or hung on to Apullius and Morirex as they hurried to join the rear of the column trailing south out of the camp.

Eyes darting, his most trusted fighting men hung back on either side of the line of refugees, ready to battle to the last. To die, if necessary, to save these innocents.

As he'd feared, the barbarians must have followed the trail of their fallen scouts. Once they'd realized a force hid in the forest, however small, it was only a matter of time before they came to crush it.

Another flock of cawing crows, so close this time he could see them blackening the sky in the patches of blue among the branches.

The Morrigan is with me. The thought bubbled up in his head from nowhere.

They'd left behind the jumble of tents and supplies, anything that might slow them down. As the column eased out of the place that had been their home for the past few days, Lucanus looked across the clearing. The last man.

Once he was certain no one had been left behind, he backed away from the golden light and into the cooling shadows. He joined the end of the column, and as they lumbered on he glanced back constantly, searching for the first signs of attack.

'Make haste,' he hissed under his breath.

The refugees were slow, but Lucanus took comfort from the fact that the going would be equally hard for the barbarians. He'd chosen their hiding place well. Only a few paths ran down the steep valley sides and none was wide enough for two men abreast. The trees leaned so tightly together they turned day to night and made it near impossible to squeeze among them.

He heard pounding feet and looked back to the column. Apullius raced up.

Lucanus frowned. 'What are you doing?'

'I'm here to fight with you, if need be. To hold back the first wave so these folk can reach the quay.'

103

'You would do better—'

'No.' The lad's voice cracked. 'I do this for my father. It's what he would have wanted.'

Lucanus nodded. Shoulder to shoulder, they edged backwards, swords drawn.

Through walls of briar the column crept, over fallen trees, and along the thin line of solid ground through a bog that would suck a man to his death in an instant.

Battle-cries rang out across the breadth of the forest. Lucanus thought there might be a thousand barbarians there. If his army could only hold fast for a little longer.

After what seemed like an age, the shadows began to ebb. A grey light suffused that preternatural world. Lucanus looked over the heads of the trundling column and saw sunlight shining. He breathed in and tasted the dank freshness of the river.

'Faster,' he yelled. 'We're nearly there.'

He crashed into the light, blinking. Once his eyes had cleared, he watched the refugees and his men lumbering along the riverbank. Some splashed in the shallows. Others clung on to overhanging branches to avoid pitching into the flow.

The thunder of the approaching barbarians seemed all around him now. The calls. The whistles. Madness. Wild beasts attacking.

'We are wolves,' he muttered to Apullius, to himself. 'Never forget that.'

He hurried along the line, showing only a cold face. It would not do for any of these folk who relied on him to see even a flicker of doubt or worry. At the quayside, he pulled himself up on to the stones where Mato was pacing, waiting for his commands. 'Put the old folk, the women and the children in boats together,' he ordered. 'If there are no fighting men with them, the barbarians might leave them alone.'

He eyed the motley collection of punts, logboats and currachs and prayed there would be enough. Since they'd taken the quay, his men had fetched any other boats they could find moored along that stretch of the Tamesis and brought them here.

'Into the boats,' he called, marching along the line. Shepherded by Mato, those who could not fight clambered across the swaying vessels, struggling to keep their balance. Fear drove them on. 'Once each one is full, cut loose and let the current take you.' They'd had no time to prepare them, and he could only hope there would be at least one person in each vessel who could guide them on the water.

Once the last of the small band of refugees was adrift, he walked to the end of the quay and studied the bank ahead while his men boarded their own vessels. A flock of crows surged out of the trees above the grey water, and he drew his sword.

Narrowing his eyes, he glimpsed movement. The first hulking shape slipped out of the shadows. Then another, and another. Heads turned towards him. A jubilant roar rolled out, leaping from mouth to mouth. The warriors scrambled along the narrow bank towards him, fighting to keep their feet.

'Come! Now!'

Lucanus flinched at the hand on his arm. Mato tugged him towards the boats, where the last of his men was taking a seat on a rowboat. The Wolf bounded on to one of the larger flat-bottomed boats. Mato jumped down beside him and cast off.

Clambering past the men crushed together in the belly of the boat, Lucanus grasped the side aft and watched their enemies stream along the water's edge. He heard the battle-cries ebb and those jubilant roars turn to yells of frustration. For a moment, he wished Catia were there with her bow.

He'd never seen an archer with a better eye, man or woman. But the thought was too painful and he pushed it aside.

In turn, the barbarians had not sent their own bowmen in the forward ranks. They'd anticipated cutting down their feeble opposition with swords and axes.

Mato clapped a hand on his shoulder. 'You saved us.'

Lucanus turned to see the eyes of all the men on him. 'Not yet. Not by a long way,' he said so only Mato could hear. 'We've clawed our way out of one trap. A bigger one awaits us.'

CHAPTER FIFTEEN

The River

A SEA OF SHADOWS FLOODED ACROSS THE LAND, POOLING among the woods and the rolling meadows. The dusk was still as Lucanus stood at the side of the boat and looked out across this unfamiliar country. The north was a hard place of rock and heather and wind like knives, and it forged men in its image. This part of Britannia was gentler, lush, with rich brown earth that was good for farmers. He liked it.

'Do you still see the daemons, Lucanus?' Amarina's voice was little more than a murmur, merging with the lapping of the river.

Amarina had her hood pulled up, as she so often seemed to do these days, hiding her eyes and her thoughts. This was how he remembered her when she had first arrived in Vercovicium to set up the House of Wishes: shadow and smile, wit and words that hid as much as they revealed. 'All the riches of Britannia are here, they say,' she said; then, correcting herself: 'Were here.'

'It's not lost yet.'

She was quiet for so long he wondered if she hadn't heard him. But then she said, 'You think you can save it, from that vast horde?'

'Not alone. But the folk of this land will heed the call. I have no doubt of that.'

'That's what I always liked about you, Lucanus.' He could hear her smile in her words. 'You see the good in people. You think the best of them is always waiting to emerge, like the leaves in spring.'

'I've seen my fair share of blood and misery. But it's never dulled what I believe.'

'It could well be that the wood-priests chose wisely when they decided you were the man, of all the men in this isle, to be the Pendragon. The one trusted to usher in their great plan.' Her tone was wry. He could never tell when she was teasing him and when she was revealing her true thoughts.

'And yet Aelius tells me you tried to abandon me.'

She brushed a strand of auburn hair from her forehead, but kept her gaze fixed on the dark landscape. 'I don't have such a burnished view of folk as you. I prefer to put my trust in myself alone. It's served me well so far.'

'I need you, Amarina.'

This time she turned to look at him, but her hood was only a well of shadows. 'What use am I?'

'Five,' he muttered, his thoughts flying back to what Myrrdin had told him.

'Five?'

'The wood-priest talks about numbers shaping all there is. Sometimes he speaks like a man in too much wine, but . . . Five is the number of strength, he tells me. Five of us will lead the way on this dark road, together. I'm the Head of the Dragon. There's Mato, who has the soul of a poet. He shows me the light in the night. And then there's you. You are, in some ways, the opposite of Mato. I sense the Morrigan's ravens swooping around you.'

She flinched.

'I know you're torn. The wyrd sisters have you under their spell.'

'You know nothing about that,' she spat.

'True. No one knows anything about your past. But I know you trust them above all others. You know how their minds work, yes?' She didn't answer, and he took that as assent. 'That's the wisdom I need.'

'I'll think on it.'

'Do that. I've accepted my destiny.' Now his thoughts twisted back to his night in Goibniu's Smithy and the strange beings who had visited him there – daemons, Amarina would call them – and the things they had told him about days long gone and days yet to come. 'My life's no longer my own. But if I'm to carry the torch into the years ahead, then I need good people to counsel me.'

'And the other two?'

He had an answer to that, but he couldn't risk angering the Fates by revealing it now. 'We'll see.'

Away in the gloom along the bank, a light flickered.

Lucanus stiffened, but only for a moment. 'Enemy,' he bellowed. 'Stay low.'

Grabbing Amarina's arm, he yanked her down. Three blazing arrows whined overhead.

He heard a cry and a crackling, and as he peered over the side he saw a man on fire in one of the smaller boats, the shaft protruding from his chest. With another strangled cry, the man pitched backwards, splashing into the dark waters.

Another burning arrow thumped into the side of their boat. The flames from the pitch licked up. Cries of terror rang through the men huddled in the bottom of the craft. One figure leapt up. Lucanus glimpsed Mato's face lit by the orange glow. His friend was gripping the baling scoop and he swung almost upside down over the side and swept river water on to the fire. With a sizzle the glow snuffed out and darkness rushed back in.

'Do we pull in to the bank to fight them?' Aelius said at his elbow.

'That may be their plan, to lure us in. We don't know how many are waiting there.' Lucanus pushed his head above the side. 'To oars,' he called.

Splashing erupted all around as oars bladed into the river. It was dangerous in the dark, but what choice did they have?

'Keep watch on those alongside,' he called again.

Another blaze of fire in the trees along the bank. The burning shaft arced, and as it dropped he froze the positions of all the boats in his mind. Mostly they formed a line along the centre of the flow, as they'd agreed when dusk was drawing in. But in a few of the smaller boats, the men had grown complacent. Some had slipped side by side, close enough to clash oars. And one was drifting treacherously close to the bank.

'Clovis,' he cried as the arrow plunged harmlessly into the river. 'Pull away.'

From the gloom, he heard muffled groans of confusion as Clovis' men realized their predicament. A moment later a clamour of screams and cracking wood and splashing echoed.

Lucanus felt his heart fall. In his mind's eye, he pictured the barbarians lurching into the shallows when the boat turned to the bank, their blades falling.

'Faster,' he cried. 'Faster.'

The dying moans of Clovis' men fell behind them, lost to the river sounds. Another two arrows whistled through the night sky. Both plummeted into the water at their backs.

'We've escaped them,' Amarina said, her voice strained. She'd been holding her breath tight in her chest.

'For now. But we can't rest, not even for a moment, because our enemy won't. They'll harry us until we reach the safety of the walls of Londinium.'

Lucanus slid his bronze sword out of its scabbard and turned it so that it caught the morning light. The black runes carved into the blade grew sharp, then faded again.

Apullius' eyes widened. 'My father said the Pendragon carried a magic sword. Is this it?'

The Wolf frowned. How quickly these tales had travelled far and wide.

'Its name is Caledfwlch.'

Sunlight glinted off the ripples around the ramshackle collection of boats. The morning was as peaceful as any he'd experienced. But as he looked around the pale, drawn faces of his men, Lucanus could see none of them had slept a wink.

But he could no longer smell smoke on the breeze. That was good. And Mato, who had better eyes than most, leaned back against the side, the familiar smile on his lips as he scanned the lush grassland.

Apullius reached out to the blade, then snatched his hand back as if it might burn him. 'That's a strange name. What does it mean?'

Lucanus pursed his lips. It was a good question. 'It's how it was told to me. A name from another tongue, I think. From the people of the west?'

'A gift of the gods,' Apullius repeated. 'My father said the Lady of the Lake gave it to you.'

This time, Lucanus stifled his surprise. He recalled diving into the freezing waters off the Isle of Yews in the far north, and finding this blade still clutched in a skeletal hand at the muddy bottom. It could have been a woman, he supposed. Myrrdin and his tales.

'I thought all you folk of the south were Christians now.'

The lad nodded. 'We are.' Lucanus smiled at the uncaring tone. Just another story. Apullius looked up, his face bright. 'I want to serve you.'

Lucanus frowned. 'I don't need a slave.'

'Not a slave. Someone to bring you Caledfwlch before battle, and to clean the blood off the blade when you have slain your enemies. Someone to feed your horse—'

'I don't like riding.'

'To make sure your food is ready when you're hungry, and to bring you wine at the end of the day. To carry messages to the other Grim Wolves . . . to allies . . .'

Lucanus shook his head, but the lad carried on speaking.

'The Pendragon shouldn't have to do these things himself. And I could learn from you. How to fight. How to do God's work . . . or . . . the gods' work. How to be a Grim Wolf—'

'No,' Lucanus said, more sharply than he intended. He felt a pang of regret when he saw the boy's face fall, but he had no intention of condemning him to the hard life of the *arcani*, or the bloodstained existence he himself endured now. 'You should be a merchant. Earn some coin. Find some comfort in this miserable world.'

'A merchant? When Britannia burns around us? There's only one kind of work these days.'

Lucanus couldn't argue with that. But he ruffled the boy's hair and said, 'You're angry with me now. You can't understand why I'd deny you. But one day, when you've found a good woman, and have a boy of your own, and sit by the hearth surrounded by the luxury your hard work has bought you, then you'll thank me.'

The children ran along the water's edge, cheering. Lucanus glanced at Mato, who was beaming. His friend waved, driving the children to louder squeals of joy.

112

'Don't indulge them,' Amarina sniffed. 'They should be working.'

'Let them have their fun,' Mato replied. 'These are the moments that bring value to life.'

Lucanus leaned over the side of the boat, cocking his head. Among the cheers, he heard one word repeated: *Pendragon*.

'They know.' Apullius had heard it too. 'Myrrdin's story is spreading faster than even the barbarian horde.'

Lucanus wondered where the wood-priest was now. Moving steadily along the drove roads, weaving magic with his words, spreading the tale of the King Who Will Not Die and igniting hope and resistance with every encounter? He'd laughed when the druid told him words had as much power as swords. Now he thought he could understand.

Ahead, a group of people jostled along a bank littered with wicker eel-pots. His gaze drifted across old men with white hair and hunched backs, mothers with apple cheeks, hands clasped in front of them. And young women, flushed and sparkle-eyed as they waved their ribbon favours at the men in the passing boats. Men who had become warriors, who had become heroes.

'Pull in,' he called.

'Is that wise?' Aelius asked.

'The men have been running for too long with death nipping at their heels. Let them hear some kind words, feel some warmth.' *And knowing what they're fighting for will give them the strength to keep going*, he thought.

The boats pulled in. Eyes widened along the bank. Those gathered could not believe they'd been so blessed.

Once they were on dry ground, Lucanus' men and the refugees stretched their legs and rubbed the cricks from their necks. Some collapsed on to the grass, closing their eyes as they turned their faces to the sun. The local folk moved among them, the older ones offering words of thanks, the younger ones demanding tales of heroism.

'You are the Pendragon?'

Lucanus looked into a face that seemed a map of the hard lands in the far north. The man's cloud of white hair floated in a halo of sunlight.

'I am.'

'I remember tales of the great war-leader, when I was a lad. We all thought your kind was gone for good.'

'Nothing goes for ever,' the Wolf replied, remembering Myrrdin's words. 'The old times are coming back.'

'The old times were hard, so I hear. Rome's brought us many comforts. And now the emperor has abandoned us. But you, you're our saviour. Sent by God.'

Lucanus felt discomfort, but this man didn't want to hear any doubts or complaints. 'The barbarians have the upper hand, for now. But this war's far from lost.'

The village elder nodded. The words seemed to give him some comfort. 'If we live through this, we'll need to build the world anew. I hear the tales from those fleeing. All has been washed away. Fields and villages burned. Forts destroyed. Towns reduced to naught but stones. The trade is gone. The coin is stolen. I have one fear now. Even if the war is won, the long night will reach out far into days yet to come. Who will save us from that dark age, Pendragon, answer me that?'

CHAPTER SIXTEEN

The Forest

Rutupiae, Britannia

CORVUS SPLASHED INTO THE FOAMING SURF.

'How does it feel to be back on home ground after being away for so long?' Pavo said as he waded alongside him to the beach.

'I can't remember much of it. Rain and mud and cold nights. The two of us running through the barley.'

'We were a couple of little bastards, and no mistake. Now we're a couple of big bastards.'

Corvus turned and looked to the ships heaving on the swell. Soldiers hefted bales over the side on to the small boats they'd towed behind them. Others gathered on the sand, stretching their legs after the cramped sea journey.

His friend stood in the prow of the nearest ship, shielding his eyes as he scrutinized the coastline. Theodosius was not good away from dry land, and Corvus had been forced to listen to his increasingly desperate prayers as their vessel bucked across the turbulent currents of the channel. One of their seasoned comrades, a squat man with a face like leather, had said this had been the smoothest crossing he'd known. Theodosius only whimpered in reply.

'No regrets?' Pavo asked.

Corvus dabbed at the sweat trickling down his brow in the late afternoon heat. 'I'm not usually one for sticking my neck out, but there was little choice this time.'

'Maybe your sister's already dead and it's clear sailing ahead.'

'We can only hope. We'll know for sure when Hecate arrives with my mother and Severus. She can ask her kind. Those witches will know, I'd wager. They and the wood-priests have been prophesying this for years, and pulling on the strands to make it happen, too.'

'You might have to drain a little blood to get the truth out of them.'

'We'll do what we have to do, as always.'

'And now?'

'The ride to Londinium.' Corvus squirmed as the sweat trickled down his back. 'It'll be a vile journey in this fiendish heat, but we're not here for enjoyment. If only this business could have been completed in Rome, surrounded by civilized people. But this is where the bloodline must arise and grow strong. The wood-priests have seen to that.' He sniffed. 'Still, at least there will be some civilization in Londinium. I've heard tell it's quite the wonder. Not Rome, exactly, but certainly a place where we can while away time in wine and good food.'

'And Mithras knows, you like your comforts.' Pavo dug a hole in the wet sand with his toe. 'One word of warning. Keep an eye on Theodosius. Most of the time he seems lost in his religion. But those Christians are dangerous when they suspect unbelievers are wandering too close.'

Corvus shrugged. 'We have our loyal band to watch our backs.' He glanced back at the milling men, all of them hand-picked from the worshippers of Mithras. 'I quite enjoy being a Heliodromus. Some respect at last.'

*

The road disappeared into the black maw of a great forest. As he peered into that darkness, Corvus felt an inexplicable shiver. The trees reached as far as the eye could see on both sides of the track. Above them, shrieking crows blackened the sky.

'Just birds,' Pavo said as if he could read his friend's thoughts.

'There's an old woman who lives by the river beyond Rome's walls who swears they're lost souls.'

'Is she also the one who eats dirt because it enables her to see at night?'

'Fair point.'

Corvus urged his horse on, but slowly. He fixed his gaze on that brooding shadow lying in sullen silence just beyond the treeline. The hairs on his neck prickled. For some reason, he felt there were other eyes in there looking back at him. 'I'm a superstitious fool,' he muttered. 'I've spent too long around men who see angels and devils behind every blade of grass.'

He glanced back. Theodosius was riding along the column of men to see what the delay was.

'Why worry?' Pavo sighed. 'We've met no resistance so far. If this is a land ruled by barbarians, all four of them are probably sitting round a fire in the cold north, picking their teeth with bones.'

'Wise words again, old crow. No doubt they heard how we crushed the Alamanni in Gaul and are quaking in fear.'

'Too true, old crow.'

The journey from Rutupiae on the coast had been uneventful. They'd taken their time, travelling only a few miles each day, sending the scouts ahead and waiting for their return before they moved on. They'd not even smelled a barbarian, and Corvus knew how much those ditch-dwellers reeked.

At one village they were surrounded by cheering country folk who saw their red cloaks and were convinced Rome had come to save the day. No one had the heart to tell them that they were all there were. But those simple beings seemed under no immediate threat. They'd heard rumours, of devastation and slaughter, but when pressed they could offer no more than whispers on the wind.

Perhaps it was the talk of a few men in their cups which had got out of hand.

'At this rate we'll be at Londinium in two days,' Pavo said. 'And then . . .'

'And then we can wake the dragon.' Corvus nodded, pleased with himself. He'd agonized over sending word back with the ship returning to Gaul that all was well and Gaia and the others could join him. But it seemed his instincts had been right when the scouts had returned that first night. There would be safety behind the walls in Londinium, at least. He needed his mother and wife with him if he was to make his move. And Father Severus would keep some steel in the spine of his men with the promise of the glory of Sol Invictus if they began to waver.

Once his sister Catia and her supporters were dead, the wood-priests would soon come round to Gaia's claim upon the bloodline – they needed this king as much as he did. He wished he had a tame druid to argue his case. But his wife Hecate would do well enough, especially when she told how he had saved her from certain death, and then given her his love and protection.

'You always look as if you're talking to someone,' Theodosius said as he rode up. He looked down his long nose, his face red from the heat.

Corvus eyed Pavo, who raised one eyebrow. 'No. Just me.'

'How goes it?'

'I'm not one to take risks, as you know.'

'There's no way around this forest. We have to follow the road through it.'

'That's true.'

'And if it's rogues and cut-throats you're wary of, they would be scared away by a column of Rome's finest.'

'True too.'

Theodosius fixed an eye on him, and after a moment Corvus nodded. He urged his mount on, sensing Pavo doing the same. Side by side, as they had been since they were children.

As the soldiers closed on the line of trees, Theodosius dropped in beside him again. 'The winter will be cold here, but not as bad as along the northern wall. There, I'm told, the snot freezes on your face overnight when you sleep in the barracks.'

Corvus shrugged. 'I've never been troubled by a little cold.' He'd have to get used to it if this was to be his home in the years to come. At least he'd have a fine villa to keep him warm. Perhaps even a palace. Somewhere fit for the head of a royal bloodline.

'Now that Jovinus has successfully finished his campaign in Gaul, for now at least, preparations must surely be under way for the campaign next year,' Theodosius mused.

'Let's hope the emperor can find enough troops. A war on two fronts, in Germania and in Britannia, will strain our capability.'

'We must trust that Valentinian knows what he's doing. He's made the right choice putting my father in charge of the Britannia campaign. He'll carve through these barbarians like a knife through a well-roasted ox.'

The column pushed on into the gloom beneath the trees.

'Birdsong,' Theodosius said, listening. 'These woods might be so dense that we can't see far, but our ears will tell us if any barbarians venture close. I met an old soldier who spent his years in Vindolanda, once. He told me those Picts and Scoti couldn't go five steps without screeching like death-hags.'

'They'll all be drunk now and enjoying their victory,' Pavo muttered.

'They'll all be drunk now and enjoying their victory,' Corvus said.

'True. If there's one thing barbarians are good at, it's falling deep into their cups and thinking they've won a war when it's only been a battle.' Theodosius laughed at his own words. 'I'm glad you're with me on this journey, my friend. It would be a far more dismal time without you.'

'We know each other well, you and I. Who works together better?'

'When we make camp, we'll thank God for our good friendship,' Theodosius said.

Corvus forced a smile. 'Oh, deep joy.'

Corvus stared into the endless dark. A few orange spots floated in the gloaming, the last embers of the fire they'd built when they'd broken the journey.

The forest was as silent as a tomb. He couldn't even hear the watchman farting.

Under his back, the ground was soft and he felt pleased he'd picked the perfect spot, nestled in the twisting roots of a venerable oak. Knowing Theodosius, his friend had probably found somewhere harder and more uncomfortable. He seemed to think his god would love him more if he embraced suffering.

The road had plunged like a dagger into the heart of the forest. At first they'd progressed cautiously, eyes darting at every creature scurrying in the undergrowth. Once they realized they could see clearly what awaited them, they'd all relaxed. By the time they'd made camp on either side of the way, laughter rang out and the conversation was cheery.

Corvus rolled on to his side, but whatever had woken him

from his slumber – the hoot of an owl, a badger's snufflings – had set him as alert as if it were dawn.

'I suppose you're deep in dreams of good wine, Pavo,' he murmured. At the thought he decided he had a taste for some drink. A couple of cups would not go amiss and it would help him sleep.

He lay for a moment, weighing his options, then decided the lure of the wine was too strong. With a sigh, he crawled away from the oak tree, feeling his way among the sleeping soldiers until he reached those few hot coals. Grasping one of the pitch-soaked torches stacked beside the fire for any night-time emergency, he plunged the tip into the hot ashes.

A patch of red glowed. The torch hissed and sizzled into life.

As the flames licked up, Corvus raised the brand high. He looked round and frowned. Something was twitching just beyond the edge of the circle of light where the watchman hunched at his post.

And then he realized he was seeing not one figure, but two, wrapped in an embrace. When the second figure raised its head to look at the trembling torch, the light washed over it.

'Mithras,' Corvus gasped.

Against the bone-white skin, one splash of colour stood out: the crimson smeared around its mouth where it had been feeding on the dead watchman. Corvus felt those unblinking eyes on him for a moment, as if the thing was marking his face in its mind. As he shuddered, it flitted away into the night.

'Awake!' he yelled. 'Awake!'

The soldiers around him leapt to their feet, swords already in hands. Corvus jabbed a shaking finger to where the watchman slumped at his post.

'Murdered!' someone shouted. 'His throat slit.'

'What did you see?' Theodosius grabbed his arm.

'I . . . I don't know,' Corvus stammered.

Torches burst into flame. Soldiers hurried with the brands to the camp perimeter, their levelled blades now aglow.

Corvus swallowed. He looked out to where the circle of light was spreading out into the dark among the trees. The forest seethed with movement.

'Stand your ground,' Theodosius barked.

'No,' Corvus croaked. 'We can't fight those things.'

Ghastly shapes darted so fast that he couldn't count their number. But there must be an army of them. An army. For the first time in his life, he felt terror drive a spike into his heart.

'What are they?' he heard Theodosius yell.

Daemons, he thought.

As the soldiers stared into the night, their swords quivering, one of the creatures rushed into the circle of light. Naked to the waist, it leapt like a savage beast and Corvus waited for its maw to stretch wide. Instead a blade thrust into a petrified soldier's chest. The attacker wrenched the weapon free and disappeared into the dark before his victim keeled over, dead.

'They are men after all,' Theodosius shouted.

And then the attack erupted in force. Corvus gaped, rooted. Reeking of loam, white faces that showed no emotion flashed into the circle of light. The things slashed and stabbed, and were gone before anyone could fight back.

A Roman fell. Another. Another.

Every time Corvus whirled, his quavering torch revealed too much.

One soldier crashed forward, blood spurting from a neck wound. As he flailed on the ground, two of the things grabbed his arms and dragged him away from the light. Lost in the dark, his screams rose into a frenzy at whatever agonies were being inflicted on him, then were cut off.

'They're eating him,' Corvus croaked.

Theodosius spun towards him, his face savage in the torchlight. 'They are men,' he roared, 'and no man born under God would do such a thing.'

When another soldier was dragged into the dark, Corvus sensed the panic rush through the Romans around him.

'Stand your ground,' Theodosius bellowed again.

'No,' Corvus shouted. 'Away! Away! This is a fight we cannot win!'

Without waiting to see if Theodosius backed him, he was running through the camp to the road. He could hear the horses whinnying in fear, but all he sensed was frantic movement, and terrible screams, and flickering torchlight.

'Pavo!' he cried. 'Pavo! Save me!'

Shadows danced around him, drawing nearer.

Corvus stumbled, caught himself, threw himself on. They were at his back. If he dared look round he would be lost.

His horse loomed up in the dark. Clawing his way on to its back, he dug his heels in. The beast hammered on to the road and he wrapped his arms around its neck.

Dark shapes raced on either side, keeping pace. The things wouldn't relent until he was dead. He imagined their swords drawn, ready to cut him down, and he dug his heels harder into his steed's flanks and roared aloud.

Through the endless dark he flew, trusting in his mount's keen sight to find its way on. But even then he felt sure he could sense those monstrous things surging through the trees on either side. Why had he been so complacent, so arrogant? What nightmare had he fallen into?

Corvus whirled on, never looking back, not caring about his comrades. Only darkness lay ahead.

CHAPTER SEVENTEEN

Queen of Fury

West of Lactodorum

'WHEN THE ATTACOTTI RETURN, YOU WILL BE THEIR FIRST meal.'

Bellicus showed a defiant face, but Erca's words drove ice into the pit of his stomach. His left eye was caked with blood, his lips were swollen, and his body sang with agonies from more beatings than he could count.

'Only because you bastards would taste like a mouthful of shit.' Solinus gave a gap-toothed grin; one of his teeth had been knocked out by Motius of the Carrion Crows two days ago.

Erca scowled, then stepped away with a grunt.

Bellicus felt proud that Solinus showed no fear. Comitinus too. The three of them had endured so much since the Carrion Crows had taken them by surprise while they prepared to scout the barbarian camp. His only joy was that Catulus had raced off into the night before they could kill him. That faithful hound would be out there somewhere, keeping pace.

For the first part of the march south, they'd been tied to stakes, each one of them supported between the shoulders of

124

two barbarians. Then Erca had set them to trudging beside the column, even though their injuries meant every step felt like walking across hot coals.

But they'd endured that too.

Now they'd broken the trek for the day, the barbarians sprawled in the grass beside the road, swilling wine from skins as they summoned up the strength to set up their shelters for the night. Erca had kept the pace hard. The horde must want to crush all resistance before the snows came. Only when Rome had no foothold in Britannia could they feel secure.

'Call yourself a good man,' Bellicus growled, 'and you stand alongside the Eaters of the Dead.'

Erca glowered at him. They were about the same size: two bears, one red, one black, each getting the measure of the other. 'Save your breath, Roman. Enjoy what's left of your miserable life.' The war-leader prowled around the three captives. 'You should never have ventured here. We rule this land now.'

Comitinus moistened his lips. 'All barbarians learn soon enough that when they invade any part of the empire they can hold on for a day, or a week, or a month. But Rome always crushes them.' His voice was soft, but that seemed only to antagonize the Scot all the more.

Erca thrust his face a finger's width from Comitinus' broken nose. 'This time things are different. You've never faced an alliance of all the tribes before. We learned our lesson long ago. We are stronger together, and before our combined force the fabled might of Rome's army melted away like an autumn mist. Send your legions to attack us. We welcome it. Fight us here in Britannia. In Gaul. Wherever the tribes gather. You'll soon learn Rome's time has passed. The season is turning. A new world is being forged.'

'A darker one,' Bellicus spat.

Erca grinned. 'But it will be ours.'

125

'Is this how you treat your captives?' Catia was observing them.

Erca's eyes flickered away from her. Was that fear he saw? Respect? Both at once?

'Only what they deserve,' the Scot said.

'How he treats his defeated enemy is a mark of a civilized man.' Her voice was low, but carried weight.

Erca's cheeks reddened. Bellicus stifled a chuckle. Catia knew how to sting, that was true.

She pushed up her chin and strode among the warriors as if she were their queen. Comitinus gasped. None of them had seen her clearly until now – Erca kept them well apart – and Bellicus felt a pang of shock as he looked at the swell of her belly.

'The time that has passed . . . the size of her . . . it can only be Lucanus' child,' he whispered. If the Wolf had known about this, he would have fought his way through waves of barbarians, to the very gates of death, to save the two of them.

'That cuts even deeper,' Comitinus croaked. 'To fail—'

'Silence,' Bellicus snapped. He would hear no talk of failure, not till the moment his flame was extinguished.

'Aye, silence, you whining cur,' Solinus said to Comitinus. 'We've been beaten within a whisper of our lives. We're surrounded by a barbarian horde, about to be eaten alive, and there's only three of us.' He sniffed. 'I've faced worse odds.'

Catia looked Erca directly in the eye. 'Three of them, chained and broken, and still you fear them.'

'I fear no one.' Erca's eyes darted. Watching for the response of his men, Bellicus knew. Any hint of weakness would be punished.

Leaning in, Catia whispered something in his ear.

Erca shrugged. 'Do what you will. I care not.'

He nodded to the men guarding his prisoners, and Bellicus felt rough hands throw him down. He lounged on the grass, turning his face to the dying rays of the red sun, with Solinus and Comitinus sitting cross-legged beside him.

Catia eased beside them, holding her belly. 'You were right. This is a fine rescue.' She forced a smile, but Bellicus saw only pity in her eyes.

'These barbarian bastards have treated you well?'

'As well as can be expected. I'm fed. No hands raised against me. No one has touched me at all, and for that I'm thankful.' She sighed. 'Why did you come?'

'We couldn't leave you here,' Comitinus said.

'I wouldn't want to see any life risked to save me.'

'And you think Lucanus would leave you to your fate?' Bellicus asked.

She winced. 'This is his child.'

'I always wondered if he had it in him,' Solinus grunted.

'Why did you come?' Catia asked again. This time her voice cracked. She leaned forward, making sure she wasn't overheard. 'You know what will happen to you when the Attacotti return.'

'I'll choke them with my gristle,' Solinus said.

'Most of them have joined the other tribes in the south,' she whispered. 'They are the best scouts these barbarians have and they were needed for the final assault, so Erca said. But a small band still travels with us, and they're expected back the day after tomorrow.'

Bellicus nodded. He'd long expected he'd die in some miserable work for the *arcani*, but never like this.

'Ah, it'll only hurt for a bit,' Solinus said.

'Aye, could be worse,' Comitinus added.

'Stop it.' Catia scrubbed away a stray tear.

'If I could see a way to escape, we'd take it,' Bellicus said. 'They don't let us out of their sight for a moment. No, make your peace with it. We have.' He hesitated, then added, 'I only wish we hadn't failed you.'

'Still your tongue,' Catia said, a little harshly, he thought. 'We are one and the same.' She pushed herself to her feet and walked away without a backward glance.

Thunder cracked the night sky. The rain drummed on the earth and a growing pool shimmered like gold in each lightning flash.

In her tent, Catia hugged her knees, looking out into the summer storm. She'd smelled the wind, seen the clouds building on the horizon in the late afternoon. She'd known this was coming.

Her thoughts flew over the dark, sodden fields, the dripping forests and the grey lakes, and she saw the Attacotti making their way back. White shapes whipping through the shadows, knives in hand, blades nicked from bones, their lips already mouthing the strange words of the solemn ritual they would utter as they began their feast. Devoid of human emotion, relentless as death.

As if in answer to her grim thoughts, she heard, or thought she heard, a croaking voice, almost lost beneath the pounding of the deluge: *'Deep in the forest, Cernunnos howls.'* Or perhaps it was her mind playing tricks on her.

The weight of her child pressed down. She could sense it drawing life from her, growing stronger, making her weary and sick in equal measure. A king in the making. What a world this child would inherit.

A shape loomed in the entrance to the tent. Her guard, a sour-faced, lank-haired Scot, eased inside after emptying his bladder. He shook himself, showering her with rain. He didn't apologize. She was less than nothing to him.

'Did you hear someone?' she asked. 'Out there?'

'In this storm? Have you lost your wits? Nobody but a jolt-head would venture out there.'

'I thought I heard something,' she murmured.

128

'Sleep,' he grunted, throwing himself down.

'When I was a girl I heard a story about a Queen of Fury. This was not long after Rome first took this isle. The invaders had her whipped and her daughters raped, so the tale said, but this queen did not submit to her punishment. She brought the tribes of Britannia together, as your tribes came together, and she led a great revolt. So powerful was her rage that she almost drove Rome from these shores.'

'As we will do,' the guard muttered.

'You do not have a Queen of Fury.'

'Sleep, or I'll cuff your ear, whatever Erca says.'

'Imagine. Within a hair of defeating the power of Rome. What a wonder she must have been.'

'Sleep!'

Catia's fingers closed around the rock she had found earlier and she bashed the guard's brains in.

Out in the turbulent night, she stalked among the tents, her blonde hair plastered to her head. The spattered blood soaked into pink clouds across her dripping dress. She paused outside one tent, where a row of round shields stood under a bowing shelter. Axes and javelins were racked behind them, out of the elements, and three bows and quivers. Catia trailed her fingers along them until she found one that suited her. She slung the quiver over her back.

The storm seemed to swallow the camp. Her ears rang with thunder. Rain lashed her body. In the centre of that growing pool, she nocked an arrow and drew her bow. Waiting. Waiting. At that moment, she surprised herself by thinking fondly of Lucanus' father, Lucanus the Elder, and remembering all the times he had leaned over her when she was a girl, teaching her how to use the bow, building the strength in her arms, forcing her to focus, and breathe at the right moment. She smiled to herself. He'd honoured her with that skill.

Lightning flashed.

Her shaft flew.

Before the white light faded, she glimpsed the arrow protruding from the face of the watchman.

Feeling around until she found his body in the dark, she dug her fingers into his furs and uncovered his long-bladed knife.

Bellicus jerked awake. Rainwater sluiced around his head in the badly erected tent; why make any effort for captives who were going to be dead before too long? But it wasn't that that had woken him.

A weight crushed his legs. He kicked out, cursing as it rolled off him.

'Can't even get a good sleep on my last night,' Solinus grumbled.

Bellicus smelled blood, and when he kicked out again felt the softness under his foot, and he realized the weight was the body of their guard. Before he could call out, the tent flap lashed open in the gale. A silhouette loomed in the entrance.

Lightning shimmered.

Catia was hunched over, the whites of her eyes shining around her dilated pupils. The guard's blood spattered her face. She drew the back of her hand across it, smearing the gore around her mouth so that it looked as if she had feasted on raw meat.

But then she drew herself up, finding once again the woman inside the beast. Her hand fell to her side and Bellicus saw she was holding a knife. Ruby droplets fell from the tip to the body at her feet.

The Grim Wolf felt her cold gaze upon him, and he almost squirmed. She spat a bloody gobbet on to the ground.

'This King Who Will Not Die,' she began. Her voice was low and strong, not a tone Bellicus expected to hear from someone who had been held captive by the barbarians for so long. 'Why should it not be a queen?'

Scrambling in, she wrenched him around and sawed at his bonds. While he rubbed the life back into his wrists, Catia turned her attention to Solinus, then Comitinus.

'Now she's embarrassed us,' Solinus grumbled. 'Showing us how a rescue should be done.'

'We're not away from here yet.' Bellicus hauled himself to the entrance and looked out into the night. It was too dark to see anything.

'The watchman?' he asked.

'Dead.' Catia's voice sounded wintry.

'They'll be changing the duty soon enough in this weather.'

'Then let's not stay here talking.' Catia thrust him aside and stalked out into the storm.

'Fuck me, we'll be out of work soon enough,' Solinus said. 'Bunch of useless Grim Wolves.'

'Why don't you shut your mouth and learn something,' Comitinus replied.

Bellicus splashed after Catia as the other two tumbled out of the tent behind him. As he lurched through the sucking mud, he felt the fire begin to creep back into his limbs after being bound for so long.

Once they'd left the tents behind and leaned into the hammering wind, he heard a cry erupt at their backs. His heart sank. It sounded as though the dead watchman had been discovered.

A torch burst into life, guttering in the gale. Erca was holding the brand aloft, and a host of other barbarians was surging beside him.

Catia sprang to Bellicus' side. Her bow was drawn, an arrow pointed directly at the Scoti leader. The torch that had revealed him had made him a target.

'Kill him,' Bellicus bellowed. 'Cut off the head and this war-band will fall apart.'

Catia hesitated for a moment, no doubt getting her measure in the buffeting wind. She let fly. The arrow whistled a hand's width from Erca's head and thumped into a man standing behind him. Bellicus frowned. He'd never known Catia to miss before. Fear and worry got the best of all of them.

The torchlight winked out. Now all were equally hampered by the night and the storm.

'Run,' he shouted. 'And don't look back.'

Bellicus, Solinus and Comitinus raced on ahead. Catia pulled herself up the slope and allowed herself one look back at the sea of dark where the camp lay.

'You are not alone.'

Catia jumped, her knife flashing up. 'Step closer,' she snarled.

For a moment there was no sound beyond the storm, and then lightning crashed across the sky. Catia jerked back. A line of people stood barely a spear's length from her. She'd had no sense they were there, never even heard them approach. As the after-image burned in her mind, she realized she was not looking at Picts or Scoti. The men were filthy, dressed in rags the colour of bark and mildew, hair and beards wild. They carried staffs and cudgels; a few bore axes.

These were the forest folk, those who had moved into the Wilds long ago, after the Romans came, living away from the sight of civilized folk. The ones who had sheltered the wood-priests after the great slaughter on Ynys Môn. Who still held the old days and the old gods deep in their hearts.

And towering over the others was a single warrior, his hands resting on a longsword. His face was hidden by a helmet of a kind she'd never seen before. The steel edged his jawline, an open section running up from his chin to twin eyeholes. A round shield hung on one arm. His tunic, cloak and leggings were filthy too.

In another flash of lightning, she saw him sheathe his long blade and step towards her. 'I am the Lord of the Greenwood.'

'A friend?'

'Of all those who believe in the coming of the King Who Will Not Die. I follow the Pendragon, whoever wears that crown.'

Catia sagged with relief. In the distance, she could hear Bellicus shouting her name.

'Myrrdin sent me to aid you. We will hold back the band sent out to hunt you down, be they *arcani* or barbarian.'

'Thank you.'

'You were well chosen, wolf-sister.'

She flinched, surprised at the use of the name that Lucanus had given her.

'Now go,' he said in a rumbling voice. As he turned back to his ramshackle band, he added, 'You will see me again, when it is darkest.'

Catia felt she had many questions to ask, but she couldn't wait. Spinning on her heels, she stumbled through the gusting wind and the thrashing rain, trying to follow the sound of Bellicus' voice.

CHAPTER EIGHTEEN

Londinium

River Tamesis, not far from Alaunodunum

IN THE BRIGHT NOON SUN, THE FIGURE ON THE HILLSIDE WAS little more than a dark blotch. A man, it seemed, though he hadn't moved since the column of boats rounded the bend in the river. He was watching their approach, there was little doubt about that, and from his position and his lone appearance Lucanus had the strangest feeling that he had been waiting for them.

'You see more than me?'

Mato shook his head. They were standing beside each other in the prow. 'Too much glare from the sun. But still, one only. How much threat can that be?'

'If he's a watchman for a hidden army, then a great threat.'

'Thoughts like that are why you were chosen as the Pendragon.'

Lucanus could never tell when Mato was taunting him. His friend had taken it upon himself to keep all feet upon the ground, and that was just what Lucanus needed.

Since they'd encountered the welcoming party on the banks of the river, they'd seen no sign of any enemy. In the hamlets and villas they drifted past, folk still went about their business. Barley fields were threshed. Wood was cut. Cows were milked. The only sign of the approaching dark was the columns of refugees trudging relentlessly towards the south-east. In their hunched shoulders and staring eyes, Lucanus had seen his mission renewed.

'Of course,' Mato added, 'we can never be certain how much of the horde has crept along the drove roads without pausing to sack the villages, just so they can get ahead of a small band of farmers with dreams of being warriors.'

'Do I hear the buzzing of a fly?' The Wolf wafted a hand. Mato grinned, but didn't take his shielded eyes off that shadow.

Lucanus looked back along the boat. His men seemed to have regained some of their fire since they'd pulled away from danger. Apullius had fashioned himself a sword from a broken branch, and he was sparring with his brother, the Mouse, on one of the benches. He was keen, Lucanus gave him that. But also searching for purpose, no doubt, after the death of his father and mother.

Amarina, Decima and Galantha lounged on a bench beyond the boys, faces turned to the sun. The eyes of the men rarely left them. The three women knew that, of course, though they never showed it. Lucanus could see it in the curve of their lips, like cats toying with mice.

And aft, Aelius sat mopping the brow of his father Menius. A good son, Lucanus thought, and felt an odd twist in his gut.

'Wait,' Mato exclaimed.

The Wolf turned back to the prow. His friend was pointing at that watcher on the hill.

'Do you see it yet?'

Lucanus squinted, and after a moment he stiffened.

He stood in silence as the boat drifted on. Dragonflies flitted among the rushes and the shadows of the overhanging branches dappled the glinting water. At some point – perhaps he had not been concentrating – the figure had disappeared from the hillside.

But as they rounded another bend in that majestic river, there the watcher was.

'I would have expected a sense of urgency,' Myrrdin called.

'I'm starting to think that the only great plan you have is to torment me.'

Lucanus stood over the wood-priest as he lay back in the prow, swilling wine from a skin that he had appropriated somewhere along his journey.

'I'd be lying if I said I didn't find some enjoyment in it.' Myrrdin smacked his lips and wiped the ruby residue away with the back of his hand.

'Why did you leave me alone at Goibniu's Smithy?'

'I had business elsewhere.'

'And you didn't think to warn me?'

'And what business is my business of yours? My business, I said. Mine.'

'I might not have found my way back to the camp.'

'Forgive me for thinking you were *arcani*, who scouted the wilderness beyond the wall.' Myrrdin hesitated for a moment, then reluctantly offered the skin.

Lucanus waved it away. 'That night . . .' His words drained away as the wonders and the terrors rushed back.

'Did you find what you were looking for?' Myrrdin asked.

'I wasn't looking for anything.'

'Is that what you told yourself?'

'Stop speaking in riddles.'

'I speak perfect sense. If you don't have the wit to understand me, that's not my problem.' He rested one hand on the staff at his side as he thought, then said, 'You are becoming

136

the dragon, Wolf. You have scales and wings, and soon you'll breathe fire. You will become the Ouroboros, and then the circle will be unbroken.'

Lucanus bunched his fists, but there was nothing to hit beside the wood-priest. He thought about it for a moment.

'If we lose this war, wood-priest, it'll all be over for the rest of us. Your kind will no doubt creep back into the forests and hide away for another few years until you find some other fool who'll play your games.'

Heaving himself to his feet, Myrrdin leaned on his staff. Lucanus felt the cold scrutiny of his eyes. 'You do me a wrong, Wolf. This is no game. There has never been a more serious business. I've given you a chance. An army . . . small, yes, for now, but growing. One that might make a difference in the war with the tribes, now Rome has deserted you.' He tapped his staff on Lucanus' shoulder, his voice softening. 'And if Cernunnos is willing, the Chalice will be brought back to you.'

'The Chalice? Catia?'

'You sent your allies to save her, I sent mine. The Lord of the Greenwood is a force to be reckoned with. You know that.'

Lucanus nodded.

'He is the power of Cernunnos in human form, and the forest folk will follow him to the ends of the earth. The hidden folk of this land' – he smiled – 'the true *arcani* will creep out from the woods and the marshes and the lonely hilltops, and they will smite down any who would harm her. Do not underestimate them, Wolf. They may not be warriors. They do not wear armour or carry swords. But they are as hard as the winter ground, and just as cold when their way of life is under threat.'

Lucanus scarcely dared believe it. He had tried to put Catia out of his mind – it was the hope that killed him by degrees. But in that moment he felt emotion rush up inside him. 'If you can bring Catia back to me, wood-priest, I will follow *you* to the ends of the earth.'

Myrrdin smiled once more, but his wintry eyes seemed to be looking to some distant horizon.

'Breathe deep,' Mato said.

Lucanus sniffed the breeze and tasted woodsmoke and shit and the acrid belching of furnaces. 'Londinium.' He felt his chest heave with relief.

'Well, Lucanus, it appears you have saved us all,' Amarina said in a wry tone.

The Wolf nodded. There had been many times when he had thought he would never see this day. When the barbarian horde had crashed across the wall in the north. The perilous journey across the high country with that wave of blood and iron at their back. Searching futilely for a place of sanctuary when the whole of Britannia seemed to be burning. When Catia was taken, and Marcus killed, when there seemed no light left in the world. And then this final leg through the green lands of the south, with the barbarians so close at their heels he could smell their sweat.

'How much of the army will have gathered here?' Aelius enquired.

'A good part, I would think,' Lucanus replied. 'They will have tried to make their way here from every garrison that has fallen. Many must have escaped death at the swords of the invaders.'

Mato sighed, allowing himself to show his exhaustion as he all but collapsed against the side of the boat. 'Behind the walls, we can see out the winter. Rest, lick our wounds, grow strong. And in that time our own army should have increased in number.'

'Food for empty bellies,' Apullius said. Lucanus could almost hear the lad licking his lips.

'And a leech who can make my father well again,' Aelius said. He gripped Lucanus' arm. 'Thank you. Menius would have died long ago without your leadership. Your own father would have been proud. Menius has whispered that to me many a time as I cared for him.'

The Wolf stepped on to the front bench and looked over the weary heads of his men to the mismatched fleet that drifted on the Tamesis beyond. 'Londinium,' he called. And as heads rose and eyes brightened, he shouted it louder still. 'Londinium!'

A cheer rose up in his own boat, growing louder as the men realized what the word meant. And then it leapt from boat to boat, moving down the river.

'Now that is fine music,' Mato said.

Oars dipped and flashed with renewed power, and soon the flotilla was speeding along the grey water. The river had widened as it meandered across the broad valley floor, the city still hidden by the bends and the trees. But as Lucanus looked around, he could see signs that they were moving closer to civilization. Small boats were moored at jetties along both banks. Creels were piled up and rods with lines were jammed in the mud. Homes dotted the fields, some shacks, but the white walls of larger villas gleamed in the sunlight in the distance. This was a place of wealth. Every now and then he glimpsed folk at their labours. They'd straighten themselves up and stare in amazement at the odd collection of vessels speeding downriver. His men waved and cheered in return, only adding to their bewilderment.

Mato sniffed the air again. 'Nearly there.'

Lucanus sensed the anticipation in those standing rigidly around him, all eyes following the flow of the river as it twisted and turned. They'd come so far, suffered so much. At times it had seemed that would be the pattern for the rest of their lives, until death ultimately claimed them. Running. Hiding. Afraid.

When their boat rounded the final turn, Londinium presented itself to them. Under a pall of smoke from the fires of homes and workshops, the city sprawled on the north bank behind a towering ragstone wall. It was as impressive a defence as he'd heard. As high as four men standing on each other's shoulders, it incorporated around a score of semicircular towers, each with a platform for ballistae. The wall also loomed up along the banks of the Tamesis, to deter any raiders from the river.

Inside those vast defences, he imagined the grand forum, basilica and amphitheatre, the bath-houses and temples and palaces that he'd heard so much about, with the fort against the north-west wall. Finally, a chance to reclaim a small portion of the life they once knew.

He nodded and grinned and looked to Mato. He felt surprised when he saw that his friend's expression was dark, and he followed the other man's gaze to the *vicus* just beyond the city walls. The vastness of the settlement took his breath away. It dwarfed the home of merchants and smiths and hard-working folk that had huddled against the wall of the fort at Vercovicium in the north. And as he stared, he realized that something was amiss.

Close to Londinium, the homes and workshops were well built. But further away the *vicus* was a shamble of poor shacks, tents and structures that were little more than leaning branches. Fires glowed everywhere, the trails of smoke twisting up to an oppressive fug that hung over everything.

And everywhere, people. More than he'd ever seen in his lifetime. Crowds shambling along the narrow tracks among the dwellings. Families hunched around those fires, filthy, their clothes hanging off them in rags. He saw hollow eyes, hollow cheeks, faces ragged with despair. Hunger. Want. Sickness. His nostrils flared at the vile stink of too many people piled on top of each other in too small a space.

In the distance, columns of refugees trudged from the hills, more arriving by the day, by the hour.

'We should have known,' Mato muttered. 'We could not have been the only ones who heard Londinium was the last haven.'

Lucanus could feel the weight of the silence at his back. He didn't look round.

Children gambolled along the muddy river's edge, waving and shrieking with excitement as the boats drifted in. Beyond, folk trudged to the bank, staring, too weary and broken to register any emotion.

From each boat, a man splashed into the shallows and secured the vessel to a mooring post.

'Put on your crown,' Amarina muttered at his elbow.

'What?'

'Put on your crown.' Her voice cracked, and when he glanced at her, her green eyes were flashing.

'Heed her,' Myrrdin murmured.

From his cloak, Lucanus pulled out the gold circlet that Myrrdin had given him that day in the land of lakes when he'd been chosen to be the Head of the Dragon. Raising it high so all could see, he lowered it on to his head, watching the reflected sunlight that shimmered off it flicker across all the faces turned towards him, driving out the dullness of hardship.

Myrrdin thrust his way to the front. He dropped into the water and leaned on his staff to lever himself up to dry land. Sweeping one hand back to Lucanus, he boomed, 'Have hope, brothers and sisters. For the first time since this war began, have hope. For here is the Pendragon, the great war-leader of old, who will build an army the like of which

141

Britannia has not known in an age. The Pendragon, who will defeat the invaders and lead us all out of the dark.'

Lucanus felt Amarina's hand shove into the small of his back. Stirring himself, he dropped into the water and waded up to Myrrdin. He knew his role. Drawing Caledfwlch, he stabbed it towards the sun. 'With this sword of the gods, I will lead that army.' His voice soared above the distant sound of hammers and bawling babies. 'I will defeat our enemies. This is my vow. Once again you will be free to live the lives you once had.'

At first there was only silence. Then faces brightened, eyes gleamed with tears and long-buried emotions rose up. A desperate, kindling hope. A lone cheer echoed. But then it spread like a forest fire, springing from lips to lips, until it raged across the entire crowd, seemingly across the entire *vicus*.

Lucanus felt humbled.

A firm hand gripped his arm, and Myrddin urged him forward. The crowd parted as he strode into the stinking settlement and that jubilant din engulfed him. The news must have rushed in like the incoming crowd, for as he marched towards the city gates with his men trailing behind him folk sped to line the way. The waves of cheering never faltered.

As he swept into the *vicus* proper, a hook-nosed man dressed in makeshift leather armour with an old sword hanging from his hip stepped in front of him. He looked from Lucanus to Myrrdin and bowed. 'Your army is gathered here, what few heeded your call. But the numbers are growing by the day. The barbarian horde made it impossible to reach you, but we prayed that you would find your way to Londinium.'

'Once we've established a base in the city, we'll meet and discuss our plans,' Lucanus told him.

The man's face fell. 'They'll not let you in.'

'They must.'

He shook his head. 'The gates are closed. The city is overcrowded already. There's not enough food to go around. Sickness sweeps through the *vicus*, and the governor fears if it gets within the walls it will be the end. Folk are dying here, Pendragon. They came in hope, and there is none. They are falling by the hour. There's not enough time, or men, to bury them. Every night the bodies are carried out of the *vicus* and burned. Our only chance is to defeat the barbarians, and soon. Otherwise, I fear few of these folk will survive the winter.'

Lucanus felt sickened, but he nodded. 'We'll find a way through this.'

His words seemed to comfort the man, for now. As he marched on, he murmured to Myrrdin, 'Is this it, then? We have fought our way here only to rule over the slow death of all hope?'

'There is always hope, Wolf. You embody it now, don't forget that. The Dragon will rise.'

'I'm starting to believe I made a mistake in trusting you, wood-priest. It seems to me that your plan is all that matters, and that you'd sacrifice everything, all these folk, all of Britannia, to see it put into place.'

Myrrdin said nothing.

Lucanus stiffened his spine and strode on. They crossed a narrow bridge over a small river running down to the Tamesis. Folk from the *vicus* tramped behind them, as if unwilling to allow their saviours out of their sight. As the walls loomed up, he looked along the parapet and saw the silhouettes of many men gathered there. Soldiers in helmets, by the look of them.

Finally the cheering died away as Myrrdin stepped up to the gate and hammered his staff on the blistered wood.

'Open up,' he commanded. 'Open up for Lucanus Pendragon and the army that will finally win this war.'

'Away with you.' The voice resounded from the rampart, punctuated by harsh laughter. Somebody hawked up phlegm, and the gobbet splattered at Lucanus' feet.

'You think these walls will keep you safe from what lies out there?' the Wolf called up.

A long moment of silence hung in the air, and then another voice said in a harsher tone, 'Away. We can't support any more.'

Lucanus drew his blade again and looked along the length of it to those shadows along the wall. 'We have no fight, you and me. We'll stand shoulder to shoulder and hold back that wave of blood and iron about to crash upon you. No one knows the barbarians as we do. We've been among them. We know their tactics, their weaknesses. You have one chance left to save the day. To live. Take it.'

'Let them in.'

Lucanus frowned. Did he hear a familiar note in that voice?

After a moment, the gates rumbled open. A cadre of soldiers darted out, swords drawn, to hold at bay the crowd of desperate, hungry folk gathered at the back of the new arrivals.

'Make haste,' Lucanus urged. He swept his arm to send his men and the refugees through the gates first in case they were denied entrance once he'd stepped inside.

At the end of the column, he marched under the arch and into the city.

Instantly, he felt assailed by the life in Londinium. He choked on a reek worse than the *vicus*. Overflowing middens and backed-up ditches. Smoke and sweat. The street ahead was thronged. His ears rang at the din. The clatter of hammers, the belch of furnaces, citizens shouting to be heard.

He could see from the bodies jammed into the street that they had already taken in more than the city had been designed to hold.

That thick bank of smoke drifted across the sun and for a moment twilight rushed in.

The gates boomed shut. The cry of despair that rose up from those left outside drove a spike through his heart.

From the corner of his eye, he sensed someone pushing their way down the stone steps from the top of the wall. He turned and stiffened.

A familiar face indeed: pale skin with a sweep of freckles, piercing eyes like a midwinter moor. Once centurion of Vercovicium, now deserter and the man who, as much as anyone, had allowed this invasion to happen, and now had the blood of all those innocents who had died on his hands. Quintus Domitius Falx.

'Surprised? You shouldn't be,' Falx said with a grin. 'In the hell that is Britannia, all roads lead to Londinium, Lucanus. You'll find many old friends here.'

Falx, who had hunted down and stolen the boy Marcus from them.

'I should kill you now,' the Wolf growled.

PART TWO

City of the Dead

At his best, man is the noblest of all animals.
Separated from law and justice, he is the worst.

Aristotle

CHAPTER NINETEEN

Summer's End

'ONE NIGHT HE WILL COME TO MY HOUSE, AND THEN I'LL cut off his cock and feed it to him.'

Amarina was cleaning her nails with her knife. She whisked the blade in the air as if imagining the act of slicing, and then leaned back against the wall on her stool. Her lips curved, but Lucanus looked into her green eyes, like pebbles on a beach, and knew this was no lie. Amarina never forgot a wrong, and it was Falx who had snatched her and Marcus and offered them up to the merchant Varro. But though she hated Falx, Lucanus knew her deepest loathing was reserved for Varro's dwarfish assistant Bucco, who had left her for dead in a pool of her own blood.

Lucanus' thoughts flew back to the first time he had seen that dwarf. All had thought him a tool mercilessly exploited by Varro. But in truth Bucco had only been masquerading as the downtrodden servant and it was he who was the true master in that relationship. Bucco, as cruel and savage as any barbarian, despite his stature, who would inflict any torture on those who stood in his way.

'We can never forget,' Mato said. 'But this isn't the time to be fighting among ourselves. Justice will catch up with Falx sooner or later.'

'On the other hand,' Myrrdin mused, 'he gave us entrance to the city and provided us with these fine comforts.' He swigged back wine, and then waved the goblet at the small, dark room. The centurion had found a few of them this house, no doubt throwing the previous occupants out on the street. Here were Amarina, Decima and Galantha, the wood-priest, Mato, Apullius and Morirex, old man Menius and Aelius. It would be cramped, but they would have space to plan and gather their strength. The rest of Lucanus' men and the refugees had been sent to the south-eastern corner of the city and told to find a place to camp. But the centurion had, at least, promised them food to fill their bellies.

'Falx is not to be trusted. Ever,' Lucanus said.

As if in answer, the door crashed open. Lucanus turned to see the centurion standing there. Falx smiled, then thought better of it. 'I understand your feelings. We've had our differences—'

'*Differences?* You certainly have a way with words.' Amarina was smiling at him.

Falx levelled his sword at her. 'Keep that witch away from me.'

'We will be opening a new House of Wishes here in Londinium, the three of us,' she went on, nodding to Decima and Galantha. 'You should visit us. It will be a night you will never forget.'

She stood up, swung her cloak around her shoulders and stepped out into the sweltering street. The other two women followed. Through the door, Lucanus could see the shadows lengthening fast, and the three companions were quickly swallowed by the gloom.

Instantly relaxing, Falx kicked the door shut, walked across the room and poured himself a goblet of wine. 'We always understood each other, Lucanus. We did good business in Vercovicium, made a little coin—'

'Until you went too far, robbed your own men, and left the wall unguarded when we needed it most.' Lucanus swallowed bile. 'And until you snatched Marcus.'

'I've made mistakes—'

'I should gut you now.' Lucanus' hand twitched towards his sword as grief stabbed his heart once again.

'I've made mistakes, like any man.' Falx swilled back the wine. 'When I took Marcus to that fat slug Varro, the world was falling apart and none of us knew if we would see the next sunrise. Survival, that's all I saw it as. And I was wrong to do it. I'm not a learned man. A humble soldier, who's given his life to Rome. Would you forgive me?'

'No,' Lucanus said.

Falx shrugged. 'Fair enough. Then will you at least work with me, in common purpose?'

'And what would that be?' Mato asked. 'Filling your coffers?'

'Coin will be worth nothing in the afterlife. The choices are clearer now. Live or die. I want to live. I'll wager you do too, all of you. You're good men, you Grim Wolves.' He eyed the others, sneering a little at the sight of Aelius wiping his father's face. 'Not so sure about the rest of you. But I'd rather have you at my shoulder than my enemy's. We need some good men, Lucanus. Let me tell you, this place is a pit of shit, ruled over by jolt-heads who don't know their arse from their elbow. It was bad enough when I first got here, and they've let it grow worse by far. Do-nothings who pray and whine, and wish like children that Rome will suddenly send a legion to the gates to save us all. Wishes won't fill bellies or gut barbarians, Wolf. You know that as well as I do. We're on our own here, and if we are going to live we have to see to it ourselves.'

Much as he hated him, Lucanus knew the centurion was right. 'How many men have you got to defend the city?'

Falx shrugged. 'This is the madness that has gripped this

place. No one has done a head-count. The rabble are barely organized. The governor has sealed himself in his palace with his advisers and slaves. No one ever sees him any more. All we have are messengers demanding this or that on his behalf; half-hearted orders; whims. But nothing gets done, and there is no punishment for it.'

'We have an army.' Aelius had finished mopping his father's brow, and Lucanus was surprised to see the old man's eyes sparkling in a manner that he had not witnessed since Vercovicium. 'You have Lucanus to thank for that,' Aelius went on. 'He is a great man now, a leader of men, as his father always believed he was.'

Falx nodded. 'I know your worth, Lucanus. And I've heard from the folk in the *vicus* that an army was gathering here. They are raw, though, yes? Farmers. Merchants.'

'But they won't run at the first sign of a fight.'

'I cannot argue with you there.' The centurion stepped to the door. 'Walk with me. I'll show you what kind of place you've found yourself in.'

Lucanus strode behind Falx into the dusty street. His skin prickled from the heat rising off the buildings. There was no breeze and the air was dry, but he could at least hear himself think now that the din had died down a little as the day wound towards its close.

Falx led him through the shadows to the river wall. They climbed the stone steps to the top and Lucanus looked to the south. The Tamesis was a river of blood in the light of the setting sun. He could see a sturdy bridge crossing to the south bank where a settlement sprawled, but much of it seemed to have fallen into ruin.

Lucanus turned to the west and looked back along the way they had come. His thoughts flew over that rich, green land to where the fires burned and the war-bands of the great horde came together and swept towards them.

'When he was in his cups, the merchant Varro used to spew words about the legend of the King Who Will Not Die,' Falx said in a low voice, eyeing him askance. 'Whoever controlled the bloodline held the ultimate power, he would say time and again. He thought that boy of the woman you took a fancy to, the married one, was key—'

'Marcus is dead.'

'I'm sorry to hear that.' Falx bowed his head for a moment, and Lucanus felt his anger rise again. 'But know now that I've got no interest in those stories, whether they're the fantasies of fools or there's any truth in them. Who cares about power and gold and kings that may or may not be born in days yet to come? Every day now is about living to the next dawn. That's all that matters.'

'We have work to do,' Lucanus agreed. 'But don't ask me again to forgive.'

Falx nodded. He turned and leaned against the stones to look back across the town. Here and there torches flickered into life. The stink of pitch rose up. Pointing to the western wall, he went on, 'When you arrived, you crossed the River Fleet and passed through the Ludgate. North of that is the Newgate, and the Aldersgate, and then the fort set against the Cripplegate. The temple precinct is over there. Plenty of places to pray for salvation. We have many of those Christians here and they have their own churches. They don't like us bowing our heads to the old gods, or going to the Temple of Mithras up there by the Walbrook, but what are they going to do about it?' He shrugged. 'They've given the Temple of Mithras over to Bacchus, but there's still a part of it we can use. Everything changes.'

Everything changes.

The Fates measured the threads and cut them, and only they knew the span of a man's life. If he died here, so be it, the Wolf thought. He'd had a good life. But those who now relied on him? That was a burden with which he still struggled.

Falx pointed to a large structure to the north, little more than a mass of shadows with the edges limned in red. 'See that?'

Lucanus nodded.

'The amphitheatre. Seen better days. Don't go up there at night, or you'll get your throat slit. But there are bath-houses still working, so at least you can get the filth of the day off you. Down here's the governor's palace,' he continued, jabbing a finger towards a complex of red-roofed buildings next to the river wall. 'And up there—'

'The forum.' Lucanus studied the silhouette of the massive structure due north, with the basilica beyond it.

'If you want to find out what's happening, who's plotting against whom, whom the gods have spoken to, who's had a vision of salvation, or damnation, that's where you go. And that, my friend, is Londinium, for better or worse.'

'What do you do for food and supplies?'

'We still have traders coming up the river from the east. Mithras alone knows how much longer that will last. We've tried to store as much as we can, for the cold months.'

'The folk outside the walls?'

'We can't do anything for them. We can barely feed ourselves.'

'So you'll let them die?'

Falx didn't reply.

'When they begin to starve, you know they'll storm the gates as eagerly as any barbarian. What then? Burning pitch? Arrows?'

The centurion held out his arms. 'I'm a fighting man. How can I answer that?'

Lucanus glimpsed a red glow suddenly flare into life beyond the northern walls.

Falx must have seen his puzzled expression for he said, 'They're burning the bodies. Same thing, night after night. Best not get downwind. The cemeteries outside the walls are filled to the brim.'

The Wolf looked out over the town and felt a chill grow inside him. They'd come so far, fought so hard, for this? There was nowhere else to run. Only the sea lay at his back.

In the distance, in the woods clustering on the high hills, he thought he heard a low, rolling yowl. Cernunnos was standing among the trees, howling. He sucked in a steadying gulp of the warm night air and for the first time felt a cool breath in his throat.

Summer was ending.

'You're right,' he said finally. 'We do this ourselves. The way we knew is long gone. If there's no good leadership, then we must provide it. If we don't, all we have is to wait here for death to claim us all.'

'Life was simpler when witches and druids took no interest in our lives. Now they say the gods are watching us too. Who wants that?'

Comitinus skidded down the bank to where Catia and the other Grim Wolves waited. At the bottom, he seemed to sense what Bellicus was thinking for he took a step behind the pregnant woman. Catia was oblivious as she scanned the horizon, her bow strung across her back.

'Stop talking like a frit child,' Solinus snarled.

'I'm not frit,' Comitinus countered. 'It's a wise man who looks to the threats on the road ahead and makes plans to avoid getting his head lopped off his shoulders.'

'Ah, you're a superstitious fool.'

'Silence, the two of you, or I'll knock your heads together.' Bellicus glanced behind him and felt his neck prickle. The forest folk and their witches and whatever other daemons walked with those haunts of the greenwood had shadowed them every step of the way since they'd escaped Erca's camp. He'd seen nothing of them. They'd speak only to Catia. Every night at dusk, he watched her traipse among the trees, to take counsel, perhaps. Who knew? She kept their secrets too. Part of the deal they had between them. But she had told them that Myrrdin had sent the forest folk to aid them, so the bastard wood-priest couldn't be all bad.

'And one day the witches who wove their spells around Lucanus will come for us.' This time Comitinus' words were little more than a croak.

'Don't talk like you're ale-soaked,' Solinus spat. 'Those wayward sisters stalked the land beyond the wall. Or do you think they turned to crows and flew here?'

'Aye. Perhaps.'

Bellicus weighed this notion. All the certainties that he had learned in his long life as a Grim Wolf had been swept aside the moment the barbarian horde had invaded. He had prided himself on knowing the way the hawk flew and the routes the floods would take in the spring melt. Now he felt he couldn't trust anything he had come to rely on. He'd discovered there was another world squatting beside the one the Romans had built with their straight roads and walls and camps, one as old as time, cheek by jowl but unseen, unknowable. The forest folk lived lives in the deep woods that barely crossed those of the men of the empire, and though he had spent all his days in the Wilds he'd never known they were there. They worshipped ancient gods, and weaved their own stories of times past, had customs and rules that were alien to him. And they still listened to the whispers of the wood-priests and the witches, as his own people had done in the days of his father's father's father.

In that world, who was to say that witches could not turn to crows and fly the length of the land?

He sensed Solinus and Comitinus watching him and he turned and whistled for Catulus. His faithful hound had sought him out the moment he'd escaped the barbarian camp.

'Move on,' he said without meeting their eyes. 'Before the barbarians catch up with us and the Attacotti eat you alive.'

'We can defeat these barbarians.' Catia's voice floated back to them, almost dreamlike.

'Why stop there? Let's take the empire,' Solinus said. Looking up, he traced the path of a crow across the sky. 'We'd run it a damn sight better than Valentinian and Valens. The whole midden heap is falling apart, like one of the shacks Clomus put up in the *vicus* at Vercovicium when he'd spent the day drowning himself in ale.'

Catia pointed to a distant gleam beyond a black line of trees at the edge of the rolling grassland. A river, catching the morning sun. 'There. We follow the Tamesis and it will take us to where we need to be.'

'Is this what your forest friends tell you?' Solinus grunted. 'How do we know they're not leading us into a trap? These days, everyone seems to be playing their own game, and we're just the pieces they shove around.'

Catia didn't look back. 'Follow me, or stay here. Your choice.'

Bellicus watched her begin to run with slow, steady strides, balancing the weight in her belly.

'You ask me, the daemons have taken hold of her. Or the witches have given her some potion to drive her mad,' Solinus snorted. 'She's with child. She shouldn't be racing across the land and fighting like a warrior.'

'Shut up and follow her,' Bellicus said.

Lucanus strode through the *vicus* outside the walls of Londinium. Everywhere he went, curious folk stumbled out of their huts and tents and watched him as if he were a god come down to earth. He felt uncomfortable. Part of it, he knew, was that he wore the gold dragon circlet, as Amarina had insisted. 'Be who they want you to be. Give them hope.'

He knew, too, that Myrrdin had been among them during the night, moving from home to home, whispering words, stories, fantastic tales of magic swords and kings who would not die. Of the work of the gods, and bringing the magic back to the land. This was how he wove his true spells. Lucanus had seen how words changed people, transformed them from whipped cur to hero, from mud-crawling scout to great war-leader.

Aelius and Apullius had insisted on coming with him that morning in case he was attacked and robbed. Coin meant nothing in that world, but a gold crown, that was still a great prize. They needn't have worried. These beaten, now hopeful folk barely dared approach him.

On the boundary where the original *vicus* met the ramshackle refugee city, he breathed in the familiar aroma of roasting venison. Following his nose, he strode up to the campfire where the deer sizzled, surrounded by a knot of squatting men. Hungry eyes watched from all around.

The men jumped to their feet when they saw him approach, and he could see from the blades they carried that these must be some of those who had answered Myrrdin's call for an army of the Pendragon.

'What's your name?' he said to a man with hair like straw who was a head taller than the others.

'Butu.'

'Where did you get the meat?'

'We went hunting before dawn, across the bridge and in the woods to the south. It's yours if you want it, Pendragon.'

'There's more where that came from?'

'The woods are rich in game, if you know where to look

for it,' Butu replied. 'I come from the land down there, near the coast, near Rutupiae. The trade routes from the southern ports are still open. The villages down that way have stores filled to the brim. They don't want for anything.'

'When you've filled your bellies, I need you to feed the refugees too.'

'We came here to fight,' another of the men grunted.

'There'll be time enough for that. Don't wish away the days until you're looking down a barbarian blade.' Lucanus walked around the men, sizing up each one. 'A few days past, I was told there's a bigger battle that will need fighting. Should we defeat the barbarians, gods willing, we'll need to rebuild Britannia so we can reclaim the lives we once knew. If not, what reason victory?'

Butu nodded. 'That makes sense.'

'We start here. We fight for the folk who followed our army. They're starving and sick, and soon they'll be cold. Take all the good men you can find and divide the camp into groups. Set the folk to helping themselves. Find men who can hunt, and if need be show them how to do it. Find women who can lead their groups. These are the ones we must save first. This is our battle now. And we can make everyone here a soldier for their own good.'

Butu looked around the others and grinned. 'We'll do what you say. Today.'

Lucanus rested a hand on Aelius' shoulder. The younger man narrowed his eyes at him. 'This is Aelius. He's a general in my army.'

Lucanus felt Catia's younger brother stiffen, and from the corner of his eye saw his face brighten with surprise. 'He'll oversee this work. He'll give my orders. And if you have any complaints, he'll bring them back to me.'

Butu nodded, and looked to Aelius with new-found respect.

Aelius eyed Lucanus slyly, shucking his cloak off his withered arm. 'It seems a half-formed man has some use after all,' he whispered so the others couldn't hear above the sizzling and spitting of the venison. Cocking an eyebrow, he added, 'A general, eh? Do I get a crown like yours? Not as grand, of course . . .'

Lucanus clapped him on the back and walked away.

As he strode back to the town, Apullius raced to keep up. 'And do you have work for me too?' he asked breathlessly. He held up the skin he'd brought in case Lucanus got thirsty in the heat of the day.

The Wolf hesitated, then took it and swilled the cool contents down his dry throat. When he'd wiped his mouth, he said, 'I spoke too harshly when we were on the boat. I'll teach you how to fight with a sword, and live for days in the Wilds.'

'You'll teach me to become a Grim Wolf?' Apullius' voice vibrated with excitement.

'This is no land for a merchant or a farmer, not any more.' He remembered the day his father had said the same words to him, and the excitement and the terror he too had felt. One day those skills might save this lad's life. That was the best way he could honour his father. And if his worst fears were confirmed, Britannia would need fighting men for many years to come.

Spikes of light glinted off helmets. A crimson banner fluttered in the breeze. Horses snorted and stamped their hooves, but the soldiers stood as rigid as sentinels in the centre of the fort.

'It's not much, but it is a new beginning,' Falx said.

Lucanus looked along the ranks that the centurion had managed to pull together from those who had made their way to Londinium and the force already garrisoned here.

Some looked ragged, it was true, with filthy tunics and dented armour. But still, here was the army he knew.

'With the men I have at my command, we may at least be able to hold back the tide for a while,' Lucanus said.

'And that's all we need to do.' Falx turned and beckoned.

A soldier with bulging eyes and thinning sandy hair strode over. He was different from the others, Lucanus decided. His chin was pushed up and he carried himself with the bearing of a man who presumed great things lay ahead.

'This is Theodosius the Younger,' Falx said by way of introduction. 'Hear what he has to say before plans are made. Theodosius, this is Lucanus the Wolf, the one they are calling the Head of the Dragon these days. In days long gone now, he was one of the *arcani* and served us well scouting beyond the wall in Britannia's northland.'

Theodosius looked him up and down, weighing. He seemed to find what he saw acceptable, for he nodded. 'Your soldiers are not well trained, I hear; not fighting men at all. But they will be welcomed.'

'They're prepared to fight and die. That's all we can ask of them.'

'I sailed from Gaul with a few good men to see the lie of the land and prepare for the campaign to come in the spring.'

Lucanus felt a wave of relief. 'Then Britannia hasn't been abandoned.'

'Rome would never let a barbarian rabble keep a part of the empire, you must know that. My own father will lead.'

'Theodosius the Elder,' the Wolf said. 'His fame reached even Vercovicium. A skilled tactician and fierce warrior.'

'A great man,' Theodosius replied. 'I hope to honour him. By gaining vital information at first hand, I can more ably advise him when he arrives, rather than having to rely on scraps tossed out by frightened and unskilled scouts.'

Lucanus stiffened at the unintended slur, but he said nothing. Theodosius could never hope to see with the eyes of a Grim Wolf.

'Good news, eh, Lucanus?' Falx said, rubbing his hands. 'Some hope at last.'

'Even now he is on his way to Bononia with the troops he already has,' Theodosius continued. 'The Batavi, the Heruli, the Iovii, and the Victores from the *comitatenses*. More will join him there, under the orders of the emperor. They'll carve through this barbarian horde in no time.'

'Then all we have to do is survive until spring,' Lucanus said.

'I've seen at first hand how these barbarians fight.' Theodosius' face darkened. 'On our march from Rutupiae we were attacked in the night. By more beasts than men, caked in white mud with black eyes and tattoos. They . . . they ate the flesh of our men . . .' His voice trailed off, and Lucanus thought how hollow his eyes looked.

'The Attacotti.'

'We lost half of our number to them. The rest of us barely escaped with our lives. It would be God's will to wipe those things from the face of the world, and I will take it as my personal mission to do so.'

'We must meet, plan our strategy—' Falx began.

'Tonight,' Theodosius insisted. 'There's no time to waste.'

As Lucanus nodded his agreement, Theodosius pulled Falx aside and whispered in his ear.

'He asks if you follow the Christ,' the centurion said with a tight smile.

What talk was this when they were in the middle of a desperate defensive campaign, Lucanus thought? The men there had other things to concern them, and many had other beliefs. Yet he replied only, 'The word of your god had not reached into the north, which was my home.'

Theodosius' thin lips tightened. 'It will, soon enough. There are many heathens here, I've learned, and I must make my peace with that. But we will work to bring you into light, and then those who follow you in shadow will find the Christ too.'

Lucanus said nothing, trying to avoid Falx's rolling eyes. As he turned to return to Mato and Myrrdin, he caught sight of another soldier striding up. More handsome than Theodosius, he had black hair and a pleasant, open face.

'Lucanus Pendragon,' the newcomer hailed him. 'It's good to make your acquaintance after hearing so many tales of your bravery. So brave, in fact, that they tell me they have given you a golden crown in the shape of a dragon. What wonders!' He flashed a disarming grin. 'My name is Lucius Aurelius Corvus, and I feel we have much in common, you and I.'

CHAPTER TWENTY

The Circle

'WAKE! WAKE NOW, LUCANUS!'
        The Wolf stirred in his bed. Someone was shaking
him roughly. He jerked up. A thin grey light was leaking into
the chamber where Mato, Myrrdin, Aelius and Menius were
still snoring.

Apullius was looming over him. 'Come,' the lad said, tugging on his arm. 'Come.'

'What is it?' Lucanus grumbled. His head still swam with
the discussion of tactics that had ranged back and forth deep
into the night in that cramped room in the fort.

'A scout has just returned, and . . . but you must see this
for yourself.' Apullius snatched up the grey wolf pelt and
helped pull it on to his master's shoulder.

'I'm regretting giving you this work,' Lucanus muttered,
his voice heavy with sleep.

'Now. But you'll thank me for it later.' Lucanus caught
the teasing allusion, and smiled as he stumbled out into the
silvery dawn light. Excitedly, Apullius hurried along the
street ahead of him until they came to the western wall and
climbed the stone steps to the rampart. At the top, Lucanus
leaned against the parapet and let the cool breeze flush the
last of the sleep from his head.

'There. See.' Apullius was pointing over the wall. A low mist was drifting across the grassland beyond the Fleet, and a row of figures stood half obscured by the haziness next to a dark copse of ash trees.

'The forest folk,' Lucanus said, squinting. And at their heart, one who was clearly a warrior, taller than the rest. The Lord of the Greenwood.

Apullius shook him and said, 'No. There.' He jabbed his finger down into the *vicus*.

Lucanus searched through the long shadows until he saw four figures running among the huts with the steady gait the *arcani* reserved for crossing the Wilds. He felt his heart leap when he recognized Bellicus' bear-like frame, and Solinus and Comitinus on either side.

And then he saw the figure at the front and thought he might burst. He all but thrust Apullius to one side and scrambled down the steps.

Once the gate had rattled open, he dashed out into the quiet of the *vicus*. His heart was thumping. He'd imagined this moment a thousand times, but still he was afraid that the figure he had seen would vanish into mist.

But there she was, sun-browned face smeared with dirt from the road, dress ragged and streaked with green, blonde hair matted and straggly. But it was Catia, and he knew then that the gods and the Fates smiled on him and all would surely be right with the world.

A moment as the hard stare formed by life as a captive melted away, and then she saw him, and believed it was truly him and not some barbarian waiting to kill her. Her eyes brimmed with tears and she threw her arms wide.

Lucanus grabbed her and swept her up into an embrace. He fell into a kiss that seemed to last an age, and then he swung her round, laughing. Only when the euphoria had subsided did he feel the weight pressing against his stomach.

Lowering her to the ground, he stared in amazement.

'It's yours, Lucanus,' she breathed.

'Marcus—' he began.

'I know.' She blinked away a tear. 'This is hope, here. Let us give thanks for that.'

Bellicus, Solinus and Comitinus were grinning. 'You saved her . . .' He paused when he saw the odd look they shared.

'Let's not get into gratitude just yet,' Solinus said.

'We are humble folk,' Comitinus added with a nod.

'Just fetch us wine,' Bellicus grunted. 'My mouth is filled with dust.'

'Wine, yes, and something to fill our bellies.' Catia gripped Lucanus' arms. 'But let's not dawdle. The barbarians are hard on our heels. From this moment on, there will be war.'

The candle guttered. Shadows danced across the faces of the five people seated in the circle. The clamour of that overcrowded town thrummed through the walls, but in that gloomy room there was only silence.

Lucanus looked around the faces: Catia, Bellicus, Mato, Amarina. Myrrdin had just entered, and now leaned on his staff in one corner. They could begin.

'No Solinus, or Comitinus?' Bellicus asked.

'Five is the right number,' Myrrdin intoned.

The wood-priest's words rushed back to Lucanus, from the time they had shared at the Heartstones: *Numbers are important. Three, five, nine. When you see those numbers, you must pay special attention, for the gods are speaking through them.*

'You'd do well giving one of them my seat,' Amarina said. 'I have no part to play here. And, as far as I can see, there is no coin to be made either.' She made to stand from her stool.

'Sit down, moon-sister,' Myrrdin said, not unkindly. That strange name seemed to cause a flicker on Amarina's face, Lucanus noticed, and she lowered herself back down. But not without a sharp glance at the wood-priest. He smiled in return.

'We gather here as equals,' the Wolf began. 'You, my most trusted friends. I will need your counsel more than ever in days to come.'

'You'd do well to have some soldiers here,' Mato said. 'I see few great tacticians in our number.'

'This is not about the coming war. We have plans abirthing there, formed by sharper minds than mine.' The Wolf glanced at Catia, then at her swollen belly. 'All has changed.'

'The unborn child,' Amarina said, understanding. 'The royal bloodline renewed.'

Lucanus shivered, remembering another child waiting to enter the world, the one in the belly of the witch, Hecate, that had come from the seed she had stolen from him. The thought unsettled him, and he pushed it aside.

Myrrdin prowled around the gathering. Lucanus' nose wrinkled at the strange scents rising off him, unguents and incense from the mysterious rituals he carried out at night in the groves beyond the *vicus*. 'When Marcus was stolen from us, it was easy to believe all hope was lost. But the gods would never let this gulf form. The King Who Will Not Die must come, as the sun must rise and the tides sweep in. And so it will be.'

Lucanus watched Mato's face harden. Of all of them, he seemed less than entranced by the wood-priest's proclamations. 'We have more pressing concerns than your games, wood-priest,' he said.

'This is not a game.' Myrrdin hammered his staff on the floor for emphasis.

Lucanus could see Mato wanted to say more, but his friend bit his tongue. Something lay between the two men, that was certain.

'The child must be protected at all costs,' Myrrdin continued. 'There are enemies who will want the power that comes with the bloodline. You know that. You have seen it before, and how much misery it causes.'

'We're among friends here,' Bellicus said.

'Enemies lurk everywhere,' Myrrdin replied.

'Wise words,' Lucanus said. 'I've learned to trust few outside this room. Falx, for one, has always kept an eye on profit. He knows the value of any child of Catia's, and if he can get a good price for it he will, whatever he might say.'

'Then we watch him like a hawk.' Bellicus unconsciously bunched his fists.

'You spoke of a sanctuary, in the west,' Mato said to the wood-priest.

Catia rested her hands on her thighs. 'The child will be here soon enough. This is not the time to be trying to pick a way through the barbarian horde, even if we could. Erca knows of the bloodline.' She shrugged. 'But he has no interest in gaining an advantage there.'

'You're sure of that?' Lucanus said.

She nodded without meeting his eye. 'But there may be others. Wood-priests move among the barbarians too.' Catia eyed Myrrdin. 'Your kind do not always speak with one voice.'

'All men have flaws,' the druid said. 'Except me.'

'So we stay here, in Londinium, till Catia gives birth.' Amarina stared into the shadows in the corner of the room, weighing what she had heard. 'Till the child is strong enough to travel. The winter would not be a good time to set forth. The spring, then.' She paused, then looked around the faces in the circle. 'When Theodosius the Elder arrives with his army.'

'In the middle of war, we run,' Bellicus said with a nod. 'The barbarians will have too much to concern them then. And no one here will care if a handful slip out like ghosts in the night. They will be too busy sharpening their blades.'

'We run,' Lucanus repeated. He looked to the wood-priest. 'West?'

'To Avalon,' Myrrdin said. 'Beyond the Isle of Apples, beyond the shining waters, there is a land where the men of Rome barely ventured. Untouched by their bloody hands, it still echoes with the voices of ancient times. The gods still walk among men there, and daemons too, and there is magic in the forests. After the slaughter at Ynys Môn, many druids took refuge in Avalon, sailing along the west coast in small boats.' Lucanus watched him lean on his staff, eyes closed, no doubt remembering how the story was told to him.

'Wood-priests,' Bellicus snorted, 'and no doubt witches too. Why would we want to visit a haunted place like that?'

'Haunted, that is true.' Myrrdin's eyes flashed open, like beacons in the night. 'Haunted by the promise of days long gone. The tribes still live there, as they always did. They remember the old stories too, and they'll help defend you, should any come searching for you.'

'And what then?' Mato asked.

'There's a place atop soaring cliffs by the shining sea that was once the home of the kings of the west. There you'll build your fortress, a sanctuary that will survive the years, and there you'll build your army. And over the years, the legend of the King Who Will Not Die will take root, and flourish, and all men and women in Britannia will know hope. And when he is needed most, the Bear-King will answer their call, and all in this land will be led out of the dark into a new age of light.'

For a moment, silence lay across the room. Lucanus knew the druid's skill with words – that was his magic, to create something from nothing with that spell – but still he felt hope rising inside him at the story. It summoned up a world he yearned for, one where peace and prosperity once again ruled. He could see from the faces of the others that the tale had stirred something in them too, even Mato.

Myrrdin was smiling, but he quickly pushed it aside. 'Until then, we do not let Catia out of our sight. She needs a guard, like any queen.'

Bellicus drew his sword and pointed it into the centre of the circle. 'I'll take that job. And I'll have Solinus and Comitinus too. We owe Catia our lives, and we will give them to protect her.'

Catia shifted with discomfort, but Lucanus grinned. 'I'd trust no men more, wolf-brother. If there are enemies here, they'll not come close.'

CHAPTER TWENTY-ONE

Cheapside

THE BLACK PALL OF SMOKE FROM THE BURNING BODIES HUNG over Londinium. Catia wrinkled her nose at the reek. 'What is this hell?'

'True, it's not the perfumed paradise you no doubt expected,' Aelius said, 'but we are beggars and have to take what we're given.'

Catia felt sickened as she pushed through the packed streets with Bellicus trailing along behind. His eyes were searching every face, his fingers never far from his sword-hilt. Her ears ached from the deafening roar of thousands of voices. Her heart ached, too, when she saw children in filthy rags as thin as needles, bawling, hands outstretched in a plea for food.

On every corner, desperate men beat each other until blood flowed into the rutted streets. Women drifted like shades, heads bowed low and shoulders slumped, greasy hair falling across their faces, so listless with despair she half expected them to crumple to their knees.

And everywhere the bodies were brought out of houses on makeshift biers, so many of them the corpse-carriers seemed to have been worn down by the task, not even having the decency to bind their cargo in shrouds or close the white

171

eyes that stared up to that black cloud. Victims of sickness or hunger or pathetic arguments that whipped sparks of hopelessness into fires of rage.

Life, it seemed, meant little in Londinium.

'A city of the dead,' she murmured.

'Hush.' Her brother grabbed her hand and tugged her away from the throng, down a narrow alley. She heard Bellicus curse as he heaved himself into the tight space. 'Think only good thoughts.'

'I've seen enough misery beyond these walls,' she replied. 'Must it corrupt this sanctuary too?'

Aelius dragged her to the banks of a stream, the Walbrook, which bisected the town. It was clogged with filth and stank worse than the corpse-fires. Soon, she was looking up at the gleaming walls of a bath-house and breathing in the sweet aroma of oils. In the warmth of the Cheapside baths, she glanced around and saw only soldiers and members of Lucanus' army. That was why there was some space to breathe there.

Her brother seemed unusually light on his feet and filled with a surprising joy that was far from the surly youth who had trudged around Vercovicium spitting venom at everyone he encountered.

'Why are you so happy,' she asked, 'in the middle of this stinking mass of suffering?'

Aelius tugged her behind a column, out of sight of Bellicus, and hugged her to him. She laughed at this unusual show of affection until she realized that his shoulders were heaving. When she pushed him back, she saw his eyes were wet.

'What is this?' she asked, incredulous.

'I thought I'd never see you again.' He dragged his good hand across his eyes.

'You should know me better than that,' she replied, trying

to make light of it. 'I've survived worse than a few barbarians.'

'So much joy has been stolen from our lives. I couldn't bear to lose you ...' He choked down his emotion, and hugged her again.

Her arms went round him gingerly as if he would crumble under her touch. She struggled to understand how she felt.

'You grew a skin of stone to survive your days with Amatius, I know,' he continued, as if he could understand her confusion. 'But don't let that keep out the ones who love you, Catia. And you are loved. By me, by Father ... by Lucanus, who would sacrifice his life for you. By everyone who has known you.'

She felt bewildered. It seemed so long since she had allowed herself to think of such things.

Aelius pulled back, smiling. 'We're a family again ... you, me, Father. Together we can overcome anything. And now I have new friends for you to meet.'

He dragged her back into the ringing echoes. Bellicus eyed them as if they were troublesome children. Aelius beckoned and two lads hurried across the flagstones towards them, one small, the other tall and gangly with a mop of unruly hair.

The older one knelt before her and bowed his head. 'I am at your service, Lady Catia. I would lay down my life in your defence.'

'Apullius,' Aelius said, 'and his brother Morirex.'

The younger one gaped at her as if she were some messenger from the gods, and then he too dropped to his knees. 'Your service,' he stuttered.

Catia stifled a smile. 'Arise,' she said. 'I am honoured.'

'Lucanus has taken them under his wing,' Aelius said, 'and is training them to be—'

'*Arcani*,' Apullius said.

'Warriors,' Morirex said.

173

Apullius' eyes dropped to her swollen belly. 'You are the mother who will bring forth the King Who Will Not Die.'

'And if you train hard,' she replied, playing the game for their sake, 'you will be my child's protectors.'

They seemed to swell with such awe, she thought they would explode there and then.

'Back to your training,' Aelius ordered, putting on a cold face, 'and if you do well, I'll take you out for the hunt with the men from the *vicus* tomorrow.'

The two lads scampered off.

'They're caught up in the wonder of the tale Myrrdin weaves,' Aelius said. 'It helps them to forget the deaths of their parents, so . . .' He shrugged.

'And you,' she said. 'A general in the army now.'

'We are all changed.'

She felt her smile grow tight at that. Shaking off her unease, she looked around the soaring arches of the bathhouse and allowed herself to sink into memories of the life that had once been. 'Myrrdin is right to be cautious,' she said, 'but after living every moment with death at my elbow, I feel safe here.'

CHAPTER TWENTY-TWO

The Shadow

A GOLDEN LEAF WHISKED ACROSS THE CLEAR BLUE SKY.
Corvus craned his neck up to watch its passage. 'The cold days will be here soon enough,' he said. 'But then you'll be used to those.'

Hecate nodded. 'My sisters and I endured long winters. But the Alamanni are a hard breed.'

Corvus glanced at his wife and thought once again how she looked nothing like the filthy witch he'd dragged away from her hovel after he'd had her sisters murdered. Now her hair was well combed, not a tangled mess of rat's tails, the blonde wisps twirling from the depths of the hood of the expensive emerald cloak his mother had given her. He breathed in the perfumed unguents she'd learned to rub into the creamy skin of her pale face, and as she reached out to stroke his cheek, he noticed that there was no mud crusted under her nails.

It seemed a little civilization could transform even the lowliest barbarian.

There, on the walkway around the walls, looking down on the fort, Corvus felt a chill wind whistle around his ears. Below them, the horses were being led out of their stables between the barracks, stamping their hooves and whinnying as if they knew what was to come. Perhaps they did. He'd always felt horses had more wits than half the men he'd encountered. He could hear orders being barked and the thunder of feet in step as the soldiers marched towards the Cripplegate.

'You must take care, husband,' she said. 'I would not lose you. You have done so much for me.'

'I've only tried to fill the emptiness you felt after your sisters so tragically died,' he replied. 'But now our destinies are entwined. A shining future awaits us.'

She smiled sweetly. Pretty, if none too bright, he thought. She would have made someone a good wife. Unfortunately, she was his, but he would make do, as he always did. Her purpose overruled all other matters.

'As soon as these barbarians are driven back, we'll see about arranging a meeting with your other sisters, here in Britannia,' he said. 'Then you can make my case to them. And they in turn will make it to the wood-priests.'

'I will,' she said, leaning in to kiss him on the cheek. 'You are a good man. You deserve all that will come your way.'

He glanced along the walkway to where Pavo lounged against the parapet, arms folded. They exchanged a secret grin. He glanced away just as quickly when he saw Hecate frown, wondering what he was looking at along the empty walkway.

'I still miss my sisters, my love.' Hecate's voice creaked. Corvus winced when he heard those heavy barbarian notes on the Roman tongue she'd muddled through learning. 'If only you could have saved them that day. Not that I'm not grateful—'

'If only I could have.'

She pressed a hand against her heart. 'I still feel them with me. When you are a Sister of the Moon, you share a bond that not even death can break. Sometimes, in the night, I hear them whisper to me.'

Corvus forced a tight smile. If they ever passed time together, she and Theodosius could witter away to each other like this till the world turned cold. Of course, Theodosius would have her swinging from a rope in a moment if he happened to learn she was a witch.

'We'll find you some new sisters,' he said, patting her arm. 'Now come. I need to have a word with my mother before I ride out to drain some barbarian blood.'

Taking her hand, he led her down the steps and through the fort, out into the town and the house he had secured in the shadow of the amphitheatre. He'd offered its worth in gold. The owner had refused, saying there was not enough space in the city, so he'd had to kill him and his family. But it was the thought that counted.

When he stepped in, he choked on the coal smoke. His mother had insisted on keeping a fire burning, even though summer still kept watch on the days. Gaia perched on a stool by the hearth, swaddled in a thick cloak. The damp Britannia climate was not agreeing with her, as she saw fit to tell him every time they met. This time she threw her arms wide, showering his face with kisses. He felt the curve of her belly against his stomach. Still early days. He wished he'd planted his seed in her sooner. Then his child, the heir to everything that mattered, would have been born before Catia's. That would have simplified matters.

Severus, the Hanged Man, stood in the corner, arms hanging at his side. He was a gloomy sod at the best of times, but since he'd arrived in Londinium with Gaia and Hecate, he seemed to excel at cloaking himself in shadows.

'Corvus,' he intoned. 'Are we any closer to realizing our plans?'

'We must trust in Mithras to guide us,' he began.

'A novel way of saying no,' he heard Pavo chirp at his back.

He sighed.

'They may have little learning, these pretenders, but they have a certain animal cunning,' he continued. 'My sister is never allowed to be alone. There're always two of those ditch-sleeping *arcani* at her side, with twitching blades. They know her worth, of course. They'll kill anyone to protect that child.'

'Put an arrow through both of them,' Gaia said. 'Poison her, and her spawn. Set fire to them.'

'You have a creative imagination, Mother. But it will do us little good if the price we pay for ending her days is facing the harsh justice of her protectors.' He narrowed his eyes at Gaia. Is that what she wanted? Then she would have complete control over the bloodline. 'Mother?'

Gaia only smiled. 'You know best, my beautiful boy.'

They'd survived the journey from the coast, with no sign of those feral barbarians. But not one of them was happy to be in Londinium. Not even in their wildest imaginations did they expect the hardships that dwelled here. And it was only going to get worse. Still, what choice did they have now? They'd shackled their futures to him, and that was all he needed.

'We four must stand strong together, come what may,' he said.

'Three,' Severus corrected.

Corvus eyed Pavo from under his brow, then smiled at the Hanged Man. 'Of course,' he replied. 'My mistake.'

A faint hammering echoed.

When Corvus wrenched open the door, he looked down at a mud-caked dwarf standing on the threshold. A wild beard trailed down his chest, but what skin was visible on his face looked like a melted candle. On his head a Phrygian leather cap perched – a sign of a worshipper of Mithras.

Corvus jerked round as the visitor darted through his legs

and rolled on his back like a whipped cur. 'I throw myself on your mercy,' he whined.

'You!' Gaia's eyes blazed. 'Kill him now, Corvus, before I have to hear any more of his lies.'

'Wait,' the dwarf pleaded. 'Slay me now and you will never learn what I know about your enemies, those pretenders who lay claim to the royal bloodline.'

Corvus froze, his sword half out of its sheath.

'Who are you?' Hecate asked.

The dwarf jumped to his feet and bowed. 'My name is Bucco. Once I called the fair city of Rome my home. But then my master, the merchant Varro, who beat me most harshly, made me a citizen of the road—'

'No lies!'

Corvus winced at the venom in his mother's voice. Her eyes were blazing. She looked as if she would kill the dwarf with her bare hands. 'The dwarf here was the master. Varro the merchant leapt to his bidding,' she said. 'They were guests in our home. And then they took the wood-priest who was to be our intermediary so they could steal the power of the royal bloodline for themselves.'

'Little good it seems to have done them,' Pavo said.

'Little good it seems to have done them,' Corvus said. 'Varro—'

'Is dead.' Bucco's chin slumped to his chest in a show of grief. 'Murdered by Lucanus the Wolf and his followers. As was the wood-priest. They tried to kill me too. They will slay anyone to keep their hands on that power.'

Hecate rested a pale hand on the dwarf's shoulder. 'Then without Bucco here I would not have been brought to Rome, and to you, my husband. Is that true? You needed me because the wood-priest was gone.'

Bucco skipped from under her hand. 'Then I have enriched all your lives. You should thank me—'

'Kill him,' Gaia said. 'And throw his body out for the ravens.'

'Let's not be hasty, Mother.' Corvus let his blade slide back into its sheath. He hooked a hand in the back of the dwarf's tunic and lifted him off the ground.

Bucco kicked and flailed. 'Our wood-priest . . . he spoke before he died. I know where they plan to go when your backs are turned. I know how you can kill them all and win the day.'

CHAPTER TWENTY-THREE

I Am in Blood

THICK FOG CLOTTED THE VALLEYS. IN THE MUFFLED STILL-ness, droplets of moisture beat a steady rhythm as they fell from the yellowing leaves. Lucanus and the Grim Wolves stood on the high ground looking into the white bank.

'It will burn off soon enough,' Bellicus said.

'It had better,' the Wolf replied. 'We mustn't lose this moment.' He pushed up the snout of his pelt and looked round at the sound of hooves.

Theodosius eased out of the dense cloud, with Corvus beside him. Falx wrestled with his mount at the rear. He was no horseman. The three soldiers slipped to the ground and led their steeds over.

'The army is in position?' Lucanus asked.

Theodosius nodded. 'We have one chance here. If we show even the slightest weakness, it will all be over.'

'Good fortune, then, that you've got *arcani* to scout the land for you,' Solinus said. 'The Grim Wolves make no mistakes.'

'When the fog lifts,' Lucanus added.

The Wolf could see the taut muscles in Theodosius' face, and Falx's fixed stare. They were anxious. And who could blame them? The force in the Londinium garrison had been depleted long before the barbarians attacked, and the new recruits were undisciplined. They still reeled from the terrors they'd experienced on the road after they'd fled their posts under the first wave of the enemy attack.

Corvus, though, was grinning. Nothing seemed to trouble this soldier. Lucanus decided he liked him. He had a good wit, and learning, so that he could spin tales well. He kept spirits up when they all drank in the tavern.

'We have the army of Britannia, led by the Pendragon, and good Roman soldiers who have never shied from a fight. What could possibly go wrong?' he said now.

'The last bastard who said that was pulling an arrow out of his eye socket a moment later,' Solinus said.

'We must pray for victory,' Theodosius said. 'Only God can help us in this, our direst need.' He knelt on the damp grass and bowed his head.

Corvus cocked one eyebrow and exchanged a look with Lucanus and Falx. 'Any takers?' he whispered.

The centurion chortled and clambered awkwardly back on to his horse.

Corvus leaned in, and Lucanus saw the other man's smile slip away and his expression darken. 'Your woman, Catia,' he murmured. 'All is well with her?'

'Mato and Comitinus keep watch on her. Why do you ask?'

'I heard whispers, in the tavern. That she had eyes for another man.' He shrugged again. 'I don't know who. It's probably nothing. Just talk.'

'Catia would never do that.'

'Of course not, my friend. Of course not. You trust those who guard her? Yes. You must. You do.' He clapped a hand on Lucanus' arm. 'Ignore me. I'm a worrier. It's just that I wouldn't want to see you cuckolded. You're a good man. You deserve better than that.'

He smiled, a little sadly, Lucanus thought, then joined Theodosius and the two men were soon swallowed up by the fog.

'What was he saying?' Bellicus demanded.

'Tactical talk, that's all.'

'I don't trust him. He's got that look about him.'

'Aye,' Solinus added. 'He'll buy you a drink with one hand, and feel up your sister with the other.'

'In these times, we need all good men to come together. What joins us is greater than what divides us.'

'Spoken like a man with a gold crown,' Solinus said. 'Now let's eat some bread. If we're going to die, I want it to be with a full belly.'

Lucanus looked back into the fog drifting among the trees down the slope, but his thoughts had flown back to Londinium, and Catia. It was true that she'd been different since she returned from captivity. He'd put that down to the hardships she'd experienced. He'd not asked her about them; she'd talk when she was ready.

But perhaps there was something more.

By mid-morning the sun was carving the fog into trailing strands. The birdsong rushed back in, and now Lucanus could hear a distant rumbling.

'They're on the move,' Bellicus said.

Lucanus marched back to where his army waited, hunched in cloaks, every face like stone. 'Make ready,' he said.

They stood, hands clasping the hilts of swords that had never drawn blood, but only been brought out from time to time to show that once their father's father's father had been a man of courage. More than anything he wished he didn't have to put them through this ordeal. But if they wanted to keep what they had – their liberty, their families – they knew they would have to fight.

Apullius dashed up and raised a skin. Lucanus took it and wet his lips. 'Remember what I said,' the Wolf cautioned. 'You stay here, whatever happens. If we all end up a feast for the ravens, you run back to Londinium and warn the others.'

'And what can they do then?' The boy narrowed his eyes. He was no fool.

'Run. Hide.'

Apullius snorted, and Lucanus cuffed him round the ear for good measure.

Then he marched back to the ridge and looked down the slope. Beyond the trees, the fog was gone. The sun drenched a sea of grassland. A shadow moved across it, though the sky was clear.

Around a hundred barbarians rode, with perhaps a hundred more following on foot. One of the larger war-bands, as they had found when they had scouted. All Picts, the fiercest fighters, roaming ever closer to Londinium.

This was where the line would be drawn.

Lucanus felt the weight of the men as they gathered at his back. He imagined their darting eyes, the breath tight in their chests. Without looking back, he raised one hand.

The world held its breath.

When he snapped his arm down, the army moved as one. Skidding down the bank through a sea of bracken, whirling by the grey trunks of ash trees. Into the last of the fog; a silent, grey world. Feet thudded on leaf mould. No one spoke.

And then he was running along the valley floor, beyond the trees and out into the glare of the hot sun.

The thunder of hooves was clearer there, and when he shielded his eyes he could make out the war-band surging towards the nearest village. Their enemies hadn't seen them yet.

'Make some noise,' he roared.

A senseless bellow boomed at his back, driven by rage, and terror too. As he ran, he saw the Pictish riders draw up, the foot-soldiers grind to a halt. Though the distance was too great, in his mind's eye he could see heads swivel towards him, grins lighting on lips at the sight of this pathetic force that dared challenge the fierce warriors who had conquered such a great part of the empire.

Now there was no turning back.

Lucanus swept up an arm and his army crunched to a halt.

For a moment, everything hung.

Eyes locked across the heaving green sea. And then the jubilant roar of the Picts rolled out, punctuated by the pounding of hooves.

The Wolf watched the war-band turn, as one, and sweep towards them.

'Back,' he yelled. 'We must not be caught out here in the open.'

Turning on their heels, his army raced back towards the shade of the valley. Lucanus heard the cries of the barbarians escalate into a frenzy, and despite his careful planning he felt his cheeks burn with humiliation.

Once they were back among the trees and lingering fog, he whisked his arm in a circle and his men scattered, scrambling up the valley sides to crouch among the ash trees and the oaks.

'Fight as if you don't expect to live to see tomorrow.' His voice drifted up the wooded slopes until it was swallowed by the muffling mist, and then he was crouching himself, behind a dense hawthorn, his gaze fixed on the golden patch of sunshine beyond the valley's end.

After a moment, he stirred, his neck prickling. In the shadows among the trees, he saw a figure watching him. All black, she was, like the deepest well, surrounded by a murder of crows, wings beating the air. In their midst, he locked on to a pair of burning eyes, and a maw that seemed always hungry. The Morrigan rarely left him these days. Since that life-changing night in Goibniu's Smithy, he had frequently glimpsed her following him relentlessly through the glades and across the grasslands, in the streets of Londinium, edging ever closer.

The Morrigan, the Phantom Queen of war and blood and death, had claimed him for her own.

The thunder rolled in like a summer storm. A shadow swept across that patch of sunlight and the Pictish horsemen pounded on to the valley floor.

Lucanus breathed in the heady mix of the musk of the horses, the rancid lamb-fat greasing the warriors' furs and the oils rubbed into their leather armour. His fingers grasped Caledfwlch's hilt.

Across the valley, the Wolf watched Solinus dart out and throw a stone. He lingered long enough for the barbarians to see him, and then he scrambled up the bank. Laughing, one rider forced his mount to follow.

Easy game. No threat.

As the horse kicked its way up, another of his men jumped out from his hiding place. The beast reared up in shock, whinnying. A spear rammed up under the Pict's ribcage, lifting him off his mount. The shaft of the weapon thumped into the ground, steadying it. On its tip, the barbarian kicked and screamed, then slowly slid down the spear until his cries ebbed away.

Lucanus grinned as his man wrenched up his weapon, flipping the body off the end. The corpse bounced down the slope to come to a halt on the valley floor.

For a moment, there was silence, and then the Picts erupted in a frenzy. Mad with rage, they threw their mounts up the slopes, just as their foot-soldiers ran into the valley.

The Wolf watched his men follow his strategy as best they could. The unseasoned warriors jumped out from their hiding places to slash at the horses to bring them down. Some succeeded. The beasts crashed down, the riders rolling off to be carved by blades. But the riders were too skilled, and most evaded the attacks. Lucanus winced as axes and swords cut down men who were too slow, or too frightened, to fight effectively.

This would be a slaughter.

And then the Picts on foot hammered up the slopes. His men would be no match for them, even with the cover of the trees and the advantage of the higher ground.

In front of him, one of them cowered with his hands on his head, face pressed into the leaf mould, as if by not seeing he could wish away the death that was coming for him.

As a Pict clawed his way up to where the former merchant whimpered, the Wolf bounded out from behind the hawthorn. Caledfwlch flashed. Lucanus felt a spike of pain in his shoulder from the jolt as the blade slammed into bone. It was enough to bring the enemy down, blood spurting from his side.

He rammed the sword into the barbarian's chest to end his suffering, and then kicked the body down the slope.

As he drew himself up, he saw Picts swarming towards him. Whether they recognized his grey wolf-pelt he didn't know. But he could see from their cold faces that they had decided he was the man to kill. He turned and pounded up the slope, leading them on, feeling the Morrigan's breath on his neck. Death was close.

When he heard the tumult behind him change its tone, he grinned. Battle-cries turned to shouts of warning. Screams ebbed as swords stilled in mid-stroke. He glanced back and saw that the men pursuing him had stopped. They were looking back down the slope to the sunlit entrance to the valley.

The army of Rome surged in on a glinting wave of steel.

The cavalry swept in first. Through a mist of blood, Lucanus glimpsed Corvus laughing like a madman as he cut down the Picts racing wildly before him.

Face like granite, Theodosius kicked his heels into his horse's flank a head behind him. The barbarians tried to form a line and fight, but the Romans crashed over them, hooves smashing them into the turf.

And behind them a wall of shields rushed in like a riptide, aglow in the brassy morning light. The neck of the valley closed off.

Aye, this would be a slaughter.

Lucanus threw himself down the slope. Caledfwlch hewed into a Pict's neck. As the barbarian spun away, the Wolf fell on the next.

The barbarians had been too confident. They'd met no resistance on their trek south. They'd looted and raped and burned and slaughtered and Lucanus understood how they could believe they were unbeatable.

This would be the end of that illusion.

He dug his heels into the loam and gripped Caledfwlch with both hands. Looking up, he watched his men do the same in a ring around the sides of the valley.

As the Picts scrambled to escape the coldly efficient brutality of the army, swords rose and fell. Bodies tumbled down the banks, littering the valley floor. Red streams flowed, turning the ground into a marsh. Caught in that trap, it was only a matter of time. Soon the clash of steel ebbed until only the moans of the dying rolled out.

Lucanus sheathed his blade. As he strode down the slope, he called, 'Leave only three men alive to return to the others and tell them how this great army smote their war-band. Only complete destruction will convince them that we can't be defeated.'

When he reached the valley floor, he squelched through the crimson puddles to the neck of the valley. In the glaring sun, three figures raced back across the grassland. He prayed that their tale would cause the horde to hesitate, perhaps to hold the line while they made their plans, long enough for winter to come. They couldn't know that this was all the men they had.

'A good plan. I can see why the wood-priest chose you to be the Pendragon.'

Lucanus looked round to see Corvus striding up. His face was streaked pink, his tunic soaked.

'One chance to hold the barbarian advance and we took it,' he continued. 'They'll think twice now.'

'Let us hope.' The Wolf glanced back and winced. 'We've lost good men today.'

'You're a scout. You had peace, more or less, along the wall. But in war, there's always sacrifice.' Corvus wiped the blood from his face. 'That's the hardest lesson any fighting man has to learn. Friends cut down. There one moment, gone the next. The most you can hope is that they've bought an advantage with their lives, and here they have. Whatever comes of this, the barbarians will know there's steel facing them now.'

Lucanus nodded. Corvus' words made sense. But he still felt a well of sadness in him for every life they'd lost. He didn't think he'd ever get used to it.

Corvus seemed to read his thoughts. The soldier clapped an arm around his shoulders. 'Come. Tonight we'll drink what foul wine still survives in the taverns. We're brothers in blood now, bonded in war. Let's raise our goblets to a long friendship.'

CHAPTER TWENTY-FOUR

Stars, Hide Your Fires

FOR ONCE THERE WAS LIFE IN THE CITY OF THE DEAD.

Across the *vicus*, fires blazed in the night. The refugees feasted on roast venison in celebration, brought in by the hunting bands Lucanus had sent out that morning in the hope of victory. Full-throated singing soared up to the clouds lowering over the city.

Lucanus closed his eyes and let the jubilant sound engulf him. He was lying on his bed, the room around him dark. He could feel Catia pressed against him, the curve of her belly, the warmth of her skin. He breathed in her musk, mingling with the rosewater she'd splashed on her hair after she washed it. All these things he had thought he would never experience again.

'You're pleased to be a father?' she murmured.

'I've never been so afraid in all my days.'

Catia chuckled. But he meant what he said. Afraid to bring a child into a world turning towards night. Afraid that protecting his new family in these times would prove beyond his abilities. He'd always thought himself fearless. What was it about the flourishing of his seed that stirred such things in a man?

In the dark, he fumbled for her hand. Now he'd found her

again, he couldn't bear to lose her. But Corvus' words squirmed in the back of his head. *Eyes for another man.* He couldn't believe it. But still they squirmed.

He felt her fingers flutter across his bare chest. 'You've bought us hope,' she said, as if she could read his thoughts, 'and that is a great and valuable thing, after all we've been through. We're safe here, within the walls. And safe we'll stay until the snows melt, and the army comes. And then we can go west, to Avalon, where we'll be safe for all time.'

She was right. All the barns were filled, and the store-houses topped to the roofs. Winter would be hard, but they should be able to grind through until the snows melted. Those out in the *vicus* and the sprawling camp beyond might find it harder, but they had their own reserves and at least now they had been taught how to hunt.

And yet still he could hear the beating wings of the ravens wherever he went, and feel the Morrigan's eyes upon his back.

The low sun painted gold along the ridges of the orange-tiled roofs. Down in the choked streets, long shadows reached their fingers over the crowds. Though the breeze had teeth for the first time in months, Catia sensed good spirits among the people she pushed through. Their bellies might be growling, but they had hope now. Sanctuary.

An end to the season of running and fear.

And there was hope for her own kin too. She glanced behind at Solinus and Comitinus, her two guard dogs, following at a distance, then back to her father leaning on Aelius. Though his steps were slow and shaky, he seemed more stable than at any time since they had fled Vercovicium. As she watched, he craned his neck up so he could study the sprawling governor's palace, a complex of buildings that was almost as large as the forum. 'Now I have an appetite to see Rome itself,' he said. 'The stories I've heard.'

'One step at a time, Father.' Aelius winked at Catia. He had grown in stature too. He pushed his shoulders back, standing tall, and he no longer tried to hide his withered arm.

'We've endured so much, our family,' the old man continued, lurching around a boy begging for bread. 'We clawed our way back from ruin once, though the price we paid was too high.' When he eyed Catia, she could see the dismay in his face. He held himself responsible for all the suffering she'd endured at the hands of her brutal husband Amatius.

'I made my own choice,' she said. And she had, once she'd learned that Amatius' money could save them all. It was her responsibility, and hers alone.

'I thought I didn't have the strength to step back towards the light,' Menius went on. 'But now, seeing you with child, and happy with Lucanus, there seems hope, even among this misery.' He forced a wan smile.

'This is the most you've walked since we arrived in Londinium,' Aelius said. 'Don't tire yourself. More important, don't tire me.'

'Yes. You have new responsibilities now. The right hand of the Pendragon.' The old man's eyes gleamed with pride, and Catia felt warmed by the reflected light in her brother's face. Nevertheless, Aelius snorted.

'As a right hand, I'm overrated—'

Before he could finish the thought, Menius stiffened, his gaze riveted to a point deep in the crowd.

'What is it, Father?' Catia asked.

'I saw . . . no . . .' His creaking voice faded away. And then he was thrusting himself into the throng. The mass of bodies swallowed him up.

Aelius cursed under his breath. He had been rooted by the old man's sudden activity. 'A moment ago he was shuffling like a man in leg-irons. Now he's bounding away like a deer?'

192

He barged into the flow, pushing his way into the old man's wake. Catia stepped into the lee of a metalworker's shop. The hammers thrummed through the walls. After a while Aelius came back.

He shook his head, baffled. 'Gone.'

Shadows swelled in the room. Only two eyes of dying embers glowed in the gloom. Corvus rocked on a stool until his shoulders rested against the wall. He allowed himself a smile. And why not? Clever men bent the world to their will.

The door crashed open and light flooded in. He blinked in the sudden glare, his eyes clearing enough to see Bucco the dwarf bound in and tumble across the floor. He leapt to his feet beside the hearth and bowed deeply.

Corvus nodded at the genuflection. 'You may be half a man, but you've matched the height of those fulsome promises you made.'

'And more!'

The rectangle of thin light darkened and Corvus saw an old man standing there, looking bewildered.

'Frail,' Pavo said from the dark in the corner. 'The years are crushing him to his knees.'

'Come in,' Corvus boomed in a cheery voice. 'Menius, isn't it?'

The old man lurched in, but he was ignoring Corvus and pointing a wavering finger at the dwarf. 'You,' he croaked. 'You are the one who tormented us . . . who tried to steal my daughter . . . who nearly killed Amarina.'

Bucco bowed again, sweeping one arm out. 'I am not forgotten. My heart leaps.'

'You died, in the marsh—'

'The mud sucked at my legs, 'tis true. That foul place wanted to swallow me whole. But I am short of stature, as you can see, and weigh little more than a leaf. One handful of reeds was all it took to keep my head in the air until I could claw my way free.'

Corvus jumped to his feet and skirted that confrontation. With a flick of his wrist, he swung the door shut and leaned against it.

'Hello, Menius.' The light voice floated out of the gloom.

A candle flickered to life. The halo of light glimmered around Gaia. How beautiful she looked, Corvus thought. Her hair gleamed and her cheeks had the rosy tint of a mother-to-be. How strong she looked, too, her lips curving into the faintest of smiles, her chin slightly raised, her gaze unflinching. She'd been anticipating this meeting for a long time, he realized; the time when she would have the upper hand. A woman like Gaia would not have taken it well to being forced to flee her homeland, to run in fear for her life, and to see all her hopes seemingly dashed. Now she was a queen returning to claim what was hers.

He looked to Menius and read all he needed to know in that crumpled face. Was the old man remembering how Gaia had cuckolded him with his own brother? How she'd stolen everything he had and left him to die in poverty? Had he thought about her in the intervening years? Yearned for her? Despaired? Surely he would never have thought to see her again.

And yet here they both were.

'Gaia,' Menius croaked.

'My dear Menius. The years have not treated you kindly. Why, you look like an old grandfather. Misery does that to a man, so I am told.'

Corvus admired her cruelty. She wielded it as well as any soldier did a sword. A warrior-queen! He felt his chest swell. But she was not done. She cupped her hands around her swollen belly to emphasize the gulf between them.

Menius gaped.

'Do you know what lives inside me?' she said in the sing-song voice of a little girl. 'Why, the seed that will become the King Who Will Not Die. Have you heard that story, Menius? Of course you have. The candle of hope in the darkest of nights. Me, Menius. I bring hope to the world. I beget kings. I was not wrong. My destiny was always greatness.'

'Gaia,' he repeated, as if his thoughts were trapped in a millpond eddy.

Corvus sighed. If the old man had nothing to say, there would be no entertainment here.

He stepped forward and rammed his sword into the man who had shared his mother's bed. As the blade burst through the convulsing chest, he found he couldn't tear his gaze away from Gaia's face. Her eyes had widened and her lips parted in almost post-coital bliss.

The dwarf gambolled around the body, clapping his hands with glee.

'One down,' Pavo said.

Corvus cleaned his blade on Menius' cloak. 'A message sent. It will kick the legs out from under them. Worry will start to claw its way into their thoughts. They'll make mistakes.'

'And then we might get close enough to your sister to introduce ourselves.'

'Keep Catia away from here,' Lucanus commanded.

Bellicus barked the words to Apullius and the lad wriggled through the gathering crowd and away to warn Solinus and Comitinus.

Mato rested a hand on his friend's shoulder and whispered, 'This is a bad business.' His voice was strained, wreathed with grief. Lucanus felt as if a blade had stabbed into his heart.

The sky was on fire and that scarlet glow sank deep into

the faces of the silent watchers. Menius' body sprawled across a midden heap at the back of a row of houses.

'Who could have done this?' Mato asked.

Lucanus didn't answer, but his thoughts were already racing through the streets of that teeming town. 'Help me.'

He scooped his arms under Menius' torso and Mato grasped his legs. The body felt no heavier than a sack of tinder.

As they carried the old man back through the streets, the memories rushed back with such force that Lucanus almost reeled. Menius, younger then, broken by his own misfortune, but waving Lucanus into his home to share bread and olives after Lucanus the Elder had disappeared into the Wilds. The old man had tried to fill the void left by his missing father, offering whatever kindnesses he could. Lucanus could never forget that.

At the house they all shared, he and Mato laid Menius on the cold floor and Lucanus threw an old blanket over him so that Catia wouldn't see the sword wound. Only then did he call for Solinus and Comitinus.

Catia rushed in, and when she looked down at her father's grey face Lucanus thought his heart would break. The woman she had become cracked away and there was only the girl he had first met, lost and yearning. She fell on the body and smothered the cheeks and forehead with kisses.

Lucanus allowed her this parting for a moment, and then he took her arm and eased her away. She seemed to have no words inside her.

Aelius hurried in with Apullius behind him. Unlike his sister, he only stood and stared. In the growing gloom, the Wolf couldn't read his features. But then Catia scrubbed away her tears with the back of her hand and Lucanus felt uneasy when he saw the expression that settled on her face. It was like a frozen lake.

'Murdered?' she said.

The Wolf nodded.

'He had nothing worth stealing. He was no threat to any man.'

Lucanus could hear her finding her way to the truth. He crossed to the door and leaned against the jamb, looking out into the crowded street but seeing none of the passers-by.

'We have enemies, here, in Londinium,' he said, 'and we are trapped with them.'

Bellicus crouched to scrub Catulus' head. 'I curse the day we first heard of the King Who Will Not Die,' he muttered.

'If this is about the royal bloodline . . .' Comitinus began.

'How can it not be, you jolt-head?' Solinus snapped. 'What other reason would there be to murder a harmless old man than to frighten us?'

'Sixty thousand people seethe within these walls.' Lucanus could hear the strain in his voice as he looked out into the town. 'More than I could ever imagine existed in all Britannia when I roamed through the Wilds. Sixty thousand strangers, and any one of them could have a blade waiting to slit our throats.'

'How will we ever know where the threat lies?' Aelius muttered from the dark of the room. Lucanus pictured him weighed down by his grief in a corner, his chin resting on his chest.

The Wolf glanced back into the dusk. 'We won't.'

'We leave here,' Catia said. 'Now.'

'And go where? West, like the wood-priest said? To this fabled Avalon?' Bellicus strode up behind him. 'What if it turns out as safe as Londinium?'

'We'll never get past the horde anyway,' Solinus grunted. 'Like it or not, we're stuck here.'

'If we get a chance to flee, we seize it,' the Wolf said. 'Until then, Londinium is as dangerous as the Wilds now, and we have to watch our backs at every turn. Survive through the winter, until Theodosius brings the army to retake Britannia.'

'And if they don't come?' Comitinus asked.

Lucanus looked up to the stars glinting in the great vault of the heavens. He let the question hang in the cool air, because he had no answer.

CHAPTER TWENTY-FIVE

Night Comes Down

D ARK FLOODED THE STREETS OF LONDINIUM. IT SEEMED TO Catia that even the lights that still burned were somehow dimmer.

'Be strong, brother.' Standing at the river gate, she stared at the turgid black waters of the Tamesis. The small raft of firewood bearing her father's meagre possessions, some bread, and a posy of flowers, drifted towards the east, towards the sunrise; towards the past.

She sensed Aelius beside her, a pillar of cold stone. She couldn't bring herself to look at him, afraid she might see another death, of the brother she once knew, but she fumbled for his good hand. He gave hers a squeeze. For now, it was enough.

'I am heartsick.' His voice was little more than a choke from a throat that must have been as narrow as her finger. 'The unfairness of it, when he'd survived so much and seemed to be regaining some of the life he once had. I miss him almost too much to bear.'

Catia watched the sum total of her father's existence disappear into the night.

'It would be easy to give in to despair,' Aelius continued.

'Remember how we used to talk about how our family was cursed—'

'You did.'

A laugh rolled out, though without any humour. 'You stolen as a babe and left for dead. My withered arm. Mother abandoning Father for his brother and stealing all we had. You forced to marry to save us—'

'I chose—'

'I know. And then the invasion, and the burning of our home, and the death of Marcus, and a torrent of misery leading to this night.' As he spoke, his voice grew stronger, harder. 'But then you told me that you could have died as a babe, but you were saved by wolves, a miracle by any other name. And Father recovered from his torment, and found new hope, and our family thrived.' He squeezed her hand again. 'And you found love with Lucanus, a love that few find in this world. When we get knocked down—'

'We get up again.'

'Someone once told me, life is good as long as you don't weaken. We must not weaken. We have to put aside all hope of returning to the peaceful life we once had. Everything has changed. This is the time to let the fire burn in our hearts, to forge us into steel. To fight.'

Catia felt a flicker of cold rage at the enemies who had stolen their father from their lives, but that was better than grief, and despair. 'You're right, brother. Tonight we are remade.'

A voice echoed behind them and she glanced back to where Lucanus and the other Grim Wolves waited on the street leading to the river gate, giving them the space they needed to say their goodbyes. Lucanus was worried that he couldn't protect her, or their unborn son, she knew. If only he understood it was not his responsibility – she could protect herself.

A small figure pushed through them and ran into the

circle of light from the lamp above the gate. Tears glistened on the Mouse's cheeks as he flung himself at Catia, wrapping his arms around her legs. She dropped down, hugging him.

Apullius strode up and clapped a hand on his brother's shoulder. 'Home now,' he murmured. 'Tomorrow we will train harder.'

As Morirex trudged away, Apullius looked from Catia to Aelius. 'I will call you sister, and brother.'

Catia furrowed a brow.

'In the west, by a campfire as I mourned my father and mother, you showed me a great kindness,' Apullius said to Aelius. 'Death changes us, you said, from lead to gold. "Once the pain you feel ebbs away, and it will, you'll find that you've been given a gift." There is hope in hardship. We share a bond – brothers and sister in the Age of Orphans.'

Catia felt her heart swell. 'Now you show us a kindness. I will be proud to call you brother.'

Aelius seemed lost for words, but he gave Apullius' arm a squeeze.

'This night I've looked inside myself,' the lad said. 'I know I have a part to play, and that it will mean sacrifice, perhaps even my own life. I'm ready for that. I'll learn how to fight, and I'll teach Morirex too. To help bring light out of this darkness, that is a life well lived.'

As he nodded and strode away, Catia thought how grown-up he now seemed, not the boy she had first encountered when she entered Londinium.

'Tonight we are all remade,' Aelius murmured.

Catia looked over the heads of the Grim Wolves and into the dark of the town. She felt a sense of unknown threats moving beyond the light, drawing closer. They would need each other more than ever if they were to survive.

CHAPTER TWENTY-SIX

The New House of Wishes

'WHY DO WE NEED TO LOOK AFTER CATIA AS IF SHE WERE a babe?' Comitinus grumbled as Mato strode on ahead through the emptying streets. 'I'm scared of her. Even with child, she could bring down any enemy who ventured near.'

Mato glanced back past the other man to where Catia stepped out of the night and into a halo of light from a torch guttering beside a door. Lucanus was huddled away with the wood-priest, no doubt trying to draw some jewels of truth from the druid's twisting words, but Bellicus and Solinus flanked her, swords drawn. Her hood was pulled up, her face lost to shadow, but he thought how regal she seemed, her back straight, her head slightly raised, her pace elegant. He could see no sign of grief.

'You saw what happened when we were on the road from Vercovicium. Those hungering for power sprang up like flowers in the spring fields. A fever seems to have gripped this world. We can't take any risks.'

Comitinus sniffed and looked up at the amphitheatre towering above them. 'One night of freedom, that's all I ask.'

'It will come, in time. Perhaps even this night.'

Mato whisked one hand towards a plain door in a plain

house in the shadow of the amphitheatre's soaring walls. The only distinguishing feature was a red rose roughly painted on the door jamb.

'What is this . . . ?' Comitinus' voice trailed off.

Mato rapped on the wood. When the door swung open, a waft of lavender-scented air rolled out. In the glow from the lamps, a familiar silhouette hove into view.

'Welcome to the House of Wishes,' Amarina said, her tone wry.

Mato shoved Comitinus inside. 'Just . . . just the three of you?' the younger man stuttered.

'There is something for every taste.' She nodded towards an open door and Comitinus saw several women displaying themselves, hands on hips, lips pouting.

'You lost no time finding friends,' Mato said.

'I know how to keep a good house.'

You know how to survive, Mato thought.

Amarina looked past him and he saw her brow knot. There was no love lost between her and Catia.

'Again?' she said, remembering, no doubt, how she had sheltered Catia once before, at the House of Wishes she had managed in Vercovicium.

'Keep her safe. Her father has been murdered, and Lucanus fears that's only the beginning. We have enemies here in Londinium who will come for us all sooner or later.' Mato looked into her face, wishing he could be more sure. 'We trust you, Amarina,' he said softly. 'You're one of us, whether you like it or not. You have duties now. But you should know that the Grim Wolves are fiercely loyal to their friends.'

'Enough of your talk,' she chided him. 'Do you think I'm a child?' She eased him aside and crooked a finger to beckon Catia inside. The two women eyed each other for what Mato felt was an unsettlingly long time. Finally Amarina said,

'One of my girls will find you a room. I'll come to you there.' She summoned one of the women from the inner room, and Catia nodded and disappeared into the back of the house with her.

When Amarina faced him again, Mato flicked her a coin. 'What's that for?'

'One night of freedom.' From the corner of his eye, he saw Comitinus frown. 'Even wolves grow weary without comfort. Lucanus has requested you find a way to put some fire back in their bellies.'

Amarina smiled. She slipped an arm around Comitinus' shoulders and ushered him in to where the women waited. Bellicus and Solinus followed, closing the door behind them.

When they'd disappeared to the bedrooms, Amarina whispered to Mato, 'Decima waits for you.' He felt his heart leap, though he knew he was a fool. Decima was fond of him, but women like her could never love; that part was missing. But he could love her, and that would have to be enough. The world was a dark place, and every candle counted.

After they'd finished their lovemaking, Mato lay on his back and watched the shadows dance across the ceiling from the guttering lamp-flame. Decima traced a finger along his jawline. Her ebony skin seemed to glow with an inner light.

'You have too many thoughts in your head. Too many for a fighting man,' she said.

'Aye. Lucanus always said I should have been a priest. But life leads us down strange paths.'

She gently rapped a knuckle on his forehead. 'And what burns in there this night?'

'I'm remembering my sister.'

'Oh.' Decima shifted. 'Are you still sad? She died so long ago, yes? When you were very young?'

'Yes. And no. The first time we encounter death, it

changes us for all time. Lead into gold; for some, a magical transformation. Others are shattered into pieces that they can never put back again.'

'And which are you?'

He brushed her lips with a kiss. 'I learned to find every crumb of joy in this life, however miserable it got.'

She laughed silently. 'You *should* have been a priest.'

After a long silence, he asked, 'Can we trust Amarina?'

Decima pushed herself back from him. 'Don't ask me to betray her. She's like an elder sister. Amarina cares for me, for Galantha, for all who shelter under her roof. I would be long dead if not for her.'

'Reassurance, that's all I want.'

'Have faith. That should be easy for a priest-in-waiting.' She popped a kiss on his nose, then let her hand stray down to his groin, a distraction and no doubt a much used one.

Mato closed his eyes, but he felt as if he had an iron rod in his spine. He remembered how Amarina had stolen the boy Marcus from under their noses and delivered him to their enemies. She had done it to try to save all their necks, or so she professed. Perhaps it was only her own neck she was interested in, or her own advantage. He had seen enough evidence of that.

What if they had delivered Catia into even greater danger?

Amarina wrinkled her nose at the candle smoke as she strode along the corridor, lighting her way before her. This place was cramped and damp, but it would suffice, for now. It was certainly larger than the House of Wishes she had built in Vercovicium. She'd fought hard to secure this place in a town as spilling with bodies as Londinium, and the merchant who owned the villa had driven a hard bargain. But he was like any man, a chariot of lust, and like any man he was easy to twist around her finger. Once he'd been promised full use of her girls, at any time, with his own peculiar tastes well catered for, he'd become remarkably compliant. But if he ever hurt one of them, she'd still cut off his cock and feed it to him.

The thump of beds and low moans echoed through the walls. Amarina breathed in the heavy scent of lavender and rose drifting on the air to mask the sour stink of sweat and spilled seed.

She paused at a door and gritted her teeth. There was no point delaying it any further.

Stepping inside, she raised the lamp so the shadows swooped away. Catia had been lying on the low bed in the dark.

'This is becoming a habit,' Amarina said.

The other woman dangled her legs over the side of the bed and eased herself up with awkward movements. In the unwavering stare and the cold features, Amarina could instantly see that Catia was not the same person she had sheltered in the north.

'Do you think I would choose to be here, cowering like a whipped cur?'

'Here with me, you mean?' Amarina raised one eyebrow, smiling.

'I don't like to run from a fight.'

'Sometimes running is for the best. Or at least walking away very quickly.' Amarina edged around the end of the bed. Catia held her gaze. 'It must be tiring, carrying that weight around with you.'

'I've carried a bale of hay on my shoulders. This is no worse.'

'A rich woman like you?'

'I was not always rich. And a purse full of coin does not always buy a path out of hardship.'

Amarina nodded. That she understood.

'I don't wish to be here. I don't enjoy being in your care. It's not in my nature to hide. But there is more than my convenience at stake here. My life, my wishes, mean nothing.'

'I can't decide if you're close to the gods, or a fool.' Amarina crossed to a table in the corner of the room where an amphora stood with two goblets. She poured herself a cup of wine, then eyed Catia and sighed, pouring the second cup and thrusting it towards the other woman. 'Life is short and filled with spite,' she said after a deep draught. 'Get out of it what little you can before the dirt claims you.'

'You think nothing of those yet to come? Of leaving this world a better place?'

'I'll not be here to enjoy it. Why should I care if everything burns to the ground after I'm gone?'

Catia sipped on her wine in thought. 'Once you have a child—'

Amarina snorted. 'Don't tell me I've been denied wisdom because I've chosen not to be a suckling sow. I could just as easily say you're addled by that thing leeching the life from you.'

'I see you, Amarina. You show many faces to the world. But I'd wager the real one is never seen. I know you have some strange kinship with the Hecatae. You speak to Lucanus about daemons in the Wilds. You understand more than your own mean-spirited life. You can see the weft and weave of all there is reaching into days yet to come.'

'And perhaps I want no part of it. I would write my own story, not have it written for me by the wood-priests.' Amarina swilled more wine into her goblet, to the brim. She could feel her blood pounding in her temple. 'Or the witches, or the forest folk, or men . . . or women . . . who seek power, everywhere. Why are you so blind? They don't care if you live or die. They spin their tales of magic swords and saviour kings, and fate and destiny and royal blood, but in the end this story is about one thing. Drawing power into their hands.' In her annoyance, she waved her goblet towards Catia and wine slopped on to the floor.

Silence swelled in the room for a long time. 'Then let us take power into our own hands,' Catia said in a quiet yet strong voice.

Amarina allowed those words to settle on her.

'Let us write our own story,' Catia continued. 'We can shape this world as well as any others. And if we can bring the light back into this long night at the same time, then all well and good.'

'An alliance? You and me?' Amarina choked back a laugh.

'You and me.'

Amarina felt an ache in her side from her recent wounds. She remembered Bucco the dwarf's knife plunging into her flesh, the sound of the steel chunking into her, the iron smell of her own blood. She winced at a spike of fear.

'Drink your wine,' she said. 'One of the girls will bring you food soon enough. Stay as long as you will. There is room enough for Solinus and Comitinus if there is still need for dogs to guard the exalted mother of our future saviour.'

In her room, she pulled on her cloak and then swept out of the suffocating warmth of the House of Wishes and into the crisp night. The sky was clear and the stars glittered like ice. Her fingers closed on the knife she had carried for so long and she walked into the maze of strange streets, driven on by the thrum of her blood.

The town was deserted and silence for once lay over that stinking mass of humanity. She hadn't gone far when the hairs at the nape of her neck prickled and she realized she could hear the faint clack-clack of footsteps somewhere at her back.

Glancing back, she caught sight of a silhouette against the golden glow of a torch.

No town was safe, not for women. Nowhere was safe. But she would go where she wanted and she would do as she pleased. Setting her jaw, she turned off the broad street into a narrow track leading south, towards the river wall. As she picked up her step, she heard whoever was at her back do the same.

Darkness swallowed her. Looking back again, she saw the patch of wavering torchlight briefly obscured. It seemed she was being hunted.

A few steps further on, she ducked behind the wall of a workshop. Her feet crunched on broken shards of pottery and her heart pattered in fear that she had given herself away.

The footsteps rattled nearer, slowed. Doubt. Perhaps listening.

As she watched the dark shape of her pursuer pass by her hiding place, she lunged. Her fingers snagged in a woollen cloak and she dragged it back, slamming the stranger against the wall of the workshop. Her left arm crushed against her captive's chest, and her knife flashed to the throat.

'It's not wise to be abroad after dark,' Amarina hissed.

'Please. I wish you no harm.'

A woman. The words were laced with a thick accent that she didn't recognize, and the voice had the slow, guttural cadence of a country-dweller. She eased the pressure on the woman's chest, but kept her blade poised.

'Following me at night is the best way to get yourself harmed. What do you want?'

With a hesitant movement, the woman reached up and pulled her hood back. Blonde hair tumbled out.

Amarina dragged her back on to the track and twisted her into the faint moonlight. A pretty face, but not the delicate bone structure of a refined woman. Still, she would have earned good coin in the House of Wishes.

'You keep the house of women by the amphitheatre. I heard talk of you among the soldiers. I watched you earlier—'

'Spying on me?' Amarina jabbed the blade a notch closer to the pale skin.

'I wish you no harm,' the woman repeated. She forced a smile, warm enough.

'Who are you?'

'I am a stranger in this place. A traveller. A refugee, seeking friendship.' She paused briefly, and added, 'My name is Hecate.'

CHAPTER TWENTY-SEVEN

Chaos is Come Again

FIRST THERE WERE BLACK WINGS AND THEN THERE WAS FIRE. Lucanus gripped the cold stone of the parapet as the cloud blackened the western sky. Crows thundered up from the trees lining the snaking river. Their shrieks swallowed even the din of a town sixty thousand strong.

'What's disturbed them?' Bellicus grunted.

They'd been wandering along the walls, discussing plans for the escape to Avalon. Here above the town the air was at least a little fresher, and they could escape the crush of churning bodies and the choking stench of filth and rot.

The Wolf watched the arc of panicked birds and felt his heart begin to pound. 'No warning from the scouts.'

The words had barely left his lips when the burning arrows lit the sky. A hundred of them, more, arcing in unison.

'Hell's teeth,' Bellicus hissed.

The fire rained down. Lucanus heard the pounding of that deluge on the edge of the *vicus*. With a roar, the shacks and the tents erupted into a wall of flame. Shrieks rang out, became one terrible, piercing cry. Bodies flooded away from the inferno. Makeshift homes collapsed, women, children, and the elderly falling before the surging tide, all of them crushed underfoot.

211

The Wolf looked up. Squinting, he peered beyond the flames, and when the billowing smoke shifted he glimpsed a charcoal smudge moving towards Londinium. It was lost in an instant, but by then he was bounding down the steps into the fort.

'How did they get past the scouts?' Bellicus raged behind him.

But they both knew the truth. An attack, long in planning. Scouts picked off, one by one, so that word never got back.

As Lucanus felt his feet touch the ground, he heard the rumble rise up. Londinium had seemed to be holding its breath, the hammers set aside, the voices stilled, an entire town of rabbits hearing a distant footfall. Far beyond the Fleet, a susurration became a roar became the sound of the heavens opening. A battle-cry caught by hundreds of voices.

'To arms!' he yelled. 'We are under attack.' His words were all but drowned out by the alarm ringing from the watchmen on the walls. They'd been caught sleeping, and they would pay the price.

Soldiers scrambled from all corners of the fort. Whatever orders had been barked drowned in the eruption of panic across the entire town, and from the *vicus* beyond.

'Do what you can to get the men together,' Lucanus barked to Bellicus. But then he was slamming his way through the churning bodies, crashing into the teeming streets, past the terrified men and screaming women.

'Open the gates!' he bellowed when he reached the Ludgate.

Faces twisted with fear looked down at him from the walls. Lucanus cursed, knowing full well what would have rushed through their minds when they heard the throoming on the gate.

A hand grabbed his arm and wrenched him back.

'Leave them,' Falx demanded. 'We can't cope with the number we have inside the walls as it is.'

'And see them slaughtered?' Lucanus threw the centurion off.

As he ran to the gates, he heard a command barked. When he glanced back, he saw six soldiers running to stand with Falx. 'Don't do it, Lucanus,' the centurion warned, half drawing his sword.

The Wolf snatched out Caledfwlch and levelled it as he backed towards the gates. A moment later he sensed Bellicus loom up beside him. Lucanus waved his blade as his friend slotted in next to him.

'The enemy is out there,' Falx raged.

Hands pounded on the gates, the desperate pleas spiralling up. Lucanus felt a pang in his heart. How could anyone ignore those cries?

'Lift the bar!'

Lucanus glanced up to see Mato on the wall. Whatever he had said, the guards on the wall seemed ready to help. His work done there, Mato scrambled down the steps. With Bellicus on the other end, he hefted the great oak beam that barred the gates and a moment later they creaked open.

The torrent flooded in. Cursing, Falx and his men dived to one side and were lost behind the flow of bodies.

'What now?' Bellicus bellowed, his raw voice almost lost in the tumult.

'Get set to close the gates when the enemy nears,' Lucanus ordered.

'And if there are still folk outside?'

The Wolf knew his friend had seen the answer in his eyes, but he replied, 'We can't allow the enemy to get a foothold inside. It'll be Vercovicium once more.'

He couldn't bear the look in those eyes. He jerked his head towards the walkway round the walls.

Once they'd clambered back on to the rampart, they looked down on a sea of flame and death. Lucanus choked on a mouthful of black smoke swirling up from the inferno rushing through the makeshift camp towards the *vicus*. Bodies littered the narrow tracks leading to the swell around the gate.

Bellicus stabbed a finger. A line of barbarians was pounding over the sole bridge across the Fleet. As they moved into the sprawling settlement, he watched axes rise and fall, cutting down those who had chosen to hide or who were too weak to flee.

'The river has stopped their army attacking as one. That's good,' Bellicus grunted, trying to find some thin hope.

Lucanus felt his heart pounding as the horde swept through the wall of flame. Leaning back, he looked down into the madness of the jostling crowd stumbling through the gate into the narrow street.

'Get them in!' he yelled.

Mato held out both hands. What could he do?

Across the *vicus* the barbarians marched, cutting down every unfortunate in their path. Beyond the edge of the settlement, the grassland stretching out along the bank of the river was black with seething bodies. Had the entire horde descended on them?

'How do we fight that?' Bellicus said as if he could read his friend's thoughts.

His heart pounding, Lucanus threw himself down the stone steps with Bellicus at his heels. Apullius had joined Mato and the two of them pressed against the gates, urging the refugees in with wild cries and waves of their arms. But they were not coming in quickly enough.

The Wolf thrust himself against the flow along the edge, shouldering his way out of the gate. He heard Bellicus yell his name, but his heart was set. He pushed his way along the stone wall until he could get to the rear of the crowd.

Among the houses of the *vicus*, a bewildered girl, abandoned by her parents, roamed back and forth, sobbing. There were others besides her: limping old men, shuffling women, more children.

Lucanus swept the girl up in his arms and brought her to the edge of the crowd. 'Take her in,' he commanded a fearful woman. Something in his voice connected with her, for she took the girl's hand. And then he was racing back among the workshops, dragging out anyone he could help.

Choking smoke drifted everywhere now. Through it he could hear the battle-cries of the barbarians above the roaring of the fire. Close, and closer by the moment.

Bellicus appeared at his side, glowering.

'Don't be a fool,' Lucanus said. 'Get back inside.'

'A fool knows a fool. And your father will haunt me until my last days if I let you die out here alone.'

Together, they threw themselves into the *vicus*, pulling out any they could find until none seemed to remain. Only then did Lucanus step back to the edge of the crowd. Legs braced, he unsheathed Caledfwlch and waited. Bellicus loomed beside him, his blade levelled.

'This isn't the way I planned to go,' he grunted.

'I'd wager you wanted to breathe your last between Galantha's thighs.'

'Every man's dream.'

Lucanus stiffened. Catia floated into his thoughts, and he felt a pang of regret. Before it could take hold, voices barked at his back, accompanied by the clatter of metal and rumble of feet. He glanced over his shoulder and saw Falx and a stream of soldiers shouldering their way through the diminishing crowd at the gate.

The men raced up, their shields clanging into a wall.

'If you've killed me, I'll make you suffer in the afterlife,' Falx snarled as he slotted into position.

Lucanus nodded his gratitude. He looked past the shield, through the drifting white cloud, and saw the first dark smudges appear. The barbarians stepped out of the *vicus*. They were more cautious now, sizing up the defences as they advanced. What they saw was enough to make them hesitate, and that was all the time the defenders needed.

'Come now!'

The Wolf recognized Mato's voice. He glanced back and saw the last of the crowd filtering in through the gate.

Keeping the shield wall intact, the soldiers edged backwards. All eyes remained fixed on the Scoti and Pictish warriors emerging from the smoke, waiting for the moment when the wave would break and they all rushed forward.

Arrows thrummed out of the fug. One shaft clanged off the side of a helmet. Another rammed into a soldier's shoulder and he spun backwards. On Falx's command, the men dropped low, tilting their shields just in time. A hail of arrows clattered.

'Back,' Lucanus yelled, 'before the next attack.'

The line of soldiers swept backwards until Lucanus felt the shadow of the wall fall over him. And then they were inside, the gates grinding shut as another volley of arrows slammed into the wood.

Without pausing to draw breath, Lucanus bounded up the stone steps with Bellicus and Falx behind him. On the walkway, he looked out through the billowing clouds. The barbarians stood like sentinels watching Londinium.

Falx frowned. 'Why aren't they attacking?'

'They don't need to. This is all there is left of Britannia.' Lucanus looked back into the town. The road from the gate was choked with bodies, perhaps two thousand more with no shelter, no possessions, nothing but the clothes on their backs. 'Seal us up, with what little supplies we have and what little more we can get at the river gate. Wait for us to starve. Or fall to the sickness. Or start killing each other.'

Bellicus splayed his fingers and stared at the back of his hand. Lucanus followed his gaze and then looked up at the lowering clouds.

Large flakes of snow were drifting down.

The season had turned.

CHAPTER TWENTY-EIGHT

Cold Season

THE SNOW CAME HARDER IN THE NIGHT. GUSTS OF glittering flakes swirled through the wavering halo around every torch. Along the walls, the watchmen stamped their feet and blew into their hands, bowing their heads so their eyes didn't sting. Soon they were crunching through ankle-deep drifts.

The wind howled along the black river. Thicker and faster the blizzard blew, until billows of white rolled up from the banks and across the fields to the hills. The land glowed and the night fell back, and silence floated across everything.

'They have snow here too.' Solinus crunched along the street towards the Ludgate at first light. 'I thought the south was all sun and flowers.'

'Enough of your grumbling.' Bellicus wiped away snot with the back of his hand. 'Or I'll send you back to stand guard at the House of Wishes. Mato never has a sour expression. A joy to be around, that one. All sunshine and light. Not a miserable bastard like you.'

'I never thought I'd tire of a whorehouse,' Solinus muttered. 'But I'm losing my wits by the hour sitting there all day and night with only Comitinus for company.'

'You've got your break. Enjoy it.' Bellicus watched Catulus

snuffling through the snow, a trail of pawprints weaving behind him. 'It's good work you're doing, keeping Catia and her child safe. Lucanus won't forget your sacrifice.'

Solinus grunted and slapped his hands for warmth.

Bellicus led the way up the sparkling steps to the high walkway. The cold north wind sliced deep. He leaned on the parapet and looked out to the west, remembering standing on a different wall looking out into a wild land filled with daemons.

The *vicus* was little more than charred bones protruding from frozen earth. Ransacked and destroyed. Beyond the Fleet, the horde's camp shadowed the white expanse. Trails of smoke drifted up from their fires.

'There's no getting out for us, is there?' Solinus said, leaning next to him.

'Miserable bastard.' Solinus was right, though. This felt like an ending. Bellicus searched the white landscape. The barbarians stopped any boat coming from the west, not that there was much trade arriving from the rest of Britannia now they'd laid waste to it. Their war-bands ranged around the town to the north and east, riding down anyone who dared venture out. The only route left free was through the river gate. A boat with a handful of men to the south bank, for all the use that was.

The barbarians could afford to sit and wait while winter sunk its teeth into them.

A cry rang out somewhere deep in the town, followed by another, and then another, until a tumult was ringing across the rooftops. The Grey Wolves straightened up.

'The barbarian bastards don't need to do anything,' Solinus said, looking over his shoulder as he turned. 'Just sit back and let us throttle each other to death.'

Bellicus stalked down the steps. At the foot, he whistled for Catulus, and the hound scampered up with an old bone he'd found. They plunged into the icy streets, following the sounds of the clamour.

Outside the gates to the forum a crowd was gathering. Folk were stumbling up from all directions, dragged from their slumber by the din. Bellicus shoved his way through the wall of bodies, a glare silencing anyone who protested.

At the centre, four men wrestled to hold a thin, sallow-faced fellow whose yells were more like the howls of a wounded animal than any human sound. At their feet lay another man, dead by the look of him, a loaf of bread lying in the snow by his outstretched hand.

'What's going on?' Bellicus barked.

'He killed the poor bastard,' one of the four men shouted as he kicked the captive's legs from under him. With a scream, the sallow-faced man slammed down on to the frozen ground. 'Killed him for a slab of mouldy bread. Give us a hand here, will you?'

'Not my job.' Bellicus relaxed his grip on the hilt of his sword.

'Some sense at last,' Solinus whispered.

Bellicus nodded. The water was already high over their heads. They were scouts, ditch-crawlers, drunks and fornicators, and somehow they'd been twisted by the words of the wood-priest to lead a ramshackle army. Keeping order in that town was not a burden he wanted.

He looked around at the faces in the swelling crowd. Some were filled with fury at the crime that had been committed. Other eyes flickered hungrily to that loaf of bread. The mood he sensed there was repeated right across the town. A wave waiting to break.

The clatter of many feet rattled up. A voice barked. The crowd parted and ten soldiers swept in with Falx at their head. 'Get him,' he snarled. No need to ask questions or weigh guilt. The centurion knew this fire had to be stamped out fast.

Once his men had dragged the murderer away, Falx came over. Bellicus read his darting eyes.

'Third murder in as many hours. This is all going to hell,' the centurion whispered, leaning in close.

'The mood swung quickly.' Solinus narrowed his eyes at the crowd, as if he thought they would turn on him next.

'We shouldn't have let those bastards in from the *vicus*,' Falx spat. 'Before that we had a hard road to walk to get to spring. Now . . .'

'One trade route to the south. That might be all we need. There're still boats coming up the river from the east.' Bellicus tapped his thigh to bring Catulus in close. The churning emotions in the crowd were upsetting the dog.

'One man was bludgeoned to death with a cudgel yesterday. Two stabbed near Cheapside baths this morning. Rows about women, rows about food, it doesn't matter. Hunger drives men mad. Once they start killing each other, it's only going to get worse, and in a town sealed up like this it'll get bad fast.' Falx stamped the snow off his feet. 'The barbarians won't let us out to bury the dead. We're having to burn the bodies by the Aldgate. Can't breathe there for smoke. The bodies are piling up. How in the name of Mithras are we ever going to keep order?'

Solinus grinned. 'Sounds to me like the gods know what they're doing. Fitting punishment for what you did in Vercovicium.'

'I made a mistake,' the centurion muttered. 'Am I to pay for it for ever?'

'Aye, I would think so. Robbing your own men and all.'

'God will set you free from this suffering,' a voice boomed, and Theodosius strode up with a knot of his men around

221

him. When he took off his helmet, his cheeks were flushed and his eyes sparkled with a preacher's fervour. 'Come to the church,' he continued loudly. 'Prayers will be offered. Only through God will we all be delivered from this hardship.'

Bellicus couldn't tell if anyone was calmed by the soldier's words, but eyes fluttered down and angry voices ebbed. Slowly the crowd broke up, and Theodosius came over to the little group.

'Londinium is a pit of sin,' he told them. 'There are men here as pagan in their beliefs as those barbarians beyond the walls.'

'I am a good Christian,' Falx lied with a devout bow of his head.

'Of course. Of course.' Bellicus watched Theodosius eye him and Solinus with suspicion, but he didn't press them. 'I have wandered along these streets talking to the citizens and many have come to the Lord. They deserve our protection. We must ensure the will of the emperor Valentinian is enforced here and Londinium is rid of those who will not follow the Christ. Only then will we stand any chance of surviving until the spring. What say you, Falx?'

'Aye, aye. Makes sense,' the centurion replied, nodding too much.

'Good. I will meet with the governor later to make arrangements. If the coward ever emerges from his chambers.' He spun on his heel and marched away.

'That's all we need, someone like him stirring the pot,' Solinus muttered.

'He's right about one thing,' Bellicus said as he watched Theodosius and his men disappear. 'Prayers might be all we have.'

Lucanus bowed his head across his horse's neck. His eyebrows were frosted with snow and his face was numb, but his shoulders felt lighter for being away from the town. He remembered how his spirits had lifted when he scouted north of the wall. Perhaps Mato was right and the Wilds were his temple.

Though there was not much wild about this countryside, he thought, as he looked across the snow-blanketed fields, dotted here and there with farms and villas.

'You didn't have to bring so many of your men. My own would have sufficed.' Corvus urged his mount up beside him and nodded his head to the column of men riding at their backs. The soldier was good company: a sharp wit, always bubbling with stories and sardonic humour.

Lucanus glanced at the other man and thought of Catia; something in his companion's features, in the almond eyes perhaps, or the shape of the mouth, he wasn't sure what. 'They're still learning. It does them no good to sit around Londinium sharpening their swords. If we're ever to drive these barbarians back, they need to be ready when the time is right. And prepared to defend Britannia should the army fail us again.'

They'd rowed across the Tamesis from the river gate under cover of darkness and tramped through the bitter night to where Theodosius had hidden the horses on his arrival. The family who kept them on their farm seemed grateful that the army hadn't abandoned them and offered fresh bread as they mounted and prepared to ride south. Every man, woman and child they'd encountered on the way was the same. A desperate hope burning. The warm expectation of spring tainted by the fear of what would happen when the snows melted.

Corvus shivered from the cold and pulled his cloak tighter around him. 'At least we'll see any stray barbarians early against this white. Unless it's the Attacotti, I suppose.'

Lucanus heard the timbre alter in the other man's voice.

He was brave enough, but any man who met the Attacotti was changed by the experience.

'I can't speak for the Eaters of the Dead – they follow their own rules. But when I travelled through the Wilds, the Scoti and the Picts retreated to their villages during the cold months. They were seasoned warriors, but they were no fools. They knew how quickly the winter could steal a man's life if he was caught out away from a fire. They'll be biding their time in their camp, I'd wager. They can afford to.'

Corvus' dark eyes flickered across the frozen landscape. He was still thinking about the Attacotti.

'Danger never goes. But we are taking good care,' Lucanus continued. 'Enough armed men to repel an attack. Few enough to travel fast. We'll do our business and be back behind the walls before you know it.'

'I'll take your word for it. This land is not so different from Gaul, but it's still strange enough.' The familiar grin brightened his face and he clapped a hand on Lucanus' shoulder. 'These are the tales we will tell our children, eh? How we saved Britannia. Two old men hunched around the fire, swilling wine and singing songs of our glory days.' He paused, thoughtfully. 'Your child is due soon, yes?'

Lucanus winced. He wished he was back at Catia's side, that he need never leave it. Myrrdin watched over her at the House of Wishes now the birth was near, along with some of Amarina's women to help when the babe came. The gods would decide if she lived or died, but he still felt the worry consuming him.

'Soon enough.'

'I haven't seen the lady Catia in a while. She is well?'

'She's got a warrior's heart. But a house full of drunken men is no place for a woman with child. She's with the midwives.'

'Ah. Where is that? I'm still getting to know Londinium. Beyond the taverns, of course.'

Lucanus squinted and peered into the hazy distance. 'We're almost at the coast. Let's ride harder. The sooner we conduct this business, the sooner we can get home.' He dug in his heels and urged his horse on, leaving Corvus, and his questions, behind.

The wind off the sea was like knives. The waves crashed on the bleak beach and the gulls mourned for all that had been lost. Lucanus led the way along the icy road to Rutupiae. After a while he could see the grey walls of the Saxon shore fortifications that had been built on both sides of the channel for protection from barbarians attacking by sea. The walls rose up as high as four men standing on each other's shoulders, and had served their purpose, so far at least.

'This is the point where Claudius' army landed when Britannia was invaded, so I'm told,' Corvus said when he once more reached Lucanus' side.

'You have some learning, then.'

'A man should know what has come before so he can see what might come ahead.'

Lucanus shrugged. 'I only know what my father taught me. How to live off the land and use a sword and stay one step ahead of death.'

'That's good knowledge too.'

As they neared, they scanned the walls of the fort and saw a few heads looking down at their arrival.

'Barely a third of the men are left,' Corvus said. 'We found that out when we arrived. The count of the Saxon shore took the rest off to the north to repel the barbarian advance. That was the last anyone saw of them.'

'As long as there are men still holding the forts along the coast, and messengers to ride between them, it will serve our purpose.'

Lucanus held up his arm and glanced at his men riding alongside the well-drilled soldiers. He could see their features hardening by the day, but they still showed their inexperience. They would learn. He snapped down his arm and they rode harder towards the gates.

The fort at Rutupiae protected a sheltered harbour on the muddy estuary. Ships creaked on their moorings and sailors and merchants milled on the quayside. Not many, but enough to give Lucanus hope.

Once they were inside the fort, the soldiers broke the ice on the troughs so their mounts could drink. The new commander wandered out of the *principia* to watch them. Lucanus thought he looked barely old enough to carry a sword. The parchment-like skin of his face was still spattered with youthful spots, and his cheeks were flushed as if he were permanently embarrassed. Probably never seen battle, the Wolf thought.

He introduced himself as Galeo, prefect of the Second Augustan Legion, and then asked with a note of apprehension, 'Londinium still stands?'

'Of course,' Corvus said. 'All is well in the world.'

Galeo eyed Corvus as if he was insane. 'Come inside where it's warm. There's wine and olives.'

'A man who knows how to provide a good welcome. We'll be firm friends, I can tell.' As he walked towards the open door, Corvus looked around at the missing tiles and sagging walls. 'Seen better days here.'

'We've been neglected for too long. Not enough men. No coin to pay for repairs or new blades.'

'I wager there are people regretting that now,' Corvus said.

Galeo waved a hand towards the western wall. 'Used to be a great arch there to celebrate our invasion, a *quadrifrons*, like the ones in Rome. The height of five men, faced with marble, and decorated with bronze statues. They tore it down. Nothing lasts here,' he added glumly.

'You sound like a man who needs good company and

better wine,' Corvus replied. 'Quick now, before we drown in misery.'

In Galeo's chamber the coals glowed red. Lucanus pulled up a stool and warmed his bones while the commander poured three cups of wine. Corvus leaned against the wall near the fire, one eyebrow cocked as he looked around the meagre furnishings.

'The barbarians haven't troubled you?' Lucanus asked.

'Not as yet,' the commander replied. 'Our fortifications along the Saxon shore have daunted them, even though a lot of good men have been lost. Nectaridus, the count of the Saxon shore, led our force towards the battle lines. He has not been heard of since. We're not fools. We know the barbarians are coming in the spring.'

'And then?'

'We die.'

'Well,' Corvus said, taking the goblet, 'if that's the way you think, why not run into the sea and end it all now?'

'Wishes are for children,' Galeo said. 'We are few, they are a multitude. We'll stand up to them when they come, like good Romans, but they'll sweep us away in the blink of an eye.'

'Any messengers from Gaul? News on when Theodosius the Elder will bring his army to retake Britannia?' Lucanus asked.

Galeo shook his head. 'A dream.'

'You don't think they'll come?'

'Valentinian is distracted by the Alamanni and the struggles in Rome among the supporters of the rival popes. If you ask me, he will let Britannia wither away.'

'Never,' Corvus said. 'Rome abandoning part of the empire? It will only give the Alamanni and the other tribes fresh hope. If they aren't stopped here, the barbarians will keep going, perhaps even to the walls of Rome itself.'

Galeo shrugged, sipped his wine, and stared into the fire.

Lucanus thought how drained he looked, like every other soldier he'd encountered since the horde had swept south.

'Even if Theodosius came, could Rome ever put right the devastation that has been wreaked on Britannia?' he said. 'If you saw the north, you would believe that this is the start of a new age.' He looked at his distorted reflection in the surface of the blood-red wine. 'The season is turning.'

'So much defeatism!' Corvus drained his cup. 'Even if Rome abandons Britannia, a new leader will rise up to lead the people into the light.'

Lucanus eyed the other man. The words could have been spoken by the wood-priest. 'Why do you say that?'

Corvus shrugged. 'Because there is a need. And so it will be filled.' He looked from one man to the other. 'It's an old, old story. Surely you've heard it? The great saviour who will return to lead the people back into the light? The followers of the Christ stole it from the cult of Mithras. The cult of Mithras stole it from religions that came before. And so on, back to when man was first made. The story lives on because the people need it, not because the gods decree.'

Lucanus stiffened. Could this be true? Not a prophecy. Not the word of the gods. Just a story shaped by men?

'Sounds like blasphemy to me,' Galeo said, eyeing Corvus over the lip of his goblet.

'Ah, a follower of the Christ! You should meet my friend Theodosius the Younger!' Corvus shook his empty cup for a refill. 'Enough of these meanderings. We are here for serious business. Londinium starves. We need your help, and those of all the forts along the Saxon shore.'

'What can we do?'

'Send messengers along the free south. Spread the word. We need supplies. Boats can be brought along the Tamesis from the east. We'll arrange a place where we can ferry what is delivered into the city.'

Galeo sighed. 'Why should any merchants risk their necks trading with a town under siege from that horde of blood-thirsty barbarians?'

'We have no shortage of coin, but we can't eat that. We need food,' Lucanus said. 'We'll pay handsomely.'

The commander thought for a moment. 'It will take a while for word to spread, and longer for trade to be arranged. Can you survive till then?'

Lucanus looked at Corvus. 'It will be hard—'

'We'll have to,' Corvus interjected. 'The sooner you get word out, the sooner we can prevent the citizens of Londinium from eating each other.'

Once the arrangements had been thrashed out, Lucanus and Corvus marched back into the cold afternoon. Flakes of snow whisked in on the icy breeze.

'Another bad night ahead,' Corvus said, eyeing the bank of clouds. 'Let's not tarry here.'

'And let's hope we've done some good. This may be our last chance.'

'You were the one who pushed for it,' Corvus said as he led the way to where the horses were tethered. 'Everyone else was too frightened to venture out from the city walls.'

'Not you, though.'

'Luckily my wits are addled.'

Corvus glanced behind them, as if acknowledging someone following them. Lucanus followed his gaze, but there was no one there. The two men bade a reluctant farewell to the warmth of the barracks and soon they were back on the road to Londinium.

Corvus pulled his mount up beside the Wolf, checked over his shoulder that he could not be overheard, and whispered, 'You're a good man, Lucanus. I can see why you were chosen to lead this army. You've got steel in your spine and a fire in your belly, and your men respect you because you're always there, at the front, putting your own neck on the block for them.' Corvus paused, looking out at the slate sea. 'I feel I can trust you, and there are few I can say that about in this world.'

'I believe in fair dealing.'

Corvus nodded, then bowed his head in reflection. 'Can I tell you a secret?'

Lucanus nodded.

The soldier sucked in a deep breath of the icy air. 'I am a follower of Mithras.'

'I know enough of those. Or knew, in Vercovicium. Most are dead now.'

'And I'll probably join them if my friend Theodosius finds out. To believe in something other than the Christ risks a death sentence in these times.'

'Every man should be free to believe what he wants. That was how it used to be. Rome never forced anyone to pray in a different temple.'

Corvus lifted his head. 'I carry it around in my heart like a lead weight. Not daring to speak a word of it, not even to my closest friend. If a man can't be true to what he believes, he's nothing.' He watched a gull arc across the granite sky. 'And you?'

'In the north, things are different. The worship of the Christ hadn't gained much ground there. Whenever I offer prayers, it's to the old gods. Like my father, and his father before him.'

'Then you'd be on my friend Theodosius' list too. We share something here, you and I. A bond. We are men who must do what's right, despite the risk. I thought you would understand.'

'I do, that's true.' He eyed Corvus, the hunched shoulders, the pleasant, open face, and felt that bond. 'Your secret is safe with me.'

'As I knew it would be. It's good to unburden oneself. These rocks can drag a man down.' He nodded. 'I'm proud to call you a friend, Lucanus.'

'And I you.'

Corvus hesitated, and Lucanus sensed there was more he wanted to say. 'What is it?'

'This is difficult . . .'

'Speak.'

'Friend to friend?'

'Aye. That's what friends do.'

Corvus pursed his lips for a moment and then seemed to decide to commit himself. 'Have you noticed any changes in the lady Catia since she returned to you?'

'Changes?'

'Does she still show her love, as she used to before she was taken prisoner?'

Lucanus felt a chill deep inside him. 'These are harder times. We all carry burdens—'

'I have no desire to cause you any pain. But a man must face up to the truth early enough to save himself.'

'Is this more of what you told me before we attacked the barbarians?'

'One of my men saw her out with another . . . no, not one of your Grim Wolves. A man whose hand she held, whose ear she warmed with her breath when she laughed.' He waved a hand in the air. 'It could be nothing, of course it could. But I would speak to her, Lucanus. Don't waste time. Go to her the moment we get back and find out what has changed. There may still be a chance to keep her, or it may be too late, but, as I say, if you act quickly you can at least save yourself.'

The snow drifted down. Under the lamp of the moon, Londinium was silent. As they tramped up from the river gate, Corvus and Lucanus kept that silence, as they had for much of the journey back from Rutupiae. Throughout that long ride, Corvus had watched the Wolf from the corner of his eye. He'd noted the strained face and the hunched shoulders, the brooding, the worry. His words had struck home.

As their men trudged away to their beds, Lucanus turned and said, 'We'll talk again tomorrow.'

'You're going to speak with your woman?'

Lucanus nodded.

'That's for the best. Good luck.'

The Wolf bowed his head into the bitter wind towards the north. Corvus watched him go, the solitary figure moving from shadow to light as it traipsed through the circles of brightness under the torches. Before it disappeared from view, another figure separated from the dark of a doorway.

Bucco the dwarf glanced once at Corvus and nodded. Then he hurried along the trail of footprints, making sure he would not be seen.

Corvus allowed himself a smile. Soon they'd know where Catia had been hidden, and then the way ahead could be cleared.

CHAPTER TWENTY-NINE

The Demand

T HE LAMP FLAME GUTTERED. SHADOWS FLICKERED AROUND the corridor and sparks ignited in Myrrdin's coal eyes.

'Stand back.'

Lucanus scowled. 'You're refusing to let me see Catia?'

'She needs her sleep. For her sake, and the child's.' The wood-priest was standing outside Catia's door in the House of Wishes. Comitinus was asleep in the warm anteroom, but Mato had ushered him through.

'You have no right—'

'I have every right.' The druid stamped his staff on the floor for emphasis. 'I am the child's protector, as are you. And I can see from your demeanour that you have not come to whisper honeyed words. What is amiss?'

The wind howled under the eaves, almost drowning out the moans of lovemaking echoing from the other chambers.

'Stand aside.' Lucanus barrelled down the corridor. As he flexed to toss Myrrdin aside, the wood-priest stabbed his staff forward and with a deft flick between the legs flung Lucanus on to his back.

Before he could push himself up, the tip of the staff was jammed against his windpipe.

'Once more. What is amiss?'

Lucanus was reluctant to speak about his worries, but he could see from the druid's eyes that the question wouldn't go away. He looked down and muttered, 'I need to know if she still cares for me.'

'You fool.' Myrrdin snorted. 'Britannia is burning around you, and you lose yourself in lovesick imaginings. You are the Pendragon—'

'I did not choose it!'

The wood-priest smiled. 'Nevertheless, it's your burden. Once you accepted the dragon crown, your old life was gone. You have one duty now. To the people of Britannia and the King Who Will Not Die. Nothing else matters.'

'I will not accept that.'

'You have no choice.'

'All I want is Catia, and the child, and a simple life. No wood-priests or witches, no prophecies, or daemons, or saviours.'

'The man who could have had those things died in the cold waters of that lake in Caledonia. You accepted the sword of the gods. You took the crown. You ate the sacred toad's-stool. What did you see in Goibniu's Smithy that night, Wolf?'

Lucanus felt ice-water rush through him. 'I visited a great forest where I met an old grey wolf, like the one I killed the night I became one of the Grim Wolves. It spoke to me.' He shuddered, though he couldn't remember what had been said. 'My eyes darkened, and when I looked again its life-blood was draining away. I heard the sound of wings, and I saw the Morrigan.'

'And after meeting her, do you think the Morrigan will let you return to the man you were?'

The Wolf slumped back. 'There's talk that Catia has been seen with another man.'

234

'Talk? There's always talk.' Myrrdin squatted, balancing with his stick. 'Hear me now. She has not ventured from this place since you brought her here. And with two of your men guarding her at all hours, do you think she is a witch who can magic herself away to another lover?'

Lucanus closed his eyes and sighed. He felt a weariness sink deep into his bones.

'You need to rest, Wolf. Tiredness tricks a man's wits.' He heard the druid stand, the end of his staff clacking on the floor as he used it for leverage. 'Worries that you would never have considered before pop up like bubbles in a marsh. Rumours become truth.'

Lucanus heaved himself to his feet. Perhaps the druid was right. He was too exhausted to think straight.

Myrrdin tapped his staff on Lucanus' chest. 'You do the work of the gods now. Never forget that. Your life is their life. But do it well and you will be well rewarded.'

'I'll settle for a day that isn't about running and fighting—'

'Lucanus?'

He turned to see Mato in the doorway at the other end of the corridor. Apullius hovered behind him.

'You must come,' the lad said urgently. 'The barbarians are calling for you.'

Lucanus frowned, but this was no time for questions. In the anteroom, Amarina was standing in a corner where the shadows were thickest, her arms lightly folded. 'Two worlds,' she said, reminding him of a conversation they had had that seemed like a lifetime away in Vercovicium. 'Beware of daemons.'

And then he was out in the cold, the frosted streets turning to grey in the first light.

Climbing the steps by the Ludgate, he found Bellicus waiting. Flecks of snow dotted his red beard and his eyes were wintry.

'Bad business,' he grunted.

The Wolf leaned on the parapet and looked down to where the frozen remnants of the *vicus* were slowly emerging from the gloom.

Two torchbearers flanked a small group of barbarians, swaddled in furs. The torches roared and danced in the wind, the orange light washing over faces of granite. At the centre was one taller than the rest, his head swathed in filthy rags. Arrist, king of the Caledonian south.

'You thought you were safe there, behind your walls,' Arrist's voice boomed out. 'Instead you have gathered in a pit to be slaughtered. How do you feel now, men of Rome? We have no need to lose good comrades in battle. We can sit by our fires, and tell our stories, and feast, and drink, while you all starve, slowly. Soon there will only be a city of the dead.'

The gale whined in his ears, and the Wolf felt his rage grow at what these enemies had done to so many innocents.

'You are this Lucanus Pendragon?'

'I am,' he called back.

'Then I speak to you as one king to another. You have a chance to save your people.'

'We will never surrender.'

'Nor would I expect you to. You've fought well, with what little army you could bring together in the night. You held us back as we flooded across the land. No. All it takes is one small sacrifice and your people can have all the food they need.'

Lucanus sensed a stiffening among the soldiers gathered along the wall. As he glanced along the row, he saw Falx leaning forward, staring intently. There was a light in his face, a hunger, that the Wolf had seen before, in Vercovicium when the centurion had sensed an opportunity to increase his wealth, usually at the expense of some other poor soul.

'Speak,' he called.

'Your woman. The one with child. Send her out to us and we will feed all your people.'

Lucanus felt a hollowness in the pit of his stomach. It seemed as though everyone along that wall had been frozen by the bitter wind.

'What is one woman to you? You've enslaved enough in your journey south.' He could hear his voice straining, despite himself.

'You know my reasons. The prophecy. We're not going to give this land up now we've fought so hard for it. We would seal our gains with this saviour-king. He will be in our hands, and he will do what we say. We have our eyes on greater things too. This is a new age now, Pendragon. The time of Rome has passed.'

'We stand together here,' Lucanus called back. 'We will not sacrifice one innocent soul.'

'Not even to save an entire city? Thousands upon thousands of people for your own selfish desires? Let us hear what they have to say.'

Lucanus recognized the cleverness of Arrist's ploy. He could turn all Londinium against him, divide the last true redoubt of Britannia. Once they'd torn each other apart, Arrist and the barbarians could take what they wanted and move on.

'Don't be rash, Pendragon. Take your time. This offer will stand, for a while. But keep this in your thoughts while you reach your decision.'

Arrist grabbed one of the roaring torches and waved it in front of him. The circle of light swooped over something that Lucanus hadn't noticed until that moment: a spike with a rotting head jammed on the top.

'Here is the fate of all who oppose us. This is the most powerful man of Rome in all the south. Nectaridus, count of the Saxon shore, commander of the army, leader of the empire's resistance, feast for the ravens.' His words rolled out across the frozen earth, and when the echoes had died away he added, 'There is no hope left now. All is dust.'

CHAPTER THIRTY

Midwinter

AD 367, Londinium, 25 December

TORCHLIGHT GLITTERED ON SHEETS OF ICE. FLAMES flickered in windows and danced outside doors. Londinium all but glowed in that bitter night. It was the day of feasts, of remembrance; of hope, perhaps, that when the light returned life would get easier.

Apullius crunched across the hoar frost, his breath burning in his chest as he ran. His sword clattered against his thigh, and with every beat he muttered another line of a desperate prayer.

Lucanus was counting on him. All of them were. And if he did not do his duty this night, they all would be dead by dawn.

'Bow your heads, my sons, and offer up your praise to Sol Invictus. Today the Unconquered Sun is reborn.'

Shadows shifted across the face of Severus, the Hanged Man, from the torches that flanked him at the altar, the only illumination in that cave beneath the old Temple of Mithras.

Corvus shuddered with a silent laugh. They'd taken a risk

gathering there, but it seemed right for this most important of days.

He thought back to how he'd crept through the shadows of Londinium to the secret entrance to the Mithraeum, where the bull was usually brought in for ritual slaughter. The rest of the temple above ground looked as if it hadn't been used in years, the shafts and tunnels to the cave long since filled in with rubble by the Christians who now dominated the town.

'*Nama*, to the runners of the sun, under the protection of the sun,' Severus' voice boomed out.

'*Nama*,' Corvus replied. Around him the ranks of loyal soldiers muttered their own response.

'On this day, Mithras was born from the rock,' the Hanged Man continued. 'He is the light, and he is the truth, and he will guide us through this age of darkness.'

'What better occasion to see all our plans reach their culmination, eh, Pavo?' Corvus whispered. 'A time of endings and fresh beginnings.'

'It's been a hard road, old crow, but you've brought us to the end of it.' His friend's voice floated to his ear from over his left shoulder.

Corvus felt excitement crackle through his limbs. All the sacrifice, the deaths of his father, his brother Ruga, all leading to this coming dawn, when he would cup power in his hands. The royal bloodline renewed, and always renewing, like the dragon eating its own tail.

Once the ritual was complete, Severus waved a hand to signal that the other torches should be lit. As light flooded the cave, the soldiers lounged on the benches, sweat glistening on their brows.

Corvus' mouth watered at the aroma of roast beef drifting in from the narthex. They'd dared not risk slaughtering a bull, as they would usually have done for this feast of feasts, even if one could have been found in that starving city. But

Severus had bribed Falx, a loyal follower of Mithras, who had bribed a merchant to deliver a cow's carcass that had arrived from the southern ports.

The Hanged Man loomed over him in his black cloak marked with the signs of the zodiac and thrust a goblet of wine into his hand.

'Drink deep, my son. You've earned your reward. Thanks to your work, this night may celebrate not only Mithras' birth, but also the beginning of his rebirth, incarnated in man, our saviour.'

Corvus bowed his head. 'The Dragon will rise again, Father.'

When Severus moved on, he gnawed on a chunk of beef and wiped the grease from his mouth with the back of his hand. The Feast of Sol Invictus would go on deep into the night, but he couldn't afford to linger. Catching Pavo's eye across the cave, he nodded.

Behind the altar, he slunk through the shadows and waited. After a while, fifteen men joined him, one by one, all of them loyal, all of whom had followed him from Rome at Severus' behest.

'You know what you need to do.' Corvus looked round the silent, trusting faces. 'No one will be abroad to see you administer justice on this night of feasts and prayer. Go to the whorehouse in the shadow of the amphitheatre. Kill everyone inside, including the women. They would see Mithras torn down, all of us destroyed, and they would betray Rome too. You'll meet no resistance. They go about their own activities, unaware that death is near.' He searched the eyes of his men, making sure they could all be trusted. 'This has the blessing of our Father, Severus,' he added. 'You do the work of Mithras this night.'

Each man nodded in turn, and then they marched up the steps to the secret exit.

Out in the cold night, Corvus' breath steamed.

'This is the end, Pavo,' he said.

His friend grinned. 'And the beginning.'

'Tonight, the barrier thins between this world of mortals and the Otherworld. Cernunnos leaves the great forest to walk along the streets of men, and daemons hover in the night outside our doors.'

Around Myrrdin's forehead holly had been entwined, the red berries glistening in the glare of the huge log blazing in the hearth. He was grinning, his eyes gleaming from the wine that he'd downed. He cupped his hand to his ear. 'Listen. That rattle on the rooftops. It's not the wind in the eaves. It's the Wild Hunt riding across the night sky, the hooves of their steeds clipping the tiles, the yowls of the wish-hounds ringing out as they run down lost souls. Listen, you damned, for the Wild Hunt comes for you next.'

'They'd spit Comitinus back out. Not worth the eating.' Solinus tossed back the last of his wine and waved his cup for more. Decima swayed across the crowded room in the House of Wishes, now festooned with mistletoe, and sloshed more wine into his goblet.

Myrrdin threw back his head and laughed, the first time Lucanus had heard him voice mirth. 'Drink deep,' he roared. 'This is Midwinter. All that was, is. And all that will be, too. Let's celebrate our good fortune—'

'We have some?' Comitinus slumped sullenly in one corner. The Wolf could see the drink had got the better of him.

'We live. That's reason enough.' With his staff, Myrrdin beat out a steady rhythm on the floor and began to sing in a tongue that Lucanus didn't recognize. The song soared up, filled with joy, until his voice rang into the corners of the room.

Lucanus nodded along as he watched the flames licking

around the ritual log that the wood-priest had dragged in from the gods knew where. Catia lay with her head in his lap, her cheeks flushed, and he brushed away stray strands of hair from her brow.

'It would be good to see the light of day,' she murmured. 'Just once.'

'We can't take any risks. It's not enough that we have enemies hiding here, ready to end our days. Now there are mobs roaming Londinium searching for you so they can toss you over the wall to the barbarians and fill their empty bellies.'

Mato waved a slice of pork in front of his eyes and winced. 'The guilt eats away at me. How can we feast when there is so much hunger?'

'You think we don't do enough for them already?' Solinus flicked his fingers towards the meat. 'Give it to me if you don't want it.'

'How much longer can we expect to survive?' Comitinus moaned. 'Another riot at the Bishopsgate this morning, folk beating each other to death over crumbs. The bodies piled so high by the eastern wall that if you stood on the top you could see the shining sea. Beggars everywhere, starving children and crying women. Londinium is a swamp of misery. And now that crazed Theodosius is hunting down anyone who doesn't bow his knee to the Christ, as if we don't have troubles enough.'

With a sigh, Bellicus heaved himself up from where he'd been nestled with Galantha, crossed the room and cuffed Comitinus around the head.

'Drink more,' he intoned as the other man rubbed his throbbing ear.

The door swung open and a blast of cold air whipped up the fire. Amarina swept in, her cloak bundled around her. She was clutching an amphora to her breast. Behind her,

Aelius and the young lad Morirex jostled to get into the warmth, each of them also hauling more wine.

'Falx has made more coin this day than in weeks.' Amarina set down the amphora and threw off her hood.

'Falx has never missed any opportunity.' Lucanus held out his goblet for more wine.

'You'd do well to learn from him,' Amarina said as she topped his cup. 'It seems to me that there's no gain in good deeds. Here you are, the great Pendragon. Leading an army that has fought to protect every man, woman and child in this town. And in one moment you've lost their trust because you won't send your woman out to the horde. You'll let them all starve to save your love. What a black-hearted cur.'

Lucanus flinched. He could hear the humour in Amarina's wry tone, but he felt her words strike home. Under the blanket that was draped across them, Catia fumbled for his hand and gave it a squeeze.

Myrrdin's song ebbed and he strode across the room to stand in front of them. Lucanus looked up at him, but his face was lost to shadow.

'You've done better than any other man could have done, Wolf. You were well chosen.' The wood-priest's words were slurred.

'Few would agree.'

Myrrdin walked back to the glow of the fire, taking a cup from Aelius as he passed. 'Enjoy this moment of peace. You've earned it, all of you. Only better times lie ahead.'

The lamp of the full moon shone down on white waves of snow sweeping across the religious precinct. At that time of the evening stillness settled on that area, close to the river, between the bath-house and the western wall.

No longer able to feel his toes, Apullius crunched through

the calf-deep drifts, following the stream of footprints. His breath clouded as he prayed he was not too late.

The black bulk of the church loomed up against the starry sky, and as he neared he could hear the drone of voices from inside. All around, the temples of the old Roman gods had started to crumble. Plaster cracked away. Self-set elders thrust out from sagging walls. Their stories were done. But the new church stood proud. The stone for the walls looked as if it'd been stolen from some of those other buildings which had once throbbed with supplicants.

Apullius heaved on the creaking door and slipped inside. He shivered; it was as bitter cold within the church as outside. Candles glowed against the whitewashed walls at the far end beyond the altar. In front of God's table, the bishop droned on, no doubt warmed by his thick robes. A gold ring glinted on his finger as he raised his right hand.

'Let us join together to celebrate the birth of our Lord on this day,' he intoned. 'Sent by God to light our way out of the darkness.'

Apullius shoved his way through the congregation. Hands clipped his head and shoulders, but he pressed on until he found Theodosius near the front of the crowd. The soldier clasped his hands to his breast, his face shining with grace. 'Is this not the greatest story of all? That our Lord will send back his only son to save us all?'

Apullius frowned. Had he not heard the wood-priest telling this very same story to Mato during their whispered discussions that reached deep in the night? But that one was not about the Christ.

The bishop lowered his hand and the congregation knelt on the cold stone floor, bowing their heads as they prayed.

Apullius wriggled in beside Theodosius and tugged on the soldier's sleeve. Theodosius elbowed him away, pressing his hands together harder and growing more annoyed as he tried to lose himself in his prayers.

'Please,' Apullius whispered. 'Lucanus sent me. He wants his woman, Catia, to be baptized into the religion of the Christ. To fall under the protection of the Lord . . . and . . . and all who follow him.' *To fall under your protection.*

'That is good,' the soldier hissed. 'But this is not the time.'

Apullius remembered the desperate look on his master's face when they discussed this plan in secret. Lucanus was afraid that once the festivities were done, the people of Londinium would rise up as one and go from house to house searching for Catia. He hadn't even discussed it with the others, or with Catia, for fear that they might find some reason not to go ahead with it. It was their one last hope, he had said.

He'd felt honoured that Lucanus had asked him and him alone. But this was harder than he thought. 'I beg of you—' he began.

Theodosius rammed the flat of his hand into his chest and he crashed on to the cold stones. 'Away,' the man snapped. Clearly irritated, he jumped to his feet and turned to search the congregation. Whatever he was looking for, he couldn't have found it, for his face hardened. When he knelt back down he glared at Apullius, even angrier than he'd been before.

'Away, I said,' he snarled.

Apullius sagged back. He'd failed Lucanus. He'd failed them all, and now they were doomed.

Corvus hummed to himself as he followed his column of men hurrying through the deserted streets. He was surprised he remembered the tune, one his mother had used to sing to him when he sat in her lap as a boy.

'There'll be plenty of time for singing later,' Pavo told him.

'Before or after I drink the tavern dry?'

'You've earned it, 'tis true. Why, a plan like this is a stroke of genius.'

'I thought so.'

'To use the cover of the midwinter feasts, when all are lost to their prayers or deep in their cups. Who would notice or care about the deaths of a few *arcani*, especially ones loathed for keeping the whole of the town hungry?'

Corvus nodded. 'You know, I might toss my sister's body over the wall anyway. Those filthy barbarians only demanded her presence. They didn't specify alive or dead.'

'And then all of Londinium will love you.'

'My genius knows no bounds.'

The bulk of the amphitheatre rose up against the night sky, and Corvus blasted a low whistle. His men slowed their step. Once he'd found the rose carved into the doorframe that Bucco the dwarf had identified, he whisked his hands left and right. The soldiers fanned out around the entrance.

'Let no one out alive,' he murmured, stepping back.

'Do you think they'll put up a fight?' Pavo whispered.

'They won't have a chance. They'll be drunk, their blades set aside. Their blood will be draining into the floor before they even realize we're there.'

'And if they raise the alarm?'

'We're soldiers of Rome. Who will the good folk of Londinium heed – mud-spattered men one step out of the ditches of the north or their cherished defenders?'

'You've thought of everything,' Pavo said with an appreciative nod.

'There's no escape for any of them.' Corvus drew his sword, and the blades of all his men sang as they were unsheathed. 'Kill them all,' he said, louder this time. The moment for subterfuge had passed.

A foot thundered against the door. Again and again, until the cracked wood burst off its hinges. The soldiers surged in.

Corvus breathed in lavender and woodsmoke and heard a man's voice booming in song deep inside the house. He felt his blood hammer into his head. He had not felt this exhilarated since he'd murdered his brother.

A half-naked woman swung open a bedroom door and shouted at the disturbance. Corvus smiled as the words died in her throat. She fell back, stabbed in the belly. The man who was with her sprawled in his own blood a moment later.

Into a larger room in the back they crashed, and the singing choked off. As his men levelled their blades around the edge of the chamber, Corvus pushed his way inside.

They were all there.

Lucanus and the woman with child. The other *arcani*, a wood-priest, some women he didn't recognize. Corvus drank in their expressions of shock, slowly shading to grim realization of the fate that awaited them.

'You?' Lucanus said.

Corvus shrugged. 'In different times, we could have been friends.'

The Wolf half pushed himself to his feet and three blades flashed towards his chest. He slumped back down, glowering.

'We were friends.'

'Words are slippery things.'

The wood-priest jabbed the tip of his staff towards him. 'What do you stand to gain?'

'From killing you all? Why, everything. Londinium deserves to eat, I think.' He waved his hand towards the remnants of their feast, and said to his men, 'See? They fill their bellies while everyone else goes hungry.'

'Take me, then,' Catia said. 'Do your deal with the barbarians.'

'Ah, if only it were so simple.' He paused, looking her up and down. How strange it was to see his own flesh and blood after imagining her for so long. There was nothing of Gaia in her. She might have been born to another entirely.

He felt nothing.

'Did you know your mother is here in Londinium?'

He watched Catia flinch and felt a wave of pleasure.

'Your mother . . . my mother.'

Her brow furrowed, the slow-witted cow. 'I have no . . .' The words trailed away.

'Gaia couldn't bear to be around you any more. She fled to Rome to escape your failings and raised children . . . a child . . . who would truly do her justice.' He could feel Pavo's eyes on his back, urging him on. How good it felt to unburden himself of all these thoughts.

The wood-priest chuckled.

'Mirth? Is this what fear for your life does to you?' said Corvus, turning towards him.

'It's always good when a rival is revealed. No more skirting each other in the shadows.'

'Oh, the skirting is long since over. In fact, there'll be no skirting for you again.' He pursed his lips in reflection. 'It's true, I have a dragon eating its own tail branded into my back. And a rightful heir awaits. All will be as it should have been before my mother was driven from Britannia.'

He sensed his men stirring around him, puzzled by the conversation. 'Kill them now,' he said. 'For Rome. For Mithras.'

He'd won.

In that moment of victory, the whirlwind struck.

Corvus jerked at sudden shouts and crashes. Bodies churned around him. Rough hands gripped his arms. Swords clattered to the floor, and through his daze he realized the room was suddenly filled with men. He glimpsed bafflement on the faces of his sister and Lucanus – not their doing. And then he spun back, dragged out of the chamber and along the corridor, a din ringing around him, faces whirling by.

In the bitter cold of the night, those rough hands flung him down. The icy street burned his cheek where his head cracked against it. Clawing his way on to his back, he looked up, trying to pierce the confusion. Soldiers swirled all around. A familiar face stared down at him.

'All the lies that left your lips.' Theodosius' features looked as frozen as the whorls of snow around him.

'My friend—' he began, but the other man's wintry glare silenced him.

'You pretended to be a follower of the Christ, even knelt and prayed with me. But all along you were a treacherous heathen. A follower of Mithras.' Theodosius' voice was as icy as his face. 'I've been watching you very closely, Corvus. I suspected you long ago, back in Rome. You're a man who understands words, and you found all the right ones to say to me, but you never seemed like a Christian. When the Lord is in the heart, a man sees these things. I've been biding my time, until I could be certain you were an unbeliever. A traitor in our midst, looking to return the empire to the worship of Mithras. But it will never be. The emperor demands we are Christians, and I will do all in my power to ensure that comes to pass. We will only be safe when your kind no longer walk among us.'

'Keep your tongue still,' Pavo whispered to Corvus.

Alas, he couldn't. 'So friendship means nothing in the face of zealotry,' he said.

'Take him away,' Theodosius commanded.

As the soldiers hauled him to his feet, Corvus saw Lucanus step out on to the street. Theodosius turned to him. 'I have my doubts about you too. But that is a matter for another time. You still have a chance for the light of God to be brought into your life. For now, know this: your woman is under our protection. We are men of Rome, and men of God, and no honourable man would throw a fellow citizen to the wolves, even to save a starving town. We will find another solution to our problems here in Londinium.'

Corvus glimpsed the relief in Lucanus' face, but that was the last thing he saw. One of the men holding him raised his sword. The hilt cracked against the side of his head.

CHAPTER THIRTY-ONE

At Still Midnight

AD *368, Londinium, 13 January*

THE SCREAMS ECHOED INTO THE DAWN QUIET. OUTSIDE THE House of Wishes, Lucanus stamped his feet and blew into his hands. Still no respite from that bitter winter. Some said it would never end, that the season had turned for good and that the gods had abandoned this world.

Of course, some had said that the previous winter too. And the one before that. Men had short memories.

The screams ebbed away and his stomach unclenched.

Bellicus clapped a hand on his shoulder. 'Catia is a fighter.'

'I've seen childbirth take women just as strong.'

His friend cracked his knuckles. 'If you listen to the wood-priest, this child will be a gift from the gods—'

'Aye. And they gave me this *magic* sword too.' Lucanus choked down the acid.

The waters had broken at the witching hour – a sign, Myrr-din had said. The child would stand at the gateway between two worlds, and show two faces, like the Romans' Janus, the holder of the key. The world of men, and the Otherworld, where the gods lived. Between Lugh, the god of the reborn sun, and the Morrigan, queen of night. Between life and death.

So Myrrdin had said.

The druid was inside now, muttering his prayers and waving his charms and burning strange herbs in the hearth, filling the room with bitter smoke. As another scream rang out, Lucanus imagined Catia lying on the birth-bed, sleeked in sweat as Amarina, Decima and Galantha bathed her head and whispered in her ear.

Three ministering women. Five people in total. He'd been told to watch out for those numbers. They were a sign the gods were active.

The Wolf closed his eyes and prayed he wouldn't lose her now that they had finally found each other.

Clattering footsteps jerked him from his thoughts and he turned to see Mato, Solinus and Comitinus striding along the street from the east. Wrapped tightly in their cloaks against the cold, they'd pulled the snouts of their pelts low over their eyes.

'Any news?' Comitinus said quickly.

'Do you think we'd be standing out here freezing our bones if there were?' Bellicus snapped. 'You and your fool questions.'

'I was only asking.'

'Go and give Catulus a bone.' Comitinus hung his head and sloped off.

'Nothing?' Lucanus asked.

Mato sighed and shook his head. 'No one in the house had seen or heard of a Gaia.'

'You ask me, that bastard was making it up,' Solinus said. 'He'd heard the stories, pretended to be Catia's brother, just so he could lay a claim to the bloodline.'

'We have to keep looking,' Lucanus said, 'for Catia's sake.'

The other men nodded, but he knew they all thought it was a waste of time. Londinium was choked with people. If someone wanted to disappear, they could do so, easily. Corvus would say nothing, however many times Lucanus questioned him in the filthy cell in the fort where he was kept prisoner. His life hung by a thread, he knew that, and he was not about to incriminate himself. Theodosius had not yet found good reason to have him executed – perhaps he still hoped his old friend would become a follower of Christ. But Theodosius was a hard man when it came to religion, and his patience for tolerating unbelievers would soon wear thin.

Another scream, cut short this time. As one, the Grim Wolves turned their heads towards the open door of the House of Wishes. Lucanus felt any warmth drain from him as the silence went on, and on.

Then, from deep in the recesses of the house, the cry of a babe.

Reeling from the rush of euphoria, Lucanus threw himself through the door and into the narrow corridor. He half heard the other Grim Wolves pounding behind him, but his thoughts were flying ahead.

In the birth-room, Catia's face was drawn and dark rings circled her eyes, but she was smiling. In that moment, he thought he might burst. Amarina looked over, and with a nod silently communicated her congratulations.

Myrrdin was whirling around the room as if dancing, his robes flying. A pink bundle was nestled in his arms. The wood-priest threw back his head and laughed, deep and long and joyously. Lucanus felt that joy infect him too. But then he looked deeper and saw how brightly the light was burning in the wood-priest's eyes, and he felt a pang of apprehension.

'A boy,' Catia croaked. 'All is well with him. The gods have given us a gift, Lucanus.'

'The gods have given all the folk of Britannia a gift,' Myrrdin roared. 'Here is the beacon that will shine for all the days to come.'

As cheers and laughter rang out, Lucanus whirled to the Grim Wolves, each man slapping him on the back.

'Another little Wolf,' Bellicus roared.

'A name, a name,' Mato chanted.

'His name has already been decided.' Myrrdin spun to a halt, and eyed each man in turn as if to tell them he would brook no argument. From the corner of his eye, Lucanus could see Catia frowning.

'He will have two names,' the druid continued. 'Both are old, and have been with us as long as the wood-priests have walked upon this green land. And it is right that it should be so, for within him days long gone are being reborn.'

'Speak,' Lucanus said.

'Weylyn is the name by which he will be known to the world. It means Son of the Wolf.'

'A good name,' Bellicus said. Lucanus tried to decide whether he should show his annoyance that the druid was trying to steal the right of naming from him, but he had to agree that Bellicus was right.

'And he will have a secret name, at present to be known only to those gathered in this room,' Myrrdin continued. 'And you must tell it to no other, for once a secret name is revealed all power is lost. Do I have your agreement?'

Lucanus watched everyone nod their assent – the wood-priest seemed to have them under his spell. When it came to him, he hesitated, holding the druid's eyes,. and then relented.

'Good,' Myrrdin said. 'His secret name is Reghan. It means "of royal blood" in the old tongue. By this name he will be known among the true followers of the path of the Dragon, and by this name his destiny will be sealed.'

A little reluctantly, Lucanus thought, the wood-priest handed the child back to Catia. She nestled him to her breast.

255

'There is hope here, brother,' Mato said, squeezing his arm. 'All the forces of evil may crash against Londinium's walls, but in Catia's arms is the beacon the wood-priest spoke of. We must never forget that.'

Tilting an amphora, Amarina splashed wine into goblets and handed them round. When she came to Lucanus, she said, 'A saviour, born in a house of whores. What stories they will tell in times to come.' Amarina's wry tone drew a bitter smile.

'And now?' Mato asked, looking round.

'Now,' Solinus said, raising his goblet for a toast, 'we only need to survive.'

CHAPTER THIRTY-TWO

The End

AD 368, Londinium, 17 March

THE RIVER WAS ON FIRE. A PALL OF BLACK SMOKE LOWERED over the Tamesis to the east, the waters shimmering with an orange glow. Flecks of ash whisked on the wind, and when he cupped his ear Lucanus could hear throat-rending screams rolling out of the inferno.

Racing along the city wall, he pushed his way through a group of watchmen to the end where the fortification met the river. Bellicus and Solinus squeezed in next to him.

Now at last he could see what was happening, and understood the anxiety in the babbling voices of those who manned the walls.

'Boats on fire. Four . . . five of them.' He shielded his eyes against the stinging ashes. The low spring sun glinted.

'They've cut off our supply lines.' Solinus gaped. He knew what this meant as well as any of them. The screams whipped up into a fever pitch of agony and he clasped his hands on his ears. 'The bastards must have tied up the men on board so they couldn't jump into the water.'

'Letting us know what's to come,' Lucanus said.

Bellicus eyed him. 'This is it, then. It's started.'

257

Lucanus watched the first blazing boat sink down in the boiling water. The barbarians must have brought the vessels upstream from where they'd taken them, and set them at anchor, just for this spectacle. That meant the horde had moved to the east, perhaps even crossed the water into the safe lands to the south.

Solinus cursed. 'We've barely made it through to spring with the food we were managing to sneak in.' He jerked a thumb over his shoulder. 'Once that lot realize even that's gone, it's all over.'

When the snows had melted, they'd readied themselves for the worst. When the trees began to bud, and the birds roosted, and there were mornings when the breath didn't cloud. Day in, day out, the watchmen gripped the parapet and searched the countryside. As each day passed, shoulders had grown tighter. They'd survived the winter, against all the odds, but when . . . when . . . when would the barbarians begin their final assault?

Every few days, messengers had ridden to the Saxon shore forts, hoping for news from Rome. No word came back. Not even any sign of the usual early ships bringing wine for the parched throats of the men on the defences. For all they knew, the Alamanni and the other tribes in Gaul and Germania could have been victorious, and the empire was crumbling everywhere.

Perhaps they really were on their own.

Lucanus glanced back across the rooftops to the north-west corner of the town. Their two armies had been waiting in the crowded fort for this day, the men under Falx's command and Lucanus' band of farmers. His own men had trained hard enough during the cold months, learning how to use sword and shield, grasping battle tactics. They would never be as good as the true army of Rome, but they would fight to the last.

Yet bellies were empty and some were too weak to lift their weapons. Others had been lost to the sickness that had swept through Londinium during the last few weeks. Theodosius and some of the other commanders had scratched out a few plans for resistance, but every suggestion seemed feeble in response to what gathered beyond the walls.

How long could they last in the face of that vast horde?

'Mato isn't back yet,' Bellicus said.

Lucanus turned his attention once again to the marshes to the east. The others fell silent. Mato had been gone for two days, using all the skills he'd learned as one of the *arcani* in the Wilds to scout as close as he could get to the horde's camp.

'Ah, he'll be good and well,' Solinus said with a flap of his hand. 'The gods look after the soft-hearted, not miserable bastards like us.'

Lucanus thought of Catia, and his son, and he pushed aside a pang of despair. Weakness would not help them now.

'They'll be coming before nightfall,' he said. 'Ready yourselves. First, I have some unfinished business.'

The door creaked open, and for a moment all Lucanus could see was an abyss.

'Misplaced but not forgotten.' The sardonic voice floated out from the dark. 'Step into my home and let us entertain each other.'

Falx leaned in and whispered, 'Keep this to yourself. If Theodosius finds out you've been visiting this unbeliever, you'll end up in the next cell.'

'You're a man of Christ now?'

'The light of the Lord burns in my heart. Come, make haste.'

The centurion thrust the lamp into Lucanus' hand and

shoved him into the cell. The fort's apple-sweet stink of horse dung and clatter of marching feet ebbed away and the door slammed shut behind him. His nose wrinkled at the reek of piss and shit, wet straw and dank walls. He shivered. It was as cold there as if he were out on the wind-blasted river.

Lucanus raised the lamp and the gloom fell away. Corvus was sitting in a corner of the cell, his legs stretched out. He looked as if he were lounging in a tavern, though his tunic was filthy, his hair greasy and bedraggled, and a new beard now edged his jawline.

'Lucanus Pendragon,' he said, forming each syllable as if he had a mouth filled with stones.

'I'd wager you didn't expect to see me again.'

'I never doubted it for a moment. We're locked together until the end, two dragons slithering around each other until one wins. And one dies.'

'We'll both die soon enough. The barbarians are massing. The final attack is coming.'

'Time to get out of Londinium, then. A boat across the river with your woman and child. Flee across the water, to Gaul, to Rome, to the hot lands.'

Lucanus stiffened. He couldn't say he hadn't fantasized about just such an escape. 'I won't abandon the people relying on me. Men answered my call for an army to defend Britannia, and put their lives in my hands.'

'That gold crown has gone to your head.' Corvus nodded, pleased with himself at the wordplay.

'You could fight alongside us. Beg your friend Theodosius for mercy.'

'Oh, Theodosius hates me for more than any professed belief, and he hates me enough for that alone. He sees me as Judas – the one from those teachings that fill his head with nonsense. The betrayer, the great devil, who seeks only to bring down the true and righteous protector of the faith.'

'I understand. You are dedicated to Mithras—'

'Gods come and go, depending on what men want from them. I'm no more wedded to following the path of Sol Invictus than I am to Jupiter or the Christ.'

The Wolf frowned. 'You'd rather die here alone?'

Corvus smiled. 'But I'm not alone.'

Lucanus ignored him. 'I'm giving you a chance to unburden yourself. You have many crimes to answer for.'

'True. I'm guilty of a great many things in my life. But the one I regret the most is underestimating my friend's stupidity.'

The Wolf set the lamp down and shadows pooled in Corvus' eyes. 'Everything you said in the House of Wishes was true?'

'About your beloved Catia, and her mother, and my mother? Oh, yes.'

'And what about the King Who Will Not Die – this prophecy of a saviour that people are talking about? This royal bloodline, chosen by the gods. Is it true?'

Corvus furrowed his brow in thought. 'Does it matter?'

'How could it not?'

He sighed. 'Surely you must have heard this a thousand times? There will come a Bear-King regardless, because men have deemed that they need one. A beacon in the night. A standard around which the poor folk can rally in their darkest hour. Something to believe in, Lucanus. Without that, what gets us all out of our beds in the morning? Gold? Lust? Perhaps, for a while. But that never quite fills the yearning, does it?' He bunched his fist and tapped it above his heart.

'And lives are sacrificed, and dreams destroyed, because

261

the wood-priests play their games of power?' Lucanus heard his voice hardening.

Corvus laughed, his eyes brightening. 'I see! You come to me for reassurance? You are a simple fellow, Lucanus. Well, in the spirit of your gracious request, I'll give you an honest answer. Look into your heart. The only truth you'll find in this world is there. What you want. What your will demands. In the end, that's all we have.'

The Wolf snatched up the lamp and hammered on the door to signal to Falx. He couldn't tell if he was annoyed with Corvus or with himself for coming there. As he stepped out into the chill morning, he heard the other man's final words floating at his back.

'We all die, Lucanus. What we do in the few short years granted us is all that counts.'

Along the walls, the sentinels stood, watching, waiting. What else could they do? The fort sang with the sound of whetstones on the edges of blades. Only the cries of babes drifted along the deserted streets. Men hunched around their hearths in silence, staring at the embers, lost to their thoughts until the call came to defend the walls. Women crooned laments, their cheeks wet with tears.

Hunger was forgotten. Want was forgotten.

The world was ending.

Lucanus leaned on the parapet, not far from the Aldgate. To his left, the vast cemetery sprawled. Ahead spread the marshes, carved up by the swords of lengthening shadow as the sun slipped down to the west. A cold wind whipped at his cloak. Winter had not yet gone.

For a while, he searched the muddy browns and mossy greens of the landscape until Bellicus lifted his arm and pointed. 'See?'

Black blurred the terrain in a wide arc from the river

round to where he lost sight of it beyond the northern wall. The line had risen from nowhere and was growing wider, a black wave, gaining height and power as it rushed towards the shore.

'Surrounded, if not for the river,' Solinus muttered.

'How many are there?' Comitinus gasped.

'Don't bother counting. It only takes one.' Solinus half drew his sword, stared at it for a moment, then let it slide back into its sheath.

Lucanus cupped his mouth and yelled 'Ho!', but the word was already leaping from the lips of soldiers along the length of the wall, a rippling exhalation, almost a prayer.

The Wolf watched Theodosius climb the steps and stride towards the wide platform at the foot of one of the crescent-shaped towers. Since his arrival, he'd grown into his role as one of the commanders in the depleted ranks. His judgement was strong and he never wavered in any of his orders once a choice had been made. If he'd still been in Rome, he could have gone far.

Theodosius boomed a command, and soldiers wrenched a sailcloth back. The ballista fell into view. Lucanus imagined the same scene unfolding on all the twenty-two platforms around the walls. He'd heard tell of these war machines, but he'd never seen any at Vercovicium. The metal weapon had two large springs that could fling a bolt even across the breadth of the Tamesis, so he'd been told in one of the many tactical meetings. But against such a vast army the supply of darts was limited, and Theodosius had overseen the constructing of skeins that would allow the ballistae to launch rubble, as they had in days long gone.

Along the walkway, soldiers trundled the one-man scorpios, smaller spring-powered war machines that could catapult a single bolt. There were several of those, but still too few to make a difference.

The black wave was sweeping towards Londinium, the line becoming a dark sea reaching out to the silvery horizon. Now Lucanus could hear a low rumble. He thought how it sounded like some great beast, slowly waking, and he realized it was the full-throated battle cries of the barbarians merging into one growing roar.

The soldier standing next to him leaned over the side and vomited.

'Where's Mato?' Bellicus muttered.

'On the south bank, hiding in the reeds, if he's got any sense,' Solinus replied.

None of them looked at each other. Lucanus knew why. Each one was afraid another might suggest the likely truth – that their friend was already dead. They couldn't entertain that thought, not now.

On the edges of the marshlands, the barbarians slowed their pace as they picked their way through the treacherous bog.

'Drown, you bastards,' Solinus growled.

On they came.

When they were close enough for Lucanus to pick pale faces out of the mass, he heard Theodosius bellow, 'Let go!'

The command rolled around the walls.

The nearest ballista cracked. The iron dart smashed into the advancing line. Bodies whirled through the air, and Lucanus imagined he felt the land shake.

Before the barbarians could recover, more bolts crashed down, splintering trees and crushing bone. Warriors staggered away, plunging into the sucking marsh. The battle-cries ebbed and in the stillness that followed only screams rang out.

Lucanus could sense their terror. To face such mighty weapons would make any man's blood run cold. Perhaps they thought this was the judgement of the gods.

But though their lines became more ragged, still they advanced.

'Look,' Comitinus cried, stabbing a finger over the ramparts.

Following his direction, Lucanus peered into the gathering gloom. At first he thought he was seeing a deer bounding through that empty land between the horde and Londinium's walls, and then, as he squinted, he realized it was a man racing as fast as his legs would carry him.

'Mato,' Bellicus breathed.

Solinus gripped the stone wall. 'Stupid bastard. Left it to the last.'

Lucanus looked past that weaving figure and saw an advance band of barbarians hunting him down. Ten of them, perhaps more. Mato stumbled, threw himself on. Ragged after two days of hiding and spying.

'He doesn't know they're at his heels,' Comitinus said. 'They'll be on him before he reaches the gate.'

'Jolt-head. What a time to stop killing,' Solinus said.

Lucanus felt the heavy gaze of his brothers on him. He nodded.

Down the steps he flung himself, having no doubt that the others were close behind. At the Aldgate, he argued with a knot of soldiers to convince them he should be let out. They thought him mad, he could tell, but the enemy was still far enough away to pose no risk to them.

At a gentle touch on his arm, he turned to see Catia, her bow across her back and her quiver hanging from her shoulder.

'We all must do what we can,' she said.

Behind her, a column of men trooped from the streets. Their heads were bowed, their step leaden, but they carried cudgels and hammers and adzes.

He felt a surge of pride at her courage. 'Always our wolf-sister,' he said. 'But Weylyn . . . ?'

'Amarina's caring for him. Until we return.' They exchanged a look, remembering how Amarina had taken Marcus as they fled south. 'I trust her,' Catia added, and that was enough.

She kissed him on the cheek. Her fingers brushed the back of his hand. So much crackled between them in those simple contacts. Without another word, she clambered up the stone steps to the wall.

The thunder of the ballistae echoed all around. Along the walls, soldiers roared their defiance, whipping up the new recruits.

'It'll only make his head swell if he sees all four of us coming out to rescue him. One should be enough,' Solinus shouted, not meeting anyone's eye.

'Two,' Comitinus insisted.

They shared a silent look and for once there was no bickering.

'We all go,' Bellicus said. 'I'll not have you two claiming all the glory.'

Lucanus turned and looked back across the darkening town. The red sun was almost gone and now fat droplets of rain were falling.

'Words, words, words,' he said, turning back. 'Never have I known men who liked the sound of their own voices more. You'd think you didn't want to go out and face a horde of barbarians.'

He raised his arm. The gate rumbled open.

Lucanus pushed past the others and bounded out.

Now there was only a sea of night stretching out from the walls. But they were *arcani* – they'd learned to see in even the darkest places. In his mind's eye, he pictured Mato weaving his erratic path towards Londinium and then he plunged along the road for a while. Where it dog-legged towards the river, he stepped off into the grasslands that ran up to the edge of the marshlands.

The rain drummed on the ground. He gritted his teeth. In that deluge, they wouldn't hear anyone approaching. But the crack of the ballistae and the thump of the darts driving into the ground cut through even this storm.

Over his head, a star blazed to earth. The earth shuddered and flames soared up.

As a copse of elders blazed, some of the dark flooded away and Lucanus saw silhouettes moving. The enemy, so close.

Another light arced down, a pitch-filled amphora with an oil-soaked wick. This one crashed into the line of barbarians. Screams cut through the din, and the Wolf watched warriors raging around as flames surged up them.

As the burning hell rained down, Lucanus saw it was driving back some of the barbarians, and slowing the advance of the others. He felt a surge of relief.

Keeping low, he glanced back and saw his brother Wolves bathed in the orange glow of one of the fires, their faces in shadow from the snouts of their pelts pulled low. He flexed his fingers and they crouched in behind him.

Weaving around the edges of the marsh-pools, they slipped into the coppice he judged to be closest to Mato's line of approach. The stark branches offered little shelter from the pounding rain, and beyond the trees dark shapes moved against the bursts of fire and the red glow reflecting off the brackish water. Soon enough they would be surrounded.

The thought had barely passed through his mind when a figure crashed into the copse, and Solinus lurched up and dragged Mato down into the mud. 'Good scouting there, brother. Did you find out if there are any barbarians?'

Mato sagged with relief, but only for a moment. 'They're close behind,' he gasped.

'Away,' Lucanus urged. 'Back the way we came.'

Making sure they weren't standing tall enough to be lit by the fires, they crept out of the coppice. A shout cracked at their backs and Lucanus whirled. Three Picts crashed out of the trees.

Lucanus heard their cries ring out to alert their comrades, and then their swords were flashing down.

Bellicus lunged, fast as a snake for a man his size. His sword rammed into the gut of one of the warriors as the Wolf hurled himself at another, slamming his shoulder into the man's stomach. They splashed into the mud, rolling as they fought until they pitched into the reeds. Forcing himself on top, Lucanus thrust the Pict's head down into the marsh water. The warrior thrashed, but the Wolf gripped tighter, holding him under until his limbs twitched and then stilled completely. When he let go, the body slipped beneath the oily surface and was gone.

When he turned back, the last Pict lay dead, but men were surging all around.

They were too late.

The five Wolves raced back into the coppice. It would not keep them hidden for long, Lucanus knew, pressing himself down into the sodden earth. The rain thumped on his back. He looked around at the others, held each man's eyes for an instant.

'I'll die with a sword in my hand,' Bellicus growled.

The Wolf nodded. He thought his old friend was going to say something more – his face seemed to grow sad – but then Bellicus' gaze flashed past him.

Lucanus rolled over, half drawing Caledfwlch, as a figure towered over him. For a moment he fought to comprehend what he was seeing, and then an exploding amphora lit up the copse. A Roman soldier looked down at him, frowning.

'We're *arcani*,' the Wolf shouted before the man could stab with his *spatha* blade.

The soldier nodded. Now Lucanus could see that the men flooding past the trees were all soldiers, their helms burnished by the orange glow of the fires.

Theodosius the Elder's reinforcements. The battle to retake Britannia had begun.

CHAPTER THIRTY-THREE

The Beginning

Sails billowed in the dawn light. Along the Tamesis, two more ships swept from the estuary towards the line of vessels already heaving at anchor along the bank at Londinium.

The storm had blown itself out and rose and silver pools gleamed beyond the eastern wall. Around them, the soldiers of the legion tramped in a show of strength that had already achieved results.

The barbarian horde had faded away into the landscape.

A retreat? Regrouping? Who knew? For now, at least, they had space to breathe, and that was enough.

Mato squatted outside the Aldgate, watching Theodosius the Elder's force take their first steps to reclaim the empire. The few ships here were only a fraction of it. Most of the fleet had moored at Rutupiae and the army was now marching north.

His heart felt light, though every bone ached from weariness. So long running and hiding to stay ahead of the rapidly advancing horde. He'd convinced himself he was a dead man, and he'd made peace with that. He'd be with his sister again, in the Summerlands. All the hardships would be over. All mysteries would be revealed. He almost yearned for it.

But his friends, his brave friends who had become more like kin, had risked their own lives to save his. And now it felt as though he was seeing all with new eyes.

Pushing himself to his feet, he walked back through the gate. Despite the early hour, the crowds milled. Laughter echoed, the first he had heard there in too long. There was still want, and need, sickness and hunger and suffering. But now there were dreams too.

Mato felt his heart swell to hear the joy throbbing through the town. He closed his eyes and pushed his head back, listening. So much despair, so much misery, for so long, and now, in the blink of an eye, this.

'Almost gets his friends killed and now resting like a babe.'

He snapped his eyes open at Solinus' sardonic voice and grinned. 'And what else did you have to do with your time?'

Solinus was gnawing on a chunk of venison, the grease dribbling down his chin. Bellicus towered over him with another handful of meat, and Comitinus was tearing knobs off a flatbread.

'Where did you get that?'

'One of those ships out there? Packed with rations. And there's more on the way,' Comitinus said through a mouthful of crumbs. 'They've already opened posts across the town, handing out food to all comers.'

Mato felt a flood of relief that the suffering was finally over. 'Where's Lucanus?'

'Theodosius the Elder has called a war council at the fort,' Bellicus said. 'Because he's got a shiny golden crown, Lucanus gets to listen to all that talk.'

'That'll teach him to do some good,' Solinus said. He

swallowed down the last of his venison and wiped his hands on his cloak.

'And what does all this mean for us?' Mato said, looking from one face to another.

'As of this moment, Londinium is once again under imperial control.' Flavius Julius Theodosius' voice was like his face, as hard as a winter field.

In the chamber in the *principia*, his commanders stood in a crescent around him. Lucanus studied them, all so different from the shabby, exhausted men who faced them across the room. There was steel in their spines, their shoulders were pushed back, eyes glittering with cold determination. Their cloaks were pristine, their armour gleaming.

The motley collection of Londinium's defenders slumped, round-shouldered, unshaven, hollow-cheeked, their clothes still sodden from the previous night's deluge. Only Theodosius the Younger stood proud before his father's gaze.

'No one will ever forget the courage you have all shown,' the older man continued. 'The names of everyone in this room will be dispatched to the emperor immediately. Rome will honour all of you.' He flexed his fingers and an aide stepped forward with an armful of charts. He set them on a trestle that had been brought in from somewhere else in the fort. 'Yes, your fight has been hard, but it is not over. Indeed, it's only just beginning. I've already sent messengers out across Britannia, to spread word to what remains of our army here. Pardons will be offered to deserters. Any other man who is able will be ordered to make their way to Londinium. This will be our base of operations now, as we drive out these barbarians. Speed will be paramount. These enemies are slow-witted. They won't realize the peril they face until it strikes them.'

'What they lack in wits they make up for in numbers,' Lucanus said. 'And cunning.'

Theodosius the Elder eyed him. 'And who are you?'

'Lucanus. I was one of the *arcani* in the north when the barbarians crossed the wall.'

'He's the one the people here crowned the Pendragon. I told you of him,' Theodosius the Younger interjected. His father nodded. 'It's an old title, from the days before Britannia was part of the empire. War-leader, so I'm told. He raised an army of farmers to fight alongside us. Without them, Londinium might never have survived.'

'*Arcani*, eh?' the commander said. 'War finds leaders in the strangest places.'

'If I learned one thing, it was not to underestimate the barbarians,' the Wolf said.

'Understood. Our scouts tell us some of the horde has already broken up into smaller war-bands. They're seeking to plunder what they can while times are good. We'll divide our troops into smaller forces to harry them. The bulk of the barbarians know they have a fight on their hands. They're retreating and trying to regroup. We will attack, again and again, ambushing and forcing them back. And as we advance across Britannia, we'll restore the chief towns. The light of civilization will return, have no fear of that.'

'The people here are broken, and starving,' Lucanus said.

'They will not be left to fend for themselves. I've already sent word to the emperor, requesting that Civilis be sent here to become the new *vicarius*. With Dulcitus offering military support, we'll organize relief. Any booty or cattle we retake will be returned to their owners, if they still live. Captives will be released.'

Lucanus nodded approvingly. Perhaps the age of darkness that Myrrdin had prophesied would never come to pass. Perhaps there would be no need for a king who would not die.

Perhaps he would finally be free.

'The fight will be hard, but have no doubt – these

invaders will be defeated,' Theodosius the Elder continued. 'Valentinian will never cede any part of the empire. And then our priority will be to ensure this disaster can never happen again.'

'It's clear now that our commanders here were too weak, too inexperienced,' his son said.

Theodosius the Elder nodded. 'Many mistakes were made. Military command should not have been divided across three provinces. When the barbarians rose against us, lines of communication collapsed. All that must change. Watchtowers must be built along all borders and along the coasts to guard against any future incursion. For now, we are not in a position of strength, but our strategy is clear. Once the rest of our troops have marched from Rutupiae, we will begin the fight immediately. Victory will be ours.'

Theodosius the Elder was confident, that much was clear. But Lucanus had heard enough about the commander's abilities, even in Vercovicium, to have no doubt that if anyone could repel this invasion, it would be he.

'God is on our side,' the commander continued. 'We were advised not to risk crossing the channel from Gaul. Winter still gripped, and the storms and the sea would destroy us if we dared attempt it, I was told. But I prayed, long and hard, and the Lord answered. Fair winds and sun shepherded us here. Now, as we begin this great campaign, we must ask for God's help again. Pray with me, so that we might smite our enemies with the full force of his will.'

As Theodosius the Elder droned a solemn prayer and the other men there bowed their heads, Lucanus found his thoughts flying out across the fort to Catia, and Weylyn, and to a hope of a new life. When the council broke up, the commander beckoned to him.

'We recognize all you have done here,' he said, 'but now that work is over. Send your men back to their homes and families, with the emperor's thanks. Leave this battle to sea-soned military men.' He forced a smile that lacked any warmth. 'We will no doubt have need for *arcani*, certainly men of your experience. Once we've established a proper command here in Londinium, come back. We will find work for you.'

He turned away before Lucanus could respond and joined his son. The two men walked away in conversation. The Wolf could see no warmth between them either.

Outside, in the chill spring morning, he breathed deeply and tried to imagine a life without responsibility. He could not go back to being an *arcani*, he knew that. He'd been changed, as Myrrdin had always said. But what could he do now? Be a farmer? That thought filled him with dread, as he knew it did the other Grim Wolves.

A shout interrupted his thoughts, and Falx hurried over, looking around. 'That's the end of making a little coin,' he grumbled. 'It's all rules and nose to the grindstone with this lot, I can tell.'

'You'll find a way to turn a profit, I have no doubt.'

The centurion grinned, but it faded quickly as he remembered why he had come over. 'You'll be interested in this, I know. Follow me.'

Lucanus trudged behind the centurion across the fort.

'No idea when it happened,' Falx said. 'Probably when we were fighting for our lives.' He swung out a hand, directing Lucanus' attention.

A soldier's body lay on the rain-slick stones, a dark pool surrounding it.

Corvus' cell door hung open.

'Is it true? You're no longer the Pendragon?'

Lucanus was surprised to hear the strain of anguish in Apullius' voice. 'This is a good thing. My part in this war is over.'

'No . . . you have a destiny . . . and a responsibility.' The lad's voice hardened and Lucanus was shocked by what he heard there: was it betrayal?

'Before we leave I'll find you a place here . . . a way to make a living . . .'

'How can I return to that life when there's work still to do?' Apullius snapped. 'I want to be at your side, learning what you know. I want to be a Grim Wolf.'

Lucanus raised his eyes to the towering walls of the amphitheatre. 'The decision has already been taken. Everyone in my army already knows. They've honoured their kin, and now they can return to their homes. They deserve that, for the sacrifices they made, and the risks they took in answering my call.'

Apullius had been almost like a son to him, but there was no point arguing further, he could see that. Yet as he turned away, he stiffened. Catia was racing towards him from the direction of the House of Wishes. Her face was twisted with worry, the braids of her blonde hair flying behind her as she ran.

He grabbed her shoulders. 'What's wrong?'

'It's Weylyn . . . he's been taken.'

'Amarina?'

Blood drained from Catia's face, and in that moment he knew she could see every threat that might lie ahead. 'Myrrdin.'

The Ludgate slowly ground open.

'If the wood-priest has harmed the child, I'll kill him.' Lucanus heard his voice as if it were rising from a deep well.

Ahead of him, the burned-out remnants of the *vicus* gave way to the bridge over the Fleet, then to the lush green landscape reaching out to the west. It would be filled with endless peril. The barbarians were still roaming in their war-bands, and it was too early for Theodosius the Elder's reinforcements to begin hounding them.

'Weylyn can't survive long.' Catia's face was as cold as her voice. She was keeping all her feelings crushed down inside her. 'The babe still needs me to feed.'

Lucanus slipped an arm around her shoulders.

'Myrrdin has fought hard to make sure this bloodline thrives,' Mato said. 'I can't believe he would put it at risk.'

Once Catia had raised the alarm, they'd begun searching the streets around the House of Wishes. Amarina had raged, but Lucanus could smell her guilt. Like a thief in the night, the druid had snatched the child when her back had been turned. None of the women had seen or heard anything. Nor had anyone in the vicinity.

Lucanus knew Myrrdin would never have risked hiding out in Londinium, not when the Wolves would have torn the town apart trying to find him. And so they'd come here, and the watchmen on the gate had told them about a hooded man carrying a bundle under one arm, who had stridden out towards the west.

'He won't have much of a head start,' Bellicus growled. 'And when we find him, I'll set Catulus to work on his bollocks.'

'You know those wood-priests – they can't be trusted.' Solinus scowled, screwing up the scar that quartered his face. 'He'll find allies with the barbarian bastards, if it serves his purpose.'

'His trail should be easy to follow,' Lucanus said.

'If you think you're going alone into a land crawling with barbarians waiting to cut out your heart, you're a jolt-head,' Solinus said.

'Lest you forget, you did that in the Wilds north of the wall and it almost killed you.' Bellicus whistled and Catulus bounded up.

Lucanus began to protest, but Catia gripped his arm. 'Hush,' she said. 'We'll need as many blades . . . and bows . . . as we can muster to fight off the Picts and the Scoti.'

The Wolf felt sickened at drawing Catia into more danger, but he knew there was no point in arguing with her. 'Six of us will make little difference—'

'More than six.'

Aelius stood in front of about thirty warriors from the Pendragon's old army, all men who'd fought long and hard for him on the retreat to Londinium. Apullius was with them, his face burning with defiance, and Morirex at his side.

'We will not rest until we bring Weylyn back to you, sister,' Aelius vowed. His eyes glittered like ice. 'Don't try to deter us, Lucanus.'

'Listen to him, Wolf. He's a good general,' said Vindex, one of the more battle-hardened men there, with a face like a crag and piercing blue eyes. 'Besides, you've ruined us for our old life. We can't go back to our homes. Our wives won't recognize us any more. They'll wonder why we wake with bad dreams. Why we can't rest when we should be watching our children play. You've ruined us, Lucanus, and now we're your responsibility.'

Lucanus winced. Though the words were delivered lightly, he knew there was a hard truth behind them. Seeing death at first hand changed everyone, a truth he had come to understand more and more.

Bellicus clapped his hands together. 'Well, they're not many, but they'll do. It'll be a brave . . . or stupid . . . band of barbarians who'll risk attacking us.'

Lucanus felt his heart swell. 'You honour me, all of you. We'll bring Weylyn back . . .'

'And then?' Apullius pressed.

'And then . . . we shall see.'

The remnants of his army churned and Amarina burst out of the ranks, her green eyes flashing. Decima and Galantha were struggling to keep up.

Amarina nodded to Catia. 'We have an agreement, do we not?'

'We do,' Catia said.

Lucanus looked from one woman to the other. 'As long as I've known you, you've made sure you turn events to your advantage. Why put yourself in danger?'

Amarina shrugged. 'You've surrounded yourself with cocks, Lucanus, and if there's one thing I know, it's that cocks always lead men into trouble. You need wiser heads around you. And colder hearts.' She smiled, and behind the hardness he saw some honesty.

He sensed there was more to it, but she spun back to the other two women. For a while they bowed their heads together in conversation. Tears pricked Decima's and Galantha's eyes and they gripped Amarina's arms, clearly trying to dissuade her. Finally Amarina beckoned over Bellicus and Mato and they moved quickly to the two other women.

'They're saying their goodbyes,' Amarina said when she came over. 'The House of Wishes is now Decima and Galantha's to do with as they will. They've earned it.'

'But only for a day or two, until we return?'

Amarina pulled up the hood of her emerald cloak until shadows engulfed her face. 'Once you leave Londinium's walls, there's no easy way back.'

PART THREE

Avalon

To have died once is enough.

Virgil

CHAPTER THIRTY-FOUR

Into the West

AD 368, 30 March

THE BLACK FIELD HEAVED LIKE THE SEA IN A STORM. RAVENS and crows stabbed down with their beaks, their shrieks ringing up to the blue heavens. Lucanus' ears throbbed from the din. As he took three steps down from the ridge, the birds sensed him and took flight as one, the rolling thunder of their wings booming across the landscape.

His nostrils flared at the stink of rot on the breeze. A carrion feast littered the churned-up mud and blood and shit of the battlefield. Barbarians in the main, by the look of it, but enough Roman soldiers to suggest the horde had put up a fierce resistance.

'No end to the slaughter,' Bellicus grunted.

'And likely not for a good time yet. No one doubted the tribes would refuse to return to their homes with only a whimper.'

Lucanus watched Mato bound down the slope to the edge of the carnage. He'd seen something.

A soldier slumped against a pile of bodies. His head lolled back and he squinted at the sound of voices. Mato knelt beside the man and leaned in, no doubt offering compassion. When he joined them, Lucanus could see the man's face was streaked with dried blood and mud, and his tunic was soaked through too.

Mato looked up and nodded. 'He'll live.'

The Wolf squatted. 'Your brothers left you?'

'They'll be back soon enough. Collect the wounded, and the dead.' The soldier hacked and spat. 'This was a big warband. One of the barbarian kings. Not going to end the chase when there's a prize like that.'

Lucanus raised his skin and sluiced water into the man's mouth. He licked his dry lips and nodded his thanks.

'The fighting goes well?'

'We're carving them up like a roasted ox. They don't want to give up the land they've taken. But they're no match for the general's strategy. They're breaking up into smaller warbands for speed, but they're being pushed back everywhere.'

'When you marched here, did you see anyone else?'

'Other than the barbarians, you mean?' He shook his head. 'Any farmers round here, they're wise enough to keep their heads down.'

Lucanus nodded. He expected no other answer.

Amarina had been right to say this quest would be harder than any of them had hoped. Once they'd crossed the Fleet, barely at the beginning of their search, Solinus and Comitinus returned from their scouting with dark expressions. They'd been tracking the mark made by Myrrdin's staff in the rain-soaked earth. On the edge of a copse, they'd found the fresh prints of many other feet.

Someone had been waiting for the wood-priest. The Lord of the Greenwood and the forest folk? Lucanus expected that was so, though he couldn't be sure. But Myrrdin's footprints joined that mass and together they'd set off towards the north-west.

Had this been a plan long in the making, and the druid

deceiving them all the while? Could a wet nurse have been waiting with the forest folk to keep the child alive? The questions came thick and fast. But his heart had been hardened by the murder of Marcus. A bloody reckoning awaited the wood-priest if Lucanus discovered he had betrayed them.

Now he and his brother Grim Wolves were *arcani* once again, the secret people, hiding, scouting, living off the country as they led their war-band in pursuit. But their prey moved faster than Myrrdin could ever have done on his own. And there were times when the trail disappeared completely, as if the wood-priest and his allies were taunting them. Of course, Myrrdin knew Lucanus would not let this rest. He must also know that there would be a confrontation, sooner or later.

Was the druid leading them all on to their deaths?

The charm of ash and holly, bone and feather, swung in the low branches.

'Witch country,' Comitinus breathed, looking up at it.

'Don't be getting all frit again.' Solinus peered into the dark depths of the forest stretching out ahead and Lucanus could see from their faces that both men were troubled.

Bellicus tugged on his beard in thought. 'Two war-bands skirted this area. It would have been easier to escape by ploughing straight on through. What does that tell you?'

'The trail goes in here.' Lucanus pointed to the grass crushed by multiple feet.

Since they'd left the battlefield, they'd continued heading west for three days. The land was rife with roaming bands of barbarians, and they'd left the west road and detoured through lush valleys and along the edges of woods to avoid being seen. From a distance, they spied on the burned-out buildings of the town of Cunetio and then continued in the direction of Verlucio. The countryside was all fertile farmland. But this forest looked as if it had not been touched.

Ancient oaks with trunks as wide as four men clasping hands. Towering ash and walls of holly. So choked with growth there was barely room for two men to walk abreast.

Lucanus peered into the depths, but even with the meagre spring growth it was like dusk beneath the branches.

'Another charm here,' Mato called from further along the treeline.

'And another,' Aelius shouted.

'Someone is telling us to keep out,' Bellicus said.

'The trail goes in here,' Lucanus repeated, his voice hardening.

Amarina caught his arm. 'Take care. Three witch-charms . . .' Her voice trailed away and a shadow flickered across her face.

She was a woman of secrets, was Amarina, and she was trying to find words that would not give anything away.

'Some believe there are places in this world that are close to the Otherworld,' she continued. 'The gods . . . and other things . . . daemons, perhaps . . . can walk there with ease. And unwise men may fall through and never be seen again. So some say.'

'You believe that?'

Her lips shifted slightly into the ghost of a wry smile. 'I believe in treading with care.'

Lucanus stared ahead, hesitating for only a moment. Then he pushed on into the forest.

Under the canopy, only the crunch of feet on dry twigs rang out. An odd mood hung in the air, although he wasn't sure if it was simply the echo of Amarina's words. All the chatter had died away.

On they pressed, clawing their way past moss-coated trees, winding through rocky outcroppings topped with fern. Every now and then, he felt his skin turn to gooseflesh as a voice whispered his name, away among the ash trees. Or perhaps it was merely the wind soughing through the branches.

The Grim Wolves took it in turns to scout ahead. Not long after Mato had set off along the trail, Lucanus jerked at the blast of a whistle. He threw himself past a dense bank of holly and found his friend kneeling by a marker stone beside the track. Though it was weathered with age, Lucanus could make out a carving, a face made of leaves. He'd seen this before, in the great forest beyond the wall.

'An old way,' Mato breathed, 'from the days before Rome came.'

'We shouldn't be here,' Comitinus murmured.

On they marched, deeper into the darkness.

Lucanus glimpsed movement away among the trees, little more than shadows. But whatever was keeping pace with them left them well alone.

In that place, night came down fast. The camp sprang up among the trees on either side of the narrow trail. Men nestled in the arms of twisted roots as thick as their waist. No song rang out to keep the approaching dark at bay; no talk. Hands were held towards the flickering flames, but the fires seemed to give off less heat than usual, so they huddled closer, their breath steaming in the growing chill.

Lucanus pulled Catia close under the thick fur of his wolfskin. He felt the knots in his shoulders loosen from the mere bloom of her warmth against his skin. Across the forest, a full moon punched shafts of white light through the thickening canopy. All was still.

'We'll find Weylyn, and return to the north, and live the life we were meant to have,' he breathed. It was almost a prayer, repeated time and again. Catia nestled closer.

As he looked out across the silhouettes of his dozing men, he felt sure he could see blue flames flickering along the trail deeper into the forest, a sapphire river pulling him on to whatever future the Fates held for him.

Perhaps it was only a trick of the lambent moon-rays and that landscape of pure light and deep shadow. But his time in Goibniu's Smithy had changed him in ways he was still discovering, and sometimes he saw more than other men, he was certain.

He felt the steady rise and fall of Catia's chest and the heaviness of her head on his shoulder and knew she'd fallen asleep. For a while, he watched and listened, wondering why there was no hoot of owl nor flit of bat. And then he drifted in and out of sleep himself, until he found it impossible to tell what were dreams and what was waking.

At some point, he felt convinced he was being watched again. Figures seemed to be gathered just beyond that flickering light, an otherworldly court with a king with antlers and a queen whose skin glowed like gold. When he forced his eyes wide, they melted away. Just twisted branch and waving frond remained.

And then, much later, in that temple-like silence, he thought he heard a dim snuffling. Some great beast circled them, pausing every now and then to snort and scrape its hooves upon the forest floor. The dark bulk of it, horns rising and falling: not a beast at all but a near-forgotten god. Cernunnos, who stands in the forest and howls.

This was the world Myrrdin was drawing him into, a place as ancient and implacable and terrifying as the deepest heart of the forest or the heaving ocean under the stars.

Lucanus slipped into a dreamless sleep.

At dawn, the interlopers pulled themselves to their feet and trudged on. Lucanus sensed an odd mood, as if everyone there had experienced something troubling during the long night. But no one spoke of it.

Through that day and another they marched, the forest

becoming thicker, the path narrower. But then, with the sun slipping down the western sky, the Wolf saw Mato's nostrils flare. He breathed in and tasted the hint of woodsmoke on the breeze. A hundred strides further and he raised his hand to halt the advance. Now he could hear what sounded like a heartbeat.

Boom, boom, boom.

The pulse of the very earth itself.

'Drums,' Bellicus muttered.

For a long moment, no one moved.

Lucanus felt a tug on his arm. Apullius was pointing away into the trees. He followed the lad's direction and saw figures moving towards that steady thrum, in ones and twos, heads bowed as if they were being summoned. Silent, like ghosts.

'The forest folk,' Apullius breathed. 'How long have they been there?'

'They pay no heed to us.' Bellicus watched them, his eyes narrowing.

'Where are they going?' Apullius pressed.

Lucanus strode on ahead, matching the pace of those distant supplicants, drawing ever closer to the sound of the drums.

'The child will be here soon.' Hecate mopped the sweat from Gaia's brow.

'This is not the auspicious occasion I'd hoped for,' Corvus said as he paced around them. His mother was lying on the roughly constructed bier their horse had dragged since they'd been forced to abandon the wagon at the edge of the great forest. He studied her flushed face, the feverish dart of her eyes. This was not a good place to give birth, but what choice did they have? 'Still, these are the trials one must face on the road to greatness,' he continued, showing a brave face.

Hecate smiled. If she had any worries, his words seemed to calm them. She'd follow him through the gates of hell, that one.

'This seed planted so long ago will soon bear fruit,' Pavo whispered in his ear.

Corvus stepped away from the two women so they wouldn't be overheard. 'Aye. If this plan doesn't fall apart, like all the others.'

'You can blame your old friend Theodosius for that. I always said he couldn't be trusted.'

'True. True. But what could be done? He served a purpose for long enough, a man of influence like that.' Corvus eyed Hecate and the tenderness of her touch as she cared for Gaia. 'She'll make our case for us when the time comes, and she'll do it out of love. That will give it the ring of truth. A wood-priest would have been better, true, but the witches still carry some weight among these pagans.'

'First you need to find someone who'll hear your case.'

'Once my sister's child is dead, that should be easy enough.' Corvus watched Severus stooping among the trees as he collected the plants that Hecate had demanded to help with whatever spells and charms she planned to brew to keep his mother safe during the birth. 'They'll be in need of a saviour or else all that they've planned across the long years will come to nothing. And lo, we'll have one, ripe and ready. An heir to the Dragon, the blood that will bring forth the King Who Will Not Die, so the story they like to tell themselves will still stand. How could they say no?'

Corvus leaned back against an oak and folded his arms. The journey from Londinium had been exhausting. If only the wood-priest hadn't fled with the child before he'd managed to reach the house of whores. Then it had been a matter of stealing a wagon and setting off in pursuit. Mithras or whatever gods there were must have been smiling on them, for they'd managed to avoid the war-bands until they reached this forest.

At some point they'd lost the trail, and found themselves adrift among the trees. But the distant rumble of the drums told him they were not too far from their prey.

'Ho!'

Corvus looked round at the cry and saw Bucco scampering around an ash tree. His ruined face was flushed and he wheezed as he bounded up.

'Faith, oh faith, it keeps us warm,' the dwarf gasped.

Corvus raised an eyebrow. He didn't trust their little helper, not at all. But if there was one thing he knew about men like Bucco, even little men, it was that the lure of power and gold quickly brought them into line. 'Your excitement tells me your search has not been a vain one.'

The dwarf pointed a trembling hand back the way he had come. 'The drums, yes, the drums, you were right. We will find the wood-priest there, no doubt, no doubt. But there is more.' He flapped his hands on his knees and sucked in a deep breath.

'I think I might die from anticipation.'

'More, yes. Drawing through the forest. Old friends. I spied them.'

'Old friends?'

'Lucanus, the Head of the Dragon, and your sister. And more. Fighting men.'

Corvus glanced at Pavo, unable to contain his smile. 'And suddenly our work becomes so much easier.'

'Not too much of a surprise. Did you expect them to give up their child without a fight?' his friend said.

'There are too many of them,' Bucco continued. 'What do we do?'

Corvus raised one finger. 'Stealth works wonders where others turn to brute force. We watch, and we bide our time.

Sooner or later we'll see an opening. A knife in the night. Tiptoe away. Our work is done.'

'In the dark, you won't have to look at your sister's face,' Pavo said.

Corvus winced at that.

As soon as Hecate had finished her ministrations, Corvus and Severus strapped the bier to the horse. When they were so close that the boom of the drums filled the air, Corvus held up his hand. 'We'll make camp here,' he said. 'Far enough away not to fall prey to prying eyes. Close enough to creep in under cover of night and do our work.'

Space to think, that was what he needed. Hecate's chirping had become an irritation, and with Bucco's constant babbling it was all he could do to keep half a thought in his head. He clambered over twining roots and found a lightning-blasted oak where he could sit and ruminate.

'Close now, Pavo,' he murmured. 'We can't allow anything else to go wrong.'

'It's in the lap of the gods,' his friend replied.

Corvus watched the sun as it crept through the branches. When it reddened, he looked away. All he could see was his brother's blood smeared on the floor of his mother's house in Rome moments after he had hacked off Ruga's right hand. He hadn't thought of it once since that moment. Why now?

He felt it squirming away inside him, like a maggot, and he realized he couldn't bear to sit in silence any more. He needed that chirping and babbling.

Pushing himself to his feet, he turned. He saw the movement first, the swarm of bodies, and then the sword-hilt crunched against his forehead.

When his wits returned, he found himself looking up at a circle of faces: barbarians, with wild hair and beards. He sensed more of them moving in the trees just beyond.

A huge figure loomed over him. The head was wrapped in filthy rags and Corvus realized this must be the Pictish king Arrist.

He grunted something in that guttural barbarian tongue, Corvus didn't know what. But then a much smaller, rat-faced man thrust his way forward. 'I am Logen of the Fire's Heart. I can understand your tongue.'

'I'm only a poor deserter. No threat to you,' Corvus said. This Logen's eyes were like nail-heads. He wouldn't find much sympathy there.

Another barbarian with a mane of black hair pushed forward. Logen turned and grunted a few incomprehensible words, no doubt relaying what Corvus had said. He heard the name Erca and remembered the Wolf talking about his sister's captor. Erca and the king spat a few more words between them. No love lost there, Corvus thought.

Arrist snarled something and hands wrenched Corvus to his feet. Back through the woods he was dragged, to the camp, where more barbarians held the others.

'They came out of nowhere,' Gaia cried. 'Oh, my son, save us.'

Arrist and Erca took turns to snarl what sounded like orders as Logen listened. When they fell silent the rat-faced man nodded and stepped back to Corvus.

'I know nothing about the army's strategy, if that's what you think,' Corvus said quickly. 'They'd crucify me in an instant if they caught me.'

Logen translated, and Corvus crashed to the ground once more at the hands of his captors.

Another man stepped forward. He was naked to the waist, his braided hair clacking with beads. Tattoos blackened the left side of his face. He crouched so he could look Corvus in the eye.

'I'm Motius, of the Carrion Crows. *Arcani*,' he said.

One of the traitors, Corvus thought, and was wise enough not to say it.

'Your army routed us,' Motius continued. 'They would like nothing more than to have the head of the great king here, and so they keep coming, and coming. We've been cut off from the rest of our own army. But we heard of a place hereabouts where the Roman army dare not venture. Where we could rest for a while and build up our forces so we can strike back. You know of it? Is that why you're here, so deep in the woods?'

'Of course,' Corvus said. 'We can lead you to it. No need to draw blood.'

'He lies,' Logen spat. 'He knows nothing.'

Before Corvus could react, the rat-faced man had translated for Arrist and Erca, and the king snarled a response.

Logen looked around the circle of barbarians. 'Kill them all. Except her.' He stabbed a finger towards Hecate. 'She's a witch, and we don't want that kind as enemies.'

'Wait, wait,' Bucco cried, his voice cracking. 'Spare our lives and I'll tell you how to gain all the power you need to keep hold of Britannia.'

When Logen had relayed his words to the barbarians Arrist flexed his fingers and two Scoti warriors let the dwarf go free. He tumbled forward, rolled and jumped to his feet in front of the king. Everyone laughed.

'Loose your tongue,' Logen said.

'I have a story to tell of a child with royal blood, and a King Who Will Not Die,' Bucco began.

Corvus saw Erca's eyes narrow, and wondered why.

'Take the child,' the dwarf continued. 'Kill all the others you find, yes, yes. They will only try to stand in your way. But take the child and power will be yours.'

CHAPTER THIRTY-FIVE

What was Old is New Again

UNDER A CRIMSON SKY, THE WILD-HAIRED FOREST FOLK whirled in ecstatic dance.

Lucanus stepped from the treeline and gaped. The silhouette of a giant hung against the incarnadine sun edging the horizon. At its feet, a bonfire roared on the edge of a vast circle of standing stones.

The Wolf blinked, trying to make sense of the monstrosity he was seeing. When it didn't move, he realized it was a statue of some kind, constructed from interlaced branches. Dark holes stared down at him from a face of leaf and ivy and fern.

He felt judged.

Through the gaps in the wood, he could see squirming inside. Bleating occasionally punctured the space between the drumbeats. Sheep? A wheel hung from the left hand, and the right clutched what appeared to be a thunderbolt ready to smash any who did not bow their head to this primeval power.

The Wolf sensed his men gradually emerging from the forest, then becoming rooted in awe. He drew Caledfwlch and that seemed to stir them from their daze.

Blades levelled.

From the numbers gathered there, and those still streaming in, they would have a fight on their hands, if that was what it came to. Lucanus swept his sword from side to side as he searched the milling crowd. Heads swivelled towards him, eyes gleaming red in the firelight. None seemed to care about the intruders.

'Myrrdin!' he yelled.

The pounding drums swallowed his cry, yet the crowd parted and the wood-priest stepped forward, Weylyn nestled in the crook of his arm. Myrrdin smiled, and Lucanus felt his anger whip up into a frenzy. He lunged forward.

As one, the forest folk surged into a barrier between him and his prey. Now they did care, and the scowls blackening their faces promised a rending limb from limb. Through the churning mass, he could still see the wood-priest smiling. Myrrdin said something he couldn't hear, and the defenders stepped back. This time the druid held out the babe, and Catia darted forward to take him, tears glimmering in her eyes.

Myrrdin whisked up one hand, and the forest folk spun back into their reel, leaving him standing alone with one hand on his staff.

'I should cut you down now,' Lucanus snarled.

'Why? For saving the child's life?'

The Wolf wavered. 'You stole him.'

The wood-priest pointed the end of his staff at Lucanus. 'Our enemy escaped his cell. He was coming to murder him.'

The Wolf lunged again. This time Bellicus clapped a hand on his shoulder to hold him back. 'Hear him out.'

Myrrdin continued: 'If that's so, you might ask, why did I need to bring him all the way here, to this place that is older than time? I have two answers to that question, Wolf. The first is that Avalon in the west is the only safe place for all of us, but you would never have come if I'd not lured you out.

You still cling on to a dream of returning to your old life in the north. And that choice would have seen you, and Catia, and the child all slain. You needed to come, all of you. The circle. Only then would the boy be kept safe.'

Lucanus narrowed his eyes. 'The second?'

'This . . . all this . . .' Myrrdin swept an arm out to indicate the bonfire, the stone circle, the giant figure, the rapturous crowd, 'is for your child.'

Lucanus stiffened, and he sensed Catia doing the same beside him.

'This is an old rite, Wolf. As old as these stones. Fire and sacrifice and carnal pleasures. Lo, a new king has been born, named and baptized before the eyes of the gods. And once this ritual is done, the word will travel to all parts of this land, and beyond. The bloodline is restored. The Dragon has risen. And soon the Bear-King will be with us.'

Lucanus' eyes widened as he looked around the festival. 'For Weylyn?'

'For the new king.'

The Wolf pulled the gold crown out from under his cloak and thrust it towards the druid. 'Take it. We don't want any more of this.'

'The title of Pendragon is yours – it cannot be taken away once it has been given. And it will be handed down to your son, and your son's son. The House of Pendragon has risen once again, and it will be known by the sign of the dragon eating its own tail. The never-ending circle.'

'Those are the games you play, wood-priest. Not me.'

'You've brought hope, Wolf. As we watched you, and listened to the counsel of those who know you best, we learned the qualities that had made you leader of the Grim Wolves. But you've grown far beyond our wildest imaginings. Head of the Dragon, yes. And Heart of Britannia too. Don't turn your back on that.'

Lucanus flinched. 'Who counselled you?'

Before he received a response, he felt Catia brush his arm. 'Listen to what he has to say,' she whispered.

'The wood-priest can't be trusted. How many times has he shown us that?'

'Weylyn is well. Our family has been reunited. This is a new dawn.' Catia heaved in a deep sigh. 'The hardships we've both endured in our lives will only mean something if we embrace this destiny.'

'Myrrdin would say anything to see his plan bear fruit.'

She smiled, sadly, he thought. 'Our lives are over, Lucanus.'

'No. I won't allow it.'

'Our lives were over a long time ago. Stolen from us, yes, but gone. All that we have left is to try to shine a beacon in the darkness that's coming. That is our only salvation. We write the ending to our story. Not the wood-priests. We do it. And that ending will be a good and honourable one, not for us, but for those who follow us.'

The Wolf felt his stomach knot. He looked at Catia and no longer saw the wolf-sister who ran with him in the Wilds, but someone more powerful: untamed, almost regal. He felt a swell of pride, and then a stab of grief.

All he could do was nod his agreement.

A moment later he was easing his way through the throng behind the wood-priest. He paused by one of the stones and rested the palm of his hand against it. The megalith was barely shaped, unlike the stones of the great circle they had paused in on the journey from the north.

'This is a *dracontium*, Wolf. A home of dragons. One path snakes in, another snakes out, and the circle at the core is endless,' Myrrdin said. 'Larger than the Heartstones that you saw in the summer. Greater. Here, there is always magic in the air. Here, the Otherworld is only a whisper away.'

The forest folk spun past him, lost to the dance, eyes fixed on inner horizons. The women tore at their clothes in their bliss, and in the shadows beyond the firelight he could see bodies heaving in congress.

'This is what Britannia was like before the Romans came,' the wood-priest said. 'Madness and joy.'

Lucanus craned his neck up, but the eerie face of the wicker man was now lost to the gathering gloom. 'Jupiter?'

'Aye, that's what you Romans called him. Taranis is his true name. God of the sky and the storms. He is one of three. Esus, lord of the forest, and Toutatis, bringer of magic and fortune, are the others. Three, Wolf, the number of power. Heaven, earth, and the waters. The beginning, the middle, and the end.' He paused, then added, 'Body, soul, spirit. They will watch over your son and ensure he achieves his destiny, and Taranis will strike down any who dare stand in his way.'

'Witches come in threes.'

'Aye. They do.' Myrrdin pulled something from the leather pouch at his waist. When he opened his hand, Lucanus saw the shrivelled remains of the sacred mushrooms on his palm. 'Eat these. You'll see with new eyes; see what everyone else sees.'

Lucanus remembered the wonders and terrors of his night in Goibniu's Smithy and hesitated. But then he popped the dried remnants in his mouth, chewed and swallowed, grimacing at the iron taste.

'I only want my son to be safe, Myrrdin. I'll kill anyone who wants to harm him.'

'I only want the same, Wolf. Believe that.'

Lucanus looked back up the soaring frame of the wicker man. No, he couldn't trust the wood-priest. He was sick of being led by the nose.

When he looked back, Myrrdin was gone.

*

Mato felt a warmth flood through him when he glimpsed Catia nestling Weylyn to her breast, protected by Bellicus, Comitinus and Solinus. There was a time on the trek west when he had feared he would never see such a sight again. But then he found his gaze inexorably drawn from the mother and child to the monstrous figure that towered over them all. The very air around him seemed to sing, as it did before a summer storm, and the hairs on his neck prickled erect.

'Stay close together,' Aelius commanded. His eyes narrowed as he searched faces for any sign of threat.

'This rite is all that matters to the forest folk,' Amarina said. 'They feel the eyes of their gods upon them. We are as nothing beside that.'

Aelius studied her for a moment, then nodded and sheathed his sword. Vindex barked an order and the rest of the men followed his lead.

Mato slipped beside Aelius as they pushed through the throng into the centre of the stone circle. 'No smiles? No relief?'

Aelius scowled. 'The worry has passed, true. Weylyn is safe. Now I only feel anger. Give me a moment with the wood-priest and I'll teach him a lesson for putting Catia through such anguish.'

'And now?'

'I'll stay by her side, of course. She'll need all of us for the rest of her days, as will Weylyn. The threats will never go away. Find yourself a saviour and half the land want to follow him and the other half want to kill him or take him for their own.' He sighed, but there was a wry smile flickering on his lips. For all the danger, he had come alive with this new purpose.

Mato glanced past him. Figures had separated from the wild dance and were coming their way. As the orange light of the bonfire washed over them, he grunted. They were young women, grubby from the dirt of their country living, their dresses little more than filthy rags, but they were smiling and holding out wooden bowls.

His nostrils wrinkled at a musty smell when one was thrust in front of him. A dark, oily liquid sloshed within.

'They want us to drink it,' Apullius said, turning his nose up.

'An offering of friendship?' Mato eyed the woman in front of him. Her pupils were wide and black. 'Part of this ritual?'

As he reached to take the bowl, fingers closed around his wrist. Amarina leaned in and sniffed the drink before flicking her hand to wave the women away. 'A brew made from the sacred mushrooms,' she said. 'You would drift away to the Otherworld until the sun rises. My advice: keep your wits about you. Catia may yet need your aid.'

'Wise counsel,' Aelius said. 'You know more than you would have folk believe.'

'Always.' Amarina fixed an eye on him. 'And never forget it.'

Mato felt a hand tugging at his wolf pelt and looked down at Morirex. He'd expected the Mouse to be unsettled by the strange circumstances in which they'd found themselves, but the lad seemed to be growing as brave as his brother. 'What is this?' he said now. 'I've never seen the like.'

'This world was always hidden, little one. A secret place, side by side with the one we knew. When Britannia first became part of the empire all those years ago, some followed the rule of Rome and made their life along the great roads. But others, the pagans, the country folk, disappeared into the deep forests and the high peaks and the moors. They took their old gods with them.' He looked around at the festival and then felt his eyes once more drawn to that soaring, judging figure. 'The old ways never truly vanished – they merely slept. And now that Rome's grip has weakened, they have woken once more.'

For a long while, they trailed around the standing stones. The mad rite never ebbed, the crowd of dancers whipping themselves into even greater frenzies. The drums pounded louder still. Logs were thrown on to the bonfire and geysers of sparks soared up almost to the giant's head. Wild-eyed men and women tore at chunks of venison, their mouths slathered with grease. On the edge of the light, rows of couples fornicated like beasts in the field.

'I can't see Lucanus any more,' Apullius said with a note of unease.

'Lucanus can look after himself,' Amarina replied.

Aelius was scanning the trees that surrounded the vast stone circle, always the general, never at rest. 'I want to know what's out there, if anything.' He turned to Apullius and the Mouse. 'Nobody will pay you any attention. Scout the edges of this place, as we taught you.'

Apullius grinned and nodded his head, and the two lads raced off towards the forest.

Hands grabbed Lucanus, spun him away, and for a while he felt his head spin as fast. Sparks and stars and flames, and the vast black canopy of night as the sun crashed below the horizon. A creamy moon, full and bright. And always the terrible judgement of the wicker man hanging over him.

Finally he dragged himself away from the torrent of bodies. In the centre of the circle, he felt oddly calmed. Blood pulsed in his head, and a sapphire light limned the stones; the druid's mushrooms no doubt working their magic.

The throb of the drums fell away, and there was only the thump of his heart.

Beyond the megaliths, the flood of bodies still surged. Lucanus glimpsed some of his men. Bewilderment was giving way to acceptance. Chunks of hot beef were thrust into their hands before they were pulled away into that wild dance. He searched for Catia and his son, for the Grim Wolves, and then Amarina, but they were nowhere to be seen.

He was alone, the watcher on the boundary between worlds.

The voice of the ancient past whispered around him. He thought he heard his name and he lurched away, towards the winding path that led out of the circle, the head of the dragon that Myrrdin had described.

As he stood with one hand on another cool stone looking out into the night, he glimpsed a sentinel standing in a pool of moonlight beyond the festivities. Hands resting on a longsword, a helmet on its head. He thought that it almost seemed to glow with an emerald hue. Was this the Lord of the Greenwood, who had helped his friends so many times now?

The figure was watching him, he was sure of it.

Lucanus pushed out of the circle. By the time he'd taken a few steps the figure had drifted away into the dark. Yet his neck was prickling and he felt himself gripped by an irresistible desire to know more about this warrior. Man or daemon, or a messenger from the gods, as the wood-priest insisted?

Stumbling away from the tumult, Lucanus crashed back into the woods.

'What do you want of me?' he called.

For what seemed like an age, he lurched among the trees until he felt the grip of panic. He was lost.

'Be at peace.' The rumbling voice echoed around him.

The hammering of his heart stilled and he gripped the rough bark of an oak to steady himself. 'Where are you?'

'I am with you at all times, even if you do not see me.'

Lucanus searched the shadows, punctured here and there by circles of moonlight. Nothing moved. 'What are you?'

For a long moment, he thought the Lord of the Greenwood was not going to answer, but then the disembodied voice drifted back. 'A friend.'

'Of this world? Or the Otherworld?'

'Heed my words,' the voice continued, ignoring him. 'Heed them, for you will hear no better advice. Find the strength to go on, though the road ahead is hard. Become what you can be. Protect your woman, and your child. Then be the protector of all those who will suffer in this coming age of darkness. This is the work we have been given, and it is good work.'

'Did Myrrdin send you to tell me that?'

'The wood-priest has no power over me. I do as I will.'

Lucanus rested his hand on Caledfwlch. It seemed to sing under his skin as if it were alive. 'And where is my reward?' he called, but the night swallowed his words and no response came back.

Hearing a whoosh and a roar, he whirled. An orange glow was wavering through the trees. Angry that he had been left alone again, he strode towards it.

Flames surged up the torso of the wicker man. Fleeing shadows twisted the features into a grotesque display of fury. Lucanus could hear the howling of the beasts in its belly. Unwitting sacrifices to a greater destiny.

Around the circle, the dance had ended. The drums stilled, so that only the crackling of the inferno raged in the night. The supplicants filed into the heart of the circle, and then stood, silent, looking up at the burning figure.

After a moment, a voice rang out. 'A new king is born!' It was Myrrdin addressing his congregation, but after that most of his words were snapped away by the breeze or lost beneath the roaring.

Lucanus watched, entranced.

In the ruddy light the shadows swooped outside the

circle, and in their distorted movement he thought he could see figures drawn to witness this event. Cernunnos, who stands in the forest and howls. A flapping of black wings that signalled the Morrigan's dark presence. And a blade of light, Lugh, the undying son, the king and saviour. All here to usher in a new age dawning.

After a while, the giant creaked and cracked and crashed to the earth in a cascade of sparks. But as the roaring of the conflagration began to ebb, Lucanus stiffened at another sound rising up in the night. A rolling thunder rushing through the forest.

Two familiar figures raced from the trees, yelling.

Apullius? he thought. *And Morirex?*

And then the rolling thunder broke into a tumult of battle-cries.

The forest erupted. An army of barbarians surged towards the crowd gathered around the burning man, scores of them, swords glinting red in the firelight.

Lucanus reeled.

Shrieks of wild panic swept up in the cacophony as the forest folk churned in the circle. Some fell, crushed underfoot.

Clawing his way through the trees, Lucanus gaped at the carnage. His thoughts raced, to Catia, and Weylyn, to the Grim Wolves and his men. And then he glimpsed the bound head of Arrist at the head of the charge, his blade swung high, and he felt his blood run cold.

And on the barbarians roared, hacking down all who stood in their way.

CHAPTER THIRTY-SIX

Blood Will Have Blood

'THIS WAY!'

Catia felt Amarina's fingers grip her left wrist. On every side, the forest folk surged, faces ragged with terror. Buffeted back and forth, she feared they would be torn apart, but Amarina held tight.

'Weylyn!' she cried above the din. Myrrdin had been holding the child during the baptismal rite. Now she couldn't see him anywhere in the confusion.

'Come, or stay here and die!' The other woman's eyes flashed.

Dragged through the flood in Amarina's wake, Catia searched for the druid and the babe; for Lucanus. Her heart thundered with desperation. But there was only the chaos of smashing bodies and ringing screams.

Somehow she stumbled out of the crowd. Amarina didn't relent. Away from the circle and the fires, into the trees, and on still she flew. Clambering up an incline, her breath burning in her chest. She sensed others fleeing around her.

At the top of a bracken-crested ridge, Catia yanked her hand free, and spun back. The terrible sounds of slaughter tore through the night.

'We have to find the others.'

'Yes, why not? With that bow and your arrows, you can probably bring down three or four before they run you through.' Amarina's words dripped with acid. She seemed to sense Catia's dismay, for her voice softened and she added, 'The wood-priest will look after your child better than you ever could. Weylyn is too great a prize to be easily given up.'

Though it sickened her, Catia had to admit that the other woman was right. She slumped to the base of an ash tree and stared at the battle. The forest folk churned in the centre of the stone circle as the barbarians herded them with a pincer movement. Some, though, slipped through the lines and scrambled away into the night and the trees. She prayed Lucanus and Weylyn were among them.

'We can't wait here,' Amarina urged. She pointed to where a band of Scoti and Pict warriors were breaking away from the rest of the army to pursue those fleeing into the forest.

Heaving herself up the tree trunk, Catia lurched away. Her legs felt like lead. Every now and then she'd glance back, tricking herself into believing she might see those she sought. But there was only ever the fire flickering through the branches, and beyond it the endless dark. As she made plans in her head to circle round and search for Lucanus and Weylyn, she looked up and saw Amarina stiffen. 'What is it?' she hissed.

Her companion snarled a curse and raced away.

Catia pounded after her. Whatever Amarina had seen, it possessed her. She scrambled over rocks and fallen trees, leapt a brook, and clawed her way up a steep slope without pausing for breath.

As they reached the top, Catia caught sight of a campfire flickering among the trees. 'Wait,' she cautioned, fearing they'd stumbled on the barbarian camp. But Amarina raced on headlong, her emerald cloak flapping behind her.

Throwing herself into the circle of firelight, she slammed

into someone, knocking them to the ground. The figure, a child it seemed, bucked and heaved beneath her. Catia glimpsed the flash of Amarina's knife and she cried out.

The blade hovered. Amarina's lips pulled back from her teeth.

Catia looked from her to her captive, and gasped.

'Please,' Bucco whined. 'I am a new man. Half a man. Humbled and broken.'

Amarina plunged the knife down, but Catia caught her wrist in mid-strike.

'Leave me,' Amarina spat. 'This filthy cur left me for dead.'

'This isn't the time for vengeance.'

'There's no better time.'

'Do not harm me!' the dwarf squealed. 'I did bad things. Many bad things. But I have learned. There is only good in my heart now. Let me show you.'

Catia felt Amarina stop straining against her grip. 'Your days are numbered,' Amarina growled, standing. 'Make the most of them.' She slammed her foot into the dwarf's ribs. He howled again, rolling over on the ground.

'Why are you here?' Catia demanded.

'He came with us.' Beyond the fire, a woman hovered, young, with an earthy appeal. Her words were thick with an accent Catia didn't recognize.

'Who are you?'

'Her name is Hecate,' Amarina said.

'One of the sisters?'

'A sister with no sisters. They were stolen from me,' Hecate said.

Catia glanced at Amarina, wondering how she knew this stranger. But the new arrival was beckoning furiously, her face drawn. 'I need your help,' she begged. 'Leave the dwarf. He knows he is only safe with us. Come, quickly.'

308

'Run as far as your little legs will take you. I'll find you when it is time,' Amarina snarled at Bucco.

In the trees beyond the fire, a pregnant woman writhed on a bier. Her hair was matted with sweat, her face twisted in agony. Catia could see she was much older than all of them, at the limit of her child-bearing days.

'The babe is coming now,' Hecate urged. 'Help me deliver it.'

The woman howled. Catia dropped beside her, and Hecate too.

'Who is she?' Catia asked. 'And why is she . . . why are you . . . here?'

'We came with Corvus.' Bucco was wringing his hands behind them. 'He is a terrible master. He beat me. The barbarians have him now—'

Amarina glared at him and he fell silent.

'Her name is Gaia,' Hecate told them. 'He is Corvus' . . . mother.'

'Gaia?'

Catia felt a rush of ice water. Her hands hung above the woman's belly.

Corvus' mother . . . her mother . . .

Gaia, who had abandoned her as a babe, stolen all that her family had and left her father broken by despair. She stared down at this woman who had haunted her thoughts for so long. She could see the resemblance now: the blonde hair, the straight nose, the high cheekbones. How long had she yearned for her mother to drift back into their home? How long had she burned with anger for what she had done? At times, those battling emotions had threatened to tear her apart.

Now, though, as she looked into that face glistening with sweat, she realized she felt nothing. Not hatred, not desire for revenge, and no, not even love. It might as well have been a stranger lying there.

Hecate leaned in and whispered, 'This child . . . it is Corvus' child.'

Catia felt a twist of revulsion and stared, disbelieving. The other woman only nodded slowly, her eyes filled with disgust.

'Why . . . ?' Catia began.

'To keep the bloodline as pure as possible, of course,' Amarina said. Catia stiffened, understanding. Amarina tugged her back and leaned in to whisper. 'This child will be a rival to Weylyn, you know that.'

'What do you expect me to do? Let the babe die?'

Amarina glanced down at the moaning woman and took longer to reply than Catia would have liked.

'You're right,' she said with a shrug. 'But you should know that a good deed here could damn your own son in days yet to come, or his son's son. This line will never back away from trying to seize power.'

'I can't do any other,' Catia said.

She dropped to her knees beside her mother. The child's head was cresting.

For a while, they told Gaia to push when the time was right, and soothed her with honeyed words in the moments when the urge receded. Catia sank into the moment, her mind locked on to that emerging babe, every fibre of her afire with the knowledge that this was the time of greatest danger, for mother and child. All sense of the outside world fell away, the distant screams dimming and then fading beneath the throb of blood in her head, and all yearning for Lucanus and Weylyn too. The world became small, and smaller still, until there was only that innocent child.

'Born in a battle,' Hecate mumbled as she hunched over a bubbling pot on the fire, and Catia jerked from her reverie. Once again the terrible howls were ringing out in the distance, didn't seem to be lessening.

310

After a moment, Hecate brought over a cloth soaked in the unguent from the pot and smeared it on Gaia's lips. The woman scowled and spat, but then Catia saw her eyes clear.

'Who are you?' she croaked.

'Your daughter.' Catia heard her voice, as flat and emotionless as it had ever been.

'My daughter?' Gaia choked back a snort of laughter. 'I have no daughter. Only a beautiful son.' Her head lolled back, but Catia could tell her mother was scrutinizing her through slit eyes.

'The child's coming,' Amarina said. 'Push down, mother.'

'Oh, joy! Oh, wonder!' Bucco cried, stamping his feet and clapping his hands.

Gripped by the pain of the birth, Gaia hissed breath between clenched teeth. But Catia could still feel those chill eyes on her.

'If only I'd succeeded in killing you as a babe.' Though Gaia's voice was little more than a croak, it burned with hatred.

'You're delirious . . .'

'I'd wrung the necks of daughters before you, but you had the gods on your side.' Gaia's lips pulled back from her teeth.

Catia felt her stomach knot, and this time tears burned. Blinking them away, she focused instead on the child, fumbling alongside Amarina to help it into the world.

'A boy,' Amarina announced, as she took the babe into her arms. Hecate whisked a cloth around it. 'Take my knife,' Amarina continued, and as Catia glared at her she added, 'and cut the cord. My hands are full.'

As Catia searched in the other woman's cloak for her blade, a snarl rang out and Gaia lunged.

Her mother's hands clenched around her neck.

Catia cried out as the filthy nails bit into her skin. The blood thundered in her head and her vision swam with

311

Gaia's twisted face. That mouth, torn wide in a silent shriek, eyes like ice.

Dimly she could hear Amarina and Hecate shouting. She grasped her mother's wrists, trying to tear the hands free from her neck, but they felt like iron. So much loathing. Gaia had found in it an inhuman strength, even after the strain of birth.

A blade rammed into Gaia's forearm. She yowled and flinched back.

Amarina snatched back her knife and loomed over the mewling woman. 'Stay down,' she said, 'or the next one will end your days.'

Catia rubbed away the burning sensation in her neck and looked down at her mother still spitting and snarling like a wildcat.

'This is what good deeds earn you,' Amarina said to her. 'Do you still hold by your word?' She held out her knife.

Catia shook her head. 'Let her take her child and go. I am not my mother.'

Amarina shrugged again. 'Your mother is fortunate she has a daughter like you, and not one like me.'

Hecate pressed the newborn into the mother's arms. Gaia continued to glower, her new prize little more than a distraction. Taking the knife, Hecate scoured the blade in the fire and cut the cord before tying off the ends.

Catia slumped back, exhausted. In that moment of clarity, she looked round and said, 'The dwarf has gone.'

'What he lacks in stature he makes up for in cunning. He knows I was ready to carve my name in his forehead.' Amarina stood up and stretched.

Grasping a moment to recover her equilibrium, Catia wandered to the edge of the camp and listened to the sounds of battle. She felt powerless, and that angered her. All she could do was place her faith in Lucanus and trust that he would keep Weylyn safe and they would soon be reunited.

When she turned back, Hecate was leaning in to Amarina's ear. For a while, the two women seemed caught in an intense debate, about what she had no idea. But then Amarina held up her hand to signal the discussion was over, and walked over to Catia.

'What's wrong?'

'Like anyone with even half a wit, she's questioning the folly of trying to survive out here while dragging a mother and babe along behind. Especially a mother like your mother.' Amarina wagged a finger. 'And before the rest of your own wits depart, don't think about suggesting we take them with us.'

'I wasn't.'

Amarina wandered off, but Catia frowned, not sure she was hearing the whole story.

'Here, here. See!'

Catia whirled as Bucco bounded in to the camp. This time he was not alone.

Her cry of alarm had barely left her lips when four Scoti warriors stalked into the camp. Their swords were drawn.

Two other men strode up behind them and Catia felt a pang of shock to see that the first was Erca. She had never expected to look upon him again. As she locked eyes with him in silent communication, she felt surprised by the warm emotions bubbling up in her. How could that be?

Before she could answer the question, the second man stepped forward. It was Arrist, towering above the others, his eyes like cold fire in the rags that bound his face. He loomed over Catia, one hand reaching out for her chin to raise her head. 'We have been searching for you, and your child.'

Then Weylyn had not been taken. Catia felt a surge of joy. Now she could endure anything.

Arrist spun her round and yanked at the sleeve of her dress, exposing her shoulder blade. She felt the calloused tip of his finger trace the distorted scar where she had been branded with the mark of the dragon eating its own tail.

'You were right, dwarf. You have earned your freedom.'

Bucco danced around with glee, until he saw Amarina glaring at him. 'I should have killed you while I had the chance,' she hissed. The dwarf scampered away into the night.

Rough hands yanked Catia back and the Pictish king studied her face. 'Until we find your child, you will do well enough. One chance to hold on to what we have won here in Britannia. Once word has spread that this royal bloodline is now allied with us, the tribes will rally and the people of Britannia will see us as the rightful rulers, not the Roman bastards.'

Catia heard the acid in his voice. So Theodosius the Elder's strategy must have already destroyed the dreams of the invading horde. 'You know I will never ally with you.' She held his gaze.

'You will. When you have been tamed.' His heavy hand fell on her shoulder. Slowly he slid it down her arm.

'You are nothing. I've endured worse in my life.'

Arrist lashed out.

Catia reeled from the blow and tasted blood in her mouth. Wiping it away with the back of her hand, she narrowed her eyes, still defiant.

Yet as she looked past the king's shoulder, she was gripped by the sight of Erca. His face was impassive, but his eyes seemed to burn with rage. He batted a hand towards the men who had accompanied them, and they nodded and slipped away into the night.

Arrist leaned over her, fingers flexing. 'We win because we tolerate no opposition,' he said.

The tip of the sword burst from his belly.

Catia gasped.

As the king staggered back, Erca wrenched his sword free, allowing the fatally wounded man to sag to his knees. The blade swung. Once, twice, three times, Erca hacked at Arrist's neck. When the head came free, he kicked it down the slope.

Catia could only gape as he dragged the body by the back of the tunic, then flung it after the head, out of sight. When Erca turned back, she could see that his left hand was trembling, with rage perhaps, or realization of the enormity of the crime he'd committed.

But when his gaze settled on her, she saw it was calm. 'We are done here in Britannia,' he said. 'Our loathing of Rome was too great, our dreams too big. Arrist was a fool. There's no gain in fighting a battle we can only lose. We'll take what booty we can and return to the north, and tell stories to our children and our children's children of the great victories we had here in the south. We've shown Rome that we are not to be swatted away. That is enough, for now.'

Erca paused as if waiting for her to ask to come with him. When she only held his eyes, signalling her thanks, he nodded and walked away into the night.

CHAPTER THIRTY-SEVEN

After the Battle, Silence

LUCANUS WRENCHED HIS BLADE OUT OF THE QUIVERING body of the Pict and whirled. Madness still reigned in the stone circle. In the orange glow of the fire, the forest folk raced back and forth, herded by the circling barbarians. But now he could see the plan in action.

The invading warriors had cut down some of the pagans to create terror, but they were not trying to slaughter them all. They were searching, for Catia, or Weylyn, or both. That could be the only answer.

His own search now even more urgent, he thrust his way through the roiling mass towards the pillar of flame rising from the remains of the burning man. It was the last place he had seen the druid.

His face seared as he lurched into the wave of heat from the conflagration. In the glare of the inferno, he glimpsed Myrrdin clutching Weylyn to his chest.

For once the wood-priest seemed relieved to see him. 'We'll need more than that sword,' he shouted above the roaring of the fire. 'Where are your men?'

'Lost in this madness.'

'Then we must make do.' The druid threw himself away from the fire towards the edge of the circle. 'The barbarians

316

would not have ventured into this sacred place unless they were driven to capture a prize worthy of risking the wrath of the gods,' he said as they ran.

'They're here for Weylyn, I know that. And I'll die before I let them get near him.'

'That is your purpose, Pendragon.'

Lucanus looked past the frantic forest folk. There had been a change in tactics, but he didn't know why. Bands of the barbarians were racing away from the circle. Had the retreat been sounded? He couldn't believe that was the case, not when they were so close to gaining what they wanted.

But a gap had opened up beyond the circle. 'There,' he yelled, pointing. They plunged towards it.

As they passed the line of megaliths, Lucanus felt a surge of relief. Open grassland lay ahead, running up to the tree-line. Yet as they ran, he sensed movement in the dark. Grey shapes moving closer.

'No,' Myrrdin gasped.

Weylyn began to bawl as if he could sense the fear in the man holding him. His cry rang out as clear as a tolling bell.

Out of the night, the ghosts danced. Mud-caked skin glowed white in the moonlight, turning ruddy as the Atta-cotti neared the blazing wicker man.

A warrior loped towards them, twirling a stone in a sling. Lucanus cried out, too late. The stone flew, straight and true.

Grey light crept through the trees. The dark fled before it. For a moment there was silence: no screams, no battle cries, only an abiding quiet.

Amarina rested against an elm, listening for the crunch of foot on dry branch, any sign that the barbarians were coming for them.

Catia eased beside her, searching among the trees. 'If they were looking for us, we'd hear them.'

'Never hurts to take care.'

'It was Arrist who wanted me. Erca knew of my value, but he didn't care. And the other barbarians . . .' Catia shrugged. 'They do as they're told without a thought to call their own.'

Amarina eyed the other woman. She'd seen the look Catia and the Scoti leader had shared. For now, she saw no gain in mentioning it. Perhaps it would be of use in some time yet to come, when she might need to bargain.

Since Erca had left them by the campfire, they'd eased through the dark on a meandering route, crawling under hawthorns or into pools of bracken whenever bands of barbarians tramped past. They seemed to be answering intermittent blasts from a horn. Perhaps it was Erca, calling them home. For a while now, they'd not seen a soul.

Neither of them had spoken about the fate which may have claimed those who had travelled with them into the west.

Catia slumped against a trunk. Her face was smudged with dirt and wood-green. Beneath it, Amarina thought she could see worry etched there. Catia would never give voice to it. She had steel in her, Amarina had to give her that.

'You don't regret your decision to leave your mother behind?'

'I would have liked to have heard her explain herself for the misery she wreaked on our family, and for Aelius to have seen the woman she truly was. But she would only have slowed us down, she and the child.' Catia paused, no doubt thinking of her own babe. 'My only regret is that we left Hecate behind.'

Amarina thought back to Gaia's parting words to her daughter. 'May you be raped and cut into pieces on your journey into the west,' she had said, making sure to hold her gaze so she could see Catia's reaction. She was a vile beast and no mistake.

'Hecate has her duty. If her husband lives, he'll make his

way back to her, and his mother, and the babe who is both son and brother.' Catia heard the scorn in her voice. '*My* only regret is that I didn't gut that dwarf.'

Amarina took a step forward and a figure dropped from the branches above her head. Crying out in shock, she whipped out her knife.

'Wait! It's only me!' The boy Morirex cowered in front of her.

'Never do that again, you little—'

'Amarina,' Catia cautioned. She ran forward and knelt before the Mouse, resting her hands on his shoulders. 'Are the others alive?'

Morirex nodded. 'They sent me ahead to scout for you. Aelius and Apullius were organizing the search for everyone else.'

Catia hugged him. 'Take us to them. Make haste now.'

In the dawning light they hurried through the trees. Morirex was following a trail of some kind, Amarina thought. The little ditch-rat was learning his scouting skills well from the Grim Wolves. Eventually the boy padded around the edge of a bog and leapt over the lip of a hollow. At the foot, the others waited.

Catia pushed past her and skidded down the slope. 'Where's Lucanus? Where's Weylyn?' She eased her way through the war-band. 'Aelius?'

As if in answer, her brother rose up on the other side of the hollow with Apullius. He ran down and hugged his sister. 'Thank the gods you're still alive.'

'Tell me,' Catia breathed.

Aelius sucked in a draught of air and steeled himself. 'Lucanus and Weylyn . . . and Myrrdin . . . are nowhere to be found.'

Choking back her feelings, Catia pushed her chin up. 'You found no remains?'

Aelius shook his head.

'Then they could still be alive.'

'The Grim Wolves haven't given up the search. They'll return to us with any news before noon.' He beckoned Apullius to join them. 'Tell them what you saw, lad.'

'I was scouting the edge of the stone circle, as Aelius commanded,' the boy responded. 'Only a few barbarians remained, searching the bodies of the fallen for anything they could loot. After a while, they drifted away in the direction of the horn blasts.' Amarina saw Apullius' eyes widen as a troubling memory returned. 'I felt eyes upon my back. When I looked, I saw someone standing at the treeline . . . white . . . white in the shadows.' He swallowed. 'One of the Attacotti. He started to come towards me. I ran.'

Apullius bowed his head. Aelius laid his good hand on the boy's shoulder. 'There's no shame in that. Any man would have done the same.'

'If the Attacotti have taken Lucanus and my son, we have to begin our search for them now,' Catia declared.

She looked around at the men there and saw that many eyes were cast down.

'Lucanus would have given his life for you.' Her voice was wintry.

'The Attacotti are the best scouts. They don't leave a trail worth following,' someone muttered.

Vindex pushed his way forward, his granite face softening a little. 'You're right: we're afraid. Those barbarian bastards, aye, we'll fight any number of them. But the Attacotti—'

'You'll do as I command.' Aelius stepped in front of the bigger man, craning his neck up. His eyes were coals.

'Heed his words.' Amarina levelled an icy gaze at the reluctant war-band. 'Catia is right. You owe Lucanus everything. Is this how you thank him?' She moved to stand beside the brother and sister.

After a moment, Vindex nodded his agreement. The other men followed.

'We ask nothing of you that we are not prepared to do ourselves,' Catia said. 'We three will lead the way into any battle. If there is no trail, we'll keep searching until we find my husband and son. And if they are dead, we won't rest until every one of the Attacotti joins them.'

CHAPTER THIRTY-EIGHT

The Attacotti

BIRDSONG. THE WARMTH OF THE SPRING SUN. LUCANUS' eyelids fluttered open to a vision of budding leaves and patches of blue sky. Tenderly, he brushed the side of his head where the missile had struck him, then levered himself up on his elbows.

He was in a camp in a clearing in the woods. Around thirty of the Attacotti were wandering around. His stomach knotted, but that was the least of his worries.

Weylyn lay on the ground, not far from a fire where a pot bubbled. One of the Attacotti squatted nearby, scraping a whetstone along the edge of a curved knife.

'Leave him,' Lucanus croaked, 'or I'll kill you.'

The white-crusted warrior didn't look up. Instead, hands grabbed Lucanus, wrenched his arms back and bound his wrists behind him. He thrashed in rage and despair, then released an inchoate howl.

A pair of sandalled feet walked towards him and he looked up at Myrrdin. 'Tell them . . . take me. Not Weylyn.'

The wood-priest squatted beside him, steadying himself on his staff. 'Don't anger them,' he murmured. 'We're fortunate that we're still alive.'

'I don't care about myself. Only Weylyn—'

'You have no power here. They won't listen to you, or to me.'

Lucanus screwed his eyes shut, fighting that rising desperation. He heard Myrrdin slump beside him, and Weylyn begin to cry.

'I've seen nothing like them before. Some say their home is in the west, or in the far north. No one knows for sure. Their tongue is unlike any other I've heard. In our schools, we're taught what little we've learned about them down the years. They have their own gods, their own rites. They don't trade with others, and, until now, have kept to themselves. What they truly want . . . who can tell?'

Opening his eyes, Lucanus forced himself to look away from his vulnerable child, only for his skin to crawl.

Bodies slumped on spikes around the perimeter of the camp: soldiers, armour splattered with blood; forest folk; even some that were clearly Picts, the Attacotti's so-called allies. Some bore the unmistakable marks of the knives of these Eaters of the Dead. All of them hung like deer for the feast.

Sickened, he imagined his own remains there, and Myrrdin's, and his son's. Such thoughts would drive him mad, he realized. Myrrdin seemed to sense his torment, for he said in a calm voice, 'Watch them.'

Lucanus turned his attention back to the Attacotti. As they wandered about the camp, they seemed lost to a dream. Their thin frames drifted around the fire, eyes focused on an inner horizon. They were lithe, fluid, almost gentle in their movements. If he had not seen their ferocity on the battlefield, or their relentlessness in the hunt, he would not have thought them capable of violence, let alone feasting on their victims.

Every now and then they would stop and close their eyes, push back their heads, and stretch out their arms as if praising the sun.

323

'They look as if they're worshipping at a temple,' he said.

'This world is their temple. The sun and the sky, the trees and the streams and the rocks. I've heard your friend Mato say the same.'

'The Attacotti are not like the Grim Wolves.' Yet Lucanus found himself gripped by these strange people. In a way, he understood them. Never was he more at peace than when he was alone in the Wilds. 'You said once that the Attacotti believe that the body of a man is nothing but clay. That the essence . . . the soul . . . is all.'

'That is also one of the secret teachings of the wood-priests. The soul is eternal. When a man dies, it moves on, and is reborn.'

The sun hung at its highest point. Together, the Attacotti lowered themselves to the ground and sat cross-legged. One of them bowed his head and made a strange keening sound. The noise was picked up by another, but lower, and by another, higher, until all of them were joined in the music. Lucanus blinked, surprised. The myriad seemingly discordant voices came together as one, in a song that lilted and soared, almost beautiful in its subtlety. He thought of a hawk soaring above a sun-drenched moor, a waterfall cascading down to a lonely pool.

When he glanced over at Myrrdin, he saw that the wood-priest had turned his face to the sun, his own eyes closed. 'My father's hand, letting go,' he murmured. 'A kiss on my cheek from my mother.' A tear trickled and Lucanus looked away, uncomfortable. 'We were taught many things at our school,' the druid continued. 'The turn of the stars, the language of birds, the magic that hides in plant and tree. But there is one lesson that gives shape to who I am: that all under the heavens are joined, as one. That the weave of everything is only visible across the span of the years. A man's life matters little. My life matters not at all. Only the part we play in shaping days yet to come. We sacrifice, and our souls move on, and through that we keep the light burning in the darkest of nights.'

Lucanus sank into his words, into the song of the Attacotti. He could feel the ground shifting under his feet. He was changing, though he was not sure what he was becoming.

The song ended without warning. The Attacotti returned to their business as if nothing had happened.

Whick-whick-whick. The thrum of the knife being sharpened, and Weylyn, who had been silent during the singing, bawling out his hunger once more.

Lucanus jerked back into the moment, and his despair rose again.

After a while, the warrior laid the whetstone aside. Lucanus tried to push himself to his feet, but another of the Attacotti knocked him back down. Only when the warrior walked past Weylyn to one of the soldiers' bodies hanging in the larder did he sag back with temporary relief. Others gathered, kneeling and bowing their heads. What seemed to be a murmured prayer rolled out in their strange, lilting tongue.

'They honour the dead,' Myrrdin said. 'Their feast is not simply to fill their bellies, if at all. They choose only the worthy. And they believe they take on their fallen foe's powers by consuming his flesh.'

Sickened, Lucanus looked away when the knives were raised.

'They will come for us next,' he said. 'Fresh meat.'

'Then let us hope our meat will choke them.'

Once their feast was done, the Attacotti grabbed sticks of charcoal stacked near the fire and smudged the black around their eyes and along their cheekbones. Their skull-like faces grew starker.

'What are they doing?' he asked.

'Preparing.'

'For what?'

Before he received an answer, the warrior who had been sharpening his knife plucked Weylyn from the ground.

Lucanus jolted, crying out.

The warrior stared once with those black, unblinking eyes, and then he bounded away from the camp into the trees. Weylyn's squalling trailed behind.

Lucanus jumped up. Hands grabbed him, but instead of throwing him back down their owner freed his bonds and thrust him forward with a blow between the shoulder blades. He ran.

As branches tore at his face, he thought, *They want to hunt. For the sport.*

He raced on, following his son's cry, until finally he crashed out of the trees. Half blinded by the glare of the spring sun, he squinted down a long slope and across a lush landscape of grassland and fields, dotted with copses.

His son's wailing rang out nearby. Searching, he almost stumbled over Weylyn in a nest of flattened grass, with Lucanus' sword and sheath lying beside him. The Wolf snatched up Caledfwlch and whirled, but the Attacotti warrior was nowhere to be seen.

Myrrdin lurched up behind him.

'What is this game?' Lucanus snarled. He picked Weylyn up and crooked him in his left arm, never once taking his eyes off the treeline. When Myrrdin didn't reply, he shook his head, baffled. 'Tell me – what does this mean?'

The wood-priest frowned, then the ghost of a smile flickered on his lips. Whatever notion had crossed his mind, Lucanus could see he was not prepared to reveal it.

'Be thankful,' the druid said. 'We are free, and we live. That's all that counts.'

The tramp of feet echoed through the still afternoon.

Lucanus peered down the slope to where a column of men was marching along a track. His men. His heart swelled when he saw Catia, Aelius and Amarina at the front, Bellicus, Mato and the rest behind them. A voice in his head whispered that this was too much of a coincidence, but he pushed aside all thought of the Attacotti and threw himself down the slope towards what he hoped were better times.

CHAPTER THIRTY-NINE

The Conversation

THE STAR SHOT ACROSS THE VELVET SKY. CORVUS WATCHED its passage through the high branches.

'A portent, Pavo. The heavens are observing us.' He looked at his friend, who was leaning against a lightning-shattered oak cleaning his nails with his knife.

Pavo cocked an eyebrow. 'And why do the gods care about the ways of men? Especially a filthy soldier like you.'

'I'd wager they like their sport as much as anyone, and what entertainment we will have here. A performance for the ages. Blood and thunder. Witches and curses and treachery, and a great victory plucked from the jaws of defeat.'

'When you put it like that, it sounds much better than a battlefield reeking of shit and piss, and a throat slit in a darkened room.'

'It's all in the telling, Pavo. All in the telling.'

The fire danced away in the dark. Corvus weaved his way through the woods until he reached the edge of the camp. Severus was pacing around the perimeter, wringing his hands. No doubt he was regretting ever leaving the comforts of Rome. No going back now.

The Hanged Man turned his head at its odd, twisted

angle, and flames flickered in his eyes. 'You spend too much time on your own.'

Not on my own, Corvus thought with a furtive glance at Pavo. 'That's the only way I can hear my thoughts.'

Severus grunted. 'This is not how I imagined it would be when you told me how you alone could save the worship of Mithras from the guile of the Christians.'

Corvus fluttered a hand. 'Let's look on the bright side for now, Father. You're no longer a captive of barbarians threatening to hang you from the nearest oak. Again.'

Hecate flashed him a smile as she swayed around the fire, rocking his son to sleep in her arms.

'How is he?' he asked.

'Growing fast. He has a hunger, like his father.' Her lips flickered, a hint of flirtation. 'And he sleeps well. But he needs a name, my love.'

'Names are difficult things. The right one, or the wrong one, can shape the course of a life, in time.'

Hecate nodded. 'Names are like spells.'

'Or curses.'

Gaia was swathed in a blanket, still lying on the bier and refusing to walk. She pursed her lips in sullen disapproval at her surroundings. Hecate leaned down to hand back the baby.

'Take that thing away from me,' she snapped.

Corvus glanced down at her. 'Maternal as ever, Mother.'

'When will we be done with this endless traipsing through this cold, wet land?'

'Soon you'll be surrounded by all the riches you ever dreamed of.'

Gaia reached out a slender hand. 'My beautiful boy,' she breathed. 'I would do anything for you.'

Corvus brushed her fingertips and moved away. He had

trodden a long hard road since the death of his father, but a family like this was a reward in itself.

Pavo was waiting by the well-worn track. A nod was all the communication that was needed and together they strode through the trees to where Bucco squatted with his dripping knife.

'You've more than earned your place here, little man,' Corvus said as he stepped into the clearing.

Bucco jumped to his feet and bowed, sweeping out an arm. 'I lack much in stature, yes.' He tapped his forehead. 'But my worth lies in my wits.'

'You've almost made me forget your past treacheries.' Corvus' smile turned to a blade and Bucco's face fell.

The wood-priest hung between two ash trees, his arms pulled back by the ropes, his head sagging on to his chest. His grey-streaked hair revealed the years over which he had amassed his wisdom. A good find, certainly. The northern tribes seemed to value these gizzard-sifters and prophecy-spouters, even though they played one off against the other.

'Apologies, I don't recall your name.' Corvus shrugged. 'If I were to be honest, I don't really care. Still, we're civilized men and we shouldn't let such things stand between us.'

The druid lifted his head. Corvus watched those rheumy eyes staring at him from under heavy brows and he nodded, pleased.

'Good, good. I have a question . . . I have many questions, of course . . . but now I'm worried about my poor son. I can't keep calling it *it*. There are family traditions, but really, this is a fresh start, isn't it? Something that looks to days yet to come, not times past, would be fitting. What do you say?'

The wood-priest worked his dry mouth, trying to find the words. After a moment, he said, 'You must choose a name laden with power.'

'Power, yes. I like that.'

'Call the child Arthur.'

'Why that?' Corvus smiled. He knew the answer well enough, but it was always good to hear it.

'Arthur . . . the bear. The protector. The brave, the strong, the leader. This . . .' He coughed and spat a bloody mouthful. 'This will mean something to those who hear it. The Bear-King is coming. The Bear-King . . . is here.'

Corvus closed his eyes and weighed the name. Yes, he liked it. 'Arthur,' he said, testing it on his tongue.

Pavo was pacing around the clearing, listening to their chat. Corvus looked past him to the fires flickering on the edge of the wood, where his army waited. Picts, all of them, the fiercest warriors in all of Britannia, so he'd been told. Once they were enemies of the empire. Now they were mercenaries, easily bought by the promise of gold and booty. And, of course, the promise of vengeance. Once they'd heard how Lucanus had slaughtered their king Arrist, who had brought them so much glory, they were easily persuaded.

'Now,' Corvus said, sitting cross-legged in front of the druid, 'let us have a conversation.'

CHAPTER FORTY

Whispers

THE GREEN LAND FELL AWAY INTO THE MISTY WEST. LUCANUS and Catia stood on the ridge, hand in hand, framed against the vast sky, Weylyn resting in the crook of his mother's arm.

Mato stared at that sight and felt a bloom of hope.

Bellicus, Solinus and Comitinus were scouting ahead, but so far they'd found no sign of the horde. Everyone they encountered said the barbarians had set off for the north, no doubt returning to their cold home.

Now nothing stood in their way. No more enemies, no death or suffering. Even the Attacotti seemed no longer a threat after Lucanus and Myrrdin's encounter with them, so the gossip among the men said.

The long war was over and the sanctuary Myrrdin had promised them waited ahead.

The wood-priest's speech when they were reunited was unwavering: 'Now that the boy Weylyn has been baptized, the path to his own destiny is almost clear,' he had said. 'All that waits is for the gate to be opened at the Isle of Apples, and then we may enter the haunted land and seek the approval of the great council.'

The haunted land.

Mato turned and surveyed the men sprawling on their backs, red-faced in the sun after the long march. Some sluiced water into their mouths from their skins. Others watched white clouds scudding across the blue, relieved, no doubt, that the fighting was behind them.

Not far away, Apullius and Morirex emerged from the trees lining a valley they had skirted on their journey here. The older boy caught his eye with a frantic wave and he hurried over.

'We followed Myrrdin as you bid us,' Apullius said, glancing back down the valley side. 'The druid is always wary and I had to keep my distance. But Morirex kept watch on him from the branches.'

Mato ruffled the younger lad's hair as Morirex grinned. 'Any army would be proud to have the two of you on their side.' And it was true. He'd never seen anyone work harder at learning the skills they were acquiring. Morirex was already a decent scout. Apullius would grow up to be a fine warrior, if the swordplay he'd already picked up from Lucanus was any guide.

'Come, quickly.' Apullius tugged at his pelt.

Soon they were prowling down the valley side in the cool shade under the trees.

'Why don't you trust the wood-priest?' Morirex whispered.

'He's not an enemy. He's helped us enough times,' Apullius added.

'Myrrdin helps himself. He only makes you think he's helping you.' Mato slowed his step. Now he could hear the drone of voices somewhere ahead. 'Myrrdin is trustworthy when his own plans align with yours. And when they don't, beware. He'll do anything in his power to trick you into walking his path.'

'So we are to keep spying on him?' Morirex asked.

'At all times, and especially when he seems to be doing nothing. Even when you sleep, keep one eye open. Tell me everything.'

The valley floor was a patchwork of sunlight and shadow. They crept alongside a tinkling brook past a stinking bog clotted with sedge until Mato glimpsed two figures deep in conversation. Myrrdin leaned on his staff. Aelius lounged along a fallen tree in the sun, his good arm folded behind his head.

Waving Apullius and Morirex to stay back, Mato eased forward until he could overhear the conversation.

'I foresee a great destiny for you,' the wood-priest was saying to the other man.

'Great destiny comes cheap these days, it seems.' Aelius' tone was as wry as ever.

'Pretend you are nothing as much as you want, but I know you're not the same acid-tongued drunk who set out from Vercovicium on this journey. The war has changed you. You've risen to every challenge, become a general who commands the respect of all here. There isn't a man in that war-band who wouldn't want you leading them into battle.'

Aelius pretended to enjoy the sun, but Mato could see him scrutinizing the druid from beneath his lashes. 'I'm happy with the part I play. Besides, what else could I do?'

'This struggle has been long in the making, and it will reach long into the years to come. If the King Who Will Not Die is to be born into the world, champions will always be needed—'

Aelius guffawed. 'Champions? Look down that long nose of yours at who you're speaking to, wood-priest.'

The wood-priest prowled around the supine man, tapping his staff on the soft ground in a steady beat. 'There is always a greater part to play, for good men and women. For one, Weylyn will need shepherding, protecting.'

'Surely that's work for Lucanus and Catia?'

Myrrdin did not reply.

Mato narrowed his eyes as he studied Aelius. He could see the younger man was considering the offer.

Weighing the moment, he pushed himself up and walked forward. 'The wood-priest makes a good argument, as always.'

Aelius jerked up. Myrrdin's face darkened, but he kept his smile.

'I came here to get away from the constant tramping and farting and bickering and now everyone I know is wandering through,' Aelius said, cocking an eyebrow.

'Think twice before you take the druid up on his offer . . . or any offer, for that matter,' Mato said. 'The wood-priests don't care about anyone. Only their schemes. Everyone who heeds them will, sooner or later, be sent marching towards the enemy to be cut down.'

'Spying on me, Grim Wolf?'

'Always.' Mato held the druid's gaze.

'Those are harsh words.'

'But true.'

'You should not make an enemy of me.'

Mato held out both hands. 'Of course not. We are friends. A bond forged in struggle, there is no greater.'

Aelius levered himself up and bowed. 'I'll leave you to your debate. Somewhere in this great wide world there must be a place where I can find a little quiet.'

Once he'd gone, Myrrdin said, 'Aelius will heed me, you know. He has a lifetime behind him of being spat upon, dismissed. The lure of importance is too great.'

'Now you're showing me how the magic works. That is never wise.'

'I tell you because there's nothing you can do to prevent it.' Myrrdin's eyes glittered.

'The schemes of wood-priests always unfold as planned?'

Myrrdin nodded slowly.

'You are not gods. Or the Fates. Only men. Never forget that.'

The druid glided past him without a sideways glance.

CHAPTER FORTY-ONE

The Call of the Greenwood

AD 368, The Western Levels, 24 April

THE MIST ON THE LEVELS SHIFTED AND THE LAMP OF A FULL
moon shimmered in the vast black pools of the marsh.
Only the creaking of the damp wooden trackway disturbed
the silence.

As he edged along the oak timbers suspended just above
the water, Bellicus gripped his sword more tightly. The fog
muffled any sound.

An enemy was waiting ahead, he was certain of it. But
who?

The horde was gone. Passing soldiers told them Theodosius the Elder had already dispatched a message to
Valentinian that he had restored Britannia to the empire.

Lulled by that news, their column of men had wound on
through the verdant landscape, following Myrrdin's directions and trading stories with the curious locals, who'd
escaped the worst of the barbarian attack. Villas still thrived,
farmland flourished and the markets buzzed with life. They
filled their bellies on fat game and slept under clear skies in
the growing spring warmth.

And then they'd crested a dizzying ridge and trudged in

the direction of the lowlands stretching out towards the great shining ocean in the west. Bellicus thought back to the wonder he had felt standing on the high ground looking down on what seemed a vast mirror reflecting spurs of golden sunlight and the blue sky above. It was almost an inland sea, a collection of lakes and pools separated by treacherous bogs that flooded every spring, so the wood-priest said. Out of the centre a great tor rose, so rare in that flat land that he could almost believe it had been shaped by the gods.

But as they neared the ancient walkway that cut a line through the flooded Levels, they had glimpsed someone tracking them. The figure had disappeared into the bank of pearly fog on the timber track, as if to avoid being seen. Bellicus grunted. He trusted his instincts and they told him to beware.

A bubble popped in the marsh and he jolted from his reverie.

On he crept. The mist was shifting all around him, revealing then hiding. He squinted, trying to pierce the white folds. Every now and then he'd pause, listening. Perhaps, this time, his instincts had been wrong.

Too late, he heard the whisper of bare feet on wood. A figure burst from the fog, and off the side he flew.

Flailing, Bellicus plunged into the marsh. As the mud sucked at his legs, he thrashed out, snatching hold of a handful of rushes. He cursed, feeling the rough fibre burn his palm. It would not save him for long.

When he craned his neck up, he stared into the grinning face of Motius of the Carrion Crows, caught in a shaft of moonlight.

'You bastard,' Bellicus snarled, kicking out to try to stop himself sinking further.

The black tattoo on Motius' face flexed as his grin grew

broader still. The Crow was enjoying watching the last moments of his enemy's life drain away.

'I have a new ally now. He bade me track you, to make sure you didn't veer from your path. And once you are all dead, he will reward me well.'

Corvus.

'You've been too confident,' Motius continued. 'You thought your battle was done and all the threats long left behind. The truth is, you've already lost. You just don't know it yet.'

Bellicus grinned, and took succour from the shadow of bafflement that crossed the Crow's face. Stifling a chuckle, he whistled through his teeth.

From deep in the mist echoed the sound of paws pounding on the wooden trackway.

Catulus burst from the fog and leapt. His fangs ripped into Motius' groin, and the Carrion Crow howled.

With a violent shake of his head, the hound wrenched away a chunk of meat. Motius stumbled back, and back, until he pitched off the timbers. A stream of rubies glistened in the moonlight and his screams snapped off as the mud swallowed him.

'Good boy, Catulus. Good dog,' Bellicus called.

Letting go of the reeds, he thrust his enemy down and held him as he thrashed. If he was going to die, at least he would take this bastard with him. Motius writhed, but only for a moment. The mud rushed into his mouth, then his lungs, and finally Bellicus felt him grow still.

The Grim Wolf spread his arms out on the surface of the bog to buy a moment or two more. 'Good boy,' he murmured, looking up at the panting dog. Blood dripped from its muzzle. He felt a pang of sadness that he would never run with his friend again, and then the mist rolled in and Catulus was lost to him.

'Take this.'

The voice rumbled through the stillness, one he had heard before, in the grove that night when they had been hoping to free Catia from the Scoti. The golden hilt of a sheathed longsword reached out of the mist and hovered in front of him. Not one to question his good fortune, Bellicus grasped it.

Once he'd been dragged from the bog, he rolled on his back and gasped in chill air. Catulus licked his face. When he pushed the slavering dog away, a man in a full-face helmet towered over him.

The Lord of the Greenwood.

'Who are you?' Bellicus found himself caught in the grip of those burning eyes.

'The champion of Cernunnos, he who howls in the forest. The wild heart of the green. I hear the roar of the oak-men and the whisper of fern and ivy. I sing the song of the wind through the branches.' He reached out a hand. 'The god is here, in everything, every leaf and frond, and in me too, and I will fight for him till I die.'

'Who are you?' Bellicus' voice cracked.

Those eyes. Unblinking, bloodshot, a stare that reached into the deepest depths of him.

Eyes he knew.

The Lord of the Greenwood grasped the side of that ancient emerald-tinged helm and pushed it up.

Held fast, Bellicus watched the strong jawline appear, skin flayed to leather by the elements, pitted and criss-crossed with scars, wounds that could have come from a fall upon rocks from a height.

Even as the Lord of the Greenwood set the helmet aside, Bellicus felt himself reeling, and for a moment he thought he was going mad.

'Old friend,' the warrior uttered.

Bellicus shuddered from a racking sob, and then he covered his face. When he finally calmed himself, he looked up and saw he was not mistaken. 'I thought you dead.'

Lucanus the Elder nodded. 'I thought so too, for a while. I remember . . . falling. Later, there was ice water, and hands on me.'

His stare didn't waver, and Bellicus tried to see loathing there, a justified desire for vengeance, but there was none.

'The wood-priests . . . the witches . . . the forest folk . . . they'd been watching me for a long time in the Wilds. Making plans that I knew nothing of.' His voice creaked like someone not used to speaking. 'For me. For my son. For Gaia and Catia. Those plans have been long in the making, and they are greater than all of us. We are just driftwood, caught on the waves.'

Bellicus pushed out his chest. 'Take your sword. I deserve it.'

Was that a hint of warmth in the Lord of the Greenwood's eyes? He couldn't be sure. There was barely a whisper of the man that had been. The rest driven out by a life lived away from human contact, with only the elements and the whispering gods of the Wilds for company.

'I hold no grudge. We were friends once. The promise of that has gone now, through no fault of either of us, but you meant me no harm that night, I know that. There was no malice there. You had a rage on you. But I knew that fire burned in your chest from the moment I met you, and I accepted it. We are all flawed. And the punishment we inflict on ourselves is worse by far than anything others do.'

'You forgive me?' Bellicus felt hot tears burn. He'd kept this secret shame inside him for so long, and the sliver of ice had grown until he was filled with hoar frost.

'There is no need to forgive. Forget your guilt. Forget your shame. What's gone is gone. We are on new roads now.'

Bellicus felt a rush of relief so great he could barely cope.

He threw himself back on his elbows, and laughed, and laughed. The sound boomed out across the black lakes of the Levels. The weight that had crushed him down for so many years was lifted. He felt as light as feathers.

'We must tell Lucanus!' he uttered. 'He will be reborn—'

'No.' The Lord of the Greenwood's voice cracked. He lifted his helmet and slid it back on to his head. 'My son must never know.'

'I don't understand.'

'It will do him no good. I am not the man I was. And he will not be the man he is meant to be, if I am there.'

'But he's your son. Is your heart so cold?'

'Do not judge me.' This time the voice rang with such steel that Bellicus feared he would be killed there and then. 'My son has grown to fill what was missing in his life. Death and grief shape a man. Harden him. If that makes him stronger, then it is well. Lucanus has been chosen for the part he has to play. And that destiny is greater than him, and me, and whatever lies between us. We are nothing. What lies in our hearts is nothing. What is to come . . . what must come . . . is everything.'

Bellicus felt an ache in his own heart. More than anything he wanted his old friend back. But he could hear the determination in that voice and he knew he could not shake such resolve.

'I will be with you, watching from a distance, as I always have. Making sure Lucanus and Catia and the babe are safe. And you.' Was that another hint of warmth he heard? 'And when I am gone, there will be another Green Warrior, to challenge, to shape, to guide. There will always be another.'

The Lord of the Greenwood thrust out a hand and hauled him to his feet. Bellicus held his friend's eyes for a long moment, and then the warrior turned and walked away into the mist.

For a while, Bellicus absently scrubbed the fur on Catulus' head, lost to his memories. His smile spread slowly, became a grin. Then he was striding back towards the camp to warn the others of what Motius had said, and for the first time in an age he began to sing.

CHAPTER FORTY-TWO

The Isle of Apples

T HE INLAND SEA GLOWED A ROSY HUE. THE RISING SUN shone from those mirrored waters as the line of men and women trailed across the timber walkway towards the tor.

Here all things change.

Mato turned over those words of the wood-priest, uttered as the chosen few had been woken in the dark hour before dawn.

'It's all rites and prayers with these druid bastards,' Solinus had grumbled as he wiped sleep from his eyes.

Always alert, Aelius had pulled himself from his tent and was soon joined by Apullius and Morirex. All three of them had been eager to join the procession. Myrrdin's firm refusal sent sparks flying from Aelius' eyes. Was this part of the druid's manipulation, Mato wondered? Pull Aelius in, push him away, make him keen for some kind of alliance? Apullius, too, was simmering. He saw himself as Lucanus' right hand, always there to serve and protect his master.

'Stay here and care for the babe,' Myrrdin had said, pouring poison into the wound.

The three of them had been left standing on the edge of the marsh, watching their friends march towards the tor.

Mato could almost feel the weight of their resentment at his back.

He watched a hawk wheel across the blue sky above that granite-topped hill. He understood the need to talk to the gods, to fortune and the Fates, even if Solinus didn't. Perhaps he would hear his sister's voice here, one final time.

When they reached the tor, Myrrdin stamped his staff once and pointed to the processional pathway winding around the hill from the base to the summit. Budding fruit trees edged the route.

'Welcome to the Isle of Apples,' the druid boomed. 'It is told that this great tor is the gateway to Annwn, the Other-world, ruled over by Gwyn ap Nudd, the leader of the Wild Hunt. If a man finds the entrance he can pass through to that land of eternal youth and endless delights. The Christians would call it heaven. And they have their own story about this place. A great man from the hot lands brought the Christ here, as a boy. The son of the Christians' god blessed Britannia. And that great man planted his staff into the ground and it flourished and grew into a tree that thrives to this day. A sign, they say, that the Christ lives on in this island.' Myrrdin smiled. 'Two stories. Which is right? Perhaps both of them, or perhaps the true story lies behind these tales. Could it be that it is not the account of what happened but the place itself that draws fables to it like hungry men to a feast?'

'Get on with it,' Solinus called.

Laughter ripped through the small group – the Grim Wolves, Amarina and Catia – and they traipsed after the wood-priest along the spiral path.

As they rose higher, curling around the tor, the landscape presented itself in a majestic sweep of water and wood and grassland. Mato felt struck by how this land must have been in the time before it became part of an empire. Time and again he'd heard the words *The season is turning*, and there, lit by the rising sun, he had a sense of what it meant.

A new age was dawning, but whether it was for good or ill, no one could yet be sure.

On the sun-drenched summit, Mato looked around. At first he could see no one, but then a figure rose up, seemingly from the rock itself, perhaps from a fissure, or perhaps he had emerged from that gateway to the Otherworld. He was another wood-priest by the look of him, with a fading tattoo crawling down the left side of his wrinkled face. Almost too frail to stand, he leaned on a staff, his long white hair stirred by the breeze.

'Is this the one?' the old man croaked.

Myrrdin held out one hand and Lucanus stepped forward. The aged wood-priest looked the Wolf up and down, his eyes settling on the golden dragon crown. He nodded. 'You vouch for him?'

'I do.'

The old man reached out one spindly arm and pressed a trembling palm on Lucanus' chest. 'Word will be sent on ahead. The council will gather.'

With a nod to Myrrdin, he turned away and walked to the edge of the summit. Standing on a flat rock, he raised his arms and welcomed the rising sun.

'We climbed all the way up here for that?' Solinus said.

'"That" has brought you a clear path to safety,' Myrrdin said. 'The journey into the west is fraught with dangers. When the Romans slaughtered the wood-priests in Ynys Môn, those who survived fled to the fringes of this island, some into Caledonia, some to Cambria, where I was raised. But many found sanctuary in Dumnonia. There, on the edge of the empire, is a part of Britannia that you have not imagined before. When you cross the Tamar, you will be entering another land, a haunted land where the witches and the gods and the Fates hold sway. The past has always lived on there.'

'And the gods and witches will give us free passage?' Lucanus said.

'Once you've been presented to the council, in the wilds of the great moorland.'

'A council of wood-priests?' Mato asked.

Myrrdin nodded. 'Now the child has been baptized before the eyes of the gods, the council will give the final assent. Then you will be free to travel into the far west where you will find a place of safety and the protection you require for your son.'

As the wood-priest turned back to the processional path, Lucanus caught his arm.

'Every time you open your mouth you promise safety and hope. Yet all I see again and again are tricks. I'll ask you one question: when I was in the far north, I saw one of your kind advising the Scoti and the Picts. Was the true conspiracy here that of the wood-priests? You brought the tribes together. You filled them with fire and set them to invade the south to weaken Rome's hold so you could see your own plan reach fruition. If that's true, your hands are drenched in blood from all the slaughter that followed. And the dark age that is dawning was caused by you, just so your saviour-king can lead the folk out into your new world.'

Silence fell across the group. Mato looked across the faces of his friends and saw that all of them doubted as Lucanus did.

Myrrdin held the Wolf's gaze. 'There is only one truth here that matters. There's no safety for you in the land at your back. The only hope you have is in the west. Will you choose it?'

Lucanus snorted and marched away. The others followed.

Mato frowned, puzzled by the warmth he saw in Myrrdin's face as the wood-priest watched the group walk away.

'I've been observing Lucanus and Catia for almost all my days,' the druid murmured. 'When I was a mere novice, I was shown them and told this was my life's work.' His smile took on a sad note. 'I've seen their loves and their losses, their triumphs and tragedies, all from a distance, yet they feel like my own blood. I could not bear to see them harmed.'

'And yet you would happily barter away Lucanus' life. We spoke of this that day among the Heartstones.'

A shadow flickered across the wood-priest's face and he looked away. 'Some things are greater than the hearts of men.'

CHAPTER FORTY-THREE

The Gorge

FOR FIVE DAYS, THEY TREKKED WEST. ALONG THE WAY, WHITE shapes flitted across ridges. The Attacotti were keeping pace with them.

'Where did they come from?' Shielding his eyes from the sun, Aelius watched the rapid movement flashing across the skyline. 'Why aren't they attacking, if that's what they want?'

'They don't have the numbers to ensure victory.' Bellicus followed the passage of the pale warriors. He felt unsettled.

'They don't care if they're seen. That's not like them.' Aelius' hand unconsciously twitched towards his sword. 'And they've got no fight with us now. Why haven't they gone with the others?'

'Something's amiss, that's for sure,' Bellicus grunted. 'But who can know the minds of those bastards?'

After the sightings, a dark mood seeped into the men as the days passed. On the fifth night, Bellicus looked around the figures hunched by the campfires and could see it etched in their faces. When the rain came, hard and fast, they crept back to their tents and sat in the entrances, staring into the deluge. No laughter, no song, features like a wintry moor.

Sodden as ditch-rats, Apullius and Morirex trudged back into camp. Bellicus eyed them as they slunk to Lucanus' tent. Not long after, they emerged and headed towards him. Something was wrong, he could see it.

He beckoned them over. 'You had sight of the Eaters of the Dead?'

Apullius shook his head, rain flying from his hair. 'We've scouted a wide area. No sign of them anywhere.' He bit his lip.

Before Bellicus could say more, Morirex blurted, 'Lucanus wants me to stop scouting. He thinks I'm too young . . . that it's too dangerous.' He seemed on the verge of tears.

'Morirex is a good scout. Better than me,' Apullius said.

Bellicus nodded slowly. 'I'll have a word with Lucanus. You've earned the right to risk your neck with the rest of us.'

For a moment, he thought the young lad was going to lunge into a hug and he wagged a finger to deter him. As the two brothers splashed away, beaming, he reached out and scrubbed Catulus' head. An unfamiliar sense of hope had settled on him and he wasn't sure why.

He cursed quietly to himself. What was he becoming?

The next day a vast area of moorland loomed up, wild and windswept and filled with treacherous bogs, carved by rivers and steep crags. Myrrdin led the way along the eastern edge until they reached a river plunging out from the heart of the moor along a steep, heavily wooded gorge.

Bellicus slipped in behind Lucanus as the column of men trailed along the side of the rushing Teign, the white-flecked waters swollen by the spring floods. In that shadowed green world, blades of sunlight dazzled through the branches high overhead. The rumble of water over rock drowned out the tramp of their feet, and the gorge hid them from prying eyes. Myrrdin had said it was the ancient route to their destination; it was one that had been well chosen.

Sensing a presence at his back, he turned to see a wry smile glinting in the depths of Amarina's hood.

'You would have been the last one I expected to accompany us into danger,' he grunted.

'Why, I'm here for the wit and the entrancing conversation.' Her voice was light, and he couldn't tell if she was mocking him. Knowing Amarina, most likely. 'And in my calculation, the danger at our backs is worse, just as the wood-priest said.'

'Mato says you've become a woman of honour.'

'No. I'd leave you to die in a ditch in the blink of an eye if I had to save my own skin.'

'Believe her, Bellicus,' Aelius said as he strode behind. He no longer made any attempt to hide his withered arm, and his mood seemed to have grown brighter as their journey became harder. 'Survival is a subject Amarina knows much about.'

At noon, they broke to fill their growling bellies with cold venison, sprawling on slabs of granite in the shade. Bellicus felt lulled by the crashing of the river and lay back, watching the flies drone through shafts of sunlight. Catulus slumped next to him.

A shadow fell over him and he looked up at Lucanus. 'The wood-priest says we need to set off again soon. We'll meet this council of his under the light of the moon. That is their way, he says.'

'Strange ways, wood-priests have. I'm sick of the lot of them.'

Lucanus grinned. 'You're not alone there. But after this we should be free.'

'Free,' Bellicus repeated. 'My brain hurts when I try to think what that means these days.'

Lucanus hesitated for a moment, then said, 'You've got my thanks for walking this road with me. It would have been easier—'

'You're talking like a jolt-head. Away with you and find some sense.'

Lucanus laughed and walked off. Bellicus smiled as he watched him go. How long had it been since he'd heard his friend in such consistent good humour? He felt his heart sing, and he prayed that the Lord of the Greenwood could see this change in his son from whatever vantage point the emerald warrior inhabited. If only Lucanus could know he had not been abandoned. But he had given his word.

For a while, he dozed, until the clatter of the men hauling themselves to their feet told him the time for rest was done. Soon they were tramping along the side of the Teign again, and he allowed himself to sink into the rhythm of the march.

The sun drifted past the high point.

'We're not alone.'

He jerked from his reverie. Apullius was tugging at his arm.

Bellicus followed the direction of the lad's pointing finger, up the side of the gorge. He squinted against the rays glaring through the branches, then shook his head. 'I don't see anything.'

Turning back, he looked into the boy's worried face. How easy it would be to brush him away, but Apullius was one of them now. Solinus had taught him how a sudden flight of birds signalled danger ahead, and Comitinus had instructed him on tracking a deer through the woods. His swordplay was rough, but he was learning fast.

'Lucanus,' Bellicus urged, keeping his voice low. 'We have company.'

The Wolf scanned the top of the gorge. 'The Attacotti?'

'If they were that close, the Attacotti wouldn't show themselves,' Apullius began hesitantly. Gaining confidence, he continued, 'I saw a man, perhaps two, darting from tree to tree. Trying to stay out of sight.'

352

'Arm yourselves,' Lucanus hissed. The order rippled along the line of men. Swords leapt to hands; eyes swept up, searching the shadows.

Bellicus craned his neck. For long moments, there was only the gurgling of the water and the whisper of the wind in the branches. He sensed the men beside him, all of them like statues, eyes used to searching out the slightest sign of threat in any landscape.

Nothing moved.

He eyed Mato, then Solinus and Comitinus. Each gave a curt shake of the head. He felt a tingle of relief. But when he eyed Lucanus he saw that his leader remained rigid, his gaze fixed high up on the gorge side.

A dry branch cracked.

A rumble resonated deep in Catulus' throat.

Further along the column, a cry rang out and Bellicus whirled. One of the men pitched back, an arrow rammed into his eye socket. Before anyone could move, he stumbled back into the rushing waters and was swept away.

'Take cover,' Lucanus roared.

Within a heartbeat shafts blackened the air, the whine and thump as loud as a summer storm.

Bellicus clawed his way into the lee of the gorge side. Along the line, men dived behind trees and threw themselves on to their bellies in a rolling sea of bracken. Little good it would do them. Bellicus peered up. Now the top of the gorge seethed with silhouettes on both sides. A warband. They were trapped, pinned down.

An arrow cracked into the trunk of an ash tree just above his head. He ducked down lower.

'They can pick us off one by one.' Lucanus had arrived beside him.

Bellicus could see his friend was right. Some of the men were crawling on their hands and knees back the way they had come. Arrows showered around them. Their enemy had closed off any retreat; doubtless they would have done the same ahead. The entire war-band was pinned down. Sooner or later, the enemy, whoever they were, would come for them.

'Picts,' Solinus shouted. 'They're Pictish bastards. Listen – you can hear their tongue.'

Bellicus cocked his head. Guttural battle-cries rolled down the gorge side. He gritted his teeth. Twisting out, he looked along the riverbank. Apullius and Morirex were both safe, flat on the muddy ground at the foot of a granite outcropping. As he watched, Apullius began to crawl away.

'Stay where you are, Apullius, you damn fool,' he bellowed. 'This isn't the time for scouting.'

If Apullius heard him, he didn't slow, and soon he'd disappeared past a group of crouching men.

The arrows rained down. Bellicus searched again. This time he saw Aelius, and Amarina. Catia's blonde head bobbed further along. She'd nocked a shaft in her bow, but couldn't find space to loose it. Little good that would do, too.

The battle-cries soared and Bellicus winced. That could only mean one thing. Pushing his head up above the cover of a fallen tree, he watched the barbarians creep down the steep, precarious path that wound among the maze of trees and vegetation.

But soon they would be here.

Lucanus caught his eye and held it for a moment, and in that look Bellicus could read all his friend's desperate thoughts.

'When the moment comes, lead the way ahead as fast as you can,' the Wolf said, jumping to his feet. 'They'll want the Pendragon more than anyone. I'll lead them away.'

'Don't be a jolt-head,' Bellicus bellowed. But Lucanus

had already drawn Caledfwlch and was scrambling up the slope.

Cursing, Bellicus leapt after him. Cries of alarm rang at his back. Wheezing, he started to claw his way up the soft loam of the side of the gorge, but Lucanus was already far ahead of him.

Iron helmets glinted as three Pictish warriors skidded through a sunbeam. One swung up a squarehead axe. Their strange, ululating battle-cry sang out. Bellicus yelled a warning, but Lucanus was wrong-footed, leaning back, unable to wield Caledfwlch to defend himself.

The axe swung down.

Seemingly from nowhere, a huge figure rose up between predator and prey. The axe clanged off the side of a green-tinged helmet, and the Lord of the Greenwood heaved up his longsword. The force of that blade all but hacked one of the skidding Picts in two.

Wrenching around, the towering warrior bellowed at Lucanus, 'Get back! Save yourself!' He kicked out, catching Lucanus on the side of the head. The Wolf spun away, slamming against an ash tree before whirling down the side of the gorge, gathering speed until he crashed back on to the riverbank.

The Lord of the Greenwood turned back, too late. The axe hacked into his shoulder. Bellicus reeled. But if his friend felt the brutal blow, he showed no sign.

The Lord of the Greenwood swung his sword again. Bellicus winced. The blade had carved into the axeman, but the strike had been faltering.

'I'm with you!' Bellicus called, throwing himself forward. But his feet slid on the steep bank, and before he could reach his friend's side the third Pict rammed his sword into the Lord of the Greenwood's chest. Wrenching it out, he stabbed again, and again.

Bellicus cried out as if he'd been stabbed himself.

His friend, his old, old friend.

Lucanus the Elder crunched to his knees. One hand flailed for purchase on a branch. For the briefest moment, he glanced back and locked eyes with the Grim Wolf. A farewell. A remembrance of times past. Of better days, and laughter, before their future was stolen from them by the schemes of others.

Bellicus howled, the anguish cracking his voice.

The Pict didn't slow his assault.

The Lord of the Greenwood crashed face down. His foe braced himself, gripped his sword with both hands, and slashed down. Once, twice, three times. The head rolled free, and the Pict kicked it down the bank where it disappeared into the greenery.

Bellicus felt a black wave of despair engulf him.

Nearby, Lucanus hauled himself up on a branch. 'He sacrificed his life to save mine.' His voice wavered and he stared at Bellicus, stunned. 'He died for me.'

Bellicus felt a desperate wish to tell Lucanus that it was a father doing as fathers did, sacrificing all for their child. But it passed, and he knew he could only be true to his friend's desire, however painful it might be. His secret would be kept unto death.

'Go,' he choked, thrusting the Wolf to one side. 'We have a fight on our hands.'

Down the dizzying sides of the gorge, the Picts swept. Bellicus threw himself into the fray.

For what seemed an age, all he knew was the clash of steel and the roar of battle-cries, digging in his heels and hacking and slashing for dear life.

Blood drenched him. Enemies fell.

At the moment when he feared all was lost, the Picts fell

back, clambering away up the sides of the gorge. He lurched against rough bark, sucking gasps of air into his burning lungs. His arm felt too weak to lift his sword.

Why had they pulled back when they were on the brink of victory?

Slithering down the bank, he collapsed next to the rushing river. His thoughts whirled, visions of slaughter coalescing into that final glimpse of his best friend and the recognition of how much he had lost that day.

When he next looked up, shadows were lengthening and the dazzling sunlight had faded from the high branches. A hand grabbed his shoulder and he looked round into Catia's face.

'Why are they retreating?' Her voice was like steel. Her bow was in her hand, her quiver empty. Where Weylyn was, he didn't know.

He shook his head, as baffled as she was.

The dusk was coming down hard. Bellicus watched shadowy figures crawl closer, familiar faces appearing out of the gloom. Eyes darted up the sides of the gorge to where whoops and howls and laughter rang out.

Catia shook him. 'When the dark falls, they'll come for us.'

Amarina was there, looming over him. 'They know every move we're about to make.'

How had it come to this, when they seemed to have escaped all threats?

'This is the only way out.' Catia snatched a knife from the folds of her dress. She looked around the other faces, and Bellicus could almost taste the desperation. Here they were, allies, friends, staring into the face of certain death. How they would go would define them all. He levered himself up and fumbled for his sword.

'We are together,' he said.

Catia looked round and her brow furrowed. 'Wait. Where's Lucanus?'

For a moment, silence descended on them all. Then Bellicus heard footsteps racing towards them, and Apullius emerged from the twilight. His eyes were rimmed with tears.

'He's gone,' he gasped, breathless. 'They took him. They took the Pendragon.'

CHAPTER FORTY-FOUR

The Two Dragons

THE BIRDSONG EBBED. THE SUN DIED. A CHILL WIND stirred the grass and moaned through the branches of a solitary tree, twisted like a broken-backed old man. Lucanus blinked away the haze in his head to look out over a vast moor turned silver by the light of the moon.

He was not alone.

Picts stood here and there, statues in the ghostly illumination. Only a few, but too many to fight. A tall man whose head hung at a strange angle. A young woman. Nearby a child bawled.

A figure strode into his field of vision and he found himself looking into the smiling face of Corvus. 'And here we are again, two dragons twirled around each other, fighting for supremacy.'

Lucanus lunged for his sword, but his scabbard was gone from his side.

Corvus paced around him so that the moon hung over his head. 'But as Pavo points out to me time and again, the central image of two dragons involved in this struggle for the ages, for power, for Britannia, for ownership of all days yet to come . . . it doesn't create a true picture. It suggests that they are equals. Perhaps that this battle is finely matched. But as you can see, you've already lost . . . everything.'

'I have an army—'

'A paltry war-band, who will all be dead by dawn. Along with your friends, your woman, and your child.'

Lucanus felt his stomach knot, but he showed only a cold face.

'Osiris needs Set. The Christ needs Judas – and God bless my good friend Theodosius the Younger for educating me into the ways of his religion. I miss his witterings. And Mithras needs . . .' He fluttered a hand, searching for the notion. 'Ahriman. Every great tale needs a hero, Wolf, and an adversary to test him. Me. You.'

'You think yourself a hero?' He heard the acid in his voice.

'The hero is the one who wins. His followers write the tale and pass it from mouth to mouth. Only victory is remembered, we all know that. The loser is condemned, spat upon, forgotten. This is history. And legend. And religion.'

Lucanus looked out across the wind-blasted moor, praying that his friends had escaped. But they were alone. 'I'm no black-hearted cur.'

'You will be, once the stories have been told.'

'Is this why you haven't killed me already? To weave your fantasies?'

'Live or die, it's not something that unduly concerns me,' Corvus said. 'There are only two things I need. But if nothing else I have an inventive mind. And it struck me, perhaps, that I could indeed weave a fantasy, one that bolstered my claim. I still have men of power to convince. But good friends will advocate on my behalf.' He bowed to the young woman. Her eyelids fluttered down.

'You need two things?'

'One thing I have learned is that symbols are important. The Ouroboros . . . the dragon eating its own tail . . .' He held out both hands. 'A king must look like a king, yes? Or else all will think him a common man.'

Corvus reached down and Lucanus saw him pick up a sword in a scabbard. His sword. As Corvus strapped it around his waist, he nodded. 'The sword of the gods. I heard tell of this in Londinium. Some are easily impressed. Still . . .' He half pulled the blade from its sheath, turning it so the moonlight illuminated the black inscriptions. 'Some name that only a barbarian could get his tongue around. I think I will call it . . . Caliburnus. No . . . Excalibur.'

'You think that will make you look like a king?'

'No, I think this will.' This time Corvus plucked up Lucanus' cloak, and from the pocket inside he pulled the golden dragon crown. Raising it high, he turned it so the moonlight played on it, and then he lowered the circlet on to his head. 'Now do I look like a king? Why, with this crown and the sword, anyone would think me the Pendragon. Anyone at all.'

CHAPTER FORTY-FIVE

The Only Way

THE NIGHT ECHOED WITH HOWLS. APULLIUS CHOKED BACK his terror as he dug his fingers into soft loam and clawed his way through the dark up the side of the gorge. In his mind's eye he saw the frenzied Picts dancing and ululating and waving their swords and axes in the air, readying for the final assault. He imagined them seeing him cowering there, dragging him out with rough hands, bending him over, swinging an axe up high over his neck.

He saw his death.

Yet still he clutched for near-unbreakable bracken stalks, caught at branches to lever himself up, moving ever onwards to those patches of starry sky that hung tantalizingly among the trees.

Would the others have missed him by now? No, of course not. He was less than nothing, and they had bigger issues to discuss: how to defend themselves when their enemy had every advantage. They were afraid, all of them, he knew; even the Grim Wolves, who had seen horrors he could only imagine. And yet not one of them showed it.

That calmed him a little. If they could be brave, so could he. He was one of them.

Even in the dark, he could feel the narrow track the deer

had made. They always found the easiest and safest path, one often hidden to untutored eyes. Comitinus had taught him that. He lifted his head and sniffed the cool breeze. Only the heavy scent of vegetation. No vinegary stink of sweat. That was good. The enemy was not too close to his current position. Solinus taught him that, before cuffing him around the ear for good measure so he would remember it. He had cursed under his breath at the time, but remember it he did.

Finally he was hauling himself up on to level ground. Pressing his back against a trunk, he tried to suck in a breath of air without sounding like a gale rushing through the trees.

Once his breath had subsided, he listened again. A snort. A cough. A fart. The Picts' watchmen were placed at intervals along the top of the gorge, as he'd anticipated. But they were looking out for an attack, not one man.

Who would be crazed enough to make a solitary journey into their midst?

Forward he crept until he could see the silhouette of the nearest guard, squatting on a fallen tree. The Pict wasn't paying attention. That was good. He had one chance.

With trembling hand, he drew the sword Mato had given him and levelled the blade, finding his balance on the balls of his feet as Mato had shown him. And then he bounded forward as soundlessly as he could manage, and swung his weapon back in the particular arc that Mato had explained, time and time again.

One chance.

The watchman fell back, dead, before he knew an enemy was upon him. Apullius ground his teeth together to stop himself crying out. The blood was pounding in his head so loudly, he wouldn't have known if the whole of the Pictish war-band was upon him.

But he couldn't rest. He found the next watchman and took his life too.

Then he was creeping back down the path he had found, unable to feel relief that he had survived. As he jumped down to the broad riverbank, he heard whispers: the others, hunched together, making their plans for their last stand.

Thrusting his way through the gathered bodies, he hovered in front of the Grim Wolves, Catia and Amarina. They looked at him, their faces drawn with worry.

'Apullius, this is not the time,' Bellicus began.

'I've found a way out,' he blurted. He'd hoped his voice would ring with all the confidence of one of the wolf-brothers, but there it was, a small thing, croaking and shaking with fear.

'Apullius . . .'

'Let him speak,' Catia commanded.

'There's a path, to the top of the gorge. The watchmen there are . . . are dead, so there's a gap in their lines.' He breathed in, trying to steady himself. 'If we're cautious, we could creep through, and surprise them. We would have the advantage then.'

He felt Bellicus' gaze heavy upon him. Comitinus stared. Solinus punched him in the stomach and he doubled over, wheezing. 'I knew the little bastard would finally earn his keep.'

CHAPTER FORTY-SIX

The Council

THE STANDING STONES ROSE UP FROM THE WIND-TORN moorland, two circles alongside each other. Under a star-sprinkled sky framing a full moon, those jagged teeth cast long shadows across the silvered grass.

The travellers trudged towards the menhirs, heads bowed as if from the weight of desolation in that place. Lucanus strained against the rope binding his wrists behind his back. The attempt was as futile as every other he'd tried since they'd departed the gorge.

All they had hoped for was lost.

When he raised his eyes, all he could see were the faces of Catia, and Weylyn, and Bellicus and the other Grim Wolves. Dead, all of them, at the hands of the Pictish war-band somewhere at his back, deep in the night. He choked down on despair, choked down on grief. Now he must feel nothing but the wintry grip of a lust for vengeance.

'Who is Ahriman?' he growled.

Corvus had been muttering to himself, nodding and chuckling in what sounded like one side of a conversation. He looked round.

'You spoke of Mithras and Ahriman.'

Corvus frowned, seemingly trying to dredge up details

that he half remembered, or cared little about. 'Ahriman is the destroyer.' He shrugged. 'There are gods and gods. Why do you care?'

'My life has been twisted out of shape. By the gods . . . or by men hungry for power.' He could almost taste the bitterness in his voice. 'Everything that is good has been stolen from me. I've been too trusting, I can see that now. I should have put all of you to the sword.'

Corvus smiled. 'That's not you, Lucanus. You don't have the fire that consumes men of achievement. You're too soft. That's why you were always fated to lose.' He looked ahead to the empty landscape. 'Now . . . how long are we supposed to wait?'

Lucanus bowed his head again, simmering. Five Picts strode around him, enough to cut him down if he tried anything. The man with the broken neck walked beside the horse that towed the bier on which the older woman and the baby lay. The younger woman, Corvus' wife it seemed, walked at the rear of the column, but she would never meet his eyes when he glanced at her. And then there was the dwarf. Bucco wisely kept his distance. How or why that treacherous toad had found his way to Corvus' orbit, the Wolf had no idea. But it was fitting those back-stabbing curs were now companions.

The grass drifted by beneath his tramping feet. If a moment came for vengeance, he would seize it, even if it cost him his life.

As they closed on the twin circles, he looked up and glimpsed figures appearing as if from nowhere. Perhaps they'd been standing behind the stones, out of sight. Now, though, around thirty men gathered in the centre of one of the rings. Druids, by the look of them, dressed in robes, faces blackened by tattoos.

Torches flared into life at regular intervals within the occupied circle.

'They have a sense of occasion, I'll give them that.' Corvus pulled out the gold circlet and set it on his head. 'And so do I.'

Lucanus lifted his head. His hands might be bound, but he would not present himself as a beaten captive. As they crossed into the circle, he stared defiantly into the faces of the waiting men. The madness of the Wilds burned in their eyes. Too long away from human comforts, too much whispering to trees and rocks, too many toad's-stools on the tongue. Their features were as hard as the stones that surrounded them.

'Greetings,' Corvus said, flourishing an arm. 'We have travelled miles to be with you.'

'You are the Pendragon?' one of the wood-priests asked. He had long hair the colour of snow, and a bald pate.

Corvus bowed his head slightly so the torchlight shimmered off the crown. Unsheathing Caledfwlch, he balanced it on the palms of his hands and laid it on the grass in front of the chief druid.

'I am the Pendragon,' Lucanus said.

'Hush now,' Corvus chided gently. 'You don't have a crown, or a sword of the gods.' He cocked an eyebrow at the leader of the wood-priests and tapped the side of his forehead. 'Nor does he have a child that carries the royal blood. I do, as you can see.' He waved a finger towards the bier and the older woman holding the baby. 'Mother?'

The woman threw off her cloak and slipped down the shoulder of her dress. As she turned, Lucanus glimpsed the Ouroboros branded into her skin.

'I have one of those myself,' Corvus said with a smile. 'So . . . all present and correct.' He flashed a look at Lucanus and nodded. 'As you might have expected, there were many enemies on the road who attempted to prevent me from reaching this place. Power-hungry all of them, like this fellow here. But I'm a merciful man. I couldn't bring myself to kill him. Of course, if that were your decision . . .'

'Where is Myrrdin?' the wood-priest demanded.

'Dead, sadly,' Corvus replied. 'Brave to the last, though. He sacrificed himself so the royal blood could survive. So the King Who Will Not Die could be brought into this world.'

'He's lying.' Lucanus stepped forward. 'My name is Lucanus, the Wolf. Your kind have watched me since I was a boy. You must know my name.'

The white-haired wood-priest nodded. 'Aye. We know of you. Myrrdin argued your claim to the crown.'

'And now this man has had Myrrdin killed. One of your own. Do you condone that?'

'Our work here is to ensure there is a suitable candidate.'

'I have no wood-priest to argue my claim,' Corvus said, 'but then neither does he. I do, however, have a strong voice who will proclaim my worth.' He beckoned without looking round and his wife walked forward and stood beside him. 'One of the Hecatae,' he said. The witch bowed her head to the druids.

'Come with us,' the chief druid said to Corvus.

Leaving Hecate standing there, the soldier stepped over Caledfwlch and was swallowed by the wood-priests who gathered around him. Lucanus could hear the throb of their voices, the rise and fall of debate, and Corvus pleading his case. He felt sickened by his impotence, and by the injustice. By rights, these wood-priests should have struck Corvus down for his crimes, but they seemed not to care. Their own plots and plans were more important than the lives of any of those caught up in their games.

Once the discussion was complete, Corvus walked back to stand next to his wife, with Caledfwlch at his feet.

'It has been all but decided,' the snowy-haired wood-priest announced. 'Let Hecate speak in your favour, and then we will have our say.'

Lucanus felt cold anger sluice through him. 'And what of all my sacrifices?'

'Only one can be chosen. We cannot allow any rival.'

The Wolf gritted his teeth. He knew what was meant by those words. 'So this is how it ends. The Bear-King will be born, come what may. No one cares how many lives have been destroyed in the process. I've long known that my own life matters not a whit. But the woman I love? My child? My friends?'

'The King Who Will Not Die must be born. If not, the night will go on for ever.'

'So your tale says. A tale dreamed up by you. But there is always another fable. Let me walk away from here and I'll dream up my own.'

The wood-priest's eyes flickered away from him. Not even worthy of a reply.

'You won't regret your decision,' Corvus intoned. 'The Dragon will rise, and all that you have worked for for so long will now come to pass.' He reached out, his fingers flexing as if he were grasping the prize he no doubt saw in his mind's eye. 'Now, Hecate. Speak your piece and we will be done here.'

The blade swept down, carving off Corvus' right hand.

Lucanus reeled, his shock as great as that he could see hewed into Corvus' face as he gaped at his stump. The agony must have hit the pretender a moment later, for he crashed on to his back. His wail rang up to the heavens.

His thoughts whirling, the Wolf's attention flew from his fallen rival to the severed hand, and then to the blood that slicked Caledfwlch.

Hecate stared at the spattered blade, drinking in the sight of it. Her face twisted in disgust, and then she tossed the weapon aside. As she turned to her husband, a cloud of righteous fury settled on her.

'I am Hecate, as were my sisters, the ones you murdered.' Her voice was trembling. 'And now justice is done.'

Corvus began to shake as if he had an ague. 'You . . . you knew . . .'

'I've always known. Did you truly think I would abandon my home, my people, to go with a Roman, the great enemy? Your head was always so swollen with your sense of your own worth, you never saw what was under your nose.' She spat on him. 'How I choked back my hatred for you, I will never know. But I forced down my bile, and waited, and waited, for the moment when I could cause the greatest harm, when you thought you had achieved all you had plotted for so long. And it is done, this long, miserable road. I care not if my own life is ended, for I will walk in the Summerlands in full knowledge that you and everything you ever fought for has been turned to ashes.'

Hecate spun on her heel and walked away, her glare daring the wood-priests to stop her.

Lucanus stared at Corvus twitching on the grass. Justice, yes. Yet he still felt as if he was frozen in the coldest winter. All of it, the lies, the games, the jostling for power, the lives ruined, the lives lost, all for this moment. All of it, meaning nothing.

He stiffened at the whisper of a footstep, too quiet for anyone who was not a Grim Wolf to hear. When he glanced round, the Picts who had accompanied Corvus lay in growing pools. Shadows moved in the dark beyond the light from the torches.

From out of the night they stepped, drenched in blood like terrible revenants from the grave. Catia, showing a cold face. Amarina, emerald eyes flickering with fire. Bellicus, crimson dripping from his beard. Solinus and Comitinus, swords still glistening. Then Mato, Aelius, Apullius, Morirex and the rest of his war-band, their graven features revealing men who had looked deep into the face of death and survived. Myrrdin walked behind them.

Lucanus looked from one to the other and felt the light come back into his heart.

Aelius stepped forward. He eyed the fallen Corvus and the rows of wood-priests. 'What would you have us do?'

Lucanus stared into his loyal general's eyes, but he was only seeing into his own heart. The wood-priests had reforged him. He was no longer the innocent who had run with his pack in the Wilds. He had died in a cold Caledonian lake and been reborn. He had died once more, in his head, in Goibniu's Smithy, and the wood-priests had taken his corpse and blown life into it, and in that moment had set him on a new road. And this night he had died one more time.

Lucanus the Wolf was gone. Now . . .

He was Cernunnos, who stands in the forest and howls. He was the Morrigan, the Phantom Queen of war and death. He was Set. He was Judas. He was Ahriman, the destroyer.

Lucanus eyed the council of wood-priests, those cold, uncaring manipulators who had twisted all their lives, and he nodded. His voice echoed like pebbles falling on a frozen lake.

'Kill them all.'

As Myrrdin cried out in horror, Catia turned her back on the coming slaughter and thrust her way through the surge of blood-drenched men to where her mother crouched on the bier. Gaia's mouth hung open, one hand flapping near it. Her eyes were fixed, no doubt still seeing in her mind that moment when her beloved son was cut down.

'I should kill you now, you and the child,' Catia said, clutching Weylyn to her breast. The wood-priests' screams tore through the night, almost drowning her words.

Gaia quivered. 'Don't hurt me. I have done nothing—'

'Still your tongue. No good can come from letting a rival live, Amarina was right. These games will go on until all hands are soaked in blood, whether it be in our sons' time, or their children's time, or beyond. It will never end. But though I come from your blood, Mother, I am not you. The past will not shape me. I choose a better road.' She looked to the tall man with the twisted neck and said, 'Take her away from here. If I see her again, or her spawn, I will kill them both.'

Catia turned back to the massacre. Amarina was standing over what looked like a bloody bundle of rags. Next to it was a spattered Phrygian cap. She leaned down and wiped her wet blade on the dwarf's remains and said with a shrug, 'Did you expect any less?'

The screams swirled up into the night. In the confusion of the massacre, Corvus crawled away. The agony was driving spikes into his head, and he felt himself growing weaker by the moment.

He would not let himself die there.

Thrusting his raw wrist into the flames of a torch, he howled as his flesh seared. Once his vision had cleared, he saw that the blackened stump would bleed no more. That gave him a chance.

The pain would not claim him, nor the blood loss. He had not come so far, beaten down so many obstacles, to give up easily. He thought of Ruga, his brother, dying at his feet with only one hand, and he sniggered. How the gods loved their games. How they must be laughing.

Through a haze of moonlight and shadows, he staggered away from the stone circles. The moorland fell away from him, a bleak expanse of scrub and rock and hollows filled with night. As he descended, the tumult at his back faded and there was only the erratic pad of his feet and the whine of the wind across the high ground.

Corvus felt a rush of euphoria that he had escaped. He'd been beaten back before, but there was always another opportunity.

And then, in the corner of his vision, he glimpsed movement and he realized he was not alone. Figures raced across the windswept grassland, keeping pace with him. When the moonlight caught them they glowed white, and he felt a wave of terror. His thoughts flew back to that flight through the nighttime forest when he had first arrived in Britannia, that moment when he had truly tasted fear for the first time in his life.

The Attacotti drew near, herding him. Blindly, he ran until he felt his foot catch a hidden rock and he spun head over heel down an incline into one of the hidden hollows. At the bottom, he splashed into an icy liquid, thicker than water. One of the treacherous bogs that covered the moorland. He had seen them in the daylight, vast pools invisible beneath a covering of moss, but able to claim a life in moments.

Corvus flailed, but that only made him sink more quickly. Somehow he clawed a handhold in the grass at the edge of the bog, just enough to stop him instantly getting dragged down to the depths, but not enough to allow him to haul himself back out, even if he had the strength.

Footsteps padded closer and he looked up into a death-mask of dried white clay and charcoal eye sockets. The Attacotti lined the edge of the bog.

'Stay back,' he gasped. 'You shall not eat me.'

Knives glinted in the moonlight, and the Attacotti bent down, leaning in, whisking those blades closer to his flesh.

Corvus felt a rush of panic that almost took his wits away. Should he let go and drown? Should he hold fast and be consumed? Madness, madness. How had it come to this?

But then the Attacotti froze as one. He watched them sniff the air above him. A change seemed to come over them and they stared at him with those sable eyes.

'Why do you torment me?' he cried. 'Be done with it.'

One by one, the knives slipped away and the Attacotti stepped back. They turned together and he watched them trek back up the slope and disappear into the night.

For a moment he felt his thoughts fly wildly, and then realization struck. He laughed, long and loud, until it ended in a choking cough.

The Attacotti, those monstrous Eaters of the Dead, thought he was beneath them, so worthless they wouldn't sully themselves with his flesh. They didn't even steal the gold crown on his head.

He laughed again and then began to cry. His fingers burned and he felt them begin to loosen.

'This is a fine mess, Pavo,' he said, snuffling back the tears. 'But there is always a way out for men like us. Tell me what to do, Pavo. You always have the answers.'

Only the wind moaned back.

'Pavo?' he called. 'Pavo? Where are you?'

His friend was always there. He'd never been alone, ever since he was a boy.

'Pavo?'

But there was no reply.

CHAPTER FORTY-SEVEN

The Haunted Land

T HE WIND WHINED ACROSS THE HIGH LAND AND IN IT Mato thought he could hear the voices of the dead. He shivered, despite himself. He'd promised himself he wouldn't give in to superstition in this place, but the desolate mood had wormed its way into him as much as the others.

Ahead, the last ruddy light of the day painted the lonely roundhouse on the scrubland.

'Is this wise?' Comitinus stuttered. 'There could be daemons inside . . . curses . . . spells . . .'

'Stop whining,' Solinus rumbled. But Mato could see his eyes were darting and he had already drawn his sword.

'We go in as we planned,' Aelius stated, unsheathing his own blade. He waved it towards the roundhouse. 'If there are enemies inside, we have to confront them. Running away like cowards will only result in our end.'

Nothing moved in the landscape. No voices echoed. Deserted, it seemed. Or a house of the dead, as many there feared. Aelius strode towards that isolated structure. When no one followed, he stopped and looked back with such a withering gaze that the men shuffled forward as one.

Mato understood their fears. Since they'd left the scene of the slaughter of the druids, moving down from the high country, they'd crossed more moorland before fording the great Tamar, a wide river that almost cut this place off from the mainland.

What lay beyond was a sliver of land reaching out into the great blue ocean, blasted by salt winds, with the crashing of the waves never far away. Of Rome's influence, there was little sign. A few villas dotted the rugged landscape, mainly along the trade routes from the harbours to the south. The folk they came across, the Dumnonii, lived much as they had before Britannia became part of the empire. At first they watched from a distance, suspicious of any strangers, as most would be in such an untouched place. But then the children came with offerings of honey cakes, and his men traded stories of the great war which had passed these people by.

Yet haunted it was. Everywhere they looked they saw standing stones, witch-charms swinging in the low branches, wells decorated with spring flowers, and every one of them experienced lurid dreams that left them troubled for much of the next day.

As they marched to the edge of another moor, one of the younger men swore his dead father came to him in the night and told him they were all doomed. His words turned the thoughts of all the war-band towards darkness, despite Aelius' acid condemnation of such superstition.

But then another warrior claimed to have seen one of the Dumnonii change shape into a beast in the forest. From then on, the reports of terrifying sights came thick and fast. Aelius was convinced the men had been gripped by a kind of madness, seeing faces in the bark of oaks and the lengthening shadows at dusk. But when the scouts found signs of night-time visitors in the trees on the edge of the camp, they had to accept that they were not alone.

And then Crax, a red-headed warrior barely into

manhood, had gone missing. Two of his fellows said they'd seen one of those shape-changing beasts carry him off.

Mato frowned. It had been all Aelius could do to stop the entire war-band fleeing back to the Tamar. He and Lucanus had argued around the fire in that hour before dawn that they were only facing men, wild men of the moors, and it was only their own fears that transformed them into dae-mons. They reached a truce, but it was an uneasy one.

As dawn broke, the scouts swept back into camp with news that they had followed the trail. To here.

'I'll go in alone if I have to. I'm not going to leave Crax to his fate.' Without looking back to see if anyone was following him, Aelius marched towards the roundhouse. Mato strode behind, and he sensed that the other men followed, no doubt shamed by Aelius' words. Catia's brother was now completely transformed from the man he had been in Vercovicium. His courage was unmatched. Lucanus' decision to make him a general had been proved right a hundred times over.

When he'd crossed half the distance to the roundhouse, the door swung open. They all froze. Mato fixed his gaze on that dark space, and after a moment a man lurched out. It was Crax. He looked around, dazed, his pupils wide and black.

Mato raced behind Aelius up to the open doorway, and Crax furrowed his brow as he stared at him. Recognition slowly lit his eyes.

'You're unharmed?' Mato asked.

Crax nodded.

Aelius edged to the door. At the threshold, he peered into the dark and then stepped inside. 'Empty,' his voice floated back.

Mutterings of relief rippled through the men, and then they found their bravery and hurried after their commander. Mato shoved Crax inside ahead of them.

'What happened?' he asked.

Crax shook his head, baffled. 'The ... the last thing I remember is being in the camp.'

'They've given him a potion of some kind,' Solinus grunted. 'Look at his eyes.'

'But who?' Comitinus asked.

Mato looked around the roundhouse. The hearth-stones had been kicked around, and the strewn ashes were old. Nothing else lay on the mud floor, no bed, no straw, no pots. No one had lived there for a long time.

'Ghosts,' someone muttered at his back.

'Is that blood?' another said, pointing to a dark stain on the ground.

'Hold your tongue,' Aelius snapped. He grabbed Crax. 'You must remember who took you.'

'Look.' Solinus was pointing into the shadows above.

Mato followed the line of his arm. A witch-charm of twigs and feathers and bones swung in the breeze.

As the men backed away from the door, Mato heard a woman's voice say, 'Make way.'

He turned to see Amarina and her new friend Hecate step across the threshold. After the witch's vengeance against her husband there had been no place for her but with them.

Aelius narrowed his eyes. 'What are you doing here?'

Amarina scanned the roundhouse, and when she saw the witch-charm her lips curled into a mysterious smile.

'What are you not telling us, Amarina?' Mato asked.

'Only that the dark days are behind us.' She arched an eyebrow. 'So let's have no more talk of ghosts and daemons, shape-changers and monsters. We still have a way to go until I can find some comforts in my life again.'

Her emerald cloak swirled behind her as she turned and stepped back out into the fading light. But Hecate continued to stare at the witch-charm, transfixed, and after a moment Mato watched a light rise in her features.

In the camp, Lucanus hunched beside the fire. Catia nestled beside him, Weylyn asleep in her lap.

'All is well,' Mato said as he walked up.

Lucanus nodded without looking up from the flames. Mato crouched beside his friend. He felt worried about the Wolf's state of mind.

'If you are still troubled by your decision to kill the druids—'

'I'm not.' Lucanus glanced at him, his eyes like steel. 'There was no other choice, if we were to be safe.'

'Still, that is a large burden for any man.'

Catia fumbled a hand to give her husband's thigh a squeeze. 'It was the right thing. For Weylyn, for me, for all of us. And if there are any troubles, they'll pass, as troubles always do.'

Mato couldn't argue with that, not with Catia, who had seen enough troubles in her short life.

'Myrrdin will never forgive you,' he said.

'Myrrdin has no choice. If he wants to see the arrival of his King Who Will Not Die, he has to ally with us. If he chooses vengeance he'll lose the thing the wood-priests have schemed for for year upon year.'

Mato nodded, but he heard a wintry note in his friend's voice that troubled him. They had all been changed, but Lucanus most of all.

'I did what the Romans never could – broke the back of the druids,' the Wolf continued. 'There are some still out there, a scattered few. Those that can are hiding out among the Christians in their churches, so Myrrdin once said. In days to come, they may be an invisible hand interfering in our lives. But for now we are free.' Lucanus' face softened. 'And you are free too, in another way. Free of obligation. You've fought long and hard, old friend. Go where you will. I'll always value what you've done for me . . . for Catia.'

'I'll follow you to the ends of the earth, you know that.'

'No—'

'Yes. I serve you, the Pendragon. This story we've dreamed up will have a good ending. We'll make sure of it.'

Catia leaned forward and took his hand. 'We couldn't have asked for greater friendship.'

'We'll all be with you. Your circle. The Grim Wolves. Aelius.'

'Aelius,' Catia repeated. She looked into the dark with a dreamy expression. 'So much suffering since the barbarians invaded, and yet I feel he has been saved. He walks a new road now.'

At the mention of Aelius, Mato looked around and realized he'd not seen the general since they'd returned from the roundhouse. Leaving Lucanus and Catia to find some peace, he searched among the tents until Comitinus directed him to a path through the grass to a grove.

As he neared the trees, he heard dim voices. Easing into the deep shadows, he glimpsed Myrrdin and Aelius facing each other in a pool of moonlight. Myrrdin rested his hands on the general's shoulders. Aelius bowed his head, and the wood-priest leaned in to whisper something.

Mato frowned. But before he could step forward to speak, the two men had melted away into the dark.

The wolf prowled across the moorland in the dawn light. Mato watched it sweep through the waves of yellow-flowered gorse and the grass waving in the salty breeze, and as it drew near it rose up on two feet.

Mato sighed, releasing the worry that had built inside him all night, and waved.

The wolf waved back.

Around him, cheers rang out from Lucanus, Bellicus, Solinus and Comitinus. They had been as fearful as he had, Mato knew. But the gods had smiled upon them all.

Apullius bounded the last short distance to the group that had gathered at the agreed point. His grinning face was streaked with dried blood from the fresh wolf pelt that now hung from his head and down his back.

Lucanus stepped forward and clapped his hands on the weary scout's shoulders. 'Brother. Grim Wolf. Welcome to the *arcani*.'

'He was the oldest in the pack, but he still put up a good fight,' Apullius said, showing the scratches on his forearm and a deeper tear along his temple. 'At the end, when I looked in his eyes, I thought he knew that his time was done and he was ready for it.'

Mato studied the dazed look in Apullius' eyes. The experience was almost mystical, like communing with the gods; they all remembered that. Each one of them there was changed by it for ever.

'The old bastards have to go so the new bastards can come on,' Solinus said. 'What's it like to be a new bastard?'

'I learned from the best,' Apullius replied.

They all laughed at that, and Mato thought how good it was to hear that joyous sound. A whoop rang out and he turned to see Morirex racing up from the camp. The lad hurled himself at his brother, almost knocking him off his feet. When he broke the hug, he spun back to the rest of them. His eyes were gleaming. 'I want to be a Grim Wolf too.'

'You'll be next, young one, and soon,' Bellicus said. 'You're one of us now.' He caught Lucanus' eye, and was pleased to see the other man smile. The strange sadness that had seemed to weigh down his friend since their journey through the gorge appeared to have lifted. Perhaps there really was hope ahead, for all of them.

CHAPTER FORTY-EIGHT

Tintagel

GULLS WHEELED ACROSS A CLEAR BLUE SKY AND WHITE-flecked waves crashed. Under the late spring sun, the two men stood at the top of the valley looking down to the ocean.

'Is this it?' Lucanus asked.

Myrrdin nodded. 'Here you will be safe.'

On the headland, a fortress perched above dizzying cliffs. Lucanus could see why the location had been chosen. Only a narrow strip of rock connected the mainland to what otherwise would be an island. No enemies could attack with ease.

Down in the lush valley, four men emerged from the trees and shielded their eyes against the sun to study the new arrivals.

'Who are they?'

'They guard the fortress,' the wood-priest replied. 'It has many names, but in the local tongue this place is called Tintagel. Once a home to kings, it has been abandoned for many a year. Only ghosts live here now, so folk say.'

'Then it is a home for us.'

Lucanus raised an arm and looked back. Catia and Amarina were frowning at the front of the war-band. All his men were still fearful of attack – and who could blame them – though their journey into the west had been uneventful. He snapped down his arm, and his followers moved off as one, down the track into the valley.

'I'm surprised that you came with us,' he said.

'You are still the Pendragon.' Myrrdin's voice was low and hard, his expression icy.

'I no longer have a crown.'

'The honour cannot be taken away, crown or not. And you still have Caledfwlch.'

Lucanus shook his head, still not understanding. 'I put your leaders to the sword. You have every right to hate me—'

'I do.'

'And yet still you persevere. Your plot is dead, wood-priest, along with all those men who thought nothing of destroying the lives of others. We have seized control now. We choose our own path.'

Myrrdin leaned on his staff as he negotiated the steep incline. 'It's too late, Wolf. This plot, as you call it, now has a life of its own. Much has been set in motion that cannot be turned around. Your heir still carries the royal blood, and the Bear-King will be born, come what may. And it is still my duty, and my own heirs' duty, to keep you and the royal blood safe until that time comes.' He paused before adding, 'Even if I am filled with loathing.'

'You have your faith, wood-priest, but I have a family to protect and I'll do so at any cost.' He strode on ahead, down past the guardians who gathered around Myrrdin, down to a wide stony beach beside a towering cave, and then up a dizzying path carved into the side of the cliff.

At the top, he could see the fortress was divided into two parts, one perched high on a headland ridge, the other across the narrow land-bridge on the almost-island. He nodded. Both seemed impregnable.

The Wolf led his war-band across the bridge and under a crumbling arch on to a road lined by stone buildings. Most of the roofs had fallen in.

'We can rebuild this place easily enough,' Bellicus said, mopping the sweat from his brow as he looked around. 'It can be made more secure than ever before.'

Lucanus watched his men collapse on to the sides of the road, laughing as they threw their heads back to take the sun on their faces. It was the first sign of hope he'd seen since they'd left Londinium.

Bellicus clapped a hand on his shoulder. 'Your father would be proud of you.'

The words sounded heavy with emotion, though Lucanus didn't know why, and when he glanced at his friend he thought he saw tears rimming his eyes. But Bellicus spun away to chastise Solinus before he could ask what concerned him.

Amarina and Hecate sat together in deep conversation, heads bowed close, so engrossed they didn't look up when Catia passed them with Weylyn in a sling across her breast. She came up and took Lucanus' hand. 'It's been a long road, but we would never have reached here without you.'

He forced a smile, but Myrrdin's words were lying heavily on him. 'What if we can never rest?'

Catia searched his face. He watched a shadow cross hers, one almost of pity, as if she'd had this thought long ago and come to terms with it. 'There's nothing to gain by running or hiding. Only by seizing the destiny that was promised us – by making it our destiny – is there any hope.'

'Wise words. You should heed them.'

Lucanus turned to see Myrrdin standing behind him, looking out over the white-flecked waves to the misty horizon.

'Here is where your power will grow,' the wood-priest

continued. 'Your circle of five will multiply; your army too. Good men and women will hear the tales of the great Pendragon in the west and will join you in the crusade to bring about better days. Here is where the royal bloodline will be preserved. The King Who Will Not Die will rise from this land.'

'This fortress will need a name,' Catia said thoughtfully.

The fire roared in the forest clearing. The sparks swirled up to the starry sky, taking with them the essence of the body blackening on the pyre.

Amarina pushed her way out of the trees lining the headland and felt the heat sear her face. Hecate stepped beside her. The patina of Rome was falling off her rapidly. Her hair was untamed, streaks of charcoal blackened her eye sockets, and she had taken to massaging bitter unguents into her skin in her rituals at moonrise.

'I have seen this before,' Hecate said.

On the far side of the pyre, two shadows edged around opposite sides of the clearing until the glaring yellow light revealed two women.

'You answered our call, sisters,' the youngest one said. Her wild eyes flickered and her smile was wide and mad. Though her naked body was caked with mud, Amarina could see that her breasts were engorged. Only then did she notice the babe nestled against her. It stared at her, calm despite the roaring of the fire, and when she looked in its eyes she felt troubled by what she saw there. Something much older, something as old as time.

'A daughter,' the young witch said when she saw Amarina looking.

'A daughter filled with the blood of dragons, the royal blood,' the matronly woman on the other side of the clearing said. She dragged her broken nails across her cheeks.

'Lucanus?' Amarina stuttered. Could it be true that he had sired this child?

The two witches only smiled.

Amarina stared at the burning body. 'Your sister?'

'The seasons wax and wane. The old moon dies, a new one is born,' the older woman said.

'The seasons always turn. It is the great wheel of life,' the younger one continued. 'I am mother now, and mother is crone.'

'We are two, but we must be three.'

Amarina shivered under the weight of those unblinking eyes. She knew what they were urging, had always known what they wanted of her, even from that first encounter in the cold north. But she had had her way out presented to her when she encountered Hecate on the streets of Londinium. She slipped her hand into the small of Hecate's back, easing her forward.

'Here is a sister with no sisters. Let her make you complete.'

For a moment she wondered if she'd angered these women. The witches were mercurial, half mad, as unknowable as the storm, and, as enemies, just as destructive. No one survived their fierce attention.

Then the younger witch flexed her fingers and Hecate darted forward. She turned to Amarina, her face glowing with euphoria. 'My thanks, sister,' she began. 'My—' Emotion choked the rest of her words away.

'We have aided you, sister, in your long flight to this place of safety.' The mother crouched, feral, still clutching her child. 'We have pulled the strands of the Fates, guiding, shepherding, protecting you from the many threats that hide away here in the land beyond the Tamar.'

'And now you must pay the price you promised, sister,' the older witch said.

Amarina felt a deep chill. This was the moment she had dreaded.

The mother crawled forward like a wolf about to leap. 'Stay at the side of the Pendragon. Stay with his child until your dying day. Listen to the whispers of the wood-priest. Heed what plans are made.'

The bier collapsed and the body of the old crone disappeared in a crack like thunder and a shower of sparks.

'Be our eyes and our ears,' the new crone said.

'We have aided you, sister. Now you must aid us.' The mother jumped to her feet and pushed the babe above her head. 'This one belongs to the Morrigan, as does her father. The crows will guide her. She will be well schooled in the dark magic, her spells and her potions. She will dance the spiral path.'

'Three children there are now,' the older woman said, giving a gap-toothed grin. 'All with a claim to the royal blood. In time we will see who is strongest.'

'Who knows?' the mother said, her smile fixed. 'Who knows?'

Amarina backed away into the trees. The waves of heat rolled off the pyre, but she felt as cold as she ever had in the hardest winter by the wall.

CHAPTER FORTY-NINE

Camelot

AD 373, Tintagel, 4 June

FIVE YEARS HAD PASSED SINCE BRITANNIA HAD BEEN TORN asunder. Five years of peace, and joy, and struggle, and grief, five years like all the other years before the great invasion.

The chamber glowed with a golden light. Through the window, the sun was setting and the warm breeze licked with the scent of brine. Lucanus perched on the stool he liked to call his throne and leaned back against the creamy stone wall the Dumnonii masons had laboured to build.

Mato absently plucked at a cithara which some visiting merchant had donated to try to win the approval of the King in the West. 'Rome has no desire to venture beyond the Tamar, so the messenger said. It seemed to me that Rome has little enthusiasm for Britannia any more.'

'More trouble than it's worth, I would wager.'

'He was dismayed that he didn't have the opportunity to meet the great Pendragon.' Mato flashed a wry smile.

'I saved him from disappointment. You're better at this business of politics than me, by far. What news from the empire?'

Mato shrugged. 'Theodosius the Elder continues to revel in his great success in returning Britannia to the rule of Rome. Not content with being the *magister equitum praesentalis* at the court of Emperor Valentinian, or with being victorious in his campaign against the Alamanni, he now travels to Mauretania to suppress the uprising of the usurper Firmus. His son, meanwhile, has been appointed governor of Upper Moesia, and charged with overseeing the war with the Sarmatians. He will go on to great things, mark my words. If you wish for royal blood, look there.'

'Lucanus?'

The Wolf turned to the door where Apullius hovered, frowning. He'd grown to be a man that any of the Grim Wolves would have been proud to call one of their own. The ragged scar along his temple flexed as he frowned, the result of his final battle with the old wolf, when he had claimed his destiny.

'Myrrdin would have words.'

'Trouble?' Lucanus read the young man's face.

'It's always trouble when Myrrdin would have words. He's never happier than when he's distressing folk.' Mato hummed along with the song he was strumming, something Lucanus half remembered from a tavern in Vercovicium. He felt a wave of nostalgia for simpler times.

'Tell him I'll come. But not because he asked me.'

Apullius nodded and hurried away.

Lucanus followed, his footsteps echoing through the great fortress that now rose on the headland. The wood-priest had been right. His army had grown as word spread of the power of the Pendragon and his magical sword that had been gifted by the gods, and his Circle of Five who placed honour above all things. They could not be challenged now. Catia and Weylyn were safe, the one thing he had wished for since he had set off along this hard road. Whatever travails he had encountered, it was worth the suffering for that alone.

He listened to the beat of his footsteps in the long hall and wondered what the Lucanus who crawled through mud in the Wilds would have thought of his older self. At the far end, Amarina waited. She pulled back her hood, unleashing her tumble of silver-streaked red hair. As he studied her, he thought how much sadder she seemed than the woman he had got to know in the north, yet how much less angry.

'Don't go,' she said.

'Where?'

'To see Myrrdin.'

'How do you know I'm going to see him?'

'I know everything.'

'That is true.'

She caught his arm, and he thought how that might well be the first time she had ever touched him. Amarina was not one for the comforts of most folk, but an island alone in a storm-tossed sea. He felt more troubled by that brief contact than by anything he had experienced for many a year.

She stared into his face for a long moment, then said, 'The seasons are turning again.'

'Who would attack us here?'

Amarina smiled and he winced at the note of pity he saw there. 'Britannia is falling into the dark. You know that. Rome will be gone soon enough. All that was predicted is coming to pass. And as the old ways fade, new things must arise.'

'You've always spoken plainly, Amarina. No riddles.'

'You're part of the old ways now, Lucanus. You shepherded in the world that is to come, but . . .'

'Now my time is done?' He smiled. 'All things must pass.' Before she could press further, he said, 'My thanks for the warning. I'll tread carefully.'

As he walked away, he could feel her eyes heavy on his back.

For a while, he stood on the road from the main gate, closed his eyes and enjoyed the last of the sun's warmth on his face. Then he made his way into his quarters. Weylyn was already asleep. Catia sat on a stool next to the bed, enjoying a moment of peace after telling their son his night-time tale. As he stood in the doorway, he felt struck by how beautiful she was, a beauty that came from the great strength he had always seen inside her, that seemed to grow more potent with each passing year. She'd faced her hardships since they'd arrived in their new home, but nothing seemed to break her. Not losing their second child at birth, nor the disappearance of her brother Aelius who walked out into the forest on the headland one twilight and was never seen again. Eaten by wolves, some said. Lucanus suspected Myrr-din knew more than he ever told.

Catia pressed a finger to her lips and hurried over, usher-ing him out. 'You came too late to see him to sleep,' she whispered.

'I was delayed. Dull business. News from the empire.' He shrugged. 'I gave up the open night skies and the peace of the Wilds for this.'

'As if you had a choice.'

That was true.

Glancing back into the room, he watched the steady rise and fall of his son's chest. 'He's growing fast. He'll be able to start learning to use a sword soon.'

Catia grinned. 'Apullius has already given him his first lesson. Bellicus, Solinus and Comitinus are teaching him how to scout. Just in the daylight for now. And Mato ... Mato tells him stories.'

'He'll make a fine King in the West with such good people watching over him. And you. More than anyone, you.'

When he looked back at her, she must have heard something in his voice, for she asked with a frown, 'What's wrong?'

'Nothing. I'm tired, that's all.'

Catia was too clever to fall for that – she could always see more in him than any other – so he pulled her in for a deep kiss to silence her. For a brief, shining moment, he was miles and years away, running with his love outside Vercovicium, unbounded.

He felt almost too much pain to let go of her hand. But then he said, 'Myrrdin wants words, as Myrrdin always does.' He pulled away, but allowed himself one last backward glance at the end of the corridor. She was still standing in the doorway, lit by the dying light, watching him. She seemed to know.

She always knew.

The chamber glowed a ruddy hue from the last rays of the setting sun. Bellicus was hunched at the window, peering out into the growing dusk. He turned when Lucanus came in.

'See this.'

The Wolf eased in beside his friend and looked out over the shadows pooling in the valley leading up from the promontory. Unmoving figures stood everywhere, heads turned towards the fortress, watching.

'The Attacotti have come,' Bellicus said.

'Here? What do they hope to gain by attacking us?' Lucanus stared at the pale figures, like alabaster statues in the last of the rays. More than the war-band that had tracked them from the east. More than he had ever seen gathered in one place.

'Leave us.'

Myrrdin stood in the doorway, one arm curled around his

staff. Bellicus hesitated for a moment, then nodded and went out. That must have stuck in his gut; he hated doing what the wood-priest told him.

'You've seen them?' Lucanus asked.

Ignoring the question, Myrrdin walked to the corner of the room and poured two goblets of wine. He handed one to the Wolf.

'This is no time for wine. Our men must be summoned from the barracks—'

'Drink.' The wood-priest pushed the goblet towards his lips.

Lucanus looked from the crimson depths to those eerie, silent figures in the growing gloom. 'What is happening here?'

'Do you remember the moment we first came face to face?'

'In the ruins of Trimontium, beyond the wall.'

'I was watching you long before that.' Myrrdin leaned against the window frame, looking out into the twilight. His voice no longer crackled. Now it was reflective, almost sad. 'I made you, Lucanus, out of the very clay. Shaped you into the Pendragon, the one who holds days yet to come in his hands. Your life has never been your own. But look, I have been kind. In the north, you were nothing more than a scout, sleeping in ditches and hiding in the deep forests. Now you have a woman you love, and a child. You have known joy that would have been far beyond you without me. And you have had glory, Lucanus. Men looking to you with pride in their hearts. A leader who will be revered down the years. All that has come from my hands, Wolf. And without me you would have had nothing.'

'I should be grateful?'

'I merely ask you to understand. Your life was taken from you, that is true. You were nothing but a key shaped to unlock a greater door. That is hard for a man to accept – that he is not the hero of his tale. That he is only there to help the journey of others. But for all that, I've tried to leaven it with kindness. What matters to you most?'

'Catia, and Weylyn,' he replied without hesitation.

The wood-priest nodded. 'Your journey has set them free. You have saved them. That is a greater victory than any battle you have encountered. True?'

Lucanus nodded.

'Good. There was a time when I thought you might not learn a thing.' Myrrdin glanced back and Lucanus was surprised to see some warmth in his eyes. 'You can't have what you want—'

'Which is?'

'You know.'

Lucanus held his gaze, feeling a terrible sadness well up in him.

'But you can buy safety and freedom for the ones you love. Sacrifice is at the heart of everything. It is writ large in every story we see fit to pass down the generations. Your father knew it well, and knew it was a lesson that should be handed on. Who we are is nothing. What we do can echo down the years.'

Lucanus listened silently.

'The Attacotti will not leave empty-handed. Spurned, they will attack and attack and attack until this place is wiped away, and everyone is dead. Your friends. Catia. Weylyn.'

'We can fight—'

'They will win, because they do not care about winning. Their concerns are larger than that.' Myrrdin drained his goblet and set it back on the table. 'Drink up,' he said, 'and celebrate what you have done.'

'What have I done?'

'You have built a beacon that will shine through the dark

days to come. This fortress, built on the very edge of the world, is more than stone and clay. It is more, even, than the place where the King Who Will Not Die will be born. It is an idea. A story. And they are more important than stone and steel, for they worm their way into people's minds, and live there, and change hearts. And by doing so they change the world around us.'

'A tale for children.'

'A tale for all men and women. They will never forget that a beacon was built, raised up on a foundation of honour and hope, and it will shine on, even when this place has been reduced to rubble by the ages.'

Lucanus stared into his wine, then swilled it back and returned to the window. Those spectres glowed in the gloom. In their silent, unmoving scrutiny, they reminded him of the supplicants in a temple, waiting to be blessed.

'You made a deal with the Attacotti, when we needed their help in our raid upon the barbarian camp. Before Marcus' life was taken.'

'Aye. But this is greater even than that. It is something that is as old as time.'

Lucanus thought of the ancient ritual that every man underwent when they became a Grim Wolf. The passing of power.

'When you slaughtered the wood-priests, you seized control of the story. And Catia has too,' Myrrdin continued. 'It does not belong to me any more. But you still have work to do.'

The Wolf nodded. He understood his responsibilities now.

'You're a good man, Lucanus. You may have been nothing but a player in someone else's story, but now you have a chance to be the saviour, the secret saviour of this tale.'

'Catia . . . my friends . . .' He felt a sudden surge of panic, and a desire to see them all.

Myrrdin shook his head. 'Here is the truth buried in all our teachings: a story that never ends is one that goes on for ever. Play your part here one final time, and when all that you know is dust, they will still tell of you, as the king who never died, the King Who Will Not Die. And when a king does return, in some long distant day yet to come, it will be him ... and you. The Dragon rises. The circle never ends. The story goes on for ever and the power remains within it.'

Lucanus held Myrrdin's gaze, and after a long moment he nodded his assent.

Catia looked around the chamber. She could hear the crashing of the waves on the shore below the fortress, but it seemed that that thunderous sound was coming from deep within her, from her heart, and filling up every part of her until she could think of nothing else.

The chamber was empty.

She stood there for a moment, breathing in the fading scent of Lucanus on the air. Then she crossed to the window and looked out into the moonless night. Beyond the line of torches that marked the boundary between their sanctuary and the wild world beyond, she thought she saw flitting shadows, moving away, but they were gone too quickly for her to be sure.

And there, in the courtyard in front of the main gate, in the wavering light, she could just make out a familiar sword with a dragon hilt rammed into a crack in the stones. Her husband's sword. Her son's sword.

Her heart felt as if it was breaking and she choked back a sob.

'I am here.' Myrrdin's voice echoed at her back. 'I will always be here. To guide. To support.'

Catia pushed up her chin and showed a cold face. She was strong, and she would continue to be so, for the sake of their son, and for the sake of all the people who would need to be led out of the dark in times to come.

'I am the queen now.'

Every new beginning comes from some other beginning's end.

Marcus Annaeus Seneca

Author's Note

The full moon hangs over Glastonbury Tor. High up there, wrapped in the balmy summer warmth and the almost sanctified stillness, you can feel the breath of the past raising the hairs on the back of your neck. Darkness still pools across the Somerset Levels beyond the town's lights, and there's a clear view of the sweep of the stars in the vault of the heavens. I breathe in the scent of cooling vegetation, and when an owl swoops by, I let my thoughts fly with it.

There's a magic to the old places.

Every book is a quest, for the author and for the reader. This one, like *Pendragon*, the novel that preceded it, was also a very real quest for me. As a writer, it's always been my belief that you should walk in the footsteps of your characters. That sense of place is a potent force that throws up levels of detail that can never be found in books or online. Not just the sensory experience, the smells, the sounds, but the *feel* of it. Such an intangible thing, yet deeply affecting.

I travelled through a great many of Britain's old places while researching this story, and that magic is still powerful. It's in the landscape and in the history, which lives on, in standing stones, and crumbling ruins, and odd patterns in the landscape. From the edge of Loch Lomond, across the shattered bones of Hadrian's Wall, south through the Lake

District, to Salisbury Plain. London. Stonehenge. Avebury. Dartmoor and west to the ends of the earth (otherwise known as Cornwall).

In these kinds of road trips, you learn as much about yourself as the places you're investigating. There's something to be said for pushing out of that comfort zone, hiking, climbing, sweating, sleeping under the stars, crunching along a deserted beach, being lashed by the wind and rain on wild land where there isn't another soul for mile upon mile. And also something to be said for placing yourself in the context of the great sweep of history. The problems of a modern person seem tiny compared to the things our ancestors endured.

As I explored each location, I was endlessly fascinated by the stories that still clung to them, most of them age-old. Religions, legends and myths, and the stories we tell ourselves, all occupy much the same place. Through them we can learn as much about ourselves as from artefacts dug out of the ground, and as such they have an important role in history. Folklore is not fantasy. There are truths embedded in those tales.

At Wayland's Smithy, the neolithic long barrow in Oxfordshire, which plays a part in this story, records from 1738 show that people believed an invisible smith lived there who would reshoe the horses of any travellers who left a coin. Visitors still leave coins today, near three centuries later (and the National Trust has to collect them all up and give them to charity). The folklorist Ceri Houlbrook says these actions 'contribute to the ritual narrative of a site'. Yet we now know that the prehistoric site was once associated with a smith-god. The story kept the belief alive in a constantly mutating form.

Stories, old and new.

There are a few things I want to mention before I wander away.

These books have the overarching title of Dark Age. A few readers have mused that it's not actually set in what we used to call the Dark Ages (although modern historians have pulled away from that term for a variety of reasons, not least because it's a very UK-centric descriptor and doesn't take into account what was happening in, say, Constantinople). But the aim was always to show how a dark age, any dark age, can arise from a time that had, perhaps, long been perceived as a golden age. Historical fiction always has lessons for today, and as we look around us, now, it's possible to see that difficult times could arise again. It's only a relatively short time since Francis Fukuyama wrote about the 'end of history' and predicted an unceasing era of Western democratic values. When the collapse starts, it's often in areas where few are paying attention.

What Myrrdin told Lucanus about the Eleusinian Mysteries is true. And it's still of relevance today. If you don't believe me, take a look at a very good book, *Stealing Fire: How Silicon Valley, the Navy SEALs and Maverick Scientists Are Revolutionizing the Way We Live and Work* by Steven Kotler and Jamie Wheal.

There's been a lot of talk about numbers in these two books, particularly three and five. Many ancient civilizations had beliefs about the spiritual significance of sacred numbers, and that there were secret relationships between numbers and the divine, or fate. The first Council of Nicaea in AD 325, which regulated aspects of Christianity, consigned numerology to the same fate as other unapproved beliefs like divination and magic.

In the section set in Londinium, I mention the River Fleet a few times. These days it's hidden in a culvert beneath London streets, but it was a key part of the Roman town's expansion. Yet I haven't been able to unearth the Roman name for the river, and when I spoke to Professor Mary

Beard of the University of Cambridge, she couldn't find it either. So I decided to stick with the Fleet name, for clarity, even though that derives from the Anglo-Saxon *fleota*. These are the compromises we have to make from time to time, sadly, and you will undoubtedly find a few more within these pages.

The legend of King Arthur lives on, mutating to fit the age in which it's told. There's a power in it that survives any telling, and a deeper symbolism. These things matter, these symbols, crowns and swords, and dragons eating their own tails.

Long may he reign.

ACKNOWLEDGEMENTS

With thanks to Professor Mary Beard for advice on Roman river names.

PENDRAGON
James Wilde

Winter AD 367, and in a frozen forest beyond Hadrian's Wall six scouts of the Roman army have been murdered.

It is Lucanus, the one they call the Wolf, who discovers the mutilated bodies. He knows the far north to be a wild place inhabited by barbarians, daemons and witches – a place where the old gods live on. It is not somewhere he would willingly go. But when the child of a friend is taken captive, he feels honour-bound to journey beyond the wall and bring the boy back home.

His quest will span an empire – from the pagan temples of Britain across the kingdoms of Gaul to the eternal city of Rome – and will ensnare a soldier and a thief, a cut-throat and a courtesan, a druid and even the emperor himself. And what it reveals will reverberate down the centuries . . .

Before King Arthur. Before Camelot. Before Excalibur. Every legend has a beginning . . .

James Wilde

His thrilling, action-packed series rescues a near-forgotten English hero from the darkest of times and brings him to bloody but brilliant life!

HEREWARD

1062. King Edward is heirless and ailing, and William, Duke of Normandy waits for the moment when he can seize the English throne. Hopes of resisting the would-be conqueror come to rest with just one man: Hereward . . .

THE DEVIL'S ARMY

1067. It seems all was lost at Hastings. The iron fist of William the Bastard has begun to squeeze the life out of this conquered land, but for one who stands in his way. He is Hereward, and he is England's last hope.

END OF DAYS

1071. Five years have passed since the Normans' crushing victory at Hastings. England reels under the savage rule of its new king. But Hereward plans an uprising that will sweep the hated Norman king from the throne.

WOLVES OF NEW ROME

1072. The battle has been lost. The Norman king William is victorious. For the beaten English rebels, the price of defeat is cruel: exile. It falls to Hereward to lead them across a war-ravaged Europe to Byzantium.

THE IMMORTALS

1073. Under a merciless Eastern sun, Hereward and his men plan a daring rescue mission. But within the corrupt heart of Byzantium there are those who would see the English warrior fail and meet his end as a feast for the ravens . . .

THE BLOODY CROWN

1081. Within Constantinople, three factions will go to any lengths to seize the imperial throne. Outside the city's walls, two armies gather. Now is the time for Hereward and his spear-brothers to ready themselves – for this could be their final stand.

THE BEAR KING
A Novel of the Dark Age
James Wilde

AD 375 – The Dark Age is drawing near . . .

As Rome's legions abandon their forts, chaos
grows on the fringes of Britannia.

In the far west, the shattered forces of the House of
Pendragon huddle together in order to protect the
royal heir – their one beacon of hope.

For Lucanus, their great war leader, is missing, presumed
dead. And the people are abandoning them. For in this
time of crisis, a challenger has arisen, a False King with an
army swollen by a horde of bloody-thirsty barbarians
desperate for vengeance.

One slim hope remains for Lucanus' band of warrior-allies,
the Grim Wolves. Guided by the druid, Myrrdin, they go
in search of a great treasure – a vessel that is supposedly a
gift from the gods. With such an artefact in their
possession, the people would surely return and rally to their
cause? Success will mean a war unlike any other, a battle
between two kings for a legacy that will echo down the
centuries. And should they fail? Well, then all is lost . . .

In *The Bear King*, James Wilde's rousing reimagining
of how the myth of King Arthur, Excalibur and Camelot
rose out of the fragile pages of history reaches its
shattering conclusion . . .